Praise for
Many Sparr

"Stunning. *Many Sparrows* is everything I want in a book: settings that spring to life, characters I love, rich historical context, heart-wrenching drama, timeless spiritual insights, and prose that reads like poetry. Lori Benton handles the conflicted eighteenth century with sensitivity in this tender tale of hope and fear, faith and doubt, loss and new life. Truly, this is an inspired masterpiece sure to stir the soul."

—JOCELYN GREEN, award-winning author of *The Mark of the King*

"Intense. Enlightening. Lustrous. *Many Sparrows* is a lesson in early American history wrapped up in a beautiful romance, one not only of the human heart but of God's heart for His creation. I cherished Clare and Jeremiah's quietly blossoming love and deeply felt their struggle to trust and reach that painful yet unburdening place of surrender. Many sighs. And many thanks to the author."

—TAMARA LEIGH, *USA Today* best-selling author of *The Vexing* and *Lady Betrayed*

"Lori Benton vividly portrays characters wrestling with a God they can't explain but desperately need to trust. *Many Sparrows* is a heart-searching story where love trumps hate, and hard-won forgiveness leads to soaring hope. Held captive to the end by the characters' inescapable conflicts, I shouted for joy when I read the masterful ending. Truly, this is history made personal and believable."

—MESU ANDREWS, author of *Miriam*

"Lori Benton weaves a beguiling tapestry of prose, pathos, and faith in *Many Sparrows,* a story as hopeful as it is heartrending. Shedding light on the ferocity of a mother's love and the beauty and complexity of Shawnee culture and community, Benton's boundless talent shines ever brighter as a rich and mesmerizing story unfolds. Each character is wonderfully authentic and honestly drawn, but it is Jeremiah's devotion to God, the tension between his two worlds, and the vow he made to a grieving woman that caught my breath many times over. Exquisitely told, *Many Sparrows* reaches all the deep spaces of the heart, abiding long after the last page is turned."

—REL MOLLET, RelzReviewz.com

"*Many Sparrows* is a beautifully threaded tapestry, rich with spiritual imagery and relatable characters, set in the boiling-pot world of the pre–Revolutionary Ohio-Kentucky frontier. With her customarily poetic voice and singular ability to bring eighteenth-century America to sparkling life, Benton weaves a story of fierce loyalty, breathtaking love, and the battles waged when faith is in crisis and survival is unlikely. Another burn-the-midnight-oil piece of literary fiction from one of the finest writers in inspirational fiction."

—RACHEL MCMILLAN, author of the Herringford
and Watts series

MANY
SPARROWS

MANY SPARROWS

A NOVEL

LORI BENTON

AUTHOR OF A FLIGHT OF ARROWS

WATERBROOK

MANY SPARROWS

All Scripture quotations are taken from the King James Version.

The characters and events in this book are fictional, and any resemblance to actual persons or events is coincidental.

Trade Paperback ISBN 978-1-60142-994-0
eBook ISBN 978-1-60142-995-7

Copyright © 2017 by Lori Benton

Cover design by Kristopher K. Orr; cover painting by Homer Dodge Martin, Bridgeman Images

Published in the United States by WaterBrook, an imprint of the Crown Publishing Group, a division of Penguin Random House LLC, New York.

WATERBROOK® and its deer colophon are registered trademarks of Penguin Random House LLC.

Library of Congress Cataloging-in-Publication Data
Names: Benton, Lori, author.
Title: Many sparrows : a novel / Lori Benton.
Description: First edition. | Colorado Springs, CO : WaterBrook, 2017.
Identifiers: LCCN 2017015973| ISBN 9781601429940 (softcover) | ISBN 9781601429957 (electronic)
Subjects: LCSH: Frontier and pioneer life—Fiction. | BISAC: FICTION / Christian / Historical. | FICTION / Christian / Romance. | FICTION / Romance / Historical. | GSAFD: Christian fiction. | Historical fiction. | Love stories.
Classification: LCC PS3602.E6974 M36 2017 | DDC 813/.6—dc23
LC record available at https://lccn.loc.gov/2017015973

Printed in the United States of America
2017—First Edition

10 9 8 7 6 5 4 3 2 1

This book is dedicated to:

*Doree Crawford Ross, whose many-times
great-uncle, William Crawford, was busy on the
Ohio frontier in 1774, taking care of business.*

*And Jeanette Puryear Johnson, a native Virginian
who made sure her children were born so too.*

Are not two sparrows sold for a farthing?
and one of them shall not fall on the ground
without your Father. . . . Fear ye not therefore,
ye are of more value than many sparrows.

MATTHEW 10:29–31

1

MAY 1, 1774
OHIO RIVER NEAR YELLOW CREEK

Jeremiah Ring had witnessed death as often as the next man on the Allegheny frontier, but in all his thirty years he had encountered no deaths more dismaying than those confronting him now.

The dead had been laid on the wet spring earth near Joshua Baker's tavern and trading post, made as decent as such desecrated bodies could be. Now the living moved among them as men whose joints had aged a score of years, tongues held captive by grief and outrage. Jeremiah's friend, the Mingo, Logan, wept in silence beside the body of a young woman, his sister Koonay.

Jeremiah felt his gorge rise as it had at first sight of Koonay. Someone had draped a blanket over her after cutting her down from the tree in which her body was found hanging, but they'd all seen what was done to her. Koonay had been heavy with her second child, but not even the unborn had escaped this slaughter. No one had yet found her firstborn, a daughter, two years old, though they knew she'd been with her mother in one of the canoes that crossed the Ohio River to Baker's post, a thing done in friendship many times before.

It wasn't only Koonay whom Logan grieved. Jeremiah choked back his own sorrow, watching the man absorb the slaughter of nearly all the blood kin he'd had in this world—his older brother, his mother, his nephew, his sister, her unborn child. The few warriors who'd accompanied them, slain along with his kin, had been Logan's friends.

For the first time since he'd met the man, Jeremiah felt chary approaching Logan, stony-faced even as he wept for his dead. Logan's warriors backed away, leaving them alone.

"Cresap." Logan didn't look at Jeremiah as he spat the name in a strangled voice. "He has done this."

Jeremiah felt his gut twist. Michael Cresap, trader and land hunter, had made it plain he meant to slaughter any Indians unlucky enough to cross his path. This was due in large part to rumors being spread by Major John Connolly, commander at Fort Pitt, who'd gone so far as to assert the Ohio Indians—Shawnees and Mingos—were on the verge of striking the frontier settlements in open war. Cresap had decided to strike first. But had the man grown so hard, so heartless, to have done *this*?

Whoever was to blame, the senseless killings were bound to escalate an already tenuous situation on the Ohio. Until now, Mingos like Logan, along with many Shawnee chiefs including their principal chief, Cornstalk, had counseled against open warfare with the whites invading their hunting grounds south of the river. These whites weren't traders, who'd come among them for years, beginning with the French. Nor were they missionaries, who'd settled among the Delawares and now had whole villages of Christian converts. These men came to blaze the trees and cut them down, to put up cabins and corn, kill the game and fill the land with cattle and hogs; an endless stream of settlers spilling down the Ohio like floodwaters.

Fiery young warriors, seeing their hunting grounds taken, couldn't always be controlled by elders who urged peace. Even the Shawnee war chief, Puckeshinwah, who'd spent the past months in talks with the Indian agents at Fort Pitt, was ready to raise the war club in the face of Virginia Governor Dunmore's inability to stem the tide of illegal settlement down the Ohio.

Three days ago, Jeremiah had left the frustrated Puckeshinwah and his Shawnee delegation in Pittsburgh and descended the Ohio with Koonay's husband, the white trader John Gibson, hoping to discover whether the alarming rumors being spread about Indian attacks had basis in fact. Assured by a band of Shawnees met on the river that their warriors hadn't been out killing whites, Gibson felt sure the rumors were false. Major Connolly was attempting to excite alarm, likely to further some land-grabbing scheme of Governor Dunmore's to snatch up the Ohio territory before Pennsylvania could claim it. Gibson had traded canoes for packhorses and continued overland toward the Shawnee towns on the Scioto River to do his trading.

Less sanguine about the rumors, Jeremiah had turned his canoe for Yellow Creek. Surely Logan's warriors weren't raiding across the river—he was known widely as a friend to the white man—but perhaps he'd know if others were.

Logan had been away at a hunting camp when Jeremiah arrived, but what caused a true disquiet was learning Logan's family had crossed to Baker's post, lured by the invitation of some white men promising whiskey. Distant shots had echoed across the river almost before the news was shared. Jeremiah had gone over by canoe with the warriors sent to investigate, only to be repelled by more gunfire. Runners had been sent to Logan's hunting camp to bring him in. That morning they'd finally made it ashore, to find the dead lying scalped and mutilated, the killers long fled.

Jeremiah sought for words to fill a mouth gone dusty. He wanted to comfort Logan, caution him not to rush to blame, say something to turn aside what could easily follow this atrocity—a full-scale border war. To mind rose memory of Koonay's lifeless face, beaten almost beyond recognition, and he thought it would take a rare man, faced with such violation, to turn aside from vengeance.

"Maybe it was Cresap. Maybe not. Surely the Indian agents at Pittsburgh will . . ."

Jeremiah fell silent when Logan's gaze lifted, knowing nothing he could say would matter. What he'd seen this day would haunt Jeremiah for his next thirty years, should he live so long. So would what he read in the tormented eyes turned on him now. Where once had leapt the flame of friendship for Jeremiah's race, there blazed a hatred mere words could never douse.

Alarm crawled over Jeremiah's scalp. Not for himself. In Logan's eyes he was no longer a white man. His alarm was for every settler fool enough to linger west of the mountains after today.

Logan seemed to read his thoughts. Lifting his shoulders until he stood lance-straight, fingers curving round the tomahawk thrust through his sash, the Mingo bound Jeremiah with that burning gaze.

"For every life here taken from me," he said though lips set tight with rage, "by my hand ten whites will die. *Ten*. In your hearing this day I vow it. Go and tell what has been done here if you will. Speak for these ones who have no more voice. But do not promise peace. Not from Logan."

2

MAY 6, 1774

VIRGINIA COLONY, WESTERN FRONTIER

C lare Margaret Inglesby, twenty-six years of age and eight months with
child, wondered how she'd come to this: trapped in a jolting wagon
advancing into perilous wilderness.

She clenched her teeth to prevent them rattling out of her head and to hold
back the flood of grievance amassing on her tongue. Though in danger of losing hairpins, cap, and sundry other trappings to the bucking of their conveyance, that was nothing to the sense of impending disaster that had dogged her
every mile they'd traveled from the place they'd last called home, the Augusta
County farm belonging to Clare's uncle, Alphus Litchfield.

In seven years of marriage, the Inglesbys had never owned a home of their
own, despite all Philip's promises.

And likely never shall, she thought, as the forest west of Redstone Fort
enclosed them in its dark embrace for a second day of misery. The men of
Redstone had warned Philip the track they followed was unsuitable for a wagon's passage, suggesting they go by canoe instead.

Philip had dismissed their advice. He was in a hurry to reach Wheeling
Settlement and hadn't the patience to wait for a canoe to be built. James Harrod and his settlers, whom Philip meant to join up with, were said to be in
Wheeling, but only for a short time before they departed downriver. If they
could reach Wheeling quickly, Philip had maintained, they were bound to
catch Harrod's party.

Always certain he could find a way or make one was Philip, no matter the inevitable disappointment that followed.

Inevitable. Precisely when had she transformed into a woman of such dark presentiment? Had this nagging expectation of doom been her companion before she became Philip's wife?

Perhaps she'd made passing acquaintance with it then, even as she and Philip ignored her father's cautioning and wed under the cloud of devastation that had settled over Philip and his mother with the self-perpetrated death of his father and the ruination of their fortunes.

Certainly she'd done so five years later when, reduced to tenancy after repeated failures to regain said fortune, she and Philip had cast themselves upon the mercy of Clare's uncle and left Richmond, with its cobbled streets, bustling shops, and established society—and painful memories—to move onto Alphus Litchfield's vacant farm in the Shenandoah Valley.

There'd been no place else to go, for Philip had flatly refused to seek the aid of her parents yet again.

"Only for a while," he'd assured her. "Until we get our feet under us." A year. Maybe two.

Clare, who'd taken to farming with a liking that surprised no one more than herself, began to hope they'd found their place at last, however modest. Perhaps one day Uncle Alphus, who operated a gristmill in nearby Staunton, might be induced to sell the land to them.

Six months later the name *Harrod* fell from Philip's lips. Hot on its heels came *Kentucky.*

She'd opposed his intention of uprooting them again and making for the Ohio frontier, where land was fast being surveyed and claimed despite King George's Proclamation meant to halt settlement at the crest of the Allegheny Mountains.

"The wording of the Proclamation isn't clear on that point," Philip had argued. "There are grants to be made to veterans of the French War, land that must be found west of the mountains." The Proclamation Line could never have been intended as a *permanent* demarcation, Philip had reasoned. "It's only a matter of time before the Ohio country is officially open to settlement. We must be among the first!"

Clare had shuddered in the face of his enthusiasm. Who could say what fate awaited them across the mountains, or who might be nearby to aid them when that fate—bedecked in war paint—chose to descend upon them, hatchets raised? Though her own troubles had risen large in recent years, she was aware enough of the wider world to know the land for which they made wasn't truly unclaimed.

Had it ever ended well when the worlds of red and white men collided?

Such collision had occurred just miles from Uncle Alphus's farm. Years ago, raiding Indians had stolen a young pregnant bride right out of her cabin while her husband was away. The husband had abandoned his farm and gone tearing off into the wilderness after his wife. Neither ever returned. Clare couldn't recall their name: Bud, perhaps? Or was it Bloom? Regardless, the story haunted her.

Now here she was pushing deep into territory where such unspeakable things still happened.

"Why not stay on Uncle Alphus's farm?" she'd pleaded. "He requires someone to work it, and he's welcomed us here as long as needs be."

"No, Clare." As always, Philip's eyes had looked beyond what rested safe in his hand to something more he wished to grasp. "I cannot abide it, farming another man's land."

"Is it the lack of ownership or the farming itself to which you object?" she'd asked, having her suspicions. "If the latter, how will it be better where land must first be cleared?"

"Better in every way!" Philip had countered, sidestepping her primary question. "The land east of the mountains is overworked. But the west—the *west* is untouched. Virgin soil. The yield there will be bountiful beyond anything we've seen. More yield for less toil. *Think* of it, Clare."

She thought of the hardships of wilderness travel. She thought of hacking out a forest of massive trees to lay bare a patch of that virgin soil. Of raising a cabin with a hatchet and their hands. Of bearing her child in a wilderness.

It was all she could do not to weep. "Why not wait, at least until after the baby is born?"

"If we wait, the best land will be claimed. You've heard how many settlers are passing through Pittsburgh and Redstone, all with the same aim in mind as have we—"

"As have *you*." Philip never seemed to grasp that distinction. "And what about Indians?"

He had waved away that most abiding of her terrors as if it were a gnat. "It's been peaceful for months. Likely there's so many of us coming downriver now they've thought better of provoking us. They'll give way. Move west. They always have. It's inevitable."

Inevitable.

Rehearsing that conversation and others like it for the hundredth time, still trying to find the thing she might have said—might still say—to divert this disastrous course her husband had set, Clare scanned the trail ahead. It leveled into a wider, straight stretch with no trees or rocks to maneuver the cumbersome wagon around. She swiveled to peer deeper into the canvas-covered bed where their son, Jacob, rode cushioned in a nest of cornmeal sacks, tucked between the few cherished furnishings they'd had room to bring along.

At four years old Jacob was, according to Philip's mother, the spitting image of his father at that age, with a mop of pale curls and dark brown eyes. Clare had adored him at first sight, squalling and pink-faced, and loved him with a devotion that gripped her at times with its intensity.

Equally intense was the rage that rose at the thought of anyone, painted or otherwise, harming her son because of his father's choices—a rage that found its target in Philip, who she hoped was prepared to use the rifle he'd bought at the outset of this sojourn, which rode now behind the wagon seat. If it came to it, she would spend her last breath defending her child with the hatchet that lay next to it.

"Jacob, would you like—"

It was all Clare uttered of the question she'd meant to ask before the right front wheel hit a rut she hadn't seen coming.

Lurched airborne, she yelped in startlement before her bottom jarred on hard wood. Pain shot through her hips and back, then arced around her belly in a tightening, terrifying band reminiscent of the pangs she'd felt at Jacob's birth.

But it was far too soon for that.

Behind her Jacob cried out, but only in reaction to her outcry, for when she righted herself and turned she could see he was unharmed. Still it was the final straw.

"Stop the horses, Philip. Now."

Philip drew back on the lines. The wagon lurched to a halt.

Birdsong and a nearby stream's steady chatter filled the silence as trail dust settled. "Clare, what is it?"

"I am in pain, Philip," she said through gritted teeth and saw her husband's face contract.

"The baby? Is it coming?"

"No!" At least she hoped not. "I've simply had enough *jolting*."

"I'll take it more slowly—"

"If we take it any more slowly we might as well be going backward." Exactly the direction Clare wished to go.

Philip clenched the lines as the horses waited, stamping and blowing, looking no happier than she.

"Let Jacob climb down to walk for a spell. I'll walk with him." She bit back harsher words, rubbing at her aching lower back.

"Clare, I'm sorry this is hard on you. We . . ." Philip caught her gaze again and didn't finish the statement. Perhaps he'd been tempted to say they would stop early and camp. But they'd barely made one tedious mile, this second day out from Redstone, and the sun was still high.

It was a relief to be on her feet once she'd finally clambered down to earth. Ahead, the wagon creaked and groaned with every rut and rock its iron-bound wheels surmounted. At least for the moment they weren't attempting to scale a ridge, or descend one. The latter was most harrowing, requiring Philp to chain the rear wheels and Clare to pray the wagon didn't go plunging down the side of a ravine, taking the horses and all their worldly belongings with it. They'd seen the wreck and ruin of more than one wagon, shattered among rocks and trees far below the trail.

"Mama? Mama! Let me show you something!"

Thrilled with his freedom, Jacob had been darting back and forth in the wagon's wake, ferreting among ferns and rocks and the massive boles of trees lining the trail, blithely ignoring her warnings about snakes. Now he held out a grubby palm, in the center of which rested a flat triangle of stone, grooved at its base on two sides, one point elongated and sharp.

Clare's mouth went dry.

"Give me that." She took the arrow point from him, intending to throw it into the woods as soon as Jacob was distracted, which occurred in short order when Philip called back to them.

"Jacob! Care to run ahead of the wagon and throw aside these rocks from the path?"

Fear came in a cold wave. Clutching the arrowhead, Clare grabbed her son before he could race away. "Philip, no. It's not safe, his being ahead on the trail."

Philip halted the horses and leaned out to view them past the canvas. "You worry excessively, Clare. He'll be in plain sight the whole while. I'll not let him range far ahead."

Clare felt the vibration of pent-up energy radiating through their son's shoulder. Jacob gazed up with hopeful eyes. "Please, Mama? I can help."

Though it went against her every instinct, she released him.

"All right, but be watchful." To her husband she called, "*Do* keep an eye on him, Philip. There may be snakes in the way."

The arrowhead bit into her clenched fist. *Or worse.*

"With all the racket we're making? I should think we've cleared the path of snakes and anything else for a mile at least." Philip smiled at her, a grin that had charmed her years ago, smoothing over many an initial disappointment and heartbreak.

It had long since lost its power to reassure.

Moving to where she could glimpse her son whenever he ran to the track's edge to toss a stone into the underbrush, Clare cupped her hands around her belly, feeling the babe stir beneath petticoats and shift.

Thankfully she thrived with the carrying of children. With Jacob she'd been ill nary a day, still able to complete her chores and walk the miles to Uncle's mill the evening prior to his birth. She'd enjoyed similar robust health with this one and expected there was time enough to reach Harrod's Kentucky settlement before her childbed was upon her.

A month, if she was lucky.

A month of this. Her gaze failed to pierce the gloom of the forest canopy around them. Childbearing didn't daunt her, but that impenetrable forest stole the strength from her knees and the breath from beneath her half-laced stays. She wished she'd taken the hatchet from the wagon when she'd clambered down. She'd feel better with it clenched at her side. Where she wanted Jacob to be. *Now.*

"Jacob!" She raised her voice to carry over the wagon's rumbling. "Enough rock-throwing. Come back to me!"

She saw him toss a final rock and turn to scamper past the wagon, flashing a grin up at Philip as he did so. Her heart seized as his tiny frame passed by the rolling front wheel. He pressed nimbly through the space between it and the immense trunk of a tree, clambered over a sloping rock embedded in the trail, and slipped through the tight spot just before the heavy rear wheel reached it.

Clare drew one easing breath before calamity ensued.

The horses must have veered, for the rear wheel rode up high on the rock the front wheel had missed and crashed down on the other side. There was a crack of breaking timber before the wheel came away from the axle, hit the tree and spun into the forest, missing knocking Jacob flat by inches.

Clare rushed forward as the wagon tipped with a splintering, clanging, and thudding. Canvas split and contents spilled. Something struck her shoulder as, shielding Jacob, she got a hand on his arm and yanked him backward.

They went stumbling and reeling until they tangled in her petticoat and fell in a heap on the trail.

3

Bruised and breathless, Clare took stock of herself. Sharp pain had shot up her thighs and back as she'd landed, but Jacob had fallen across her lap. Surely that had been its cause.

"Jacob? Are you hurt?" She swatted aside her hampering petticoat, ignoring the pain still throbbing in her lower back.

Even as she grappled for him, Jacob scrambled to his feet, nary a graze in evidence, eyes wide and focused on the trail ahead.

"Papa?"

Clare got to her knees, pushed herself upright, and with Jacob her shadow hurried past the listing wagon, terrified of finding Philip cast aside in similar broken state.

"Philip, are you—" She halted at sight of her husband sitting up in a bed of ferns, brushing leaf matter from his coat.

"Merely chipped and dented!" Philip retrieved his hat and shoved it onto his head, then winced as he examined a torn stocking, the exposed skin scraped but scarcely even bleeding.

He'd managed to jump free of the wagon as it lurched sideways, he explained. Once he'd seen she and Jacob were likewise whole, he turned his attention to the horses, for which Clare had given scarce thought even as she'd rushed past them. Pinned by their traces to the listing wagon, they stood twitching and nervous but unharmed.

"I'd say we've come through remarkably unscathed," he pronounced. "This might have fallen out a good deal worse."

That he'd said it at all was stunning. That he'd said it *smiling* . . . Clare gaped, mouth trembling like her hands and knees.

"Philip—have you even *looked* at the wagon?" The contraption would have been on its side had it not fallen against the tree; one wheel missing, a second cracked nearly through, likely a broken axle, canvas gaping, possessions scattered on the trail. *"Unscathed?"*

Philip's smile faltered. "Granted, the wagon does look bad, but . . ."

Clare never knew what else he might have said, for that was when her shaking stopped and fury surged high. Her husband had never taken to gaming to restore his family's fortune, but apparently he was willing to risk their very lives, which could be lost without warning at any bend of that terrible trail—as had just been proven.

"Why wouldn't you heed the men at Redstone? Better still, never left Uncle Alphus's farm in the first place! What were you thinking? What was *I* thinking to have come this far with you? To bring Jacob into this? You're going to get us killed!"

Philip raised placating hands. "Calm yourself, Clare. Let me—"

"I'll not calm myself!" Infuriated, she stepped back, hands cupping her belly. "I ought to have taken Jacob and gone back to Richmond months ago as my parents begged of me!"

Philip's face drained of color, leaving the fresh sunburn across his nose a stark red blaze.

What had she said? Richmond, her parents begging . . . *Oh, no.*

She'd concealed from Philip the letters her father had penned, letters imploring her to return to Richmond with their grandson. Her father had declared his lack of faith in Philip to provide them a living after so many years. Desperate to deny her own doubts in that regard, she'd never replied.

The truth was out now. Philip's face showed the marks of its wounding. "I wish you would trust me, Clare. At least in this one thing—I will not get you or Jacob killed."

"*Trust* you?" She put her back to her husband, too overcome to scream, to sob, though the need for both pressed hot in her throat.

"Mama, I want to live with Papa!"

Shame washed over her at Jacob's urgent words, broken by sniffling gulps. That she'd revealed such doubt—hers and her parents'—to Philip was bad enough. To have done so in front of their son was unforgivable.

"It's all right, Jacob," Philip said. "Your mother was frightened, is all."

Tears blurring her vision, Clare reached for Jacob. The boy rushed to her, arms stretching around her belly in an attempt to embrace her. She pressed his head to her side. His tousled hair was sweaty, his cheek wet with tears.

"It's all right." Hearing Philip's powerless words coming from her lips, she amended, "It *will* be all right."

As soon as they were headed east again.

She met her husband's imploring gaze and felt her will harden. She would do what she must to protect her children, no matter the cost to Philip's dreams. Or his pride. It would be all right, for she would make it so. One way or another, she and Jacob were going back to Uncle Alphus's farm.

They said no more until Jacob was comforted and sent to play at a stream a few paces from the trail, well within her sight.

Philip drew near, putting his hand on her arm. Meant as a comforting gesture, no doubt.

"Clare, if your parents have lost faith in me, I'm to blame. But should *you* find it in you to give me one last chance to prove I can provide for you, for Jacob . . ." He dropped his hand to her belly. "For this one. Can you do that?"

He was doing it again. Sweeping aside her concerns with a quick apology, a gentle pleading for her to see it his way. Do it his way. No matter if his way screamed of folly.

"Can we just go home, Philip? Please."

Philip's hand slid away. "All right."

Before she could fully take in those glorious words he added, "Unless it proves I took the wrong turning this morning, back where the trail forked."

As he spoke, Philip began gathering up large stones from the trail's edge, dropping them beside the broken wagon, going back for more.

"Perhaps I'll find someone who can help us fix the wagon, perhaps the axle can be saved."

"Even if the axle is still functional, Philip, the wheels aren't. We have one spare but need two."

"Just let me do this, Clare," Philip said, voice stiffening with that familiar bullheadedness as he went on doggedly piling stones that clacked together as the pile toppled and fell. "Let me see what help I can find. I'll take one of the horses, ride back—it wasn't much more than a mile if memory serves—check out that other trail. Perhaps you can be sorting through your things while I'm gone."

Clare's chest tightened with apprehension as she watched her husband hunker beside the tumbled stones and begin to stack them. He was being unreasonable. Utterly unreasonable. And it frightened her.

"Who do you think you'll find, Philip? Someone who just happens to have an extra wagon wheel they're willing to give us? What are you *doing*?"

The answer to that last question grew clear as she voiced it. He was piling the gathered stones beneath the broken axle to support the wagon.

"I ought to have listened to the Redstone men," he said, pausing in the work and lifting his gaze. "I will own to that. But even if I find no help, we can still catch Harrod at Wheeling if we sort through everything, figure out what the horses can carry . . ."

He'd gone back to piling stones. Clare watched, too weary to reply to this preposterous notion. He would have her walk to Wheeling Settlement? That was simply not going to happen, but she thought she could just manage to walk back to Redstone, and for that she would have to sort through the wagon's contents. Stabilizing the wagon so they could clamber around within was a step in that direction.

"All right. I'll do that."

Perhaps this accident was a blessing in disguise. Philip would find no better path, or help. He'd already admitted to his misjudgment about the trail. He would return to them that evening and admit the full defeat, which wouldn't be defeat in Clare's estimation but triumph. She only wanted to retrace their steps before something worse befell them.

They pitched a camp where the wagon had broken. Clare listened dully as Philip pointed out the amenities of the site—the stream, the clearing where the horse he wasn't taking was picketed to graze.

"As if the Almighty Himself chose the spot," Philip said without meeting her gaze.

Do not bring God into this, she wanted to say. Her husband was a man of faith, though she no longer knew in what exactly he put his faith—the Almighty or his own schemes and hopes.

They were strangers to each other, it so often seemed.

In the clearing Philip built a fire and erected an open-faced shelter out of pine boughs. It was barely past midday, the sun high in a clear sky, and Jacob had fallen asleep inside the shelter, when Philip saddled his favorite of the wagon team.

"I'll be gone no more than an hour or two, Clare. You'll be fine."

"I know." Her heart gave a lurch at the lie. Philip was leaving her with a loaded pistol and his hatchet, taking only the rifle for himself.

"I'll shoot us some supper while I'm gone," he added as he mounted up.

She was fairly certain he had never fired the piece.

He grinned down at her, but she turned her back to set about sorting through the contents of the wagon that had spilled during the crash. "Have the stewpot ready."

She heard the attempt at lightness in his voice but didn't reply.

"Clare?"

She straightened without facing him. "What?"

"It's going to be all right. I love you."

She could only wonder at the hope in her husband's voice—from where did it spring? And the rare note of vulnerability.

Her throat burned. Her eyes burned. She didn't let him see she wept.

"Just return before nightfall," she said, expunging all trace of tears from her voice. "Please."

And in the morning let us put this Kentucky foolishness behind us and go home.

"I will," Philip said. "I promise."

She cringed at the word, even as her heart took desperate hold of it.

Saddle leather creaked as the horse took its first steps away from her. By the time she turned to watch him go, Philip had disappeared around a bend in the trail.

4

The day was cool for early May, despite the sun high in a cloudless sky, yet Clare had worked herself into a sweat retrieving their scattered belongings from the trail and piling them in the wagon's shade. She dragged sacks of cornmeal, rolled casks of salted beef, and toted a trunk of Jacob's clothing and sundry other items, some damaged.

Seething, she checked on her son, found him still sprawled in sleep beneath the brush shelter, then heaved herself into the wagon—judging Philip's prop of stones stable enough—and began sorting the chaos beneath the bows, shoving and pushing with more force than necessary, once kicking aside a coverlet that dared tumble from the pile upon which she'd set it.

"Foolishness. Utter foolishness!"

As she snatched up the offending bedding to refold it, her fingers closed as well over a small wooden crate beneath it; the crate slipped from her grasp. The shattering of its contents as it hit the boards found its echo in her heart.

"No . . ." Lowering to her knees, she snatched the coverlet aside and attempted to pry open the crate's lid. Philip had nailed it fast. She took firmer grip, straining with gritted teeth, giving a shout as the lid came away with a screech. What remained of its contents—six delicate, blue-flowered china cups—slid away from its straw packing and fell around her in shards.

They had been a wedding gift from her mother.

Perhaps the cups had broken in the wagon's tipping, before she let them slip. Perhaps all she'd heard were the pieces clinking together inside the crate. In any case they were but cups, unsuitable for the life toward which they'd been making. They couldn't bear her and Jacob to safety, defend them against danger, provide a single bite of sustenance.

Yet it felt a monumental loss.

"Mama? I'm hungry."

Jacob's voice, thick with sleep and need, had her wiping her eyes and pasting on a smile as she turned to see him peeking over the wagon's gate. "Awake and hungry? Let me get down from here and I'll . . ."

Her words died on an indrawn breath. As she'd begun the awkward climb out of the wagon she'd felt a twinge, low in her back, sharper than the dull ache she'd experienced in that region off and on for days. Halfway out of the wagon she froze, heart beating hard, all her focus turned inward, searching the depths of her child-burdened flesh.

There came no second twinge, only a tug upon her petticoat and Jacob's voice, threaded with whining.

"Mama, *hungry.*"

"All right, Jacob." With her feet on solid ground she looked at the forest, at the clearing through the trees where the horse grazed. Shadows had deepened. The sun was setting. No wonder Jacob was hungry. Much more than an hour or two had passed since Philip's leaving.

Her gaze went sharp and searching to the bend in the trail leading back to Redstone. There was no sign of him.

He promised. Bitterness coursed through Clare as she sat before the open fire, Jacob asleep in the shelter behind her, darkness closed in thick beyond the firelight's reach. Would she never give up hoping Philip meant a single word he let cross his lips? Why had he left them alone in the perilous dark? Who—or what—had prevented his return?

Questions tormented her through a night spent dozing before the fire, waking to feed it with sticks she and Jacob had gathered before daylight fled. She kept the pistol and the hatchet close, but nothing came near in the dark. Or nothing she heard.

But in the morning the horse was gone.

Once the first clutch of shock released her, Clare surmised that its picket must have loosened, allowing it to wander off. Unless it had been stolen.

A chill having nothing to do with the cool mountain air night had ushered in gripped her. Philip had assured her the trail from Redstone to Wheeling would be safe, at least from raiding Indians.

He'd also promised to be back before nightfall.

"Mama? Mama, let me ask you something!"

Clare knelt at the fire and scraped a long-handled spoon through the cornmeal mush she was cooking for their breakfast, while Jacob jumped about like a flea, rested and bubbling with questions. He'd exhausted several subjects already, including the horse gone missing and his father's absence.

"Ask it then, Jacob."

"Will it rain?"

"I expect it will."

Thunder had worried the damp air since the predawn dark lifted. Now leaden clouds sagged above the clearing.

Jacob ceased his prancing and hunkered at the fire's edge, skinny arms wrapping dirty knees. "But how do you know it will rain?"

She ladled mush into a wooden bowl, found a spoon, put both into Jacob's hands, and said the first thing that entered her mind. "Rain most often follows thunder."

Directly on the heels of her words thunder rumbled again; seconds later scattered raindrops hit the trampled grass.

Jacob dropped the bowl, which landed miraculously upright, and stared at her open-mouthed.

Clare might have laughed if she wasn't drowning in fear and helplessness below a thin veneer of calm. Gazing about the secluded mountain clearing, she had never felt so threatened or exposed.

A tug on the sleeve of her gown. "Mama? Mama! Let me ask you something. Where did the horse go?"

She put the bowl back into his hands. "I told you, Jacob, I expect it got loose and wandered off to find more grass."

"Will it get wet in the rain?"

"I suppose it will. Now *eat*."

"Will we get wet?"

With a padded rag to protect her hand, she moved the rest of the corn mush from the flames. "We'll stay dry. We have this shelter Papa built."

Clare turned a critical eye to the lean-to, roofed in a layer of pine boughs that might keep off a light rain.

Jacob was at last shoveling mush into his mouth. Around a mouthful he asked, "What about Papa's horse?"

The child could be as fixated on a thing as could his father. "Swallow before you speak. What about it?"

Jacob swallowed. "Will it get wet in the rain?"

"Doubtless it will." Though for all she knew that horse was tucked up dry in a stable somewhere. Unless it was wandering the wilderness too. Riderless. Or bearing some painted heathen who'd stolen it.

She shook off that last chilling image and what it implied.

"Mama? Mama, let me ask you something!"

Clare bit back a sigh. "Ask it, Jacob."

"When will Papa be back?"

"Soon." She reached to tousle his sleep-mussed hair. "I'm sure it will be soon."

"But how do you know?"

If she heard that question another time . . .

Clare forced a smile and ladled more mush into Jacob's bowl. She had no answer, but her son had abandoned the bowl and the subject of Philip and was up again, his little body bursting with energy.

"Mama? Mama, is this where we're going to live?"

Finally a question she could answer with certainty. "It is *not*."

"Then when are we going to *leave* here?"

The very question she'd been pondering since the darkness lifted. She hadn't felt another menacing twinge, but if she was going to walk back to Redstone with a four-year-old, a loaded pistol, and food enough for the journey, she'd better start sooner rather than later.

Or should she wait a little longer?

As she turned to call out to Jacob, who was racing about the clearing now, the scattered raindrops that had continued to fall transformed without warning into a pelting deluge.

"Jacob! The shelter!"

Jacob raced to her and scrambled beneath it. Clare went to her knees and crawled within, dragging her petticoat behind her, and knew immediately the structure was an insufficient barrier to the rain. It barely slowed it.

"Run for the wagon!" Thunder cracked, momentarily deafening. Jacob gaped through runnels dripping from his hair. "Go, Jacob. I'll be right behind you!"

Wide-eyed, the boy shot like a cannonball into the falling gray, reaching the wagon almost before she'd extricated herself from the low shelter. Rain sharp as needles pounded her shoulders, her sodden cap.

Jacob was crouched beneath the wagon, peering out as she staggered toward him. She'd meant him to climb inside, but by now they were already soaked and muddied. The oiled bonnet should keep things dry inside and maybe the rain would be brief.

Once more she crouched and dragged her petticoat through mud that clung to anything it touched. Rain drummed on canvas, wood, earth, and leaf. Thunder cracked and lightning flared with a violence that made Jacob huddle against her and pat her thigh.

"Don't be afraid, Mama. Don't be afraid."

Her little boy was trying, in the midst of his own fear, to comfort her. *My little brave heart.* She pulled him close, wishing she still had a lap for him to occupy.

"I'm not afraid, darling. Not as long as you're with me."

The rain continued through most of that day. The little stream swelled until it threatened to overrun its banks. The trail became a quagmire. They huddled under the broken wagon, save for a few brief spells when the rain looked to be letting up, seeking its cover again when the deluge returned.

When at last the rain ceased and the sky began to lighten, Clare gave Jacob and herself a cursory wash, found dry clothes to change into, and made her decision.

Philip was gone. The horse was gone. But she still had two strong legs and so had Jacob. They would start the walk back to Redstone as soon as she gathered up what they would need—enough food to feed them on the way and what spare clothing they could carry. They would be back in Redstone in two days' time, maybe three, come rain or shine.

But not come childbirth.

The first unmistakable pang ripped through her while she was inside the wagon sorting through Jacob's clothing. More than just a throbbing in her lower back, this time a tight cramp arced around, gripping the sides of her belly.

She'd put off announcing to Jacob their return to Redstone until she'd made ready. She hurried now, panic gnawing at her, stuffing clothes and a bag of meal blindly into a knapsack, mentally reworking what she would, or could, carry.

She was climbing out of the wagon when a second pang gripped her. Lowering herself to the ground, she stood and waited it out. Waited several moments more just to see.

Just when she had breathed a sigh of relief, a third pain swelled, tightened, and receded. Then a fourth.

She would never make it to Redstone in time.

Hiding her dread and increasing discomfort, she prepared a supper, watched Jacob eat it, then settled him to sleep in the wagon early and made ready for what was coming, wondering how she would keep Jacob from having to witness it. She stripped to her shift and tried to sleep as well, waking with each pain and disturbing Jacob's sleep until finally she pulled a shawl across her shoulders and crept out of the wagon in darkness.

She paced the clearing near the shelter, wetting bare feet and the hem of her shift until, overcome with weariness, at the clearing's far edge she settled against a mossy tree, massaging her thighs and lower back as best she could between the pains that wouldn't cease, dozing between them. At some point, out of utter exhaustion, she fell into a deeper sleep, to be awakened at last by a pain so intense she couldn't stifle an outcry.

She blinked, disoriented by birdsong and sunlight.

Using the rough bole of the tree for support she got to her feet, then bent with her palms pressed to it, waiting out another wrenching pain.

When she caught her breath she called toward the wagon, visible across the clearing. "Jacob?"

All was quiet.

Halted twice to bend over her knees and gasp, Clare finally reached the wagon and peered within. The place she'd laid Jacob to sleep was mussed, but abandoned. He wasn't in the wagon. He wasn't under it. He hadn't been in the brush shelter.

The stream? Dread clenched her. But the water level had abated in the night. It was too low to have carried off her sturdy son even if he had fallen on slippery stones.

"Jacob! Where are you?"

Gone to see to the necessary? She turned in a circle, scanning the forest, expecting to see his blond head bobbing, his small frame emerging from the brush, struggling to button the front flap of his breeches.

"Jacob! I'm going to fix . . . breakfast!" Another pain gripped her halfway through the word.

No, baby, please. Wait a little longer. I need to find your brother.

She listened but there came no answer to her calls. No sound of boyish footsteps trampling the wood. Aside from the twittering of birds, the morning was still.

Waking to find her gone, Jacob wouldn't have wandered off without first calling for her. She'd have roused to that surely. Had he been prevented from doing so? Had he—she could hardly think it—had he been snatched away in the night? She'd heard Indians could move as silently as panthers.

An odd metallic taste flooded her mouth. *Not Indians.* Settlers more likely, passing through in the night. They'd found Jacob alone and took him. Out of kindness. On to Wheeling? Surely so. Settlers went west, not east.

Her relief at the realization was short-lived. Why hadn't Jacob told them she was nearby? Did he think she'd abandoned him? Is that what they all thought?

"Jacob . . . JACOB!"

Clare Inglesby screamed her son's name until her throat was raw. Until her voice broke with weeping. Until she felt a gushing beneath her shift and knew she was going to deliver this baby in the middle of the wilderness, while Philip was who knew where and Jacob was being carried off by strangers.

5

There were fresh tracks—Clare found them farther down the moist trail just out of sight of the wagon, beyond where her own panicked feet had obliterated all else. The prints led westward. She took a step in that direction, then halted, breathing hard. All she had on her person was the shift she wore and the hatchet clutched in her hand. She didn't recall snatching it up.

She studied the tracks. Two, perhaps three pairs of feet had made them. None with heeled shoes.

That didn't mean Indians. White men on the frontier wore moccasins. She'd seen plenty at Redstone.

There were no tracks of a barefooted little boy. Jacob had been carried. Relieved, or terrified and struggling?

Where was Philip?

She bent over and vomited onto the trail. On the heels of the sickness came the next pang. She endured it, breathing hard through clenched teeth. When it loosed its grip, she pushed all thought of Philip aside. She'd no more attention to spare him, either to hope for his return or to rage at his absence. She'd only attention to spare her children. There was no one to help her find the one lost or bring forth the one coming into the world.

Too soon to survive in it?

She headed back to the wagon, thoughts fixed on present needs. She would deliver the child. It would live or it would die. Either way she would press on. She would—

Where the trail took a bend around a stand of sapling maples, Clare halted, shot through with fresh alarm. At the wagon a man crouched, looking at the ground. Though his back was to her, she glimpsed dark hair, long and tailed, buckskin leggings, breechclout, fringed hunting shirt, rifle tucked into the crook of an arm.

Her gaze went back to the hair, straight, and so dark it might have been black. He was hatless. An Indian?

Gripped by another pang, she backed into the maples and lowered herself to a squat, clenching the hatchet. She waited out the pain with mind abuzz and heart slamming, then peered through the foliage at the man.

Still hunkered in a crouch, he cast his gaze in her direction. She was too far away to make out his features, but several days' growth of dark beard shadowed his cheeks.

She didn't think Indians were bearded.

Relief was again short-lived, replaced by suspicion. Had *he* taken Jacob? She saw no sign of her son, but perhaps he was nearby. Perhaps this man had come back for . . . what? Her things? Her?

A low groan escaped her, which she managed to muffle almost at once, but soon enough the agony of childbed would reveal her presence. Before another pain came she grasped a sapling and pulled herself to her feet.

A stick cracked beneath her settling bare heel.

As if it had been a gun's report, the man shot up from the ground, rifle leaping into his hands, its long barrel aimed with uncanny accuracy at the spot where she hid.

An everlasting two seconds passed before he spoke, calling out in a voice hard as seasoned hickory, carrying the trace of a western Virginia drawl.

"I know you're there. Might as well step on out where I can see you proper."

Clare stayed still as a cornered rabbit, fingers melded to the hatchet's handle. She'd use it if he came at her. Strike him with it. Then get to the pistol and . . .

The man took a step toward her. "Reckon you're unarmed else you'd have shot me by now."

Pain gripped her again. Encompassing. All-consuming. A moan tore from her mouth.

The man had taken more steps but now halted, gaze searching the maple thicket, trying to make her out.

"You hurt?"

Body and soul. Her every fiber screamed the answer. All that emerged *was* a scream as she burst from cover like a pheasant taking wing, hatchet raised, running at the man in what she knew, even in the midst of half-blinding fury and fear, was a ludicrous waddle. His lean face as she reached him—mouth agape, dark brows shot high, eyes wide—was an equally ludicrous mask as, still screaming, Clare aimed the hatchet at the throat just below it.

Her belly was her undoing. Robbed of balance, she staggered and missed her mark. Still she saw red bloom across the back of his hand as he raised the rifle between them. The hard barrel banged her knuckles, knocking the hatchet away.

Resorting to fingernails, she clawed for the face looming above hers. "Where is he? What have you done with my baby?"

He held the rifle crosswise, keeping her at bay. She tried to thrust it aside; it was like trying to shove a mountain from her path. He freed a hand and grabbed one of hers and she smelled him—leather and grease and smoke and male—as his dark eyes looked down at her bulging belly pressed against him, nothing between but her filthy shift.

"Miss . . . Missus." His voice was tight with the effort of restraining her. "Reckon your baby's right here between us."

Recoiling, she wrenched free, not expecting the stranger to simply let her go, nearly falling when he did so. She caught herself and faced him.

"My son. My four-year-old son. *Jacob.* He's gone!"

The words were little more than a wail. Even so those eyes above strong cheekbones flashed understanding and concern.

"Your son is lost?"

Was it concern? Or was it cunning?

"Not lost—taken. You know it! *You* have him!" Clare lunged for the hatchet, but another pain gripped her and she halted, holding her breath, hands fisted against her sides.

The man took a step back, rifle still raised between them. "I haven't got your boy."

His gaze swept her, seeing far too much, but when the pang loosed its grip she stood straighter, uncaring what he could or couldn't see. "Someone does!"

"You didn't see him taken?"

"I was asleep! If I'd seen—"

The next pain came so swift it stole her breath. She bent over, panting, unable to mind the man or anything except getting to the other side of that agony.

"God in Heaven," she thought he said but she was groaning so loudly she couldn't be sure. When at last she looked up, his sun-browned face had gone ashen. "You're having your baby *now*?"

"They don't ask *by your leave* to be born. Now get out of my way!" She pushed past him and made for the wagon, all but certain by the look of him he'd be no help to her—not that she meant to ask. Limbs shaking, she started to climb into the wagon.

"Wait, Missus." The man was beside her, a hand encircling her arm. For all his strength she could feel him shaking. "Let me get whatever—"

"Leave me be!"

He didn't release her. "What sort of man would abandon you like this?"

"My husband, for one!"

Now here was this stranger offering the promise of support. She wanted to collapse into it, trust in it, but knew better.

But if he would at least fetch and carry . . .

"I need bedding. Get it from the wagon and take it to that brush shelter yonder. I'm going to have this baby there. Wait," she added as he set the rifle against the wagon's gate. "Before you touch anything, go wash at the stream."

She wrinkled her nose in his direction, though he wasn't soiled or greasy-looking, unlike many of the frontiersmen she'd seen at Redstone. In fact, he was in far more presentable state than she. Not looking to see if he obeyed, she headed through the fringe of trees between the wagon and the clearing where she and Jacob had camped.

Jacob. How would she find him? How long until she could start? *Don't let it rain again. Let those tracks stay clear.* The sky above was clouded but looked to be clearing. If it didn't there was nothing she could do about it. The weather—and her body—were beyond her control.

Don't let me die.

The going was slow, halted twice by pangs so stunning she could do nothing but stand and ride them out. By the time she reached the shelter so had the man, beard and lashes wet from washing, arms full of bedding. This he spread beneath the shelter; then took off running back toward the trail.

Clare lowered herself to the ground and crawled inside, thinking that was that. He'd lost his nerve.

Before she could grind her teeth over the thought, he was back, a pack and the rifle in hand. He propped both against the shelter, along with her hatchet. Tucked into the sash belting his shirt was her pistol. He removed it, testing its weight.

"This primed, loaded?" She grunted affirmation. He set the weapon aside. "What else can I do?"

"Water . . . and my simples box . . . the wagon—"

She'd brought along supplies for this hour, though she'd hoped not to need them until they had a cabin raised or at least were among a party with other women. Before she could describe the box in question, the man spied the small kettle at the edge of the ashes, snatched it up, and was off again.

In moments his footsteps returned. The kettle thumped down, dripping full. The box appeared beside her.

"Open it," she said.

He obeyed, fumbling with the latch, clearly rattled. She told him what she needed: shears to cut the cord, twine to tie it, clean rags to wash the baby, a vial of oil she needed to use immediately. He set each item beside her.

"Turn away now. I don't want you watching." Knowing what the man was eventually going to see—if he stuck around long enough—it was a pointless command, but he put his back to her obligingly. She rucked up her shift and used the oil to lubricate delicate flesh about to be very much abused.

But please not torn. The baby was early. Perhaps it would be small. *But please not too small.*

She pulled her shift back over her knees. The man had gotten the fire going, the kettle over it. Now he ran a hand over his bound hair, an agitated gesture.

"May I turn around?"

She'd have to let him do so at some point. "Fine."

He turned, still kneeling. "Can I do more?"

She pushed up on her elbows as the next pain built, expecting to feel the urge to push. It didn't come. "There's no helping me now."

"I know *that* well enough," she thought he muttered. Louder, he asked, "How long since your husband left?"

Time had muddled. It felt like moments. It felt like weeks. "Days. Two, I think."

The man wore an odd expression. Pity? Regret?

"And your son? He was taken when?"

"In the night just past. My pains started. I went into the woods so as not to frighten him." The anguish and frustration were almost too great to bear. Jacob was being carried away, and it was her fault, but she was trapped here with his brother who'd chosen the worst possible time to be born. The man was staring at her, thoughts moving behind his eyes.

"Do you know who took him?" she asked.

It could never be so easy. But the man didn't say *no*. He hesitated, looking as if he'd something to tell her he'd no wish to say.

Jacob isn't dead! She wanted to scream the words at this stranger with eyes full of doom, but the baby was coming, the undeniable need to push gathering at last in flesh and bone. The man hovered near, terror in his gaze again, but his next words evidenced some notion of what was next to come.

"Where do you want me? Behind you or . . . ?"

"Someone has to catch him." No thought of modesty now, she rucked up her shift and he knelt between her knees.

She strained and pushed and wasn't quiet about it. At last she gasped for breath. "He's early. Can you . . . see him . . . yet?"

"I don't think so. Hold on . . ." While he hemmed and hawed, she pushed again. "I see his head!"

The man's eyes were huge. She felt his hands on her as the baby's head emerged. She pushed, rising up enough to see him pull the baby out of her, a blur of purplish limbs. Then she lay back on the coverlet, feeling the hard ground beneath, and simply breathed with the visceral relief of it, until she realized she'd heard no newborn's cry. No sound at all.

She struggled to her elbows, spots swirling as she raised her head. She blinked them clear to see the man still kneeling between her knees, but his attention wasn't on her. He'd snatched up a rag, was doing something with water, or was it the twine?

"Is he alive? Tell me!"

The man looked up, eyes still round but no longer glinting with terror. As though the worst had happened and there was no more need for fear.

"Your baby's breathing, Missus—thanks be to God." He'd spoken with relief, but those eyes beneath level brows met hers warily, as if to gage her receptivity to some less favorable news of the child. "It's only . . ."

She wanted to claw the tangled shift away to *see* but hadn't the strength. "Only what?"

"Only it's not what you've been saying," the man replied. "Not a *he*. A *she*. You got a baby girl."

6

It had all come right in the end. The woman had survived. The baby girl seemed strong, if a tad on the puny side. He had kept a tight lid on his nerves and done what he'd had to do.

Jeremiah Ring rehearsed the facts, giving thanks for the Almighty's deliverance, yet his hands quaked as he knelt at the trail-side creek. He winced as the bloody score across his hand touched the water's flow. She'd dealt him the scratch before she knew he meant to help her.

A fighter, that one. Not that Hannah hadn't been . . .

He took that thought captive. Instead he pictured the woman from the wagon, blond hair streaming, green eyes aflame, coming at him with that hatchet like she meant to take him down—alone and in the grip of childbirth.

Desperation could lend a body strength, and to Jeremiah's reckoning there wasn't much more desperate a woman could face than birthing a child. But was she strong enough to bear what he'd yet to tell her? And what was he to do about her once she grasped the extent of her plight? He'd his own business to be about, and it lay in the opposite direction she would need to go.

The first whispers of the tragedy at Baker's had outpaced Jeremiah to Pittsburgh, where Major John Connolly proved more interested in securing Ohio land for Virginia's Governor Dunmore than in a few lost Mingo lives. A seething Alexander McKee, the Indian agent, had enlisted Jeremiah as one of the carriers of a message to the Shawnee chiefs—and to Logan—inviting them to a council in Pittsburgh in hopes of turning aside reprisals for the Yellow Creek killings.

Jeremiah feared the plea would fall on deaf ears in Logan's case. The

Mingo's words as he stood over his murdered kin tolled in Jeremiah's memory. *"For every life here taken from me, by my hand ten of the whites will die."*

"Not that I don't sympathize with Logan's desire for revenge," McKee had said. "In his place I'd want it. But if he takes it, we could find ourselves plunged into an all-out border war, one no side can win, save maybe Dunmore."

He'd promised McKee to do all he could to keep the peace, as well as to take word of the summons down the Monongahela to Redstone Fort, cautioning every man there against interfering with any Indians on the river heading for Pittsburgh. From Redstone he'd meant to travel west to Wheeling by canoe, then on to the Shawnee towns on the Scioto River, but while at Redstone he'd heard talk of a settler who'd taken his family down a packhorse trail against urgings to the contrary—in a wagon.

Nursing a bad feeling about that settler, Jeremiah had taken to the trail. Rainfall had washed out most sign of the wagon's passing, but here and there Jeremiah saw the scars of small trees the man had removed from the path, rocks dislodged where he'd made way for his wagon's wheels, ruts where those wheels had mired.

Then he'd found the man, stripped, scalped, and left for carrion alongside the trail he'd labored to bend to his will. Or Jeremiah supposed it the man. The absence of a family didn't surprise him. They'd be taken captive. But where was the wagon or its charred remains?

He'd buried the man, piled him over with stones, and decided to press on to Wheeling.

It was while lifting the last stone onto the makeshift grave he'd found the timepiece, its gilded case half crushed so that it wouldn't yield to prying. He'd slipped it into his knapsack, thinking he'd force it open when next he paused to rest, hoping for an inscription inside. It was still in his knapsack, leaning against the shelter where the woman rested with her newborn. He could see her lower half, muddy shift, long pale calves, dirty feet.

Returning to her, he crouched at the shelter's opening, half hoping she'd be asleep.

She was awake, gazing at the babe beside her, wrapped in a blanket he'd fetched from the wagon. The blanket, tiny and blue, had stirred his heart with pity. She'd prepared it for this day, planning for the child's advent. A busted wagon, a vanished son, a brush shelter in the wilderness, a stranger to midwife —none of that would have figured into those plans.

She'd yet to learn the worst of it.

The baby's tiny features were knotted, scrunched and red. The small head was capped in hair surprisingly dark for a fair mother and, best he could tell by what remained of the man's scalp, an even fairer father.

Shoving those thoughts aside, he cleared his throat.

"Reckon we ought to introduce ourselves, Missus. The name's Jeremiah Ring, lately out of Fort Pitt."

The woman looked him over with those clear green eyes, an assessing gaze. He wondered what she made of him. He'd never gone wholly native as some men did, living long stretches among the Shawnees, but squatting there in breechclout, leggings, and quilled moccasins, he didn't much resemble the Virginia farmer he used to be.

The woman dropped her gaze. Tired bruises ringed her eyes.

"Clare Inglesby," she said, then frowned. "Mrs. Philip Inglesby, I mean."

He'd noted her momentary confusion, the coloring of her cheeks. He felt it too, the disconcerting intimacy that oughtn't to lie between two people just exchanging names. As if shy of him seeing her bare skin now, she tucked her feet beneath the dirty hem of her shift.

Again he cleared his throat. "What were you doing when I found you, Missus? You weren't trying to follow those ones who took your boy, were you?"

"That's precisely what I was doing." Mrs. Inglesby pushed herself up to sitting, hair falling in golden ropes to her lap.

Now he had space to really look at her, Jeremiah noted she'd a comeliness undiminished by months of child-carrying or the ordeal just past. She'd eyes wide-spaced, a nose not small but nicely sculpted, a sharp jaw ending in a delicately pointed chin.

"What else was I to do?"

He'd no answer to that. None she'd want to hear.

"Why don't you tell me what's happened." Maybe she'd let fall some clue as to who killed her man and made off with her son. Maybe he'd find it wasn't even her man he'd buried.

She told the story from the busting of the wagon to her husband's insistence on leaving them, the long wait, the vanished horse, the labor coming on, up to that morning when she woke to find her son vanished as well.

She spoke precisely, unhesitating, and somewhere in the midst of her tale he realized she was what his mama would've called *gentle-born*. Virginia seaboard by her accent.

By the time she'd reached the part where he entered the tale, Jeremiah couldn't say for certain who'd been the death of Philip Inglesby, nor who'd taken her son, nor if they were one and the same, but his gut was telling him who it had been.

Logan.

"I can wait no longer for Philip." She leaned forward and gripped his arm, catching him off guard. "Can you tell me where to go from here? Where do I begin to look for Jacob?"

He stared at her hand clamped above his wrist, then into her determined face. "*Look* for him?"

She released him. "You cannot imagine I would simply abandon him?"

"I don't . . . You've just . . ." Did she think she was going to cross the Ohio, march into Logan's town at Yellow Creek, and—if his gut was even correct about that—simply demand her son back? Just delivered of a baby?

But he'd yet to tell her the one thing that might bring her around to seeing sense.

"You're right, Missus. There's no point in waiting any longer for your husband."

She blinked at him, a rising dread overshadowing her determined gaze. It crystallized into stark knowing before she banished it with a blink.

"Why would you say that?"

"Because I found the man dead on the trail yesterday, about a mile from here." Scalped, mutilated, probably tortured, but she didn't need to know that part. "I buried him. It was getting on toward sunset," he added lamely.

The woman was wagging her head. "But how do you know? How *could* you know it was Philip?"

"I said I was out of Fort Pitt, and that's true. But I've come by way of Redstone, where I heard tell of you and your husband. I was bound for Wheeling so decided to come along after you. There's been other killings." He told her about the massacre at Yellow Creek, again sparing the gruesome details. "In my hearing, Logan vowed his revenge. I don't know was it him and his warriors killed your husband or took your son. Probably was. Unless it was a passing band of Cherokees. But as I said, I came along the trail and found a man lying dead—"

"And as *I* said," Mrs. Inglesby interrupted, "you cannot know it was Philip!"

Jeremiah rose to retrieve his knapsack. "You're right, Missus. I don't know. Maybe you can say."

He fished inside and found the object he sought, withdrew it, and thrust it at her, resting on his open palm.

"This recall itself to you?"

Mrs. Inglesby stared at the battered timepiece; Jeremiah was watching her face when the blood drained, leaving it pale as chalk.

Oh, Philip. He'd been so proud of that timepiece, an heirloom of his grandfather's given to him on his eighteenth birthday, one of the few of his family's treasures he hadn't sold to pay his father's debts. It was battered and broken now, as if a rock or a boot heel had come down on it. She took it in her hand, which shook from exhaustion and the grief crashing over her like a smothering sea-breaker. Philp wasn't coming back. Philip was dead. Buried by this stranger with sense enough to come down that trail after them.

A second wave, as relentless as the first, broke over her and washed away grief, flooding her with rage and determination. Philip was lost to her, but Jacob would not be. He would not know this yawning emptiness, this terrifying abandonment she now faced and to which she could see no end. Not for one second longer than he must.

She was going to find her son. No matter if Philip had left her to do it alone.

Despite her pallor, Mrs. Inglesby hadn't swooned. She'd taken the timepiece from him, closed her fist around it, drew back her hand, and hurled it past his head, out into the clearing.

She didn't weep. Didn't tell him her husband couldn't possibly be dead. Didn't say anything at all. She put her back to him, lay down with her baby, and appeared to go to sleep.

For the rest of that day, Mrs. Inglesby napped, saying no more than was necessary when awake. Jeremiah found foodstuffs in the wagon and fixed a meal of corn cakes in the fire's ashes. He fetched and carried for her. She tended her baby, rising once to make her way into the wood to tend herself. He watched for her return but didn't aid or interfere. Her stark, preoccupied face was a daunting sight.

She slept that night in the brush shelter, in a clean shift, on fresh bedding. He washed the soiled things in the creek, spread them on the wagon's gate, then slept by the fire, his last thoughts troubled by what the morrow would bring.

What it brought was Clare Inglesby on her feet before the sun was up, gowned, shod, capped, baby in a makeshift sling across her breasts.

"Will this trail lead me to Wheeling Settlement, Mr. Ring?" Her gaze burned him as her lips formed the words.

"Aye, it will, but oughtn't you to be heading back to Redstone?"

At this sensible suggestion the woman radiated impatience. "I have no intention of returning to Redstone. Not without Jacob."

He rubbed a hand behind his neck, for a moment at a loss for words. What was the Almighty thinking, saddling him with this woman when he'd pressing need to be elsewhere? Already her plight had stirred up memories, ones he'd spent the last ten years laying to rest.

"Missus, exactly how do you mean to find your boy?"

"By following this trail to Wheeling Settlement. I can travel neither far nor fast at present, but I am determined to start today."

The woman waited, arms laced beneath the bulge of her newborn, looking for all the world mere seconds from starting off down that trail. He stood by the fire with the rising sun shedding no light for his tired brain, not liking the lift of her stubborn little chin. She'd gone stony since hurling the timepiece away, the only emotion she'd exhibited since he gave her the news of Inglesby's death. He'd found the piece in the weeds while she slept and slipped it back into his knapsack. In case she changed her mind about wanting the thing.

"What," he began carefully, "makes you think your son is in Wheeling?"

"He must be!" For the first time, Jeremiah detected a hint of desperation behind her stubbornness. "I know it's my fault. I fell asleep and . . . they must not have known, mustn't have realized Jacob wasn't abandoned."

She nearly choked on that last word, ducking her head toward the tiny infant in her sling, hunching over the child as if she feared the baby being snatched away as well.

He was trying hard to fathom her train of thought. "They? I thought you said you didn't know who took your boy."

"I don't! I . . ." Mrs. Inglesby clamped a hand over her mouth, but her eyes gazed at him, searchingly. When she spoke again, it was from behind the shield of her hand, as if she wished to hide from the words. "My parents . . . They warned me not to go through with it, not to marry Philip. Not after . . . everything."

"Everything?" He'd no idea where she was going with this and was pretty certain he didn't want to know.

The woman's face twisted as she fought for control of emotions that seemed to be surfacing now, whether she wanted them to or not.

"Philip's father . . . He lost their family's fortune on the eve of our wedding, then took his own life. It was our fathers who arranged the marriage, and after Philip's . . . my father advised me to break the engagement, but . . . I couldn't. I couldn't abandon Philip. Now he's abandoned me. But I *will not* abandon Jacob!"

There was panic in her eyes, raw and pleading. Jeremiah felt a wrench in his chest and realized he knew this woman—leastwise her anger, her grief, her terror, the desperate hope that wouldn't let her accept her son was lost to her. Ten years, yet memory of that driving need was as fresh as though it had entered his soul yesterday.

Though he feared to reach for her or make any move that might spook or offend, to his surprise words came bubbling out. "You got to keep steady now, Missus. Don't let fear drive you beyond reason. I know it seems like nothing's ever going to be right in your world again, but that's a lie. I promise you, it's a lie."

The panic in her eyes receded some, but not the pain. "How can you know it's a lie?"

Jeremiah clenched his teeth to keep from telling her how he knew, or how hard-won was the knowing. "Missus, you got another child to think of. There's only one thing to be done now." He drew breath to tell her again what that one thing was—return to Redstone—when, amazingly, he saw something like calm overtake her. As if she'd heard his words, inadequate as they'd been, taken strength and comfort from them, and would allow herself at last to be sensibly led. *Hallelujah.*

"You are correct," she said, the steel coming back into her tone. "There is but one thing for me to do now. One thing with which I must concern myself, with all my heart and strength."

Clare Inglesby straightened her spine. Up went that chin again. "I am going to find my son, Mr. Ring, and you . . . surely you are meant to be my guide."

7

Darkness had fallen, busy with insects and the stirrings of night creatures. The fire Mr. Ring had built was small, growing smaller since he'd ceased to fuel it. What light it cast showed his face, so needful of a razor's attention that it might properly be called bearded, but did little to push back the blackness pressing close. The twisting flames made the shadows edging their camp shift like stealthy figures darting through the brush.

The wagon had been no true protection from peril, but away from it now Clare felt stripped of its comfort, the last tie to a life taken from her piecemeal, severed. Now all that remained was the wrenching need to recover the piece that mattered most.

Jacob. He was her life now, along with the baby in her arms. Not the son she'd envisioned, the playmate for Jacob whom she'd intended to name after Philip.

The baby's arrival, Jacob's disappearance, Philip's death, the man seated across the fire—it might all have been a merciless nightmare from which she couldn't wake. The one hopeful turn was Mr. Ring's agreement to escort her to Wheeling where, no doubt, she would find her son in the company of whomever had needlessly taken him into their care.

Never mind what *he* had to say on the matter. *Not Indians . . .*

She laid the baby on the blanket spread over moss, enduring the visceral need to feel not this tiny infant in her arms but Jacob's solid weight. Did someone hold him? Was he hungry? Did he cry for her?

Unable to stem her tears, she turned her back on the fire, giving her attention to the baby's soiled clout. She sorted through the items Mr. Ring had ap-

proved her bringing, parceled out in packs they'd each carried, until she
unearthed fresh wrappings and the cloths she needed to tend herself.

He'd argued for stopping well before dark because of the spring, the faint
burble of which his keen ears had caught, issuing from under a rock.

The spring had been an excuse. Clare knew he'd thought her too spent to
press on until nightfall. Perhaps she was. Once they'd stopped she'd grown
aware of a ravenous hunger and a thirst that had been building all that day, no
matter how often they'd stopped to quench it, as well as muscles aching from
the birth, the pain in her breasts as her milk began to come in.

That latter was going to worsen—at least it had with Jacob—before it got
better. The thought of wearing her baby in a sling against those breasts again
was quailing.

That was tomorrow's worry. For now she needed to find the strength to
stand and wash out the soiled clout.

"Let me see to that, Missus."

Clare looked over her shoulder to find the man come silently to his feet,
hand extended.

One thing he could not be called was *garrulous,* this Jeremiah Ring.
They'd spoken little since leaving the wagon that morning. Their exchanges
since pitching camp had been marked by wariness, uncertainty, and, on Clare's
part, the rawest, bone-achingest exhaustion she had ever known.

"You needn't feel obliged, Mr. Ring. I'm well able to care for my child."
She all but cringed, hearing the words. Were they true, she wouldn't have allowed Jacob to be stolen from under her nose.

"Of course you can, Missus. Just thought the mite would be hungry and
you'd need to feed her. I'd not have that clout stinking up camp, drawing in
whatever it may draw, before you get the chance to see to it. Nor the little one
crying to feed while you clean that clout."

Too tired to argue with his logic, she gave the bundle into his hand.

While he went into the dark, she draped her shoulder with a blanket, unpinned her bodice, unlaced her stays, and pressed the baby warm against her sore flesh. She winced as the tiny mouth latched on with a strength she'd forgotten a newborn possessed, but was glad she hadn't to struggle over getting this one to nurse. Unlike Jacob, she made no fuss over suckling but seemed to know what to do from the first time Clare put her to a breast.

She'd been a quiet baby thus far, not squalling incessantly as Jacob had done his first weeks. Granted, she'd come early, though perhaps not as early as Clare had thought, given her ability to thrive.

She glanced at the shadows where Mr. Ring had vanished, then moved the blanket aside to observe the baby.

This was her child, every bit as much as Jacob. Where then was the overpowering love, the consuming passion, that had engulfed her at first sight of her son? In its place was a maelstrom of resentment the child didn't deserve. She hadn't chosen the timing of her birth. Yet the thought wouldn't dislodge from Clare's mind that had it not been for this baby, she and Jacob would never have been parted.

Mechanically she stroked the baby's cheek, then ran a fingertip over the cap of soft, dark hair. Jacob's hair had been the same startling shade at birth. It had long since been replaced by fair curls, a process she'd found fascinating.

Footsteps in the brush snapped the sweet thread of memory.

Mr. Ring set his ever-present rifle near to hand, spread the wet clout before the fire, and resumed his place opposite, legs crossed. Clare looked away from his sun-browned thighs bared by breechclout and leggings. She'd seen such immodest clothing at Redstone, a distinguishing feature of frontiersmen. By the look of him, Mr. Ring had long acquaintance with the wilds, though she didn't think he was many years older than she, despite the weathering around his eyes.

He had nicely shaped eyes. Kind. A little sad.

Self-conscious about nursing her child in front of him, even under the concealing blanket, Clare did her best to discreetly settle her daughter against her other side. She avoided looking at Mr. Ring again until she had spread the blanket on the moss, put the baby down, and readjusted her stained clothing.

The baby squirmed in her wrappings, little face clenched, pink gums baring in a fretful mewl. Clare hurried with her pins, then picked up the baby with tired arms and hoisted her against one shoulder. She patted the tiny back until she'd elicited a soft burp. Hoping that would suffice, she laid the baby down.

The little face scrunched tight.

"What is the matter?" Clare asked, as if the infant could convey such knowledge. She rolled the little body gently aside and felt under her with a hand. No stones or roots met her searching palm.

The baby's crying escalated. Stifling a sigh, Clare scooped her up again.

"Mind if I hold her for a spell? You look to need a rest."

Surprised by the man's offer, Clare's first instinct was to deny any such need, but her arms were sagging under the tiny weight. Reluctantly she handed her daughter over.

"Mind her belly stump. And her neck. Take care how . . ." But he already had one big hand splayed protectively behind the baby's head, steadying her wobbly neck.

"You've held a baby before."

Mr. Ring met her gaze across the fire's embers. "A time or two."

But not his own. He'd told her as much that morning as they'd locked horns over which direction she would head from the wagon. Mr. Ring had wanted her to start for Redstone, abandoning all they could not carry. After all, she'd no business, a woman alone with a newborn, being in the west.

"No business?" she'd retorted. "You know very well what my business is, Mr. Ring. Jacob. Have you so soon forgotten?"

The man hadn't backed down in the face of her indignation. Taller than she by a head, he'd gazed at her with seemingly unruffled calm. "I've not for-gotten him, Missus. But it might be best if you try to. Chances of you getting him back—"

"You've obviously no child of your own," she'd asserted, cutting him off. "Or you would never suggest such a thing!"

He'd flinched at that. "I have no child."

"Then do me the courtesy of ceasing to pretend you've any understanding of the need that compels me." Her chin had trembled but she'd ground her teeth, refusing to cry again.

"Yet I do grasp the enormity of what you propose to do, far better than you possibly could."

She'd gazed at him, desperate to refute the stark words, and into her mind popped a phrase. "With God all things are possible."

She wasn't sure if that was Scripture. It sounded like it. And it sounded brave. Determined. She needed him to believe she was both.

"With God, yes," Mr. Ring had agreed. "If we're certain sure it's His leading."

"Of course it is." Why wouldn't the Almighty wish her to find her son? To do all in her power to recover him?

"I've lived among both Shawnees and Mingos, Missus," Mr. Ring had said. "They aren't going to harm your boy. He's not suffering right now, not in any want. He's safe among them."

Face blanching, she'd raised her hand to halt such talk. "Jacob is in Wheel-ing, Mr. Ring. Of that I'm certain. You are headed in that direction regardless, are you not?"

"I am. But—"

"Then take me with you. Once there I shall go my way and you yours. There will be others willing to help me, surely."

He'd caught the reproach in her words, though this time the flinching was only in his eyes. He'd opened his mouth as if to argue but then shut it, shaking his head.

"I mean to go to Wheeling Settlement, Mr. Ring," she'd reiterated. "Should you attempt to force me back east, I promise I shall go kicking and screaming the entire way. Still, what you do or don't do to aid me from this point is up to you."

With that, she'd started walking westward, away from the wagon. Foolishly. Blindly. Without a scrap of food or anything on her person but the baby.

In moments she'd heard his footfalls coming fast behind her and thought he meant to brave the kicking and screaming, throw her over his shoulder, baby and all, and carry her east to Redstone.

"All right. All right, Missus. Will you . . . just stop!"

She stopped. "What?"

The man held her gaze, his own resigned. "I said all right, Mrs. Inglesby. I'll help you get to Wheeling, but I'm telling you, you won't find your son there."

"But I shall." Clutching her baby close, Clare turned her back on the man, returning to the wagon to pack her things.

Of the wagon's contents, they'd taken what could be borne on their backs—provisions, bedding, the pistol and its ammunition, the contents of Clare's simples box though not the box itself. Gowns and wrappings for the baby. The hatchet.

As for the rest, though no word of it passed between them, Clare knew she would never see any of it again.

Mr. Ring had remained taciturn throughout the day's sojourn, slow as it was. She'd been content to let him remain so, it needing all her willpower to put one foot in front of another.

Now, in the firelight, Clare studied the man, who seemed absorbed in like inspection of her daughter, cradled along his forearm. He'd worn a battered, round-brimmed hat for most of the day but had removed it, baring dark hair pulled back into a tail that fell below his shoulders. His forehead was high, his brows level and thick, the bridge of his nose long and narrow. From that head-bent angle, his cheekbones appeared prominent, though his face was longer than it was wide, rather mournfully cast until . . .

Her gaze traveled downward to his mouth, which had softened in a smile. It crinkled the corners of his eyes, which captured a glint of firelight as though sight of her baby's face had kindled warmth behind them.

It was the first time she'd seen him smile. It made his sober face seem almost handsome.

Clare had thought it wise to refrain from inquiring exactly how long it would take to walk to Wheeling, for she supposed that would depend upon her stamina. She'd pushed herself over a trail that had twisted along creeks, climbed wooded slopes, and plunged down ravines, proving the men of Redstone correct beyond any doubt; had they made it to Wheeling, it would have been on foot with the wagon abandoned—the wagon they'd meant to trade for river passage. Had he survived, Philip would have led them into utter ruin, destitute on the frontier.

She supposed he'd managed to do it, even in death.

Mr. Ring lifted his head and caught her staring. "You settle on a name yet?" he asked, that soft smile lingering.

"I— No." The question disconcerted. "I'd a boy's name chosen these months past. Philip John, after . . ." When she hesitated at the painful closing in her throat, Mr. Ring cleared his own.

"Did you never think on a girl's name?"

Not only had she never considered a feminine name during her pregnancy, she'd yet to give a name for her daughter a moment's thought. "I suppose I could still name her as I'd planned."

Mr. Ring raised his brows over the baby asleep in his embrace. "Call her by a boy's name? Philip or John?"

"Neither, of course. I'd call her Philippa. Philippa Joan, perhaps."

The name didn't resonate in any particular way. Nor did it with Mr. Ring, apparently. He frowned at the baby, as if searching her tiny features for some indication the name suited.

It suited Clare well enough. "Philippa Joan will be her name."

Mr. Ring's gaze lifted, but he didn't comment on her choice.

"Don't know whether I've mentioned what my business is along the Ohio at present. You recall what I told you about the Mingos? About Logan and his kin at Yellow Creek?"

"You told me they were killed." Why was he bringing up that savage's name? She didn't want to think about the manner of Philip's dying. What he must have seen. Had his last thoughts been of her? Their children?

She cut off that line of thinking fast as Mr. Ring said, "I was with Logan when he found their bodies. It was the cruelest, most barbarous sight I hope I ever see in this life."

Clare drew in a breath. "Worse than the sight of my husband lying dead?"

Mr. Ring glanced up briefly, giving his answer in silence.

"After we got his kin back across the river to their town, I left Logan in mourning and returned to Fort Pitt. From there I was sent out by McKee—he's the deputy Indian agent—with a message for Cornstalk, the principal Shawnee chief, in response to the killings. I'm on my way with it now."

And she, with her plight, had slowed him down. That must be what he meant to imply. "Once I have Jacob safely in my custody, I will find a way to return to Staunton."

"Come from Staunton, do you?" He looked surprised. "I'd placed you farther east."

"I am from Richmond, if you must know, but we lived the past few years on my uncle's farm in the Shenandoah."

The man was searching her face, his gaze sharpened, though she'd no notion what he was looking for. Thinking she preferred his silence, she reached for the baby.

"Give her to me, please."

As he held the baby toward her, one hand splayed protectively beneath her head, Clare noticed the angry red scratch across its back, just below the knuckles. She took the baby and laid her down asleep, then turned back to him.

"Your hand. Did I . . . ?"

He turned his hand over to view the scratch, as though he'd forgotten it was there. "Don't bother yourself. I'll tend it."

By the time he found the unguent he carried and smeared it over the wee scratch, Mrs. Inglesby was asleep. Jeremiah sat wakeful, watching her. A puzzle she was, with some pieces beginning to fall into place in his mind and others that, try as he might, he couldn't make fit. He couldn't know the nature of the Inglesbys' marriage. Arranged, she'd called it. Yet when she might have broken off the engagement, she'd married the man without his fortune. Perhaps there'd been love in it once. Jeremiah was fair certain there'd been pain—older than the tragic events of the past few days.

He glanced at his knapsack, where McKee's missive was tucked away, an obligation he oughtn't to ignore even if he wasn't the only messenger sent. No telling whether the others had got through already, or at all, but someone had to reach the Shawnees. Ought he to abandon Clare Inglesby in Wheeling, regardless of what she did or didn't find?

He'd been where she was now. He knew the screaming need in her, had once let it master him, let it drown out reason, wisdom, even the Almighty's leading.

There were two paths before him, but he couldn't walk both. Could he?

Show me, he prayed. *Better yet, show me wrong. Let the boy be in Wheeling.*

The faintest of breezes crossed the fire's remains, stirring embers, briefly showing him a long blond braid, a curving hip, the stained folds of Clare Inglesby's petticoat.

He lay on his back with his rifle near, gazing at the slow march of clouds across a bright half-moon and remembering . . . fear, grief, regret, and the voice of a warrior telling him in all kindness the hard, cruel truth of what it meant to be a captive, embraced and adopted, white identity washed away in the cleansing waters of the river.

He awoke some hours later, judging by the moon's new position in the sky, disturbed by a sound out of place in his surroundings. Whimpering, but not that of an animal. His fingers tightened on the rifle before he remembered the baby.

Pippa. He'd stopped himself saying it aloud, what sprang into his mind when the woman announced her daughter's name. He'd been looking at the baby asleep along his arm, feeling a roil of grief and anger remembering Koonay and her and Gibson's unborn child, yet finding in the face of the tiny mite he'd helped into the world a healing of sorts. A balm. There was a sweetness about this girl-child that touched him in a way nothing had in a long time. Then he'd heard the name pronounced upon her seemingly without thought to the child herself.

Maybe it was down to the years he'd spent with the Shawnees, who didn't choose their offsprings' names without some study of the child or the circumstances of its birth. He hadn't meant to force the issue of a name, only talk about it with the woman. Then it was done and he'd been left staring at the scrunched little face thinking, *Pippa.* It had settled easy on the infant laid across his arm.

Jeremiah smiled, half his mind attuned to the forest around them, sifting sounds and smells and deeper senses. The smile faded as the whimpering escalated and he realized it wasn't the baby making the noise. It was her mother, crying in her sleep.

"Jacob!"

Jeremiah's heart wrenched, as if an unseen hand had grasped it and jerked it down one of the two paths facing him, making the choice for him. He'd agreed to guide Clare Inglesby as far as Wheeling but knew now their paths wouldn't diverge there.

I don't know why You seem bent on my trying to do for her what I couldn't do for myself, but all right. How am I to do it?

It was a question flung to heaven. The reply came back to him, a still, small voice.

With God all things are possible.

He chuckled softly at that. It was what *she* had said. And it was true enough. The Almighty could, and would, do whatever it pleased Him to do. In His way and time. But Jeremiah knew better than to promise everything was going to turn out the way Clare Inglesby so fiercely hoped it would. Sometimes the ways of the Almighty were beyond a man's understanding, even looking back, after he'd weathered the first crushing grief of a loss he'd thought sure to kill him.

He thought about something else that warrior in his memory had told him. *"Not a sparrow falls to the ground without Creator seeing, and you, a man, are worth more than many sparrows. That is what the words of the One the whites call Jesus say. But His word does not say that sparrows will never fall."*

Jeremiah had to agree. They were never promised that.

Uncle Alphus's fields have been neglected. So many stones, big and small, buried in the clay-rich soil. "Like raisins in a cake," she says, making Philip sigh dramatically and her little boy laugh and repeat her words, "Raisins inna cake!" More often now he has his own words to impart. "Mama, let me tell you something!"

They've been a month on Uncle Alphus's farm, carving out a life Clare never imagined for herself, a life devoid of the comforts she's known since birth. It's a life of constant work, sunup to sundown, blisters on hands, cracks in shoes, backs that ache at night and yet . . . watching her husband and son carrying rocks out of the field they hope to make yield life-giving food, it strikes her that she's never been so happy.

Uncle Alphus hadn't made a farmer, and she never expected Philip would, but on this day closing in with its aches and weariness and a supper still to fix and her filthy little boy to wash, she dares to hope her husband has finally found a life to which he can settle, that he can be content with its simplicity, its honest toil, as she finds she can be. She dares to hope and embrace the joy.

Fingernails caked with reddish earth, she pauses to watch her little family. Philip has hefted a stone from the ground. His face twists into a comical mask of strain—Jacob is at his side, watching every move—as he staggers toward the line of piled stones that might, with more skillful stacking, become a fence. Jacob spies a much smaller stone and, covered in Virginia clay to his eyebrows, pries it loose and totters with it toward the pile, a miniature of Philip . . .

It is a different time. Later. She carries another child beneath her heart, another son, she thinks, but her joy has vanished like the mist it was built upon because Philip stands before her with that gleam in his eye telling her about a man, James Harrod, and a place, Kentucky, and a weight heavier than the baby she carries is forming in her chest. Tears roll down her cheeks though she knows she was too stunned to cry when this actually happened and that she is only dreaming about it now.

But the weight . . .

They are piling the stones on top of her. Philip and Jacob. Stone after stone. Burying her. "No, please. You will crush the child. Jacob, your little brother!"

A last stone covers her face, and Philip and Jacob are gone and only the stones remain. And the child? Not a son. A daughter . . . but where is she among all these stones . . . ?

Clare came awake with a groan, hands scrabbling over moss and earth, groping for her baby, hair and face wet with tears wept in her sleep. It had been a terrible dream. But the weight still lay heavy on her chest. Something was wrong. Dreadfully wrong. The weight . . .

Philip was gone. Jacob was gone. She was alone.

No. The baby. Where . . . ?

"She's right here, Missus," a voice said, sending shock through every nerve before she remembered him, too.

"She woke a bit ago, but I thought to let you sleep. She's been quiet."

Mr. Ring sat by the fire that blazed again, holding her daughter wrapped in the blue blanket, and Clare Inglesby, remembering everything, longed to forget again.

Dawn had come stealing over the mountains, down the ridge near which they'd camped. By the light of the fire he'd watched the graying bring the woman into focus. She'd wept in her sleep again and awakened the baby. He'd scooped her up and held her until Mrs. Inglesby sat up, groping as if for something lost. He gave the baby to her and wanted to give her more.

Words came to him. "Wait on the Lord. Be of good courage. He will strengthen your heart."

She stared at him, desolation in eyes that bared a soul she'd tried to keep hidden, but there on the edge of her dreams, with the barriers thinned, she couldn't.

"How?"

"For now, Missus? Let it be one moment, one breath, at a time. Just keep crying out to Him. He brought us together, led me right to you in your need. Don't you think He'll finish what He's started?"

Whatever that was.

She looked at him for several of those breaths, then pushed herself resolutely to her feet, took her baby a little distance away, and put her back to him.

Wait on the Lord. Be of good courage.

He thought about telling her who had said those words to him when that desolation had filled his heart but knew it would uproot whatever seed of good they might sow, hearing it was Logan.

8

Whatever Clare expected to find on the banks of the Ohio the day she followed Philip out of Redstone, it wasn't what greeted her as she descended the final ridge to the sight of the settlement huddled on a stretch of stump-pocked river-bottom land. The reality of Wheeling was nothing short of a reflection of her own inner landscape—a hive upturned, swarming with frantic activity.

Catching the scents of cooking on the warm air, she spied cabins scattered near a two-story timber blockhouse—built, Mr. Ring informed her, by the Zane brothers, Silas and Ebenezer. Not far from the blockhouse, a stockade was going up, men dragging timbers, shaping them with axes, hoisting them upright. Everywhere women milled about, wrangling children and animals, striding hither and yon. Many families had pitched camps along a creek winding down from the ridge. Fires from camp and cabin spiraled smoke into a cloudless sky. Beyond it all the Ohio River swept past, broad and bluish, with an island in the center of the wide sweep. Canoes, rafts, and flatboats crowded the bank.

Pausing on a bluff overlooking the scene, Mr. Ring nodded toward the rising stockade as another timber was dropped into place, the gap at its base filled with earth, tamped by booted feet.

"Connolly's doing." Catching her questioning gaze, he expounded, "Major Connolly, commander at Fort Pitt. He's ordered a fellow, Major William Crawford, to bring four hundred men to Wheeling to fortify the place. Don't look as if Crawford's arrived yet, but word must've gone ahead to get the work underway."

Mr. Ring had yet to say how long he planned to remain in Wheeling, but he'd made it plain he meant to cross the Ohio to the Indians, and she'd made it plain that was fine by her. To judge by the number of rivercraft coming and going, there would be someone with room enough for two small children and a woman, even one who presented a less than respectable sight.

She was come down out of the mountains footsore and bug-bitten, sunburned and blistered. The soles of her shoes were worn near through, threatening to part at the seams. Her petticoat and short gown begged repair and a good washing. But her insides no longer felt raw. Her baby was reasonably clean and had made the mountain crossing in more comfort than her mother.

The second morning on the trail, she'd awakened to find her guide sitting by the fire. On the ground beside him was a narrow contraption built of sticks whittled flat and woven into a backboard, with something like a leather sack attached to its front, stitched up the center, open at the neck. Leather loops of varying length attached to the woven back hung limp across the sack. A broad flat piece like a hat brim jutted from the top.

Its purpose had wholly escaped her.

Turning her back to feed the baby, she'd reached up to massage her aching neck as soon as she'd a hand free. The cloth she'd used for a sling the previous day had proved insufficient support. Much of the time she'd had to lend a hand to it—tricky when she needed both to manage the trail's rougher spots, places so steep or stony they were climbing more than walking.

Behind her Mr. Ring had said, "I noticed, Missus, you carrying the baby in a sling is causing a strain. Thought you might get on better with a cradleboard, like Indian women use to tote their babes. I can show you how it wears."

Clare had looked again at what he'd made, interest sparking until she thought, *Carry my baby like an Indian?* But if it would help her walk faster, farther each day . . .

She'd allowed him to strap her daughter into the thing, finding it suited perfectly, between sack and leather cords and woven bits to shield her from the sun, keeping her snug and immobile, even her tiny head. He'd put the baby on his own back and walked around the camp to let her see her daughter was secure.

The baby whimpered now in the carrier on Clare's back. She'd have to see to her daughter's needs before she could begin her search for Jacob.

They moved on down the trail, Clare's feet aching, her heart thudding with hope, and soon came in sight of the camps along the creek. Mr. Ring pointed out a place where the water tumbled over mossy rocks and made a pool. Several women were tending to their washing there. Some paused to take curious note of them.

"How if I leave you here?"

The time for parting had come.

"Thank you for getting me this far," Clare said, "and for helping me when I was alone." Such inadequate words for what the man had done. Clare swallowed, choked by the unexpected depth of her gratitude. "I'm sure I'll be fine from here."

Jeremiah Ring stared at her, brow creased deep. "I don't mean to leave you for good, Missus. I'm just going off to find Ebenezer Zane for a talk. I'll come back for you once I make arrangements. Tend to your things meantime, then rest a bit."

It was her turn to stare. "I've told you there's no need for you to arrange anything concerning me."

The baby wasn't growing any happier on her back as Mr. Ring, clinging stubbornly to the notion that Jacob had been captured by Indians, said, "I mean to take a canoe to Yellow Creek, see if Logan's people have Jacob in their keeping and might be willing to return him peaceable-like."

"If you truly mean to help me, don't go rushing off, but talk to your Mr.

Zane and anyone else here you will about Jacob. Two of us will cover the ground more quickly."

She could tell he was exerting effort not to argue outright with her plan. "You meaning to talk to every soul in this settlement?"

His incredulity only hardened her will. "You are free to leave me any time, Mr. Ring, as I've repeatedly said. I have two strong hands and can work to feed myself until I find my son, and truly I must see to this child on my back right now." With the baby setting to wail, she glanced over at the women doing their washing. "I'll stay here for the present."

It was as good a place as any to begin her search.

He found Ebenezer Zane outside the blockhouse lighting a clay pipe in a rare moment of idleness. The two exchanged news, Zane keeping a watchful eye on folk passing near the blockhouse where stores were kept. Jeremiah told of finding Philip Inglesby dead and scalped and his widow in distress of childbirth, having discovered her son missing from the wagon where she'd left him.

"A killing that close to Redstone?" Zane lowered his pipe to cast a grim look at the wooded slopes hemming Wheeling up against the river. "Ye're thinking 'twas Logan or his warriors done it, then took the boy?"

"No telling for sure till I see the man. But I expect so."

Zane confirmed he'd had no word of a boy found in a wagon and brought in to Wheeling. "Not likely settling folk would've taken him in the middle of the night without a look round. Or without the boy calling for his ma."

"Tracks told another tale, but the mother won't believe it. She's bound and determined she'll find him here."

Zane chewed the pipe stem and shook his head. "Her boy's across the river by now."

Jeremiah gazed in that direction. It was a place he knew—its people and perils—well enough to know it was no place for Clare Inglesby, even though the woman did have fortitude. She hadn't complained these past days, though the mountain crossing had been hard on her. She'd gone quiet once he'd agreed to take her along to Wheeling. Done what he asked of her. Tended to that dark-eyed baby girl.

Watching her cope with the shattering of her life was like seeing himself ten years back. From his present vantage he knew, despite her single-minded pursuit of her son, there was no guarantee it would end like she hoped, with or without his help.

He felt the boring of Zane's gaze. "You going over to look for the boy?"

"Least to Yellow Creek. Just not sure what to do with the mother."

Zane gestured at the men at work on the stockade. "We'll keep 'em safe till ye come back this way—with her boy, God and Logan willing." The younger man paused, studying him. "You and Logan go back as I recall, but Lord have mercy, Ring, this don't seem the best time for a white man to be trading on that Mingo's friendship. Even you."

Jeremiah needed no reminding. "Bad timing or no, seems the Almighty picked me out for the task." Speaking of time . . . Feeling it slipping past, inexorable as the river's flow, he glanced through the open door of the blockhouse.

Zane read the gaze. "You need anything for the journey, or the woman while she's waiting on you?"

Thinking of Mrs. Inglesby's ruined shoes, provisions needed—he'd no intention of leaving her to feed herself—he said, "I do, but what goods I have I need to keep, in case it comes to trading for the boy."

Zane clapped his shoulder. "Take what you need. Bring me some prime furs next time you come through and we'll call it a trade."

He'd have welcomed being proved wrong. In truth he'd have danced a jig had Clare Inglesby found her son in Wheeling.

"These ones here haven't seen him, I take it?" Finding her at the creek, he'd nodded at the women still washing. "Neither has Zane."

She'd stood there, a wrung clout dripping in her grasp, while Pippa, fed and content, slept in the cradleboard.

"Have you spoken to everyone in Wheeling?" she'd asked, knowing he'd done no such thing.

"To those who'd know if your boy was brought in by anyone other than . . ." He'd searched her face, trying to judge whether she'd grown more accepting of facts.

She'd raised her chin, and it was again as if he saw the younger man he'd been. Her life had shattered out of her control. She was exerting her will in whatever way she could, desperate to gather up her pieces, to reassemble what remained, far from accepting it could never be done. Not by her hands.

He hoped she figured it out quicker than he had.

"I mean to make a thorough search. If it vexes you, then you need take no further thought to me, Mr. Ring."

"On the contrary, Missus," he'd told her. "I'm giving you considerable thought."

"Do you mean to prevent me doing what I need to do?"

"You're free to do as you will, but—"

"Good. Then I bid you farewell, and thank you again for all you've done. I . . ." She'd hesitated while the women on the creek bank watched and listened. "Had I saved it I would give you Philip's timepiece in payment for all your trouble."

His face had flamed at the notion of her paying him for his help—and at the presence of that timepiece in his knapsack.

"I've asked no payment."

"Very well then." She'd made him an awkward curtsy and turned her back.

He hadn't known what else to do but leave her to go her willful way, telling himself he could be patient, as others had been patient with him. More than patient.

He pitched camp as far from the point where he saw she'd begun her search as possible, then spent the day talking to those of his acquaintance in Wheeling to be sure no one had heard of Jacob Inglesby and neglected to tell Zane of it. He'd kept track of Mrs. Inglesby throughout the day, careful not to let her catch sight of him.

As dusk was closing in he found her again at the camp of one of the creek women who'd let her spread her washing to dry under the watchful eye of an older child. As he neared he spotted her at the edge of camp, baby on her back, washing in hand, seeming in no hurry to quit the other woman's company, as if she hoped to be invited to spend the night. But the woman was overrun with little ones, two of them screaming and flushed as though ailing.

Jeremiah had come upon them soft-footed, in the shadow of a nearby oak, moccasins making little sound on the mulching leaves and acorns underfoot. He'd nearly reached the camp when he saw Mrs. Inglesby turn wearily to head away into the gathering night, hiding her fear and disappointment until she faced his way. She took two steps from the camp, not seeing him in her path, before the sole of her right shoe parted from its upper and she stumbled over the broken pieces.

He reached her in time to prevent a fall, grasping her by the arm. She reared her head back. "Mr. Ring?"

"You all right?"

Pulling away from him, she knelt to pick up the pieces of her shoe, voice trembling as she asked, "Is there some way to repair this? Perhaps I can tie it together?"

"Better to replace the pair of 'em."

"How?" She sounded on the verge of tears. "I've no coin. Nothing to trade. And I've yet to look for paying work."

"No need for either." Jeremiah opened his knapsack and took out a pair of moccasins, much too small to fit his feet. "Trade those shoes for these, Missus, then let's get you to a fire, a meal, and a place to sleep for the night."

She reached to take the moccasins from his hands, hers trembling, and instead sagged toward him as though her legs wouldn't hold her up another moment. He caught her with an arm around her waist, led her to a nearby stump, sat her down and removed her other shoe, nearly to the point of disintegration as well, and slipped the soft moccasins on her blistered feet, while she wept behind her hands and the baby whimpered on her back, wanting again to be fed. He fetched the washing she'd dropped, drew her to stand, and led her to his small fire and the shelter he'd raised—an oilskin tented over a sapling frame.

He settled her in front of it, put her washing inside the tent, took the cradleboard off her back, removed Pippa from it, and handed the baby into her arms. Turning his back, he set about fixing them something to eat, knowing she didn't like him looking at her until she'd settled the baby and covered herself.

"You're still here?" she asked at last.

Though the answer to that was obvious, he didn't say so. Likely she thought he'd taken that canoe downriver and was on his way to bring the Shawnees the message she'd delayed him in delivering. But he wasn't going to Cornstalk's Town. Not yet.

He faced her.

"I never intended leaving you here without so much as your next meal." It was a choice he thought any man of worth would have made in his place so was unprepared when Mrs. Inglesby burst into tears and hunched over her suckling baby, rocking herself with the streaming flood.

He'd been fixing corn dodgers. He moved them away from the heat and gave her his full attention.

"If only Philip had listened to me," she was saying, half-choked by her tears, "or to Uncle Alphus. Have I lost Jacob now as well?"

Uncle Alphus. Jeremiah hadn't heard her name that connection before.

"I'm sorry, Missus, but you got to believe me when I say you could spend a week asking these folk if they've seen your boy and it's not going to help you."

She looked at him with pleading eyes. "Have I wasted this entire day?"

"Not if it's helped you see matters different." He didn't say a day more or less likely didn't matter now. "There's no going back to change what's past," he said, the truth of the words searing him deep. "But we can advance from this point and make the best choice we can with what we got to go on."

"I must find Jacob. That's all my world now. All my hope."

If he'd ever before heard the essence of a human soul distilled in so few words, Jeremiah couldn't recall it now.

"You aren't going to, Missus. Not here in Wheeling."

Pippa gave a hiccup, then settled back to feeding. Mrs. Inglesby looked at him with green eyes darkened in the firelight to the shade of a high-country spruce.

"You're sure?" she implored, though he could see she was finally ready to believe him.

"What I'm sure of is that Indians took your boy out of that wagon. Indians left the tracks we saw. And Indians wouldn't have brought him here."

Clare Inglesby had ceased her crying and was looking at him with an intensity that rattled him, yet compelled him to help. Knowing it would be the last time he did so, whatever her response, he said, "Our best chance of finding your boy is at Yellow Creek, and the less time passes before I head upriver, the better the chance of getting him back before someone decides to keep him. I'm leaving at first light. Ebenezer Zane will find you a place here while you wait."

"Turn around please," Mrs. Inglesby said, and after a second of staring, he realized she needed to readjust the baby.

Behind his back all was silent save the rustle of garments against skin and the baby's smacking, until finally she said, "You truly are going upriver, not down to the Scioto? You may turn around now."

He turned. "I'm going to find Logan."

He saw the terror wash over her features at his words. But love and need rose up stronger, and he knew what was coming an instant before the words tumbled out of her mouth.

"Then I'm going with you. I'll not be left behind to wait. There's much I find I can bear, Mr. Ring. More than ever I knew. But I couldn't bear that. If you're going to the Mingos, then I'm coming with you." She made her voice firm, as if expecting a battle from him. "I'm sure you mean to tell me it will be dangerous, but I will face any danger—even death—for Jacob's sake."

There went that chin lifting and it nigh broke his heart, knowing what that show of bravery cost her. He held her gaze as he asked, gently as he could, "How would your death help either of your children?"

She'd no answer to that, but words spilled out regardless. "If I'd stayed at the wagon, we would have been captured together, Jacob and I. I'd prefer even that to this unbearable separation."

"I understand," he said, knowing she could never grasp just how much. "But if you'd been taken together out of that wagon and they let you live despite birthing a baby on the way, you'd not have been kept together long. I couldn't say what would've happened to you, but Jacob still would've been taken and given to someone who'd lost a son or brother or sister."

He saw the sweat bead up along her hairline. "They wouldn't keep a child from a mother standing right in front of their eyes, would they?"

Rather than answer that, Jeremiah asked her a thing he'd been mulling over for days. "Would you consider Jacob to be brave?"

Her gaze sharpened. "Why do you ask?"

"I ask because the Indians might kill a tearful, whining child afore they got him back to one of their towns."

He might have phrased that better. Even by firelight he could see Mrs. Inglesby blanch.

"He is brave," she said. "This wild country didn't frighten him. He went boldly where I feared to go, but now I shall follow him and be no less courageous. I am in earnest, Mr. Ring. I won't be left behind."

Her color had returned as she spoke, but Jeremiah figured his next words would steal it again. They had to be said.

"I see that plain, Missus. I just want to be sure you know finding your boy mightn't be the hardest part of getting him back."

9

It was small for a canoe. Constructed of elm bark, it was meant for two, three bodies at most. With the cradleboard propped against the pack before her, braced between her knees, Clare clutched the sides of the conveyance as Mr. Ring shoved away from the bank. There came the buoyance of the water's embrace, the push of the current, the rocking as Mr. Ring boarded. Clare expected the canoe to tip, but in seconds he'd settled his lean frame before her, paddle in hand, and was guiding them upriver along the Virginia shore. Forsaking civilization as she'd known it. Her belly twisted at the thought as she fretted over what lay ahead, including coming face-to-face with Philip's murderer. Logan.

"They wouldn't keep a child from a mother standing right in front of their eyes, would they?"

Mr. Ring had evaded that question. Thinking of why that might be, sweat prickled along Clare's hairline and a clammy weakness washed down her limbs. She'd heard of white children taken by Indians, taught their words and ways, absorbed into that life until they forgot who they'd been . . .

"How would your death help either of your children?"

She glanced down at the tiny face looking back at her from the carrier's confines, wide eyes dark like Philip's blinking at the sun-glare off the water, oblivious to the peril into which she was bound.

Was it fair to this child, endangering her for her brother's sake?

Fair or not, Clare had made her decision. Still she couldn't help looking back over her shoulder at the settlement shrinking in the canoe's wake, at the shifting traffic of rivercraft and people along the muddy bank.

"The Beautiful River."

She'd only partially caught Mr. Ring's words. "I beg your pardon?" she asked, turning to view the back of his head.

Mr. Ring showed her his profile. Like his face in general, his nose was long, with a slight arch near its base. His beard, fuller than it had been at their meeting, still hugged the contours of his jaw. "It's what the French call the river—*la Belle Rivière*. The Senecas call it *Ohi:yó*. Good River. To the Shawnees it's the *Spaylaywitheepi*."

She didn't ask what that last name meant. Perhaps the same as its other names. *Good. Beautiful.* Clare found the river neither, despite its impressive features—over nine hundred miles long, a mile wide in places, though not that far upriver. Philip had talked of it rapturously. To her it was the place on the map's edge where men drew the figures of strange and forbidding creatures. A hazard to be crossed only under the gravest compulsion.

They were passing the mid-channel island, the river widening to the left. To their right a flock of ducks veered away into a stand of cattails growing thick along the bank. A high ridge on the Virginia side closed in, its feet planted at the water's edge. It loomed above the river, thickly wooded, blocking the sky. Clare glanced back for a last glimpse of Wheeling before the ridge moved between, closing off the sight and any possibility of remaining in its relative safety.

She faced forward as Jeremiah Ring's strong shoulders bent to the paddling. At least she still had this man to guide her, though he might be taken away at any moment. Or choose to take himself away. No matter. With or without him she would keep looking until she found Jacob. She would search under every stone, behind every tree, inside every heathen hut she could force her way into.

Either she and her children would emerge from that wilderness together, or none of them would.

"Yellow Creek's just there, other side of that bluff. Town's farther up the creek."

Mr. Ring's voice startled Clare. It was the first he'd uttered for hours and, lulled by the river's rushing, she'd dozed while the baby slept. Looking ahead, she saw the bluff that met the water's edge, then looked across the river to the Virginia side and saw a stretch of bottom land, log structures visible among the trees. The scene was peaceful, bathed in the slanting gold of late afternoon. "Is that it—Baker's post?"

"It is, but look there."

She followed his nod to see a lone warrior in a canoe had rounded the bluff at the mouth of Yellow Creek, coming toward them with grim face, purpose in every paddle stroke. As fear gripped Clare, Mr. Ring called to the warrior, a stream of gibberish that flowed off his lips with a rhythm odd to her ears.

Recognition came into the approaching Indian's face but didn't soften his expression.

The warrior was bare-chested, tattooed across his cheekbones and down his arms. A leather band held black hair back from a low brow, revealing ears pierced and ringed with copper hoops and beaten discs; one side of the headband secured a hawk's feather, its tip dangling above the warrior's bare shoulder. As he brought his canoe alongside theirs, his dark gaze flicked past Mr. Ring and settled on Clare, as far from welcoming as winter was from summer.

As words were exchanged, Clare sat mute in the canoe behind Mr. Ring with nary a clue to discern whether they were being warned off or it was the weather being discussed, but when the warrior's gaze dropped to the cradleboard at her knees, a fresh surge of fear burned in her throat.

Abruptly he tore his gaze away and dug his paddle deep and propelled his canoe back toward the creek mouth. Jeremiah Ring dipped his paddle; they followed in the Indian's wake.

"What is happening?" Clare demanded as they approached the creek mouth. "Was that Logan? Did you speak to him of Jacob?" She hadn't heard her son's name uttered. She *did* hear the near-panic in her own voice.

"Steady yourself, Missus. Whatever may come, you need to stay calm. Silent too, can you manage it," he added with a touch of wryness so faint she might have imagined it. "I know that warrior. Tall Man was with us the morning we made it across the river to Baker's. I told him I wished to speak to Logan."

"You didn't ask—"

"I told him you travel with me. Under my protection. We've been given welcome, but also an escort, for which I've been beseeching the Almighty since I got into this canoe."

"Why? I thought you were friends with these Indians."

"I am, but these people are grieving a great loss and betrayal. Hold that notion in your mind, whatever happens."

"Will they deny us aid as revenge . . . because I'm white?"

Mr. Ring glanced back at her. "No telling how this'll go, other than they won't harm you. Not while you're with me."

Clare's mouth had dried. Fear spread through her like a poison, seeping outward from her center.

The moment she caught a whiff of wood smoke, they glided around a curve in the river and she spotted what must be Logan's Town among the trees, though it looked like no proper town she'd ever seen and more populated than she'd expected.

The creek bank seemed thronged with the figures of men, women, children—most brown-skinned, some showing white blood, a few African— moving toward the creek out of a warren of log cabins and humpy structures walled in bark. The humid air was abuzz with unintelligible speech. Those nearest called to others who came running to stand like a wall of flesh, every last one of them, it seemed, focused on her seated in the canoe.

Mr. Ring was out with a splash, dragging the canoe up the sloping bank with a strength impressive after the strenuous upriver journey.

Jarred by the vessel's halting, she reached to steady the cradleboard. The baby was wide awake and screwing up her face to cry. Clare jiggled the carrier, but there went her daughter's little mouth opening in a protracted squall, to the general rise of interest among the women on the bank.

With her heart banging twice as hard as when she'd met the stare of the warrior, Tall Man, Clare put her baby on her back, took the hand Mr. Ring held out, and stepped from the canoe.

Mr. Ring looked down at her, face stiff with unease. "Logan isn't here."

Clare had the baby to a breast as they stood beneath an arbor attached to one of the cabins—that of Tall Man and his plump wife, whose name no one had told her—where Mr. Ring had left her to tend the baby while he conferred nearby with several warriors dressed much like himself. As Tall Man's wife peeped at her from behind the hide that served as a door, Clare shot wary glances at other women hovering near, trying surreptitiously to scan bark lodges—*wegiwas,* Mr. Ring called them—cook-fires, and every knot of children for Jacob. Now here was Mr. Ring returned with the news that Logan wasn't even there to petition. After all her battling to get this far.

"He was here. But yesterday he took twenty of his warriors and went raiding again across the river. Only reason they told me that much is 'cause I was with them at Baker's and after. Besides I lived with Logan for a spell, years back. Some here remember that. But they don't want to talk to outsiders about what's happening now."

"Me?" Clare fought to ignore the Indians edging nearer while they spoke, ringing them about beneath the arbor.

"I suspect the pair of us, just now." There was hurt in Mr. Ring's eyes, in the lines tracing their corners.

"Why didn't Tall Man tell you so at once?"

"Maybe on account I didn't ask. Likely he grasped our purpose here the instant he saw you in the canoe with me. Or guessed it."

Mr. Ring had a habit of raising more questions than he answered.

"Does that mean he's seen Jacob?" She glanced at Tall Man's wife, peeping again from behind the hide, and though her mouth felt stiff as a board she forced herself to smile at the woman.

The dark eye peering out at her vanished.

"So far no one has owned to knowing anything about your boy," Mr. Ring said, "but there are others I may speak to. Will you be all right here while I do? I may have to sit for a spell, smoke a pipe, come at this cautious-like."

"I'll be all right." It was all Clare could do to keep from clutching the man's fringed shirt to keep him near as he left to see about their business, falling in with a few older warriors who led him away through the town.

She settled herself on a crudely hacked seat beside the doorway of Tall Man's lodge and tried not to look at those Indians who hadn't lost interest in her and drifted away.

Across the creek the sun had reached the tops of the trees. The light streaming through the village had mellowed to a peachy hue, the muggy air cooling as shadows crept between lodges.

While she nursed the baby, she tried to appear at ease in this alien place where it seemed anything at all might happen. The smells were strange, the speech impenetrable, the sights alien to her eyes. She'd seen Indians before, of course. But whether in Richmond or in Staunton, those brief encounters had happened in the safety of her own familiar world. *They* had been the interlopers, the strayed sparrows. Never she.

An unreasoning fear crept in upon her mind. Mr. Ring was never coming back. He'd been tomahawked somewhere out of sight. At any second those women hanging back would rush at her, pry Philippa from her breast, and . . .

At a rustle close by, Clare started with a half-swallowed yelp. A musky smell of deerskins, smoke, and sweat enveloped her as the rounded form of Tall Man's wife emerged from her lodge, moving between her and the light of the setting sun. She spoke, but even had it been English, the blood pounding in Clare's ears would have drowned the words.

The woman raised her hand. She was holding out a gourd cup. Though terribly thirsty, Clare had no way to know what was in that cup. Still she didn't want to refuse the unexpected offering. More than that, she felt she mustn't.

Looking up into a face younger than her own, with a mouth curved like a bow, she met a gaze not hostile but shy as a deer and tentatively friendly.

Clare took the cup and sipped. It was only water. After a longer swallow she said, "Thank you."

She'd no idea whether Tall Man's wife spoke English, but her round face softened. She ducked back into the lodge and emerged next with a chunk of corn cake.

Clare's stomach rumbled audibly, but dared she accept food from an Indian? What else might have been baked into the meal? Something she'd as soon not put in her mouth?

The water had been just water, given in kindness.

Suppressing caution and distaste, Clare took what was offered and made a show of biting into it hungrily, which seemed to please the woman. She chewed, ignoring the grit of stone in the bread.

Tall Man's wife looked over her shoulder, then vanished into the cabin.

Clare looked up to see why; Mr. Ring was already returning, striding toward her with a disturbance in his face.

"I'm sorry, Mrs. Inglesby," he said without preamble once he reached the arbor. "I did all I could without arousing anyone's ire, but no one admits to having seen your boy, and I don't think they're hiding him here."

He reached for the pack he'd brought out of the canoe, propped against Tall Man's lodge, as though fixing to leave.

Clare took a hasty gulp of the water and stood, pulling the baby free of her breast and handing her to Mr. Ring while she fastened her bodice fast as she could.

"Can you be sure of that?" She reached for the baby and settled her in the carrier, practiced now and swift. "Is it because I'm with you?"

He didn't answer that directly, but she saw a flash of affirmation in his gaze. "Like I've tried to tell you, this is a bad time for these people. It might be different among . . ."

When he hesitated, clearly reluctant to say more, Clare straightened from the carrier and searched his face. "Among *whom*, Mr. Ring?"

He studied her while she willed him to share with her whatever chance he might have glimpsed, no matter how slim.

"I won't sweeten this, Mrs. Inglesby. There's no telling where Jacob might be now. But there's something happening might make it possible to discover his whereabouts. Maybe get a lead, I don't know. I don't want you to raise your hopes high, but it's all we have."

Might. Maybe. She grasped at the flimsy words. "Tell me."

"There's a council happening at Wakatomica. That's a Shawnee town to the west, on the Muskingum. There'll be chiefs gathering to discuss McKee's invitation to Pittsburgh." Mr. Ring patted one of the bags that hung from his shoulder. "The message got through to Cornstalk and the other chiefs. Problem is, there's scarce time to reach Wakatomica before the council ends if I start out now, and I'd need to take you on to Fort Pitt or back to Wheeling, first."

She was aware in her periphery of warriors gathering, eying them. Mr. Ring knew it, though his back was turned. She sensed his unease. They needed to leave that place.

"Take me with you." She was shaking again with the terrible need that compelled her deeper into that wild land, among forbidding people, with a man she couldn't fully trust. "To the council at . . . wherever you said."

"To Wakatomica?" Mr. Ring wagged his head. "No ma'am. That's not going to happen. I cannot take you traipsing across the Shawnee nation with maybe war brewing and no firm idea whether . . ."

In the midst of this refusal, he glanced aside, brows drawn tight, then snapped his gaze back to her. So focused was she on the man attempting once again to thwart her, Clare didn't at first register the cause of his distraction or what had interrupted him. Then she heard the words emanating from the other side of the door-hide. Jeremiah Ring never took his gaze from Clare's, but he was listening intently to whatever Tall Man's wife was saying, her voice low and urgent.

It took all Clare's self-possession to remain still, searching Mr. Ring's face, finding in it no clue as to what he was hearing. At last Tall Man's wife stopped speaking. Mr. Ring uttered a few words, then his gaze sharpened on Clare. "Put the baby on your back. Follow me to the canoe. Don't say a word," he added as he took up the pack.

Clare did as he directed, too alarmed to disobey. She didn't look at the faces of the Mingos who parted to let them pass back through the village to the creek. She took her place in the canoe, and Mr. Ring pushed it out into the flow, but her hope was plummeting and her heart breaking as she turned for one last look at Logan's Town.

Then she realized Mr. Ring hadn't turned the canoe downstream toward the Ohio but upstream toward the darkening foothills and the orange blaze of the sun nearly set. She held her peace until the river bent and the Mingo town, cast in dusky shadows, had vanished behind them.

"Mr. Ring, where are we going? What did Tall Man's wife say to you?"

Not slackening his strokes, Mr. Ring turned his face to the side to be sure she heard him.

"I know where your boy is, Missus. And who has him. But I need to get us a fair piece from here 'fore daylight's gone, and just now I need my breath for paddling."

The man might have needed all his breath for paddling, but the words he'd spared struck Clare a blow that stole the breath from her lungs.

The dusk-shadowed creek banks slipped past as she stared at Jeremiah Ring's back, waiting for her next breath. At last she sucked in a gulp of clammy air, parted her lips to speak, then clamped a hand across her mouth to stifle the sob that emerged.

Bent over the cradleboard, she kept her muffling hand in place so her weeping wouldn't attract the attention Mr. Ring seemed eager to avoid.

"I know where your boy is, Missus. And who has him."

The words were lightning flung against the bare ground of her heart, searing a path terrible and sweet.

She didn't know how long they traveled thus, only that when she felt the canoe scrape bottom it was full dark. Mr. Ring vaulted from the canoe to tug it toward the bank where a feeder creek entered the flow. A half-moon broke through clouds, shedding light enough to see. Ducking branches, she climbed the bank as he pulled the canoe into a concealing thicket.

"Reckon we've come three miles," he was saying, barely loud enough to hear above the water's rush. "We'll camp here tonight. Come morning see whether—"

"Mr. Ring!"

He was beside her in an instant, a hand across her mouth. The smell of him and his recent exertions enveloped her.

"Logan's warriors let us go, and likely we're in no danger from that quarter. All the same we best keep quiet-like."

Over his hand she fixed him with a glare.

"You got questions," he said. "I aim to answer them best I can. You going to keep your voice down?"

Knowing she'd get her answers sooner if she complied, beneath his infuriating hand she nodded. His fingers released her mouth, found her arm, and tugged her through the trees.

"Up the bank there's a clear space, big enough we can both stretch out to sleep. We'll have a cold supper. I'm not risking a fire."

She didn't care about a fire. Or food. Her daughter cared about the latter, judging by the mewls coming from the cradleboard, which would escalate if ignored. Wanting to hiss at him to take his hand from her, Clare let the man lead her to where he wanted her to be, then knelt on the ground, thankful to find it dry. Surrounded by rustling leaves and croaking frogs, she set about freeing baby and breast and uniting the two, while Mr. Ring rolled out blankets and delved into his pack. While the baby settled with a contented grunt, Clare fixed him with a stare that surely penetrated the dark.

"Where is Jacob? Did Tall Man's wife tell you?"

Squatting on his haunches, he held out a strip of jerked meat. She didn't take it.

"She warned me to get you away from there."

Clare suppressed a frisson of fear. "That's all? She said nothing of Jacob? I thought . . . You said . . ."

"Listen now. She didn't tell me outright where your boy is, but what she *did* say was enough for me to guess. She said a hunting party of Shawnees passed through two days back and left with more than they came with."

Clare held the nursing baby close, arms aching and unfulfilled. "And from that you deduced . . . what?"

"What they left with was your boy."

Try as she might, she couldn't follow his leap in reasoning.

"*The warriors left with more than they came with.* Those were her exact words?"

"Near about."

"But that could have been a sack of cornmeal!"

"Only it wasn't," Mr. Ring replied. "She named the warriors. One of them was Falling Hawk, and he's . . ."

In the pause following, Clare's mind filled with all manner of dire possibilities of what the warrior named might be, starting with *bloody-minded savage.*

The answer Mr. Ring gave wasn't on the list. "He's my brother."

His brother? "But—you aren't an Indian!"

"Not born. Adopted. Nigh on ten years ago."

He paused again, long enough for Clare's spinning thoughts to settle on the horrible realization that the man had lived through what those savages likely wanted to do to Jacob. Adoption. Assimilation.

Mr. Ring had seemed a man of two worlds, yet not wholly of either, rootless, drifting about the frontier carrying messages between white men and red. Yet she'd thought if he claimed any identity it was surely as a white man. He worked for the Indian agents at Fort Pitt.

And called a Shawnee warrior his brother?

Nigh on ten years ago. He was surely no more than thirty now. He'd been old enough to retain his identity, to forget none of it but what he chose to forget. The same couldn't be said for Jacob. If she failed to recover him, he would become savage through and through, stripped of any memory of his life before. His memory of *her*.

All this swept through her mind while Mr. Ring was clearing his throat to continue.

"Well, see, back in Virginia, 'fore ever I went west of the mountains, I had another—"

"Mr. Ring," Clare cut in, less concerned with his past than with Jacob's future. "Are you saying this warrior—whatever his name—has taken Jacob to be *his* son? Taken him where? You must know if he's your . . ." She couldn't get the word *brother* to pass her lips.

Mr. Ring seemed to need a moment to shift his thoughts from whatever he'd been about to tell her. "He's called Falling Hawk. And aye, he's likely headed for the Scioto River, to Cornstalk's Town. That's some days' journey west, quickest being back down the Ohio."

Digesting that, Clare frowned over the soft head of her daughter. "Then why have we come this way? If this Falling Hawk has my son, surely you can get him back for me! Why not make for this other river, Scioto, as directly as possible?"

"Hold on now, Missus. Falling Hawk is days ahead of us. By the time he reaches the Scioto, he'll be farther ahead still, given the pace we'll be traveling with you and the baby."

His words sank in. "You'll take me to this other place—Cornstalk's Town? But you were adamant against taking me to Wakatomica."

"That was before we had us a solid lead on Jacob. Now there's no time to take you back east, not if we want to overtake your boy before he's claimed by . . ." He paused, drawing a breath and continued in a calmer tone. "Listen. I'm fair certain I know why Falling Hawk took your boy—bought him, traded for him, whatever exchange was made back at Logan's Town. It wasn't for himself. He has a wife and children. But I know someone who doesn't, and so does Falling Hawk. I'm thinking he means to give Jacob to his sister."

Bombarded by this new information, Clare's thoughts skittered from relief to dread and back again, blown like swirling leaves. "Who is Falling Hawk's sister?"

"She's called Rain Crow, and since she's Falling Hawk's sister that makes her mine, too, though she hasn't lived in Cornstalk's Town since my coming to the Shawnees and I barely know her. What I do know is that she's come to the end of a year of grieving and I'd wager a winter's fur take that Falling Hawk is bringing her a son to replace the one she lost last year to smallpox, same as carried off her husband."

Clare wondered that the milk hadn't curdled in her breasts, so deep was the pang of nausea that roiled beneath her ribs. "Jacob is *my* son."

"By the time we reach them," Mr. Ring said, "in the eyes of every Shawnee in Nonhelema's Town, he'll be the son of Rain Crow—if he pleases her."

Clare hadn't realized she was weeping until she tasted the salt of her tears. She willed them away, determined to untangle all the information he was throwing at her. *Too fast. Too fast.*

"Nonhelema? Who is that?"

"She's Cornstalk's sister, chieftain of her own town, across Scippo Creek. That's where Rain Crow has chosen to live."

"A woman chief?" This was an astonishing piece of news, and suddenly hopeful. "Surely a woman would understand a mother's need to have her child returned." Philippa was done feeding. She dealt with the child, changing her wrappings in the dark; the baby's waste-smell stained the air. "Can we not try to catch up to them? I can keep going."

"No ma'am," he said. "I mean to go to Wakatomica."

"But why? If it's as you say and Jacob will be adopted soon, you must take me there first—to the Scioto towns."

But he wouldn't. She knew so before he spoke again.

"Listen to me. There's a chance Falling Hawk has gone to Wakatomica himself. It might be we'll find him there—with your boy—before ever he reaches Rain Crow. That's worth taking the time, because I do know this: if Falling Hawk's gone straight to the Scioto, it won't matter if you half-kill yourself and Pippa trying to overtake him. We'll be too late. And I have my reasons for needing to be at that council."

Clare sat back, trying to steady her galloping heart. She recoiled from putting her trust in this man, still so strange to her—more so with every revelation. Yet he was offering his continued aid, and if she fought him every step of the way, there *would* come a breaking point. He would change his mind, abandon her, leave her in some dire strait among these cruel and unfathomable people. He was willing to take her to Cornstalk's Town. Eventually. She would have to content herself with that.

And maybe, just maybe, she wouldn't need to go that far.

Clare picked up the baby and held her to a shoulder, and only then did it strike her what Mr. Ring had called her daughter.

"Her name is Philippa, Mr. Ring."

"I know," he said. "She looks like a Pippa to me. But if it vexes you, Missus, I'll not speak the name."

Clare huffed a breath, then relented. She needed him to hold the baby, which he seemed more than happy to do. "Call her what you wish," she said, laying her daughter into his arms as her braid slipped down and bumped against his chest. "I'm going to the stream to wash."

"You won't fight me over going to Wakatomica?" he asked as she grabbed up her pack and started for the moon-glint on the water through the nearby trees.

"No, Mr. Ring. We'll go first to Wakatomica."

As if she'd ever truly had a say.

As she tramped off through the screen of foliage to the creek bank, Jeremiah held the tiny girl-child along his arm, enjoying the warm, contented weight of her, thinking about what Tall Man's wife had said, the part he hadn't told Clare Inglesby.

"Those ones out there, those warriors," the young woman had whispered through the door flap. "They might not be inclined to let the woman with you go from this place unless she is not just traveling with you but is *your* woman. That is what some of the women are saying."

They had made it out of Logan's village without his having to tell that lie, to claim Clare Inglesby as his own. He still wasn't certain what to make of the fleeting disappointment he'd felt about that as they'd shoved off in the canoe and Logan's warriors let them go unchallenged. He glanced into the darkness, able just to make out the woman's shape through the trees, bending over, seeing to her bathing.

How would she take to the notion?

He quailed from even asking. But if it came down to saving her life and Pippa's, or to finding Jacob . . . he reckoned the woman would find a way to make peace with a lot worse things than pretending to be his wife.

10

Wakatomica proved a collection of villages built along the creek bearing that name. In one, the gathering Mr. Ring was keen to attend was still in progress, inside the council house—*msi-kah-mi-qui,* she thought he called it. Unlike the bark lodges the people lived in, this structure was log-built, some eighty feet in length. It loomed high in the village center surrounded by a broad, well-trodden ground, a little like a village square.

Though most of the men of Wakatomica were gathered in the council house, Clare's heart still banged against her ribs at plunging into the midst of so many Indians—more than she'd faced at Logan's Town. Gazes turned when they caught the swish of her petticoat passing between their lodges, where cook-fires burned and children played and dogs lay in the sun.

These people were Shawnees, different from the Mingos but to Clare's eyes indistinguishable. Mostly copper-skinned—a few lighter, a few darker—their clothing a mixture of deerskins and trade cloth. Even their gazes were like those she'd endured at Yellow Creek, unwelcoming at best. As more stares followed, piling up like stones, she longed to take the baby off her back, fearing a set of hands would pluck her away and make off through the warren of bark huts as they'd plucked Jacob from the wagon.

No one molested them, however. Some called greetings to Mr. Ring.

They'd almost reached the council house when he raised his voice, addressing one of the few adult male Indians Clare had seen outside the structure. Dressed in the usual breechclout, moccasins, leggings, and shirt, this one had been squatting outside the council house but stood swiftly at their approach.

Mr. Ring wasn't a small man, but the Indian was even taller, and younger, nearer Clare's age. His features were angular, well-molded, but his eyes made the most striking impression, a startling amber that contrasted with his darker skin, with a daunting pair of eyebrows that soared above them like ravens' wings. A breeze stirred the Indian's black hair, tied in back with a hawk's feather that twirled behind his lofty head.

He regarded her while Mr. Ring spoke to him in Shawnee. Whatever he said had the Indian pulling those fierce brows tight. He said something in reply, gave a brief nod, yet uneasiness swept Clare as Mr. Ring turned to address her at last.

"I need to go within before the council is over. Wolf-Alone will watch over you and Pippa while I'm inside." As she glanced at the Indian, doubt surely evident, Mr. Ring added, "Wolf-Alone is also my brother."

"How many Shawnee brothers do you have, Mr. Ring?"

He gave her a swift smile. "Just the two. Wolf-Alone was with Falling Hawk's hunting party that came through Logan's Town."

Sucking in a breath at this more significant news, Clare swung her gaze back to the warrior, still regarding her with those striking eyes but giving no sign he understood a word they'd exchanged. Excitement surged, warring with panic at the thought of being left in the keeping of this fearsome being.

"Is Falling Hawk inside this . . . this . . ." She gestured impatiently at the structure looming over them, having forgotten what he'd called it.

"Msi-kah-mi-qui," Mr. Ring said. "Wolf-Alone parted with Falling Hawk on the trail to the Scioto. Our brother went on to Cornstalk's Town, with Jacob."

"No!" The protest was out of her before she could stifle it.

Mr. Ring looked as if he sorely regretted mentioning Falling Hawk.

"I'll tell you more, soon. Right now I need to be in there. It's important, what they're discussing. To you and me as well as to them. Some thirty chiefs and sub-chiefs are gathered. They've got the message I was sent to deliver. Now they're deciding whether they'll go to Pittsburgh or make war. It's all but decided, so this won't take long. I need you to stay with Wolf-Alone. Don't leave his side."

Giving her no chance to speak further, he caught the tall warrior's gaze, nodded, then hurried inside the *msi-kah*-whatever-he'd-called-it.

Furious and impatient, Clare was on the verge of taking a step in pursuit, unmindful of anything but calling him back, when the Indian he'd left her with started speaking. His voice jarred her sensibilities enough to realize it would be a mistake—perhaps a deadly one—to follow Mr. Ring into that building full of warriors, uninvited. Warriors perhaps on the brink of war—with her people.

She drew a steadying breath, then turned to look at Wolf-Alone, who went on talking. She thought she detected concern in his tone, along with a notable wariness that matched the look in his eyes, and wondered if he'd ever been this close to a white woman before, whether she unnerved him as much as he did her.

Or he had done at first. As she drew in the air of that place, pungent with wood smoke and tanning hides, sunbaked earth and drying fish, she felt herself calming as she focused on the guttural, rolling syllables that were nonsense to her ears but apparently not her soul. Or maybe it was simply that she found his voice pleasantly pitched.

When at last he fell silent, her gaze shifted beyond him as she took in the crowd of small Indians that had, without her noticing, gathered near; children ranging from chunky toddlers to gangly pre-pubescents stood gawking, some craning their necks to glimpse the baby on her back.

Wolf-Alone spoke a word that scattered them, then tugged her toward the side of the council house, where a pack rested in the building's shadow. Crouching, he removed a skin bottle from the pack and thrust it at her.

Conscious of her thirst, she took it and drank a tentative sip. Water, cool and quenching. She gulped it down.

When her thirst was slaked and she gave him back the skin, he gestured at the straps of the carrier, inviting her to remove it, to rest and tend her baby. She obeyed, though Philippa had been quiet, likely sleeping, having nursed before they reached Wakatomica.

She was surprised to find the baby awake, eyes wide as if in astonishment at all she'd seen these past few moments. It struck Clare then that the only life her daughter, less than a fortnight old, had ever experienced was traveling the wilderness on her mother's back.

Wolf-Alone sat with his back against the log wall of the council house, legs bent, long thighs exposed between the tops of his leggings and the tail of his shirt. Leaving the baby in the carrier for now, propped against the wall in its shade, Clare sat with the pack between her and the Indian and tried not to stare at him. Instead she watched those outside the nearest wegiwas, searching for a fair head though she knew it was useless. Jacob had never come there.

Disappointment was crushing. She wiped angrily at tears she couldn't suppress, wanting to rock herself and groan.

"How long can I bear this?"

Realizing Mr. Ring's brother could hear her, even if he couldn't understand, she glanced aside to find the Indian studying her. He said nothing though, and she looked away, going back to scanning bark huts—helpless to do otherwise—and drew in a breath sharp with astonishment and wonder.

The child was playing in the dirt across the village center, outside a wegiwa no different from those surrounding it. A child half-naked like most, but this one with skin and hair too pale to be an Indian. Much too pale.

She caught but a glimpse before the child was swept up by a Shawnee woman who'd noticed her staring. The woman carried the child out of sight behind a rack of meat strips suspended over a smoky fire. But a glimpse was all Clare needed. With a sound in her throat half whimper, half growl, she was on her feet in a scramble of petticoats, convinced Wolf-Alone was wrong about Falling Hawk or else had lied to Mr. Ring about it. Or Mr. Ring had lied to her.

Jacob was here.

She ran, aiming for the spot where the woman and child had vanished. "Jacob!" The name tore from her, wrenching her chest.

She was vaguely aware of her Indian guard's wordless exclamation of surprise. She was keenly aware of the Indian women straightening from their fires, alerted to her swift approach. Some snatched their own children close. Others moved to bar her way. Clare dodged their grasping hands, slapping and thrusting away those she couldn't elude, saw the woman bearing Jacob deeper into the village, and hurtled after her, lunging and barreling past crowding bodies, screaming all the while for Jacob, that he might know she was coming, she was near.

Darting between bark lodges, she caught another glimpse of Jacob riding the woman's hip, feet dangling, bare and dirty. The woman's long black hair swished like a curtain as she vanished between yet more wegiwas.

Clare ran harder, ignoring the pinch in her side. She burst again from between huts, nearly tripping over a basket of fish fresh from the nearby creek. Beside it on a woven mat sat an ancient Indian woman, a wrinkled bundle of brown sticks capped in wisps of white. Clare barely noticed her, for the woman holding Jacob had turned at bay. She was young, her copper-brown skin a stark contrast to Jacob's. His head was pressed into the woman's shoulder, blond hair obscuring his face. The woman's was set in defiance. She pulled back her lip and loosed a stream of angry gibberish.

Clare slowed her approach, wary as if confronting a snarling dog. "Jacob? Darling, it's Mama. Jacob, look at me!"

The woman swung Jacob to the ground and thrust him behind her, ready to battle over his keeping. Jacob cowered for an instant, then peeked out from behind the woman's skirt, eyes wide with terror.

Blue eyes.

Clare stopped short, noting for the first time the cut of the child's clothing—a skirt like the woman's that wrapped and tied at the waist. And the length of that pale hair, longer than Jacob's had been. And the small, snubbed features, too delicate for a boy's. The child was a girl.

It seemed to Clare the earth tilted beneath her feet.

Not Jacob. The truth swelled to encompass her thwarted purpose; courage fled, and rage with it, as beneath her breastbone surged the first awareness of her peril.

It came too late.

The first blow landed between her shoulders, sending her sprawling into the reach of the woman she'd pursued. The woman grabbed her, fingers pinching. A slap landed across Clare's face before she staggered several paces. Somehow she stayed on her feet, whirling to face her attacker.

Attackers. She was nearly surrounded now by Indian women, young and old, some clutching sticks, menacing as they neared, some scolding her in their incomprehensible tongue. Dark, hostile eyes condemned her, labeled her all manner of names that needed no interpretation. *Intruder. Threat. Enemy.* Face stinging, a throbbing between her shoulder blades, Clare backed away in the only direction that remained unbarred by angry Indians, toward a gap between two wegiwas behind her.

She didn't dare turn her back. "Please, I didn't mean . . . I thought . . . I'm sorry! I thought she was *mine.*"

No abatement of hostility showed in their faces. She looked again at the youngest of the women closing in on her, those with babies in their arms, and blanched in horror. *Philippa.*

She'd rushed off and left her baby in the keeping of a warrior she didn't know, in the middle of a people who habitually stole white children—*had* stolen Jacob.

Panic coiled around her mind, freezing her in place. *Help me. Oh, help me find her.*

The woman nearest her, that tiny, wrinkled bundle of sticks that had been sitting by the fish, raised a club in fingers like gnarled roots and screeched with a force of astonishing power, a sound as blood-chilling as a war cry.

Clare turned and blindly ran, taking whatever path looked least obstructed, least barred, least defended, but knew almost at once she was lost. Lost in a warren of wegiwas that looked identical.

She slowed her steps, gaze darting, seeking anything familiar. Children cried out in surprise at sight of her, some in fear, others in curiosity. It didn't seem the women who had chased her were hard on her heels, but others were emerging from their homes to see what the commotion was about.

Her mind latched onto the only source of guidance she could produce: the image of the council house, tallest structure in the village. If she could spot it, she might yet find her way back to its relative safety.

No longer running for fear of attracting further pursuit, she kept moving steadily, drenched in the sweat of fear, trying to look as if she knew where she was going so no one would attempt to stop her. At last she glimpsed the council house rising above the lodges ahead. Keeping that structure in her sights, ignoring all who spoke to her, at last she broke into the cleared ground at the village center. The council house was before her, the back of it at least, but all around it milled the lithe and intimidating figures of warriors.

She'd no choice but to head toward them, though many had caught sight of her and stopped in their tracks to stare.

Knowing she'd never pick Wolf-Alone out of that crowd, she searched instead for Jeremiah Ring as she swerved to avoid as many as she could, making for the side of the structure where she'd left her baby, refusing to look into those frightening faces and thus failing to notice the tall warrior who turned the corner of the council house nearest her—until her nose collided with his hard, blue-shirted chest.

Enveloped in a miasma of musky bear oil, male sweat, and pungent pipe smoke, she tried to step back. A hard grip clamped her arm, imprisoning her. With pain exploding in her bumped nose, she tried to yank her arm free but in vain.

Clearly by his choice, the warrior released her. When he remained in her path she jerked her gaze up to meet his. The sight of her had surprised him, but surprise was fading now, leaving the Indian's dark eyes cold, dead of feeling, as if she were no more than a beetle he'd as soon crush under his foot.

Or maybe not so dead. There *was* something in those eyes to be read, rising up like a dark shape approaching the still surface of a pool.

Hatred. Clare's knees nearly buckled under its force.

The Indian's hand fell to the hilt of a tomahawk shoved through his waist sash, fingers curling around it as if they itched to pull it free. This was alarming enough. Then Clare's gaze fastened on what hung beside the tomahawk. A man's scalp, blonder than her own.

Philip's scalp.

Logan. With the blood rushing in her ears, she looked into the hard face of the warrior, too stunned to scream, seeing what must have been Philip's last sight on earth, those hate-filled eyes looking at her as if he knew exactly who she was.

She wanted to run, to flee this monster who had murdered her husband, yet she couldn't move.

The Indian's lips pulled back from strong white teeth, not in a smile.

"I would take that golden scalp off your skull," he said in perfect English, "and hang it with this one at my belt, if one I swore never to harm had not this hour claimed you."

A clammy chill washed over Clare. Her vision tunneled. She was going to faint, in the midst of all these warriors, at the feet of this one who wanted very much to kill her.

"Clare." An arm as solid as a young oak tree was suddenly around her waist. Then her legs were moving though she could but half-feel them for the numbness washing down her.

Mr. Ring had found her. Was taking her to . . .

"Pippa?" There was no answer. She looked aside and saw why. It wasn't Mr. Ring but Wolf-Alone who'd found her, who'd spoken her name when she hadn't known he knew it.

She heard her baby then, a gurgling near her ear. The Indian was cradling Philippa in his other arm. They were back in the shadow of the council house. There was the pack and the carrier and the skin of water she'd drunk from. Still the spots danced in her vision. She swayed.

Wolf-Alone pushed her to the ground. She landed hard on her rump as he squatted beside her and, with a hand behind her head, pressed her face lower still, between her raised knees, fingers splayed behind her sweaty head. She struggled until she realized it was helping. The wooziness was passing. Wolf-Alone was speaking, had been for some time, she realized. She'd no idea *what* he was speaking, but again she found his tone soothing.

"I'm all right," she said, hoping her voice wouldn't belie the words. When she tried to lift her head again, Wolf-Alone slipped his hand away.

She sat up. He cradled Philippa against his chest, tiny in his keeping.

"I'm all right," she repeated. "Let me hold her."

Amber eyes searched her face, then he grunted and gave the child over to her. Relief flooded Clare like medicine at the weight of her daughter in her arms.

"I'm sorry," she whispered, breathing in the baby's scent, love for her daughter welling stronger than she'd ever felt, with it the bitter taste of guilt.

"I'll never leave you like that again. I love you." She whispered it again, heart-broken that she'd never once said it aloud to this easy-natured girl who could comprehend it no more than could the Shawnee warrior beside her. Clare could feel her heart swell, expanding to include the daughter she'd not allowed herself to fully embrace or treasure, until she'd nearly lost her. "Pippa, I do love you."

Behind her came swift footsteps on the packed earth. She looked up as fear jolted through her.

"Clare!" Mr. Ring's face was a reassuring sight—for the second it took to register his fury and realize it was aimed at her. "Where did you go? Wolf-Alone said you went tearing off alone. What did I tell you before I left you?"

Clare blinked at the man, who didn't crouch beside her as Wolf-Alone had done but remained standing, hands fisted.

"You told me to stay with him," she said, aware of the village full of Indians beyond Mr. Ring, most too preoccupied with their own concerns to pay them more than passing glances. "But I didn't think when—"

"Right enough you didn't! This is no place to lose your head and go rush-ing off as you please. You might've been killed a dozen times over!"

"Once would have sufficed." Back still throbbing, she gathered her baby against her and stood. "Will you allow me to complete a sentence before you again berate me?"

Mr. Ring made a choking sound, then ran a hand over his bearded chin and clamped his lips shut. Clare had never seen the man lose possession of his temper so thoroughly. She glanced at Wolf-Alone, still squatting by his pack, and thought she caught the trace of amusement in the curve of his mouth.

"I know it was a reckless thing to do, but I saw a child, Mr. Ring. A white child Jacob's age." The speaking of his name brought a rush of tears that nearly prevented her finishing. "It wasn't him!"

"I told you Falling Hawk never came to Wakatomica."

Clare bent her head to the baby. "I know."

Mr. Ring was silent for a moment; then he said, "Clare, look at me."

He stepped near enough to put a hand to her chin, raised her face, and turned her cheek to the sun's slanting light. His fingertips traced the place that still stung, then jerked away as though she'd burned him.

"Are you hurt?"

She fixed her gaze on Philippa. Tears had fallen on the baby's downy head. She bent and kissed them away. "I dare say no more than you think I deserve."

She didn't care what Mr. Ring thought. She was thinking of that little blond girl who hadn't been Jacob but was someone's child. At that moment she hated all Indians. Even Mr. Ring, who'd made himself one of their race for his own inscrutable reasons. She raised her gaze to him at last, but before she could speak, Wolf-Alone's voice broke over them.

His words were in Shawnee so she could only guess what he was saying, until Mr. Ring, clearly alarmed by it, said, "He's telling me he found you with Logan. That Logan threatened you. Did *he* strike you?"

She shuddered, recalling the hatred in those deadened eyes, but quickly shook her head. "Not him. It was a woman—women—but I got away. Or they let me go."

Mr. Ring turned to speak at length with Wolf-Alone, who answered with a grunt, then bent for his pack.

"Best we go," Mr. Ring said shortly. "Wolf-Alone will travel with us, if you're ready."

"I'm ready," Clare said, reaching for the carrier.

"You're sure?"

Arrested in her preparation, hands full of baby, she nodded at Wolf-Alone, standing by with his pack on his back, waiting. "He's seen Jacob. We know where he is. We *are* going to Cornstalk's Town?"

"I only meant are you sure this—going on with me—is what you want to do, now you've had a taste of what you're in for, what you'll be facing among the Shawnees?"

Clare stared at the man. What else could she do but press on? Leave her son to become a savage? Spend a lifetime never knowing his fate?

Not while she'd breath and strength to prevent it. Which meant her only path forward was trusting a man whose loyalties she now suspected were divided—trusting him to somehow prevail against the wishes of his Shawnee kin and return Jacob to her; or help her steal him back if he couldn't manage to obtain him any other way.

She knew better than to mention that last desperate plan. She would wait and see if he remained true to his promise, or if whatever loyalty he bore to these Shawnee brothers of his—and their sister—proved stronger.

Kneeling to put her daughter in the carrier, she said, "We're going with you, Mr. Ring. To Cornstalk's Town. Nonhelema's Town. Any other place we must. You need never again question my resolve."

11

They'd gone a mile along a trail that wound southwestward, descending low wooded ridges and crossing wet bottomland, before Clare let herself relive that horrifying encounter with the Mingo, Logan. Until then she'd occupied herself by glaring at Jeremiah Ring's back, stiff-set beneath its pack, speared alternately by shadow and sunlight as he moved ahead of her on the forested trail. His tension hadn't abated since leaving Wakatomica.

"It wasn't just Shawnees in attendance," he'd told her. "Delaware, Wyandots, Mingos too. Puckeshinwah—our war chief—spoke for driving all settlers back over the mountains, but in the end even he agreed to try again for peace. They're sending a delegation to the Indian agents at Pittsburgh."

A runner had been sent to Cornstalk and his sister, Nonhelema, both of whom would be pleased with the council's outcome, Mr. Ring had said. He expected the principal Shawnee chief would lead the delegation. "Won't be a large contingent, else it'll look like a war party . . ."

As he trailed off, Mr. Ring had looked thoughtful, wistful even, leaving Clare to surmise he wished he could accompany the delegation to Fort Pitt.

Since that brief exchange, they'd barely spoken. Wolf-Alone had trudged behind her, equally taciturn. She hadn't earned either man's approval at Wakatomica.

The whole interlude was a muddle now, save the moment she'd been imprisoned by the hand of Philip's murderer. She shivered despite the forest's muggy warmth. What had Logan said to her? Not the part about taking her scalp. That, and the gut-churning sight of Philip's, she would never forget. But something else . . .

The forest receded to a blur of green as she strained to recall. Something about a promise not to harm someone who'd claimed her. Who else could that be but Jeremiah Ring, who called himself Logan's friend?

"What claim have you on me, Mr. Ring?"

The man marching ahead of her missed a step on the trail, then rounded to face her, brows tight. "What did you say?"

Behind her came a scuff of moccasins as Wolf-Alone halted.

Clare ignored his presence. "I asked about the nature of your claim on me. Logan said he wouldn't scalp me, but only because he'd sworn not to harm someone who'd claimed me."

Color blazed above Mr. Ring's beard. "Logan threatened to *scalp* you? Why haven't you said so till now?"

"I might have had you seemed interested in anything other than berating me."

The man returned her look with a disconcerting intensity, mingled with a consternation that had him shaking his head. "Missus, I doubt you've the smallest notion what interests me."

"Don't I?" She'd had time to think about his interests—about the fact that the Indian who had her son, this Falling Hawk, was his so-called brother, that this brother was taking Jacob to be the adopted son of their sister. His loyalties had split asunder as surely as if he'd come to a fork in the trail. The man couldn't go both ways.

"Perhaps you would enlighten me," she challenged, as from behind her came the sound of her daughter waking. "For it seems, Mr. Ring, you're wishing mightily you'd never crossed my path." The man's gaze skimmed from her to the Indian lurking behind her, as the baby's mewls transformed into a full-throated wail. "Since you learned it's your brother who has Jacob, it's been clear you—"

Clare bit off her words, seeing by the alarm on Mr. Ring's face that the baby needed quieting. While Wolf-Alone held both aloft, Clare shrugged out of the carrier's straps and turned to unlace the baby, avoiding the Indian's gaze. But when she had the baby in her arms, patting her and pacing a short section of the trail in an attempt to quiet her, it proved futile.

"Come now, Pippa. You should be sleeping still."

And here I am, she thought, *calling you Pippa.* She looked into her daughter's scrunched, unhappy face and thought the name did suit. Not that she'd admit it aloud. She bent and kissed the wailing infant, put her to the other shoulder, sang a snatch of lullaby, then in exasperation said, "I suppose she needs feeding."

Mr. Ring had been standing in a shaft of sunlight, watching her. He looked away before their gazes met. "We can make another mile or two before we lose the light, unless you're calling a halt now."

Clare jiggled the crying baby. "I can nurse her while I walk."

She'd never done so but wasn't going to be the reason they halted early.

Far from looking pleased by her accommodation, Mr. Ring began, "You needn't—"

"I need but a moment of your averted gaze," she interjected. "Let me settle her, then we may walk on."

Mr. Ring stared at her with that confounding scrutiny, then spoke a word to Wolf-Alone. Both men put their backs to her. Clare unpinned her bodice and put the clouted baby to her breast.

Blessed silence at last.

The baby smelled of urine. So did the wrappings she wore in the carrier. Clare needed to wash them, but the urgency to reach Cornstalk's Town—and her pride—forbade it. They would simply have to stink, she and Pippa. She covered herself as best she could with the pungent wrappings.

"I'm ready." Clare reached for the cradleboard, uncertain how she was going to manage it one-handed, but Wolf-Alone shook his head and stepped out of her reach, letting her know he would carry it. She thanked him, thinking it ironic she should find it easier to communicate with this savage who spoke no English, whom she'd known less than a day, than one in whose company she'd journeyed nearly a fortnight.

Perhaps Mr. Ring entertained similar thoughts as he resumed their trudge down the trail. She'd never known him to be so out of sorts.

They'd gone a quarter mile before Clare realized she'd never gotten an answer to the question that began their exchange, but hadn't the heart to wade through another argument to satisfy her curiosity.

"Claimed me," she murmured, thinking perhaps she didn't want to know. There was something she wanted him to know. "Mr. Ring? It *was* Logan who killed my husband."

He halted again and faced her. "What?"

She needed to swallow hard before repeating it. "I said it was Logan who killed Philip. He wears my husband's scalp. I saw it."

She tried to read his face, the thoughts that seemed to convulse it, but they passed too swiftly.

"I'm sorry, Missus," he said, before he turned and continued on.

"So, Brother. Do you mean to finally tell me how this woman and her child come to be in your keeping, or will you go on sitting in silence stealing looks at her while she sleeps?"

Caught in the act of doing so, Jeremiah tore his gaze from the golden braid peeking from the blanket Clare Inglesby had wrapped herself and the baby in to sleep. His brother held one sweeping brow aloft, yet firelight showed concern as well as humor in those amber eyes as he added a stick to the small flames.

Jeremiah sighed. "Remind me what I already told you."

Though he spoke in Shawnee, same as Wolf-Alone—no chance of the woman he'd ceased for some time now thinking of as anything but *Clare* waking to hear herself discussed—he kept his voice low, not wishing to wake her at all after the day she'd had.

There'd been scant time to tell Wolf-Alone much of anything save the bare facts of Clare's plight and his promise to help her. Wolf-Alone said as much. "But you did not tell me how you let yourself be talked into carrying her across the Spaylaywitheepi, a white woman with a newborn. Nor did you speak of her children's father, though maybe of him I have no need to ask."

"Dead," Jeremiah confirmed. "Found him on the trail west of Redstone. Buried him there. Logan wears the man's scalp. She saw it at Wakatomica. Reckon I did too, just didn't know it for his."

"After they killed the father, the Mingos found the boy, but not the mother?"

"She was off in the woods in the night starting her labor, not wanting to wake the boy. She never heard them come."

Jeremiah skimmed his gaze over Clare, tracing the curve of her slender back, thought of that back braced against a tree as she waited, wracked with pain, willing to birth her daughter on the ground in the dark to spare her son having to watch the ordeal. Now she was willing to go among a people she deemed murderers to get the boy back. What else was she prepared to risk?

"Logan took the boy to Yellow Creek," Wolf-Alone said, "just in time for our brother to pass through and see him." He paused, thoughtful, studying Jeremiah. "Had you known that part sooner, about our brother, would you have agreed to help her?"

Jeremiah sought for the truth of that. He'd never have left a woman alone in the straits in which he'd found Clare Inglesby, but would he have agreed to help her recover her son knowing Falling Hawk's intention of giving Jacob to their sister?

"She was nigh to birthing that one," he said, nodding toward Clare as Pippa emitted a gurgle in her sleep, "when I found her."

Wolf-Alone raised both brows. "You tended her through the birthing?"

"Who else was there? Afterward I tried to talk her into returning to Redstone, but she would not hear of it. She would have gone on alone to Wheeling—or died trying—had I not agreed to guide her."

Wolf-Alone had been gazing at Clare. "She has a strong heart to have come so far. That does not surprise me, having seen her son. I am less certain about her wisdom."

"I am less certain about a lot of things."

Jeremiah's unguarded statement brought Wolf-Alone's gaze back to him. "Our sister? Yes. I am thinking much of her. She will want the boy."

That piqued Jeremiah's curiosity about Jacob Inglesby, hardly more than a phantom until now. "What can you tell me of him?"

Wolf-Alone thought for a moment, then said, "He was afraid when we took him from Yellow Creek, but even that first day on the trail with us he did well. He is strong of spirit and does not cry or refuse the food given him. He did not need to be coddled."

Jeremiah knew these were words Clare would wish to hear translated. Though she'd kept silent while they'd eaten a simple repast and she tended Pippa, washing out wrappings at a nearby stream, he'd caught her casting looks at Wolf-Alone, looks that burned with a need to speak.

"But he chatters like a bird as soon as he opens his eyes in the morning. On and on, the questions. So Falling Hawk says," Wolf-Alone added with a glance at Jeremiah. "He would be good for our sister, once they got used to each other. She will want him."

Wolf-Alone said it as firmly as before, but now his eyes revealed the questions he hadn't put into words. What was Jeremiah going to do when they reached Cornstalk's Town? Which mother's cause would he plead?

Jeremiah might once have said there was no question. The boy was white, taken against his will. He'd a mother who wanted him back. But Jeremiah was no longer that farmer from the Shenandoah Valley he'd once been. Nor was he just a frontiersman in the sporadic employ of the Indian agents at Fort Pitt. He was also Shawnee. He'd called Cornstalk's Town his home—as much as he had a home—for the past ten years. He'd hunted with them, danced with them, helped clear the women's fields. He'd known his greatest grief among them. A few of them he loved. One of those was Falling Hawk, who'd taken him to his heart as a brother born. And Wolf-Alone, adopted a few years later. But Rain Crow . . .

Ten years younger than Falling Hawk, born to a different Shawnee father, she'd lived most of her life with their Delaware mother who years ago professed belief in the Christian God and went to live with the Moravians and the rest of their Delaware converts. First in Pennsylvania, then among David Ziesberger's converts in Schoenbrunn, his mission village on the Tuscararas River. There Rain Crow had married a Christian Delaware called Josiah. She'd borne him a son and, to the best of her brothers' knowledge, had been content—until her husband and son contracted smallpox and died within days of each other. Soon after, Rain Crow, also called Abigail, returned to her mother's people, coming to live in Nonhelema's Town, across Scippo Creek from Cornstalk's Town, near its joining with the Scioto.

Their sister's time of formal grieving had passed. Now Falling Hawk was bringing her a son to fill her heart. He wouldn't be keen to hear of that son's white mother wanting him back.

"What was it this woman was saying to you, back on the trail? Something that made you angry."

Wolf-Alone's question pulled Jeremiah back to the present. A tightness gripped his chest; he sidestepped the question. "She can see my loyalties are torn. I want our sister to be whole again, but I have promised this woman to help get her son back."

"That is what makes you angry?" his brother asked. "Having to choose between this woman and our sister? Or is it something about that woman herself?"

Jeremiah reached for a stick and stabbed at the fire's embers, spilling sparks. Wolf-Alone was probing close to what bruised like truth. When his brother had slipped into the *msi-kah-mi-qui* at the council's ending and whispered urgently that Clare had run off into the village, screaming Jacob's name, the intensity of his fear for her had taken him aback. Once he saw her safe, that fear had translated into fury at her for putting herself in peril.

He wasn't certain what to make of such powerful feelings. He'd handled them badly.

"Is it that she reminds you of . . ." Wolf-Alone began, stopping when he caught the sudden warning gaze Jeremiah shot him.

"You think I look at her and see Hannah?" The name still trailed pain across his soul.

"No, Brother. She is nothing like that one. I was going to say she reminds you of yourself when you first came into this country, following the warriors who stole what was yours, as she follows now."

Well, that much was true. He'd thought it more than once himself. Was that all it was then? That he saw himself in Clare Inglesby—himself at his most vulnerable, a time he would rather now forget but that she kept rekindling like a fire that wouldn't die? She was certainly stirring memories he'd thought he'd laid to rest.

When Jeremiah could find no words, his brother remarked, "You have not told me what she said to you on the trail."

"She asked me . . ." Jeremiah's face grew hot. "I claimed her as my wife, in front of Logan. He must have told her so. She asked me why I did it."

Since Yellow Creek he'd suspected it would come to it, and sure enough, Logan had seen him at the back of the council house and drawn him away from the others. One of Logan's warriors had seen Jeremiah and Clare enter the town moments before and had already told Logan he'd come with a white woman. Logan asked about her. Jeremiah had told Logan exactly who Clare Inglesby was, that they'd been to Yellow Creek looking for him, that they were looking now for the boy he had taken, but that Clare Inglesby and her baby were his.

Logan had looked long at him, as if trying to decide whether he believed Jeremiah. No warmth filled his gaze. No memory of friendship.

Finally Logan had nodded. "When I made my vow in your hearing, I let you go in peace. I will also let this woman you claim and her child go away from this place in peace. I will not touch them. As for that boy—her son? He is no longer in my hands."

Jeremiah shared with Wolf-Alone all that had passed between him and Logan concerning Clare.

"She would not have left Wakatomica alive, I think," Wolf-Alone said, "if you had not done what you did. Called her your wife."

"But it is the last thing she wants from me, no matter the reason I did it. I do not think things were well between her and the husband she had before. Knowing I claimed her as mine would only give her one more thing to fret about."

"She has told you these things?"

"Not all of it."

"Then be careful of thinking about her as if such things were true. You cannot see her heart. You cannot know her mind. Even the things she says may be colored by her own untruths."

Jeremiah shook his head, then laughed softly. "Sometimes you speak in riddles to devil me, I think."

Wolf-Alone himself was a riddle, or at least his past. Jeremiah remembered well the day, seven years ago, when the warrior came into his life. He knew how to make an entrance, Wolf-Alone. It was on an early spring morning when the creeks were running full that the big Delaware, just eighteen years old, had come floating down Scippo Creek like one dead, only to rise from the water like a hero out of legend, giving the women come to bathe a proper fright. Dressed in only a breechclout, with no adornment or markings to proclaim his origins, he'd said not a word but strode past them into the town, straight to the *msi-kah-mi-qui* where he was met by Cornstalk himself. He hadn't spoken Shawnee at the time—only the tongue of his mother's people, the Delaware—but had made it clear his intentions were to stay with them, become one of them. So he had done, after being forced to run the gauntlet.

The Delaware stranger who would become Wolf-Alone had taken a hard beating, but he'd stayed on his feet and run the gauntlet's length, to be set upon at the end by one young warrior who he finally bested by snatching the man's war club out of his hand and landing a blow to the head that ought to have caved in that warrior's skull but hadn't.

That young warrior had been Falling Hawk.

Once he'd recovered from the ordeal, Falling Hawk had asked what they'd done with the bold Delaware who wanted to be Shawnee. He was told they had tended his wounds but were holding him captive, Cornstalk being undecided what to do with such a one.

"Good." Falling Hawk had said. "I know what to do. I will make him my brother."

So that was what they'd done. Some of the women took the stranger, who had told no one his name, down to the creek from which he'd come and washed away his Delaware blood, and whatever other blood ran through his veins, and he became Shawnee.

It was a good story and had been told many times, but what had come before it . . . if anyone but Wolf-Alone knew, Jeremiah had never heard it repeated. There was something about the big warrior that forbade his asking, a barrier that, for all Wolf-Alone's loyalty to his adopted family, no one was allowed to cross.

Jeremiah turned from the fire to look at Clare Inglesby, thinking of a change he'd noted in her since leaving Wakatomica. It was in her tending of Pippa, the way she held her daughter, looked into her face, a devotion that had been missing since the baby's birth. She'd run off into the village and abandoned Pippa with a warrior she didn't know; Wolf-Alone had had the baby in his arms when he came into the *msi-kah-mi-qui* seeking Jeremiah.

Had she come to her senses, somewhere in the village, and feared she'd lost her daughter as well? Maybe that fear had broken open a place in her heart for the child, a place she'd kept sealed tight, reserved for the son she couldn't reach with her arms.

If so, that was a good thing to come of it. But as he and Wolf-Alone settled to sleep, Jeremiah found himself praying she wouldn't repeat such a rash act in Cornstalk's Town or wherever she finally set eyes on that son.

12

They'd begun encountering Indians on the trail two days ago. Hunters mostly, though twice they met runners bearing word from Cornstalk to the chiefs at Wakatomica. Now, emerging from thick forest into a more rolling, gentler landscape than any she'd crossed these past weeks, Clare was astonished at the prospect opening before her—broad tracts of cleared earth occupied by women bent over hoes or on their knees with hands in the dark soil, sowing some crop not in rows but in large hillocks that made the land look as if it were infested with giant voles. Accustomed as she was to the sight of Virginia steadings, her mind calculated the area of cultivation—what she could see as they advanced between fields—and translated that into a rough approximation of the numbers such acreage could sustain.

Cornstalk's Town would be larger than any she'd yet seen, and it was but one in the vicinity. South of Scippo Creek was the village of Cornstalk's sister, Nonhelema. Other towns lay across the Scioto River. The sheer number of Shawnees inhabiting this landscape pressed upon her, but it was those nearest demanding her immediate attention.

Most stopped their work to stare. Some called out to Mr. Ring or Wolf-Alone. With memories of Wakatomica fresh, Clare was afraid to return their stares but couldn't keep herself from studying the children playing. Spotting no fair head among the dark ones, she bit back a groan of longing, comforted only by the solid weight of Pippa on her back.

She would conduct herself with proper decorum in this place. She would do nothing to jeopardize her goal—leaving with both of her children, unharmed, as soon as possible. She'd show Mr. Ring it had been no mistake to bring her this far.

"I need you to listen," he'd told her as they lingered by what would be their last fire, camped in forest where Shawnees hunted, where others called Miamis, Wyandots, Senecas, Patawatomis might be encountered. "I'm going to tell you how things will be for us when we reach Cornstalk's Town tomorrow, best I can foresee."

Clare had known how they would be. The Almighty hadn't brought her this far to deny her Jacob, whatever dire prediction the man was about to make.

"First I'll have to ascertain if Jacob is in our sister's keeping, as Wolf-Alone believes." Mr. Ring had glanced at his brother, sitting across the fire; Wolf-Alone's enigmatic gaze had moved between them, though he showed no comprehension of their exchange. "If so, I'll learn whether he's been adopted, then whether our sister is willing to meet with us and talk."

Clenching her teeth against dismay at the notion, Clare kept her mouth shut and waited.

"It's going to take time." Mr. Ring said the words carefully, as if unsure she would grasp his meaning. "Longer than you'll wish."

"How much time are you thinking it will take, Mr. Ring?"

Again his dark eyes shifted, gaze going to Wolf-Alone before he shook his head. "That'll depend on Rain Crow, Falling Hawk as well. We'll need him on our side if we can get him there. But I caution you not to count on that."

"I will count on the Lord," she said, more desperation than conviction in her voice.

He leaned forward, bringing his face into fuller firelight, features thrown into shadowed relief. "I need you to trust me, let me see this through for you. You cannot do what you did in Wakatomica, not in Cornstalk's Town. It matters what these people think of you."

More than ever she felt he resented being put in this position, pulled between her and his Shawnee kin. *She* wished he wasn't in this position, wished she and Philip had remained in Virginia, content to be dirt-poor farmers raising their children by the strength of their backs.

Mr. Ring had asked for her trust. Pippa set to crying, relieving her of saying more than "I understand."

Next morning Mr. Ring had shaved off his whiskers. She'd blushed when first she saw him, finding it impossible not to stare, disconcerted that she missed the beard, though she noticed now that his mouth was nicely shaped, wide and full. The skin on the lower half of his lean face wasn't much paler than that across his cheekbones and brow. She supposed he kept himself clean-shaven among the Shawnees, only letting his beard grow while traipsing about the wilderness or wherever his Indian agency business took him.

He'd altered his dress that morning too. Gone was the battered hat. In its place he'd tied what looked like turkey feathers in the leather whang that tailed his hair. Though the leggings and breechclout were the same, the shirt he'd donned was of billowy linen sewn with beads at the collar instead of the worn, linsey-woolsey hunting shirt he usually wore.

Taken altogether he seemed more *Indian* than before.

Walking between him and Wolf-Alone as they pushed past the Shawnees' fields and into the edges of the town—a mingling of wegiwas and, to her surprise, squared, split-log cabins that might have been plucked by some great wind from any of a hundred Virginia farmsteads and dropped across the Ohio—Clare felt like a sparrow strayed into some alien flock that promised no welcome. The babble of voices enclosed her as women and children left their tasks to trail behind.

Thus surrounded by her enemies, with more doubt in the man who stood between them than she cared to admit, Clare Inglesby straightened her back and followed Jeremiah Ring into Cornstalk's Town.

The warrior called Falling Hawk met them within sight of the *msi-kah-mi-qui*, a structure in the town's center Clare recognized on sight. She had no need to be told of his identity. Somehow she knew, in those seconds his bent head emerged from a nearby lodge and he straightened, lean and muscular, with thick black hair that fell halfway to his waist worn loose and flowing. He wasn't as tall as Wolf-Alone or even Mr. Ring, whom he caught sight of and greeted with an expansive smile, but he strode toward them with a carriage so straight he seemed tall.

Mr. Ring called a greeting to the approaching warrior, then turned to her. "That's my brother. Keep quiet 'less I speak to you. I'm going to explain things now."

Her mouth was a desert. She couldn't have spoken had she wanted to. Sensing movement near, she looked up. Wolf-Alone didn't look at her, yet it seemed he was offering what he could—his familiarity and the substantial force of his presence. The depth of her gratitude surprised her, but she was distracted by the greeting being exchanged by Mr. Ring and Falling Hawk. The two fell to talking, and Clare strained to listen, though she couldn't comprehend a word. Falling Hawk looked her way, surprise lifting feathery eyebrows. Something Mr. Ring said drew reactions from Indians nearby. Noises of surprise, curiosity. More glazes flicked to her as Falling Hawk crossed to Wolf-Alone and greeted him as warmly as he had Mr. Ring. The two exchanged a few words, then the warrior turned to Clare.

"Good you here with my brother." He added more that she didn't catch, but the gist of what he'd said was plain despite his imperfect English. He'd welcomed her.

"Thank you," Clare said, sounding breathless with nervous relief. "Thank you so much. I . . ." Truth warred with necessity before necessity won out. "It is good to be here with you."

Jacob's name was on the tip of her tongue when she heard Pippa waking in her carrier. Falling Hawk heard too and asked a question in Shawnee, turning to Mr. Ring, whose face reddened slightly as he replied. Clare sought to catch his eye. He sensed her gaze. She knew he did. But he wouldn't look at her.

Her belly turned over, as around them bodies smelling of bear grease pressed close and she felt the touch of fingers. Were they touching Pippa too? She wanted to remove the carrier and hold the baby, shield her, but feared to cause offense. She could feel her nerves unraveling like a spool of ribbon with each moment's passing. She yearned to ask about Jacob.

Just then a woman emerged from the lodge Falling Hawk had exited moments before. She stood and looked their way, smooth-skinned, slender, and arresting.

Assuming this was Falling Hawk's wife, Clare took a second look and realized it wasn't the set of the woman's features that rendered her striking, though the bones beneath were strong in shape. What made her so arresting came from within, a joy that radiated from shining eyes as she caught sight of Mr. Ring and Wolf-Alone and blazed a dazzling smile.

That smile betrayed the woman's true relationship to Falling Hawk, for Clare had seen its twin moments ago. Not wife. Sister.

The woman called to them in Shawnee. Mr. Ring turned at the sound, just as Clare felt the breath go out of her in a rush. She was no longer looking at Falling Hawk's sister but at the child she was turning back to coax out of the lodge. A child emerging from the bark hut into sunlight that shone almost blindingly off curling pale hair.

The woman took the child by the hand.

The world narrowed until it included nothing but those clasped hands.

Slender graceful brown hand. Small trusting white hand. Bonded in a manner that seared her soul with violation.

Jacob. She could neither speak nor move, so paralyzing was the shock, the joy, the outrage coursing through her.

"Clare," was all Mr. Ring had time to say before Jacob saw her too.

Her son's face hung expressionless and remained so for a breath . . . two . . . long enough for Clare to fear that already he'd forgotten her. Then Jacob's face broke with recognition and a relief so wrenching Clare knew it matched her own. His features screwed up as tears came in a flood.

"Mama! Mama!"

Shrieking at the top of his considerable lungs, her little boy twisted in the grasp of Falling Hawk's sister, yanked free, and hurtled toward Clare, who fell to her knees in a billow of stained linen to receive him, the agony of the past weeks lifting away.

"Jacob—*Jacob.*" She closed her eyes, feeling little arms clamped around her, smelling soft hair, tasting the salt of tears and sweat—familiar, beloved—while above and around them voices rose, exclaiming, querying, protesting. They collided like waves crashing. An island amidst the breakers, Clare paid them no more heed than she would such waves. Not even that high, desperate voice calling the same Shawnee words over and over. She cared not. Jacob was found. Safe. *Hers.*

Then hands were on her, pulling at her gown, her hair. Pulling too at Jacob. Her grip on him tightened as a growl escaped her lips.

A blow glanced across her cheekbone. Still she clung.

Pippa was wailing, still strapped to Clare's back . . . until suddenly she wasn't. The weight of baby and carrier lifted away, the straps falling slack into her lap. For an uncomprehending second she stared at the severed leather. Then, still crouched, Jacob clinging to her burr-like, she whirled to catch whoever had taken her baby, ready to battle for both her children against an entire Shawnee village.

Wolf-Alone stood just out of reach, holding the carrier with Pippa in it, the baby red-faced and squalling. While above the din Mr. Ring shouted something in Shawnee, Clare surged to her feet, Jacob clutching her petticoat.

Holding her iron gaze like a lodestone, Wolf-Alone backed away a measured step. Enraged by his betrayal, she staggered after him, hampered by Jacob's clinging. In that instant her son was yanked away. She felt the wrench of her garment, heard the tearing of seams as his grip broke.

Turning in desperation, she saw Falling Hawk's sister sweep Jacob into her arms and be folded into the crowd of Indians as if a mouth had opened and swallowed them whole.

"*Jacob*—no!" Arms came around her. She struggled.

"Clare, let them go!"

Mr. Ring held her fast. She jerked in his arms, loosening his grip enough to manage a turn, ready to fight her way to Pippa next but found Wolf-Alone standing well within her reach.

"Give her to me!"

Wolf-Alone handed the screaming baby over. Clutching the carrier to herself, Clare sought for Jacob, but she'd lost all sense of direction. The village, the people, their faces, seemed identical no matter which way she looked.

Falling Hawk had taken command of the situation. He was the one talking now, scowling at Mr. Ring with more than a hint of the betrayal that was coursing through Clare as she seethed against Wolf-Alone, who'd done the one thing that could have provoked her into relinquishing Jacob. She met that amber gaze now, blazing mutely in her rage. Wolf-Alone looked calmly back, showing no remorse.

Not her ally, after all.

But what of Mr. Ring? What had he said to Falling Hawk and the rest? Did they understand Jacob was her son?

Mr. Ring was speaking again, his tone firm, reasoning. Other voices quieted. Falling Hawk, stone-faced, waited until he ceased to speak, then made a cutting motion with his hand. That seemed to end things. Or decide something. Everything was a dizzying blur to Clare. Faces, voices. Falling Hawk turning his back, striding away. Hands were on her again—Wolf-Alone and Mr. Ring—forcing her in the opposite direction, past bark lodges and Indians moving aside, opening a path she barely heeded. Mr. Ring pushed her head down and they were inside what must be a wegiwa. A hide fell across the entrance, muting light and noise.

Stunned, she looked around at the dim interior, seeing little of it before sunlight flashed and Wolf-Alone ducked back out. She would have a thing or two to say to that Indian later, never mind he wouldn't understand a word. For now she faced Mr. Ring, Pippa still mewling in the carrier she clutched.

"You let them take my son away!"

"I had to." Mr. Ring looked beset, but when she opened her mouth to speak, he raised a hand to stop her. "No. Listen to me."

So unyielding was his tone that she hesitated. Aware suddenly of the fullness of her breasts, another reason for Pippa's fussing, she crouched on the earthen floor—it was strewn with reed mats around a central fire pit, above which a smoke-hole in the roof streamed sunlight—and began unlacing the baby. Turning her back on Mr. Ring, she settled herself on a mat and opened her gown.

"I didn't know Jacob would be here," Mr. Ring went on, the strain of the scene just past evident in his voice. "Rain Crow has been living in Nonhelema's Town, across the creek. She happened to be visiting Falling Hawk, wanting to show off . . . her son."

The words stung like hail. Her hands shook. She had trouble getting Pippa to latch on to suckle. Gently she coaxed the baby as she forced out the hateful question. "He's adopted then?"

She knew the answer, had seen it in the Indian woman's face as she looked at Jacob, his tentative, half-fearful trust in putting his little hand in hers.

"They had the ceremony at the river yesterday. He's called Many Sparrows."

Clare swallowed back a churn of nausea. "His name is Jacob. I am his mother."

She heard Mr. Ring take a step nearer. "I'd hoped to get us settled, then approach Falling Hawk on the matter in private, reason things out between us and our sister. Now the entire town knows of it, and Cornstalk isn't here to arbitrate the matter."

She gazed down at the dome of Pippa's head, at rounded cheeks and busily working mouth, and with an ache asked, "What of Nonhelema? Can she do nothing for me?"

"She's gone with Cornstalk to Pittsburgh for the council. Even were they here I don't know what they'd think of this situation. I doubt it's a thing that's happened before, a white woman come seeking a son taken captive. But there's a thing you need to—"

"What do you mean?" Clare shifted so she could see Mr. Ring, but he stood in shadow. She couldn't see his face. "Have these people never been confronted by the kin of a captive they've stolen? Surely in the French War, or after it, they were forced to return their captives. They brought them back to the forts. Back to their true families."

"It's less common for those families to come to them."

"But such has happened? A father, a brother maybe, come after one they lost?"

"It's happened."

She didn't like the wariness she heard in his voice, as if she'd forced him to say a thing he hadn't wanted to utter. "Have you seen such a thing, Mr. Ring? Here in this town?"

"Once."

Impatience gripped her. Why was she having to drag every word out of the man? "And how did it end?"

"Not in the way that man hoped."

What did that mean? Had the Shawnees made a captive of that man as well as his kin? Tortured him? Killed him? Or merely sent him away without the one he sought?

She turned her back again, hunching over Pippa, uncertain which fate would be the more intolerable. "Had you no hope at all that it would do any good once we found him?"

"Clare," Mr. Ring said wearily. "I told you this won't be a simple matter to unravel. We're going to have to wait now. Until Cornstalk and Nonhelema return from Fort Pitt. Then we'll see."

Joy and relief at finding Jacob had been cruelly cut short. Back was the stone lodged in her chest. "And do what meantime?"

"You can take steps to gain ground with Falling Hawk, if not Rain Crow—or let me do it for you. I've got my own amends to make. They're both vexed with me. Don't understand what I'm doing, or why."

"What *are* you doing, Mr. Ring?"

"For now, I'm going to find Falling Hawk, try and smooth things over, see if he can overlook what happened before."

"They're going to let us stay?"

"Of course we're staying. This is my home."

But not hers. She was a guest, an unwelcome one. Regardless, she was there, and she'd herself and one child at least to keep fed, clean, and clothed. "Where will Pippa and I sleep?"

"Right here. This is Wolf-Alone's lodge. It's where I live when I'm with the Shawnees."

She'd not yet had the presence of mind to wonder whose lodge this might be, though evidence of it being a dwelling was strewn about. "Not with Falling Hawk?"

"He has a wife and children. Wolf-Alone hasn't."

She looked around, taking in the place. She'd seen them aplenty from outside, but this was her first time past a door-hide. The bark-slab walls were adorned with woven reed mats such as covered the floor, as well as netting, clothing, and sundry other trappings. Around the walls platforms had been built. Under and on them items were stacked—kettles and pans, moccasins, baskets, boxes made of bark. Two were piled with furs and trade blankets. Her roving gaze fastened on the nearest of those.

"Is that a bed?"

"It's mine." Mr. Ring swallowed audibly; she shifted her gaze to him. "Actually it's ours now."

"*Ours?*"

"Well, yours but . . . they think you're my wife." Even in the dimness she could see the man's deepening color as he added, "It's for your protection, nothing more. Being married to me makes you all but Shawnee to them as well. It was the only way I could assure your welcome here after . . ."

After the scene she'd caused. Her heart was pounding so hard that she was amazed Pippa was still nursing. "You did this at Wakatomica, didn't you? This is what Logan meant when he said I'd been claimed. He thought I was your wife; that's why he didn't harm me."

"That's exactly why, Clare."

Indignation flared. "Why do you address me so familiarly? We are not married, whatever these people think, and I never gave you leave."

He was silent a moment before saying, "I'm sorry, Missus. I'll not do it if it vexes you so."

His calm accommodation filled her with shame. Deftly she shifted Pippa to her other breast and said, "Though why I should make issue of it now that we're to share a roof, I do not know."

Mr. Ring crouched beside her. "You're making issue of it on account you feel helpless and need to lash out against it. Better you lash out at me. I give you leave to do it, as often as you need. I can take it."

Deeper shame washed over her at his words. She'd never meant to place him in such a situation, torn between his promise to her and his love—or whatever he felt—for these people, but it was her fault he was in it. He didn't deserve her constant pique.

"You even renamed my daughter," she said, disgusted that she couldn't heed her own admonition.

"I thought you liked the name. You've used it."

"I know," she said, though it sounded like a protest. "Oh, call us whatever you will."

"You mean that?"

"Yes," she said, only a little testily.

He smiled at her and stood. "I need to leave you for now. You'll be safe here. I'll bring in the packs before I go; you can get settled."

"I want to go with you." She wanted to see Jacob. There was a chance that might happen if Rain Crow was with Falling Hawk. But Mr. Ring was backing away.

"It's too soon. Best you stay out of sight for now."

She was little better than a prisoner. And Jacob was so close. She'd seen him, held him, saw he was safe but . . . he'd looked different. Older. How could he already look older?

She resented the days apart, of being deprived of even a moment of her son's life.

"Fine," she said, turning so he wouldn't see her face crumple. "Go. I'll sit here and do nothing."

His retreating footsteps paused at the door. "There's one thing you can do. One thing I need you to do."

She didn't look at him. "I'll do anything."

"Right now," he said, "I need you to pray."

He found his brothers outside Falling Hawk's lodge. Falling Hawk's arms were crossed as he listened to the unhappy voice of their sister emanating from within and whatever Wolf-Alone was saying. Though they were drawing glances from those within earshot of Rain Crow, neither man looked desirous of entering the lodge. Jeremiah heard Crosses-the-Path, Falling Hawk's wife, from within as well, but her softer tones were drowned by their sister's strident voice.

Jeremiah halted in the dooryard, near Crosses-the-Path's kettle fire, with the eyes of both men on him.

"Brother," he said, addressing Falling Hawk, "I am sorry for the disruption our arrival has caused. I had thought our sister would be across the creek at her home, that I would be able to speak to you."

Rain Crow's voice fell silent an instant before the door-hide whipped aside and she emerged. She had eyes for no one but Jeremiah; her gaze seared the words from his tongue.

"Why did you wish to speak first to our brother?" she demanded. "Did you mean to get him on your side in this? He is the one who brought my son to me!"

Jeremiah steeled himself to remain calm. He knew there was much pain and likely fear behind Rain Crow's mask of anger. "Sister, I am sorry. Please, will you let me explain?"

"No!" Rain Crow's lips drew back from her teeth, so vehement was her denial. "What is to explain? You have brought a woman to this town who wants to take my son from me. And you—" She swung toward Falling Hawk, who took a half-step back, bumping into Wolf-Alone. "*You* brought Many Sparrows to me, telling me how he was found in the mountains alone. That he had *no* mother, *no* father. No one!"

Falling Hawk raised his hands as if warding off attack. "That is what I was told at Yellow Creek! Was I to know it was not true?"

"Is it true?" Rain Crow turned back to Jeremiah. "Or is *this* the lie, that woman you bring here? What am I to think?"

"If you will let me," Jeremiah began again, "I will tell you what is true about that boy and his mother."

"*I* am his mother!" Rain Crow put her back to them and pushed aside the buffalo hide that hung across the doorway and in English called, "Many Sparrows! We are going home now."

Jeremiah stepped forward, putting his hand to her arm. "Will you not stay? Will you meet with the woman who has come here with me?"

She jerked free, glaring at him. "I have nothing to say to that one. I never want to see her white face again."

Falling Hawk cleared his throat. "That is going to be a hard thing, since she is our brother's wife."

The words fell like stones in a pool of frogs, bringing utter silence. Wolf-Alone looked at Jeremiah, then raised his slanted brows with a look that said plainly no good was going to come of any of this, then he backed away from them and took his leave.

Coward, Jeremiah thought, but when he caught his sister's glowering gaze he didn't blame Wolf-Alone. *He* wanted to slink away like the lowest of snakes.

Inside the lodge Falling Hawk's wife and daughters were speaking, their voices cajoling. The boy didn't seem to want to come out.

"Many Sparrows?" Rain Crow ducked inside and in seconds was out again, the boy clutched by the hand.

Jacob Inglesby, though clearly frightened and confused, wasn't struggling or crying. He saw the men gathered outside the lodge and looked up, straight into Jeremiah's face. The boy's eyes widened in recognition. They weren't his mother's striking green but a rich dark brown.

"Mama?"

"Come," Rain Crow said again. "We go home."

"Where's Mama?"

Rain Crow was tugging him along, the look on her face riven with pain. The boy twisted to look back as his little feet stumbled along, barely keeping up with Rain Crow's strides. For as long as he could, he kept them in his sights, searching for Clare, pleading wordlessly with Jeremiah—or so it seemed. Then they were gone down the path to the creek.

Crosses-the-Path peeked out of the lodge, but Falling Hawk waved her back inside. The warrior heaved a sigh. "All I wanted to do was bring gladness to the heart of our sister."

"That is a thing I want to do as well." When Falling Hawk looked at him with disbelief, Jeremiah added, "You know I have grieved with her for the ones she lost."

"That is not all you grieve," Falling Hawk said bitterly.

"That is true. It puts my heart on the ground to see how she has turned her back on the Almighty, whom she professed to love and serve."

Falling Hawk's face hardened. "It is good she has done that thing. I wish our mother would do so, but at least we have our sister back."

Jeremiah said, "Here is a thing about the Almighty, my brother, that you might not understand. He is a jealous God. Whatever she calls herself, our sister is His. He will not let her go far before He woos her back with His love."

He had to say the words, though he knew there was little chance of them changing Falling Hawk's heart. No lover of the missionaries or their God, his brother saw their sister's faltering faith as a good thing.

Was his challenging her right to Jacob Inglesby going to push her further from that faith? That was a thing he hadn't foreseen until this moment.

He had to do something. He had to fix this.

"I will go after her," he said and took a step in that direction, ready to cross the creek that separated the towns. "I will talk to her."

Falling Hawk's hand on his shoulder stopped him. "You will talk to her, but not now. She will hear nothing you have to say now."

And that was all it took to remind Jeremiah. He didn't have to *do* anything, fix anything, not when he couldn't see the path ahead clearly. Not until, unless, he was sure it was of the Almighty's leading. Even if doing nothing was the hardest thing of all.

Maybe especially then.

Meanwhile, the Lord Himself would fight this battle. But he very much hoped Clare was doing the one thing he'd asked her to do.

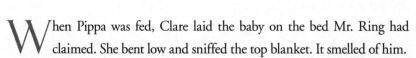

13

When Pippa was fed, Clare laid the baby on the bed Mr. Ring had claimed. She bent low and sniffed the top blanket. It smelled of him.

She straightened and paced the confines of what was to be her shelter for an undetermined period of time. If only it could shelter her from the memory of Jacob's cry. *"Mama . . ."*

She clamped a hand across her mouth, pressing hard.

"Right now I need you to pray."

A reasonable request, all things considered. Clare tried, but her mind skittered over the constant pleas she'd sent heavenward a thousand times already, latching onto nothing but *"Mama . . ."*

Groaning, she halted with her arms pressed to her ribs. How long must she wait and do nothing while Mr. Ring made whatever negotiations he deemed necessary to pry Jacob from his sister? Memory of Rain Crow's grasping hands, her voice calling what must have been the name she'd given Jacob, made Clare grit her teeth. *Many Sparrows.*

"His name is Jacob!" she said, loud enough to startle a squeak out of Pippa. Clare held her breath, waiting. The baby settled back into sleep.

If only *she* could sleep and forget her grief and worry until all was accomplished and she and her children were safe. What if Mr. Ring's efforts proved in vain? Ought she to devise a plan? Something less desperate than snatching up her children and running from that Indian town into the cornfields surrounding it, then into the forest surrounding them, then finding the distant Ohio River and following it home.

Such an impossible-seeming thing had been accomplished before, Clare knew. And by a woman. Mary Draper Ingles, heavy with child at the time, had been taken captive by Shawnees during the French War, forced into the wilderness with her two small sons. Her escape and return from captivity, months later, was a feat of endurance most Virginians could still hardly credit. Yet it hadn't come without staggering cost. Mary had abandoned her children with the Shawnees to make that daring escape.

Clare would sooner become Shawnee herself than leave either of her children behind. But she had an advantage over Mary: a man willing to stand between her and these savages. To be her advocate. One who, presumably, was doing that advocating while she stewed in this bark lodge, staring down a mountain of uncertainty, in the shadow of which she must find a way to survive. For now.

Crossing the space to Pippa, she looked down at her sleeping daughter, thinking of Wolf-Alone and how he'd exploited her fear of losing another child to distract her from Jacob. Now here she was, virtually a prisoner in his lodge, surrounded by his possessions—including a crude puncheon table with block chairs drawn up to it, very like what one might find in any settler's cabin along the frontier, if cut lower to accommodate the sloping roof.

But this was no hewn log cabin. Sturdy peeled poles, forked at the top, framed the structure at each end, two rising like slender pillars in the center. A long pole laid across their forks, tied with rough fiber cordage, formed the apex of the roof, against which more poles were bent and tied to complete the oblong frame. Flat sheets of bark, secured over the frame, created a surprisingly snug interior.

Her belly gurgled, making her aware of hunger. Ought she to pry into the baskets stacked about in hopes of finding something recognizable to eat?

Before she could act upon the thought, a rustle at the door-hide had her tensing, thinking it would be Wolf-Alone returning or Mr. Ring, though she hadn't expected him back so soon.

It was neither man. The hide pushed inward, and a boy, five or six years older than Jacob, poked his head within. Sunlight streamed across his tousled hair, which wasn't the black of an Indian's but a light brown ribboned with paler streaks. His face, while brown, looked to have gotten that way from the sun, not by birth.

The boy blinked, gaze adjusting to the dimness within, and in a cautious voice only someone inside the lodge would hear said, "Wolf-Alone? You here?"

Shock held Clare mute. The boy's English, heavily accented but unmistakable, was a peal of thunder in her brain.

The boy pushed his way into the lodge and stood, poised at the edge of the smoke-hole's light streaming down. Before Clare could summon speech, he looked her way and nearly jumped straight off the ground.

They stared at one another, agog, until finally the boy spoke. "You English lady?"

"N-not English. I'm a Virginian." Clare took a step nearer the boy, wanting to be sure her eyes weren't playing tricks. "Are *you* English?"

His features weren't remotely Indian. His hair was light. So were his eyes. A striking golden brown that seemed . . . familiar. "You're white, aren't you? Who are you?"

It was almost comical, the way the boy's color drained at the mention of *white*. He stepped back from the smoke-hole's light and said something in Shawnee, shaking his head.

Sensing imminent bolting, Clare smiled in reassurance. "Come now, young man. You've already given yourself away. Stay and talk to me, would you? You're a friend of Wolf-Alone's?"

The boy's eyes were wary, yet he couldn't seem to tear his gaze from her face, her braided hair, her full-skirted gown with its waist already fitting her trimly again.

He didn't answer her questions.

"My name is Clare. What is yours?" She nearly sighed in relief the instant she saw curiosity outweigh the boy's wariness. Pointing at his narrow chest, he said something in Shawnee. Clare shook her head. "What does that mean in English? Do you know?"

"It mean . . . Little-Cat-That-Scratches."

Clare couldn't help smiling at the whimsical name. "I'm pleased to make your acquaintance, Little-Cat-That-Scratches."

The boy had slender brows, a little darker than his hair. They drew together as he pointed to himself again. "Little Wildcat. Easier you say?"

"Much easier, Little Wildcat."

The boy's frown deepened. He thrust out a jaw surprisingly firm. "No more *little*. Almost man grown."

This time Clare bit back the smile, nodding gravely. "Ah, yes, I see. Shall I call you simply . . . Wildcat?"

The boy flashed a grin. With the issue of his name settled to his satisfaction, he tilted his head, studying her with interest. "You . . . Wolf-Alone . . . his woman now?"

"His . . . ? Oh goodness, no. I'm no one's . . ." She remembered in time she *was* meant to be someone's wife, at least as far as these people were concerned. Was she truly going to play along with this charade?

If it helped get Jacob back . . .

"I'm the—the woman of Jeremiah Ring. Do you know him?"

"Ring?" The boy nodded. "But he is—" A complicated string of syllables flowed from his lips. When she stared blankly he laughed. "How to say name . . . Big-Cat-Looks? No . . . Panther-Sees-Him!"

Clare wondered why it had never crossed her mind that Mr. Ring would have another name among his adopted people. A Shawnee name.

"Panther-Sees-Him?" She suspected a story lay behind the name. She considered asking, but just then Pippa made a noise in her sleep and kicked, distracting the boy.

"Baby?"

She wondered where he'd been earlier, during the scene of her arrival. Not among the crowd they'd drawn, else he'd not have been surprised at Pippa's presence. "Would you care to see her?"

Needing no more invitation, Wildcat moved to the bed platform and bent over Pippa, who went on sleeping, unaware she'd become the center of attention. Clare knelt beside the bed.

Wildcat crouched beside her. "What name?"

"Her name is Philippa Joan, but Mr.—Panther-Sees-Him—calls her Pippa."

"Pippa." The boy repeated it, all but cooing over the baby.

Clare was startled by the ache of tenderness the child stirred, the deeper ache of grief, for while his presence was some comfort, screaming through her mind was the thought that somewhere someone probably longed for this boy, worried for him, grieved for him.

"Who are your parents, Wildcat?"

Showing no disquiet at her question, the boy went on gazing at Pippa's sleeping face. "Wildcat father Split-Moon. Mother . . . gone."

Gone. Had his Shawnee mother died? Looking at his face in profile, the stiffening of his mouth, she sensed it was so, and not long ago. Desire to gather the boy in her arms nearly overpowered her. She fought the urge, knowing he thought himself a man—almost. "What was your name?"

"I say. Wildcat."

"And it's a good name. Truly. But I meant what was your name before you became Shawnee? When you lived with your white parents?"

Wildcat glanced sidelong at her. "No white parents."

"But you had them. Everyone has a mother, even if . . . they get another later."

"No—yes! But no . . . memory?" Wildcat looked at her, questioning his choice of words.

"You don't remember your parents? But you speak English still. Surely it cannot be so long since you last saw them."

"It much long. Not know me before *Wildcat*. Before this." He made a gesture meant, she suspected, to indicate the town surrounding them, ending with that finger pointing at his chest again. "Not know before."

His explanation was clear enough, but it begged a question she couldn't contain. "Then . . . did someone teach you English?"

Wildcat started to reply, then shook his head as if he didn't understand the question. But she saw the flash of awareness in his eyes as they darted toward the door-hide.

"I go." He was making for that hide before she could get to her feet, but stopped short and turned to her, like a child belatedly remembering his manners. "Good-bye, Clare-wife."

He ducked outside in a flash of sunlight quenched by the falling hide. Just beyond it he spoke again.

"You back!"

A man's voice spoke in reply, sounding for all the world like a gentle scold, but the words were Shawnee, the voice too muffled by the door-hide to recognize.

Jeremiah Ring, she hoped.

The boy switched to Shawnee, and the two exchanged a few more words before the hide moved again and a man's large figure pushed within.

Wolf-Alone. Clare's heartbeat quickened with surprise and dawning understanding.

Wolf-Alone looked at her briefly, then turned to drag in the pack he'd carried from Wakatomica. He set about pulling items from it and putting them away beneath the other bed platform.

Clare sat on Mr. Ring's bed and smoothed her hand over Pippa's downy head.

"Please try to be quiet. The baby is sleeping." She watched the Indian closely, but while he glanced at her to acknowledge she'd spoken, he didn't look at Pippa or show he'd understood. "Did you find Falling Hawk? Or see Jacob?"

This time Wolf-Alone didn't so much as look her way.

She thought a moment, then said, "While you were gone I had a visitor. Maybe you saw him leaving? He called himself Little-Cat-That-Scratches." She put a smile into her voice. "Then he said he's nearly a man grown—no longer *little*—and he wishes instead to be called Wildcat."

Wolf-Alone was reaching into his pack, his face turned in profile, but the pull of his cheek muscles into a smile would have confirmed her suspicion even without his involuntary, "Huh."

Clare felt a surge of triumph, followed by outrage.

"He speaks English surprisingly well," she continued, jaw muscles tightening over the words, "for one who claims to have no memory of his white parents. But I suspect that's no surprise to you."

Wolf-Alone froze, hand inside the pack. Slowly he faced her, features catching light from the smoke-hole, and she realized with surprise why Wildcat's eyes had looked familiar. They were nearly the same shade as Wolf-Alone's.

"You taught him, didn't you?"

The Indian said nothing at once, as if he needed time to decide whether to acknowledge the accusation or go on pretending ignorance.

Confident in her deduction, Clare was content to sit and glare and wait for it.

A deep-chested sigh flowed out of Wolf-Alone as he sat back on his haunches, lips twisted in what might have been a rueful smile; it faded quickly.

"Yes ma'am, I taught the boy. But that's a thing between him and me. Not even my brothers know of it."

Clare gaped. Wolf-Alone spoke English like one born to it. More precisely, one born to it in *Virginia*. What he'd actually said was slower to register. "Not even Mr. Ring knows you speak English?"

"He doesn't, for a fact." Wolf-Alone's gaze hardened, holding hers. "It's going to stay so. You hearing me?"

Clare was hearing him, though the need for secrecy was mystifying. Wolf-Alone stood, waiting for her to speak.

"If that's what you want . . . I suppose I'll keep your secret."

"I'm looking for more than *suppose*."

"All right then. I promise."

"Good." With no further explanation, Wolf-Alone pushed aside the door-hide and left her again in solitude, save for Pippa, who'd slept through it all.

"Well," she said, and remembered the scolding she'd meant to give the man over his recklessness with her daughter. As if she'd ever find the courage to do any such thing now.

14

It took Falling Hawk, at Jeremiah's urging, two days to persuade their sister to come back to Cornstalk's Town and listen to Clare's petition for Jacob's return. The place of meeting chosen was the neutral ground of Falling Hawk's lodge, though as they took seats around the central fire, Jeremiah sensed their brother's sympathies still rested with Rain Crow. Not for the first time he wished for the wisdom of King Solomon, when presented with a similar dilemma of two mothers claiming one son.

"What would you have me do, Brother? Take my knife and cut the boy in two?" Falling Hawk had demanded, unknowingly echoing Solomon's revealing decree.

"I would have you do no such thing," Jeremiah had said. "Only listen to the words of the woman I have brought here. Help me persuade our sister to listen. That is all."

"Our sister's heart has found the sun after a long night of sorrow. You would make it dark again?" His brother's pained eyes had flicked to him, not quite accusing but coming near it.

"Never willingly." Yet the impossibility of the situation being resolved to everyone's content had burned in Jeremiah's chest. "What of the one who bore that child, who had him stolen and wants him back? What of her sorrow?"

Falling Hawk closed his eyes, as if to gather patience, then met Jeremiah's gaze. "I am glad my brother has at last taken a wife. I know you have walked through your own darkness. But why did it have to be *that* woman? Why the mother of a child who is now Shawnee?"

Jeremiah was tempted to ask his brother why *he* had to be at Yellow Creek when Logan and his warriors brought Jacob Inglesby there, why *he* had to be the one to take him—to their sister of all people?

"I found the woman and made my promise to help her before I knew of your connection to the boy. To her, the boy is *her* son. He will always be her son. You understand this?"

"I understand," Falling Hawk said. "But you have been Shawnee long enough to know the boy is now Rain Crow's son in her heart and in the eyes of the People. As you and Wolf-Alone are the brothers of my heart."

For all its calculation, it had been an expression of honesty. Falling Hawk had welcomed him into his family without reservation. Jeremiah owed the man his loyalty as well as his affection and consideration. But something had happened those days on the trail from Redstone, finding Philip Inglesby dead, then Clare alone in dire straits. A bond had begun with Pippa's birth. He hadn't expected to fall head over heels in love with that baby girl or to feel something more than obligation for her mother as well.

For a time Falling Hawk had looked toward the creek where their sister had vanished. At last he'd said, "I have not forgotten how you came among us. I see why your heart would be to help this woman, even if she were not your wife. You see yourself when you look at her."

It was what Wolf-Alone had said to him on the trail. Jeremiah didn't refute it.

Falling Hawk had sighed, as though resigning himself. "I will talk to our sister. I will see what she is willing to do."

Listen. That was all Rain Crow was willing to do. It was more than she was obliged to do, and Jeremiah was thankful.

So was Clare, but as Jeremiah seated himself to her left at Falling Hawk's fire, he was concerned by her pallor, the sheen of sweat beading her brow. In a sling across her front Pippa slept, fed and cleaned, unaffected by the tension of those around her. Wolf-Alone, who'd joined them as part of Falling Hawk's family, took the space on Clare's right. But it wasn't Wolf-Alone she looked to for reassurance. Firelight deepened the green of her eyes, but the dimness of the lodge didn't hide their anxious appeal as she met his gaze.

"Will Jacob be there?" she'd asked when he told her of this meeting.

"Not likely."

Sitting on the bed platform, she'd touched her cheek where Rain Crow had struck her at their meeting. "What will you say to them? To her?"

"I'm going to introduce you formally—as my wife. Then you're going to speak to them."

Clare's face had gone ashen. "But I don't speak Shawnee."

"Falling Hawk speaks English well enough." Rain Crow even better, though his sister balked at uttering the language now. "I'll interpret anything that's said to be sure everyone takes everyone else's meaning rightly." When Clare still hadn't looked convinced, he'd added, "It's best they hear you speak, Clare. It's in their coming to know you that we have any hope of my sister re-linquishing Jacob."

"Relinquishing?" Clare gripped the edge of the bed's frame, knuckles white. "Do you mean she'll be allowed to keep him unless she gives him back voluntarily?"

"I don't know. Just tell them your story. If that's well received, tell them what it is you want them to do."

"How will I know if it's well received?"

"You'll know. But look to me if you need guidance. I'll be right beside you."

He'd no idea where things would go should this effort fail to soften his sister's heart toward Clare. He'd need to make certain of the Almighty's lead-ing before rushing ahead with another plan toward that end. That kind of waiting was hard to master when the need was great, the desire pressing.

Looking at her now, furtively watching the faces of those around her—all but Rain Crow gathered—he knew a pang of doubt about Clare's patience.

As the silence lengthened, awkwardness mounted. Falling Hawk cleared his throat, flashed a look around the incomplete circle, but didn't speak.

Falling Hawk had never split or stretched his earlobes, as many Shawnee men did, but wore several copper bands on his lean brown arms. Crosses-the-Path, who'd pinned every trade brooch she owned to her calico shirt and donned every bangle and bead necklace in honor of this occasion, sat quiet by his side, stealing curious glances at Clare and the baby.

With her one free hand, Clare gripped a fold of the petticoat she'd tucked around her knees, twisting the worn fabric until Jeremiah feared it would shred. He needed to get her something else to wear. He'd appeal to Crosses-the-Path and hope Clare would be agreeable to whatever she could find.

He was starting to think his sister had changed her mind about this meeting when the buffalo hide shifted and she entered with a flash of sunlight.

The strong bones of Rain Crow's face, her slender frame and regal bearing, made her a woman most people looked at twice. She wore the black sheaf of her hair in a braid down her back. Unlike Crosses-the-Path, she hadn't bedecked herself in finery for this meeting, as if she wished to show it was to her of no significance. Pausing inside the lodge doorway, she swept them with a gaze that skimmed over Clare as though she wasn't there, before she crossed to the empty place at the fire and sat gracefully beside Falling Hawk.

Jeremiah saw no sign of Falling Hawk's pipe and realized his brother intended to forgo the ritual of smoking.

Falling Hawk cleared his throat again and spoke in Shawnee, looking at them each by turn, his gaze when it reached Clare carefully inscrutable. When at last he gave a nod, Jeremiah turned to Clare, tense beside him.

"My brother has stated the particulars of this situation as he understands it and that they've done as we asked. Our sister has come to listen to what we have to say. I'm going to introduce you to them now."

He held Clare's gaze, then switching to Shawnee, said, "This woman is called Clare. She is my wife, and the mother of that one now called Many Sparrows, whom she calls Jacob. He was taken from her in the midst of much sorrow and loss, and I have promised to help her get him back."

Rain Crow stirred at this, lips pressed tight. She looked as if she meant to interrupt, but Falling Hawk made a sound in his throat and she subsided.

She hadn't so much as glanced at Clare.

"I am heavy in my heart to learn my sister has adopted the son of this woman I promised to aid," Jeremiah continued. "That my sister has found joy again is a good thing. It is what everyone who knows her has wanted for her. But it means this woman, Clare, has more sorrow to bear." He looked deep into the eyes confronting him across the fire and poured all he could of compassion and regret into his gaze; Rain Crow dropped hers. The low-burning fire sizzled and sparked between them. "That is all I mean to say for now. This woman will speak to you as only a mother can."

In the silence that followed, Clare looked at him with alarm—perhaps because he'd spoken so briefly.

"You may speak," he told her after explaining all he'd said, wishing he could take her fear into himself. "Take your time. Stop when you need to gather your thoughts and I'll interpret what you've said."

Clare drew an audible breath and lifted her gaze to those across the fire waiting warily for her to begin. Though her voice shook, she plunged in without hesitation, addressing Falling Hawk and Rain Crow.

"Thank you for allowing me to speak to you about my son, whom you have here in this place, who was taken from me and whom I have searched long for and come a great distance and through much trouble and fear to find."

Jeremiah heard her swallow as she paused for breath. He judged it a good beginning, no doubt well thought out. She'd made no accusations. She'd acknowledged their graciousness and, without boasting, her own bravery and determination in finding her son.

He put a hand over hers, still gripping the petticoat, hoping to signal her to silence. To his surprise she turned her palm to his and clutched his hand, nodding to show she understood.

She waited while he translated her words. By the tautness of her grip, he knew she was bending all her senses to interpret every nuance of expression and posture of the one person who wouldn't return her gaze.

The tension strung between the two women was palpable.

When Jeremiah nodded her to continue, Clare told of her plight in the mountains, of Jeremiah's arrival as her daughter was being born. He found himself watching his brother and sister, who would understand much of what was being said before he translated it. Though their faces remained guarded, their gazes dropped to the sleeping infant Clare cradled while she spoke.

He signaled with a squeeze of his hand for her to pause and let him put into Shawnee the tale of his delivering her baby.

Clare next spoke of Wheeling, of failing to find Jacob, of her determination to go to Yellow Creek with Jeremiah and what they learned there.

While she spoke, Falling Hawk raised his eyebrows and looked at Clare as if he might be truly seeing her at last, but Jeremiah could sense the rising tension in Rain Crow, see it in the set of her shoulders, the flash of her eyes, the pulsing at the base of her throat. Her agitation increased until Jeremiah could see her trembling from across the fire, as he translated the part of their story that happened in Wakatomica.

"This woman has stood before the warrior who killed her children's father. She has seen his scalp hanging from that warrior's belt. He is the same who stole her son. That warrior is Logan."

Crosses-the-Path drew in her breath and looked at Clare with something near to admiration. Clare didn't seem to notice. She was leaning forward in her attempt to see past the thin screen of smoke from the fire, to read Rain Crow's expression—a mask of impassivity that cracked and shattered as Jeremiah finished and Clare drew breath to speak again.

"When?" Rain Crow demanded in Shawnee, her gaze fixed on him. "When did you make that one your wife?"

He'd felt Clare start as his sister's voice cut through the wegiwa's warmth. "In Wakatomica."

"That was how many days after you found her in the mountains?"

"Why are you asking this?" Jeremiah replied, pricked with uneasiness.

"You say in Wakatomica you claimed her as your wife," Rain Crow replied. "But you both say you found her right after she lost a husband to Logan's revenge. How is it she so quickly accepted you in his place? Has she no heart to mourn the man who was father to Many Sparrows?"

Jeremiah's heart plummeted as he grasped the magnitude of his misstep. Among the Shawnees, mourning for a spouse would normally last a year, though among Virginians it wasn't uncommon for a widow to remarry within weeks of a husband's death, nor unheard of to stand at the grave of one husband by the side of the next.

Clare hadn't understood his sister's words, but their tone needed no interpretation. Rain Crow looked at her at last, and Jeremiah knew that look must sear.

"If you have no heart for a man who was your husband," his sister said, "to mourn him properly before you take another, why should I believe you have a heart for a son born of you? Find another and put him in the place of the one taken from you—who is no longer that person anyway. There is only my son, Many Sparrows. What more is there to say between us?"

Clare must have been holding her breath through Rain Crow's disparaging speech, for she all but gasped as she looked to him. "What did she say?"

The words came barely whispered; she knew it wasn't good.

Jeremiah translated, his face hot with mortification. Around the circle now everyone allowed their grief, anger, or discomfort to show. Only Wolf-Alone appeared impassive, though Jeremiah could tell he wished this meeting to be over.

"You needn't answer, Clare. This is my fault. I'll set it right. I'll tell them—"

"No," Clare said before he could confess the lie. "I'll answer."

Rain Crow looked at her with narrowed eyes. Clare leaned forward and spoke directly to her.

"I do mourn my husband. Philip was trying his best to provide for me, for Jacob. For the daughter he will never know. He didn't deserve to die as he did." Tears welled, still Clare's voice was firm, though Jeremiah guessed it was taking all her strength to make it so. "But I needed help. Not just someone to help me birth my daughter, but one who could help me find Jacob. I wouldn't be turned aside from my purpose. I was going to find him or die trying, but Mr. . . . Panther-Sees-Him wouldn't let me go alone. And he made me see I was safer traveling as his wife."

She glanced at him, in the look a mingling of resentment and acceptance. He wanted to tell her again he was sorry, that she needn't pretend to a thing distasteful to her, but she had no more attention to spare him. This had become a conversation between two mothers. The rest of them were merely witnesses.

"He believes the Almighty brought us together on that trail," Clare said. "I don't know about that. I haven't felt God's presence or heard His voice in a long time. I hope what he says is true. I need it to be true."

Jeremiah's heart leapt at her words. He hadn't realized she remembered that conversation. He glanced across the fire at Rain Crow in time to see it in his sister's face—the merest hint of the softening he'd hoped to illicit in her.

Of all things. Was it Clare's faltering faith that had pierced his sister's defenses?

Rain Crow pressed her lips together, then said in a voice stripped of its harshness, "My brother's wife has spoken of . . ."

A commotion of voices outside the lodge swelled, causing Rain Crow to hesitate, jarring each one around the circle to blink like sleepers rudely awakened.

At a nod from Falling Hawk, Wolf-Alone rose and hurried to the doorhide. In seconds he was back. "Cornstalk and Nonhelema have returned. Silverheels is with them—he is injured."

Wolf-Alone said no more but slipped out of the lodge, leaving the rest gaping after him. Falling Hawk rose, looked down at Clare and in English said, "This to you important, and to sister, but that outside is important to all Shawnees."

Falling Hawk and Crosses-the-Path went out after Wolf-Alone. Rain Crow shot Clare an enigmatic look, then rose and followed, leaving Clare and Jeremiah alone.

Clare looked stunned. "What is going on?"

"Cornstalk and Nonhelema have returned. Their brother—he's called Silverheels—sounds like he's met with some injury." All of them were back too soon for any talk of peace to have taken place in Pittsburgh. He started to rise, but Clare held onto his hand, detaining him.

"What was your sister saying there at the end? She sounded less . . . angry."

"I don't know," Jeremiah said, though he had his suspicions and rued the untimely interruption. "She's still angry with me."

"Was this all for nothing?"

"Don't think that way. I've told you this is going to—"

"Take time, yes. But how much time?"

Standing, he reached to pull her up. "I'm not going to leave it at this, but Cornstalk is here now. And Nonhelema. Maybe that'll be a thing in our favor. For now let's hear their news."

With one arm cradling Pippa, she took his hand and let him pull her to her feet, disappointment brimming in her eyes.

Mr. Ring hadn't released her hand, but under the circumstances she was thankful. He'd led her through the crowd gathered to meet the returning chiefs and warriors who had ridden in on horses still bedecked with the ornamentation of ceremony. Ribbons, fringe, and feathers fluttered in a breeze that bore the scent of coming rain as the sky, scudded over with clouds while they'd been inside Falling Hawk's lodge, sagged low and threatening.

These people were formidable on their own feet, but astride horses they were a daunting sight. Standing half-concealed behind Mr. Ring, Clare had no difficulty identifying Cornstalk, still mounted on his spotted horse as he spoke to the people. Gray threaded the scalplock hung with silver ornaments and feathers, and his broad face was lined with care, yet Cornstalk's body was that of a warrior in his prime, lean and muscled, marked with tattoos, his voice strong and carrying.

Murmurs rippled out from the center of the gathering as, she supposed, word of what their chief had said passed to those come too late to hear it for themselves. Cornstalk swung down from his horse and turned to aid the dismounting of a slightly younger man who resembled him in feature and whose torso was bound in strips of blood-spotted linen. But a third rider had been quicker to dismount, a woman who bore resemblance to both men.

Nonhelema. It must be. But no one had thought to mention to Clare the most astonishing thing about Cornstalk's sister. Nonhelema was as tall as her brother, who stood over six feet in height. Clare couldn't take her gaze from the woman who, with a strength to match her height, all but lifted the wounded warrior from his mount and stood him on his feet.

Someone in the crowd called out a question, to which Cornstalk replied while Nonhelema steadied their brother. Some among the people exclaimed in anger, others in dismay.

"What is he saying?" Clare asked.

Jeremiah's reply was grim. "The peace talks never happened. They were just come to Pittsburgh when they were attacked."

They'd been escorting some white traders they'd met up with in Mingo territory, he explained, seeing them safe through country where Logan and his band roamed, striking whites indiscriminately in their vengeance for the killings at Baker's post. The men of Pittsburgh, not bothering to inquire whether the Shawnees were friendly, had fallen upon the delegation at the gate of Fort Pitt. Silverheels had been badly wounded, though thanks to the help of Alexander McKee none of them were killed. Understandably outraged, Cornstalk, Nonhelema, and the war chief, Puckeshinwah, had called off the peace talks. The agents had secured an escort to take them back across the Ohio without further molestation.

"Cornstalk says McKee was in a towering rage over it, but no undoing the damage done by a few reckless fools."

Nonhelema had her arm around Silverheels's shoulders. The warrior was laughing at something said to him, the only indication of his suffering the tightness around his eyes. Nonhelema smiled at whatever her brother found humorous, though concern was in her gaze. Clare could well imagine her ferocity in the moments following his wounding. She'd never want this woman's enmity, but if she could gain her sympathy, might the battle for Jacob be won—in one fell swoop, instead of the long, tedious, torturous, process Mr. Ring envisioned?

Heart slamming at her temerity, Clare started for the woman, pulling easily from Mr. Ring's grip, having caught him off guard. She couldn't let Nonhelema out of her sights, though thought of addressing the woman set off a quaking in her limbs that woke Pippa, nestled against her in the sling.

"Clare!" Just before she reached Nonhelema, Jeremiah Ring had her by the arm again. Clare turned in annoyance, and that quickly, Nonhelema and her brother moved away.

She started to call after the woman, but Mr. Ring bent close and said, "Not the time."

Thoroughly awake now, Pippa let out a hungry squall.

Not the time. Clare knew he was right. What had she been thinking?

Not thinking at all. She'd been desperate beyond reason. For all her planning, preparing, hoping, praying, nothing had gone right this day.

Blinded by disappointment, there was nothing to do but let Mr. Ring hurry her away to Wolf-Alone's lodge, where at least she could give way to her tears without offending anyone.

Inside the *msi-kah-mi-qui,* Jeremiah sat in council with Cornstalk, Puckeshinwah, and many of the warriors of both towns on Scippo Creek, even the wounded Silverheels who'd insisted upon being present though he was flat on his back, fevered, and watched over by his sister—a fierce, brooding eagle of a nursemaid.

Perhaps Silverheels's presence was a thing Cornstalk regretted allowing, for when all had heard of what happened in Pittsburgh, an alarming number of warriors had been in favor of joining Logan in his raids against the settlers south of the Spaylaywitheepi. While Cornstalk managed to persuade most of them that this would only drive their people closer to open war with the Long Knives at the cost of much life, a small contingent of the most militant warriors remained firm in their resolve.

"We will go from this place to find Logan—or are we no longer a people with the heart to push back when one of our own is done such grievous wrong?" The warrior who stood as spokesmen for those who wouldn't be pacified swept his hand toward Silverheels, on the edge of consciousness with his sister hovering, impatient for the council to end.

Cornstalk accepted their decision. He had no power to force the warriors to remain at peace and had said all he could to persuade. At least for now.

As the council broke up and the men dispersed, Jeremiah felt the looks cast his way. The warriors were no doubt wondering what he would choose to do, having returned to them at such a time with his own disturbance.

Jeremiah had given hard thought to that question as he listened to the warriors debate. No denying the pull he felt to head east and warn McKee that what was once merely rumor was likely to become reality—Shawnees raiding south of the Ohio. But he couldn't imagine what it would take to force Clare to leave this place without her son. Nor could he imagine leaving her and Pippa here without him.

For himself, whatever else he did in the coming days, he was determined to remain neutral as long as possible on the issue of war between his peoples, having no desire to fight against either. Remaining neutral between his sister and Clare seemed a more treacherous and uncertain path to walk. Was the issue of Jacob Inglesby, or Many Sparrows, going to force him to have to choose between them?

Let there be some middle road.

Cornstalk lingered in the council house, overseeing the removal of his brother to his lodge. Nonhelema paused to exchange words with Cornstalk, who turned and looked at Jeremiah waiting in the shadows.

Jeremiah stepped forward as Cornstalk was momentarily left standing alone in a shaft of sunlight streaming from one of the openings in the high roof.

"Panther-Sees-Him has traveled much of late and seen much," he said as Jeremiah approached. "But now I am told he has also found himself a wife. A white woman."

Jeremiah nodded, wavering on the point of confession, but before he could do so, the older man spoke again. "She must be a notable woman for you to have met her and claimed her as your own so quickly."

"She is that," Jeremiah said, finding he could agree to this without a speck of untruth in his heart.

He proceeded to tell Cornstalk the story of his first encounter with Clare and their journey thus far, watching the principal chief for reaction all the while. But this was a man much experienced in keeping his counsel. He was unreadable.

"I had hoped to get the boy back while he was still among the Mingos. The last thing I expected was to find my own sister had adopted him, and for this unhappiness I have brought her my heart is on the ground. But I have given my word." Knowing the likely futility of it, he asked, "Would you speak to Rain Crow, persuade her to give the boy back to the one who birthed him?"

Cornstalk pulled in his long upper lip, still giving nothing of his thoughts away in his countenance. But Jeremiah knew what they must be, on the heels of what had passed in that council house.

"As you have seen and heard, I cannot even persuade all my warriors to do as I would wish them to do. How then can I tell a woman to give up the son she has adopted? Or," he amended, "I can say the words, but if she does not wish to hear them, then she can take herself and that son away to live among others who will not tell her to give him up. You know this."

As deep as his own bones, Jeremiah knew it.

That seemed to be the end of the matter as far as Cornstalk was concerned. The Shawnee chief was going to let them work out the situation between them as a family, he and Falling Hawk, Rain Crow and Clare.

He wondered what Nonhelema would say about it.

Cornstalk read his thoughts. "My sister has heard about the situation and is of the same mind as I. She is a Shawnee mother. She will not force another

Shawnee mother to do this or that with her child. It will have to be the mother of this boy—not the mother who is your wife—who decides. Unless . . ."

Here the chief's lips pressed tight, and he wouldn't finish whatever thought had been in his head. He didn't need to. As their gazes held in shadowy light, Jeremiah knew exactly what he'd started to say. The choice about Many Sparrows was going to have to be Rain Crow's, unless that thing Cornstalk desired to avoid happened—unless there was war, and the Shawnees lost that war, and the Virginians forced the people to give up *all* their adopted sons and daughters born white as a term of the peace treaty that would follow, that they would be made to sign.

Torn as he was about the boy, Jeremiah would never wish such a thing upon the People, neither the defeat, nor the loss of those who had become dear to their hearts.

15

It had been only a few days since the meeting with Falling Hawk and Rain Crow, but Jeremiah knew that every moment without her son was an agony to Clare.

He'd gotten her Shawnee clothes, a wrap skirt and hip-length shirt that belted at the waist with a woven sash. They'd left her alone so she could wash, as well as could be managed with a kettle. She wouldn't go to the creek to bathe with the women. She wouldn't leave the wegiwa at all unless Jeremiah accompanied her. If they brought in food, she cooked it. If something needed washing—and one of them fetched water for it—she washed it. All the while her anxious expectation filled the lodge, setting nerves on edge.

After learning neither Cornstalk nor Nonhelema would aid them, he'd told her to give Rain Crow time before they approached her again. Time to get used to the idea of Clare's presence.

She'd railed at him. Argued and pleaded.

"Another day, another week, isn't going to change the fact that I'm Jacob's mother, not Rain Crow. He's my son!"

When none of it availed, she'd settled into silent stewing, and it wrenched Jeremiah to see her misery.

"Clare," he'd said early on the fourth day, after Wolf-Alone left with rifle and shot-pouch to spend the day somewhere her anxiety didn't disquiet the air. "I'm done drawing water for you. Go down to the creek. The women will welcome you. If any don't, they won't harm you. They think you my wife."

"I don't want to disturb Pippa. I just got her to sleep."

She wore the clothes he'd acquired and seemed to find it easier to move about in them, squatting at the fire to tend a kettle or rummaging through their stores. But clothes didn't change what was inside her. Fear was the bitter spring from which her stubbornness sprung. And mistrust.

Considering the calamity Philip Inglesby had led her into, little wonder she'd no faith in a man she barely knew, who'd led her into what must seem greater peril and uncertainty than anything she'd known with Inglesby.

"I'll mind Pippa. If she wakes and cries, I'll bring her straight to you." Thrusting a waterskin into her hands, Jeremiah all but propelled her past the door-hide.

To his amazement she went, if stiff-backed and tight-lipped. He stood there as the hide fell shut, fully expecting it to swish aside and Clare to march back in.

When he heard the scuff of moccasins on the path leading from the doorway, he felt his shoulders ease.

She'd lasted three days inside the lodge before the need to do something—*anything*—to alleviate the torment of waiting outweighed her fear of having to do it in view of a people who thought abducting a child and forcing him to become one of them an acceptable practice. A people Jeremiah Ring insisted she must try to understand. Even *befriend*.

The man must be sitting in that bark hut thinking he'd cajoled her into taking the first step. He was quite wrong. Had she not already determined to do so—she'd been summoning the nerve since waking—he could never have forced her past that hanging hide.

Only now was she having second thoughts.

From the instant she'd stepped from the lodge, she'd been scrutinized. There was nothing she could do about her hair, plaited in a braid, or her skin, but at least she was dressed like the women taking note of her. A simple stroud-cloth skirt and a long shirt that bound her with nothing but the woven sash securing it at her waist. Going about without stays cinching her ribs left her feeling naked, yet it had made so many tasks, especially nursing Pippa, remark-ably easier.

Being outside the lodge without the baby either in a sling or cradleboard left her feeling naked as well, but she wasn't worried for Pippa. Mr. Ring was good with her daughter, who sometimes settled for him faster than she would for Clare. And she wouldn't be gone long. How much time could fetching water take?

That would depend on how hard it proved to find the creek. Mr. Ring had described the route . . .

Uncertain of her path, she halted and looked around with the same disori-entation she'd experienced in Wakatomica. All the lodges looked alike. All the faces staring at her.

Her chest grew tight, her breathing labored, but she calmed herself. *They aren't going to attack you. You're married to one of their own—so they think.*

She began to see the wisdom in the subterfuge, however disagreeable the notion.

Thrusting down fear, she decided to do what Mr. Ring had urged for days: make contact with one of these women. But for all their staring from the kettles and fires outside their lodges, not one would actually meet her gaze. Were they waiting for *her* to do something? Ought she to hold up the water-skin and point? Make a show of drinking from it?

She was raising the skin to give that last idea a try when a slight, round-faced woman hurried into view around a nearby lodge, trailed by two little girls; Falling Hawk's wife, Crosses-the-Path, out of breath but striding with purpose to intercept her.

Halting in front of Clare, she opened her mouth, then shut it, coppery complexion deepening in the wordless silence. Finally she cleared her throat and said, "You . . . butterfly . . . come out . . . cocoon?"

Butterfly? At least she hadn't been likened to a snake slithering from under its rock. Clare smiled in pure relief. "Yes, I have come out of the lodge—the wegiwa," she said, adding the Shawnee word when she detected no understanding in the woman's gaze.

Crosses-the-Path's daughters—the youngest about Jacob's age, the other perhaps two years older—clutched their mother's skirt and peered up with dark eyes. Clare offered them a smile. The little one giggled, then hid her face.

"I'm trying to find the creek." Clare raised her gaze to their mother, who noticed the waterskin and babbled something at Clare, whose turn it was to stare blankly.

Crosses-the-Path tried saying just one word.

Clare didn't know it.

The woman shook her head, brows bunching, then grabbed Clare's wrist. With her other hand she beckoned, backing along the path through the lodges.

Clare took a reluctant step.

The woman backed away another step, repeating that one word, as if trying to coax a frightened animal to come along. Was it the word for *creek*? Clare hoped so because she was coming along now, the little girls in their wake, chattering to each other.

Crosses-the-Path faced forward, still clutching Clare's wrist, seeming pleased by the stares of those who watched them pass. Clare came with pounding heart and mounting confusion, feeling at once ridiculous . . . and touched. She'd had no idea this woman felt anything remotely kind toward her. At their meeting three days ago, her focus had been all on Rain Crow. She'd given Falling Hawk's quiet wife spare regard.

They reached a stand of trees where fewer lodges stood, then it was all trees for a distance and the land dipping down, then the woods opened to the creek where women crouched or sat along its bank, some busy with tasks Clare couldn't discern from a distance, others filling skins and bladders and trade kettles from the creek's flow.

At that point the creek widened around a bend, though not so wide she couldn't have tossed a stone across it. The broad gravel beach there made it seem wider, and the creek flowed shallow and chattering. Most of the women were gathered in that spot. A little ways upstream where the water deepened, a few bathed, completely naked.

Clare looked away, cheeks blazing.

Crosses-the-Path released her hold on Clare's wrist, pointed at the creek, and said that word again. She made a motion of drawing water, as if Clare mightn't yet have made the connection. Obligingly Clare nodded her understanding, raising the waterskin between them. "Yes. Thank you. Thank you so much for showing me the way."

Her tone conveyed what her words couldn't. Crosses-the-Path nodded.

Forcing herself to move, Clare chose a spot on the gravel beach downstream from a knot of women who made a show of minding their business. She caught a wary glance to two, but they seemed content to let her be. Children were about, most playing quietly; they had no compunction about edging nearer for a look at her. She glanced along the stony beach, offering smiles to the children, trying to read the body language of their mothers, the sidelong looks they gave each other and her.

She hadn't asked Mr. Ring what was being said about her outside the lodge. Did these women know Rain Crow well? Falling Hawk's sister didn't live in Cornstalk's Town, though at that moment Clare wished she did. She'd have ventured from the lodge sooner had there been the slightest chance of catching a glimpse of Jacob.

With a stab of longing, her thoughts returned to her son. She yearned to touch his hair and kiss his face. Hear his laughter and incessant chatter. Let him ask her a thousand questions. Feed him. *Smell* him.

It was a visceral, burning ache to think of another woman doing those things in her place.

She pulled up the dripping skin and stood, flinging her gaze and her heart across the creek into the woods beyond. There was a path there, the beginning of one. The path to Nonhelema's Town? It lay somewhere across that creek, but how distant? She saw no one on the path, no indication anyone was near, and yet . . . she felt the burn of a gaze upon her.

She looked toward the women to find half of them had left the creek. Those remaining were minding their tasks. Even the children had drifted off upstream to play.

Turning, she saw Crosses-the-Path still standing where she'd left her, apparently waiting to escort her back into the town. Clare relaxed, thinking it was the other woman's gaze she'd felt.

Just then the older of Crosses-the-Path's daughters came racing up and tugged at her mother's shirt hem with some urgent need. Crosses-the-Path called to Clare, beckoning.

Clare shook her head. She didn't wish to return to Mr. Ring's lodge yet. It was pointless perhaps, but she wanted to stay at the creek, if only to gaze across it and yearn for Jacob.

She waved the woman away, hoping she would go.

Crosses-the-Path looked unhappy about leaving her, but with a last half-worried glance she hurried along the path, leaving Clare wondering for the first time if Falling Hawk hadn't told his wife to watch her—and not out of kindness.

Putting her back to the women on the creek bank, Clare made her way downstream, moving without seeming purpose, hoping to draw no attention.

She wasn't a captive but a guest. One who had brought trouble, but a guest who could go where she wished, within reason.

And *still* feeling like she was being watched.

She halted and looked back, but a clump of wild roses overhung the bank now, hiding the spot where the women gathered. None had followed to spy.

She should return to the lodge. What was it going to solve, standing there staring across the creek? It only deepened the pain. She started to turn away, heart dragging like an anchor, when she caught movement in the shadows beneath a tree, directly across the creek from where she stood.

An animal too shy to come and drink? A deer perhaps?

From the shadows beneath a tree, a man stepped into the cloud-filtered light. A white man. And he was looking at her. He was tall, fair-headed, and from that distance looked enough like Philip that the shock of it rendered Clare's fingers numb. The waterskin dropped from her grasp to the pebbles at her feet.

The man stepped nearer the water's edge, arm lifted in supplication. "*Mademoiselle, je suis désolé*—my sincere apology. I intended you no startlement."

He hadn't shouted to be heard, for he seemed to know his voice would carry across the water, which ran smoothly just there, quieter than its chattering around the beach upstream.

A Frenchman. Not Philip, of course.

He wore the long, fringed shirt of a frontiersman and, with it, fawn knee breeches and a pair of stockings that must have been donned that morning for they were remarkably clean. The moccasins on his feet seemed a bit incongruous, but all in all he gave the impression of a man who hadn't forgotten where he came from, whatever turn of events had brought him to this place.

Clare composed herself but didn't reach for the waterskin. "It's all right. No harm done."

"*Merci. Bonjour, Mademoiselle.* I was downstream a small distance engaged in . . . well." The man peered across at her as if to gauge from her appearance some clue as to what she might be willing to abide when it came to the details of a man's morning toilette.

"You were bathing, *Monsieur*?"

"Just so." The man smiled engagingly. "And then I come along to the trail," he went on with a nod to indicate the path she'd noted, upstream, "when I see you across the creek. At what do you gaze, Mademoiselle? I see nothing out of the commonplace."

"Actually, it's *Madame*," Clare said, hesitating to answer him directly. Had it been his stare she'd sensed? Despite his explanation she wondered how long he'd been watching her from the shadows.

"*Je vous demande pardon, Madame,*" the man said. "May I begin over with a proper introduction? My name is Jean-Paul Cheramy. I am a trader out of Montreal." Mr. Cheramy bowed, the movement gracefully executed save that it made the wide satchel hanging from his shoulder swing precariously forward. He grabbed for it and, straightening, said with unperturbed aplomb, "May I have the honor of knowing your name, Madame?"

"Clare Ing—Clare Ring. Jeremiah Ring is my . . . husband. They call him Panther-Sees-Him here." She was too far away to read the man's expression clearly but thought it shifted when she said Mr. Ring's name. "Do you know him?"

"Do I know him? Not well. I prefer to do my trading in the town of Cornstalk's sister. And you, Madame? I judge you a Virginian by your speech. This is true?"

Stifling impatience at this irrelevancy, she answered, "Yes. Born and raised. But have you—"

"Ah. For me it is Quebec—*born and raised* as you say. Though the trading keeps me much away."

With her mind teeming with questions about Jacob, Clare could find no suitable reply to this. Perhaps noticing her lack of interest, Mr. Cheramy shrugged the subject of himself away.

"But *you* I see here on the bank of this creek looking across as one who has great interest. What is it over here that so engages you? Will you tell me?"

Clare looked down as wetness seeped into her moccasins. In her eagerness to inquire about Jacob, she'd stepped up to the creek's edge. Ought she to cross over to speak to the man? The water there looked deep, with no convenient stones exposed as they were upstream. Crossing would be difficult.

"Have you been long in Nonhelema's Town?"

"A fortnight perhaps," said Mr. Cheramy.

"Have you seen a little boy? A white boy, hair about your shade. He'll not have been there long."

The trader's brows drew together. "A boy four, five years of age?"

The jolt went straight to the pit of Clare's stomach. "Yes, he's four! His name is Jacob. He—"

A sudden tug on her hand made Clare yelp. She turned to find Wolf-Alone's young friend, Wildcat, clinging to her.

She tried to pull away. The boy clung tenaciously and shot a scowl across the creek.

"Clare-wife. Come away to *your* man and baby. Leave that one."

"Where did you come from?" She hadn't seen him among the children playing along the creek. "Were you spying on me?"

Wildcat dropped his gaze, his grip on her loosening. She pulled her hand away.

"Did Mr. Ring set you to follow me?"

The boy dug a bare toe into the pebbles of the bank. "No."

"Wolf-Alone then?"

"Yes."

"Why?"

"He want you . . . safe. *Safe* is word?"

"I have no notion what Wolf-Alone is thinking. Is that the only reason?"

Wildcat didn't understand that question. Or pretended he didn't.

"Come," he said again with a look across the creek. Mr. Cheramy had stood watching them. His genial smile was gone, but he gave her a polite nod before striding back into the forest.

"Wait!" Clare called as Wildcat snatched up the waterskin and thrust it into her hands.

The trader had gone.

"All right," she said and followed the boy back along the bank to the gravel beach. "Why didn't you want me to talk to Mr. Cheramy?"

The boy shook his head and would answer only vaguely, "Not good, talking much to traders."

"But why? Do they cheat your people?"

"Sometimes cheat. Lie. But not all," Wildcat added, as if trying to be fair. Still the scowl between his brows remained.

They'd nearly reached the first of the lodges. Clare put a hand on the boy's shoulder to halt him. "Should you not cease speaking English, if it's meant to be a secret between you and Wolf-Alone?"

It was a lot of words at once, but the boy appeared to understand. He lowered his voice. "I speak you, Clare-wife, they think you talk me?"

Clare stifled the urge to smile. "That's what people will think, is it? Was that Wolf-Alone's idea?"

Wildcat nodded, looking pleased. "You talk Wildcat?"

"Will I *teach* you, do you mean? Maybe I should. Your English could use improving."

The boy grinned. "English bad. You make good?"

Clare lost her battle with the smile. The child was too appealing with his lively amber eyes, his hawk-feathered hair, that impish grin. "All right. And while we're at it, maybe you can teach me to speak Shawnee."

"Wesah!" the boy said with enthusiasm.

"Wesah?"

"This means . . . *good*. Your first word?"

It wasn't quite the first, but she nodded, letting him think so.

"We have treaty, me and you." With confidence that she would follow now, Wildcat continued along the path into Cornstalk's Town.

The boy left her outside Wolf-Alone's lodge and scampered off into the village. Clare ducked past the door-hide, expecting to find both Mr. Ring and Pippa grown impatient for her return. She felt a stab of guilt. How long must she be torn between a baby's demands and doing everything possible to free her son from captivity? It was eating her alive with each passing day, fearing Jacob would forget his life before—forget *her*. That he would let Rain Crow take a mother's place in his heart.

Now her mind spun with possibilities, thinking of Mr. Cheramy. Had she found the means to get Jacob back at last? She could envision so many ways it might unfold, how the man might help her . . . if she could convince him to do so.

She'd expected to hear a hungry infant's fussing long before now; all was quiet when she entered the lodge, which produced a momentary clutch of panic.

Then she saw Mr. Ring, stretched out on the sleeping platform he'd given up for her, dark hair loose against a heap of bedding that pillowed his head. Sprawled across him, pale little arms splayed wide, wearing nothing but a clout, was Pippa.

Both were sound asleep.

One of Mr. Ring's big hands covered her daughter's back, fingers slightly curled, as her tiny body rode the rise and fall of his broad chest. The soft dome of Pippa's head was tucked up against his neck, her little mouth and chin scrunched against his collarbone, visible in the opening of his shirt.

In all of Jacob's infancy, had she ever seen Philip do such a thing? Memory failed to supply a single instance.

Scarcely daring to breathe, Clare lowered the waterskin to the ground. Rather than her daughter's face, her gaze settled on Mr. Ring's. There was light enough in the lodge to trace the contours of his profile, the narrow bridge of his nose, the dark line of a brow above the hollow of a closed eyelid, the sweep of lashes against a cheekbone.

Pippa jerked in her sleep, emitting a soft whimper. Mr. Ring opened his eyes and saw her. Across Pippa's head their gazes held. Clare smiled gently, flustered to have been caught watching him sleep.

His gaze dropped to the waterskin. "How did it go?"

Pippa wasn't settling again. Mr. Ring sat up, swinging both legs off the bed platform and shifting Pippa higher on his shoulder. Like Jacob before her, Clare's daughter had gradually lost her dark birth cap of hair. Only a few patches remained; soon that would be gone, replaced by a pale down so fine it needed the right slant of light even to see it.

Pippa would be fair like her brother.

Clare bent to retrieve the skin, found a small kettle, and poured water into it. "No one tried to drive me away with sticks."

She'd meant to make light, but Mr. Ring didn't laugh. He waited, clearly expecting more. She had no intention of mentioning Mr. Cheramy, so she told him of meeting Crosses-the-Path, the woman's friendly overtures. And she mentioned Wildcat. "He asked me to teach him English."

"He *asked* you?"

Clare looked up at Mr. Ring's startled tone. He was patting Pippa's back, but his gaze pinned her, questioning. It was strange, knowing something about Wolf-Alone and Wildcat that Mr. Ring didn't know. But she needed to be more careful. She'd nearly revealed their secret.

"He has a few words. He made his wishes clear enough."

Mr. Ring seemed content to let it go. "I'm glad you made the effort to go among the women."

Finally, she supposed he was thinking. "I was surprised by Falling Hawk's wife. I didn't expect . . ."

"That she'd be curious about you? She's been waiting for you to come out into the village for days." A smile played at the corner of Mr. Ring's mouth.

Pippa was growing red in the face. Mr. Ring stood. Clare did as well. "Let me take her."

Their hands brushed as she took the baby from him; she blushed unaccountably at the contact. "I'll fetch the water from now on," she said.

She turned her back as she customarily did while tending to Pippa, so she didn't see Mr. Ring's face when he replied, "It's only going to help matters, showing yourself friendly."

"As you keep saying . . . and no doubt you are right."

"Am I?" he replied, sounding pleased. Thinking she was falling in with his plans at last?

She was thinking about returning to the creek tomorrow morning, and the next, and next—until she saw Jean-Paul Cheramy again. Until they could continue their conversation about Jacob.

She'd see Crosses-the-Path as well, and yes, she would show herself friendly if it aided her cause. But she dared to hope it didn't matter now because eventually Mr. Cheramy would bring her word of Jacob. Perhaps he'd even contrive to bring Jacob with him, out of Nonhelema's Town, down to the creek that ran between. She'd noticed that Indian children, even those as young as Jacob, weren't tethered to their mothers every moment of the day. They ran together in packs, the oldest looking after the little ones. Perhaps Rain Crow would let down her guard.

She bent over her nursing daughter, biting back a groan of longing. Surely it could be no coincidence, she and the trader ending up at the creek at the same moment. He wasn't Shawnee. Not even adopted, far as she knew. He would be sympathetic to her plight, not torn in his heart like Mr. Ring. Not bound to any Shawnee kin. He would see the captivity of her son as a white man should—a thing to be undone.

He would help her.

16

JUNE 12
REDSTONE FORT, VIRGINIA COLONY

A person could vanish on the Virginia frontier without much fuss and bother. A hunter gone out for meat meets instead with mortal mishap crossing a river—or a bear—leaving his bones to bleach lonely on a mountainside. A child playing in the dirt of a cabin yard is snatched by tawny hands and carried off to grow up Seneca or Shawnee. A man pulls up stakes, carts his family over the next blue ridge westward, never to be seen again.

It happened in a hundred different ways and not just to strangers, so why it never entered the mind of Alphus Jacob Litchfield that it could happen to his niece, her husband, and his namesake great-nephew, he couldn't rightly have said. Maybe the notion had tried to slip its way in and he'd slammed the gate on it like a skunk come nosing. Clare was like a daughter to him, the nearest he'd ever know, confirmed and grizzled bachelor that he was at forty-nine. Thought of her disappearing from the face of the earth was unimaginable.

Until now.

It still rankled that Philip Inglesby couldn't stay put on the land Alphus had planned eventually to give the man—*give*—in exchange for working it. Of course one didn't generally rebuild lost family fortunes farming in the Shenandoah, but for crying after spilled milk, it would've been a life worth living, one many a man would trade places for given half a chance. Philip was accustomed to better, and he couldn't let that go. He'd thought he could find it, or the start of it, in Kentucky. Of all places.

It wasn't that Alphus didn't understand the allure of the frontier. As a second son with no prospect of inheriting the family's Richmond estate, which had passed to Clare's father, Lawrence, he'd gone west himself, back when the Shenandoah *was* the frontier and Shawnees still had a village or two tucked between the Blue Ridge and the Allegheny Plateau.

Those Shawnees had since moved west themselves. Civilization had caught up with Alphus in his gristmill on the banks of Lewis Creek, near Staunton. He reckoned Kentucky was the next generation's gold at rainbow's end.

Philip was after gold, but Alphus had never pegged his niece's husband as having gumption enough to go chasing down a perilous path like the Ohio to find it. He'd tried to dissuade the young man of the notion. Clare's father had done the same by letter. When the combined efforts of the Litchfield brothers had failed to carry the battle, he'd been the one to watch them rattle off along the Great Wagon Road.

The dust of their creaking Conestoga had hardly settled before murmurings began about the Yellow Creek killings and that Mingo Logan's about-face from friendly Indian to the white man's mortal foe. Then those fools at Pittsburgh attacked a peaceful delegation of Shawnees come to talk to the Indian agents. Now not only a few Mingos were riled but an entire nation of warriors already agitated by the overrunning of their hunting grounds south of the Ohio.

The whole frontier was set to go up in flames, with Clare and her family gone straight into the fire's heart.

So he'd done what Lawrence would've done were he in Alphus's place. Decided not to wait and see if Philip came to his senses and brought Clare and the children—she'd have had that second baby by now—back to Augusta County. He set out to find their girl and see her safe home himself.

Leaving the mill in the hands of an apprentice, he saddled his horse and rode northward up that hard-traveled road to discover how far the Inglesbys made it before news of Logan's raids turned them back. He wouldn't have been surprised to come across them a mile down the road, headed back his way. Certainly he'd expected to encounter them before arriving at Redstone Fort, way on up the Monongahela. Mile after mile his horse trod, and he met with many a settler heading east to wait out the threat of Indian uprising, but not Clare and Philip.

Redstone proved busy with settlers who'd abandoned their Kentucky holdings, or their dreams of such, but no one had word of the ones Alphus sought.

"Got no news of Harrod," was the general response from those camped around the fort, until finally a trader turned back after shaking his head to add, "Though come to think on it, I did hear Governor Dunmore sent out a couple scouts to warn Harrod's party to come in. Boone was one."

"Daniel Boone?" Alphus asked, pulse giving a leap.

"The very man."

Alphus knew Boone. They'd served together during Braddock's doomed campaign back in '55, when Boone was a wagoner. A stout fellow. Knew the wilderness better than most and how to stay alive in it.

Hope took an upswing.

"Why the interest in Harrod's party?" he was asked. "Got kin among 'em?"

"I do." Alphus was inclined to keep his business his own but decided opening up to a man with more notion than most of how things were unfolding to the westward mightn't be the worst concession he'd ever made. "My niece and her family. Inglesby's the name. They'd planned to come through Redstone, meet up with Harrod before his party left, go by water down to the Ohio . . ."

He stopped talking, catching a light in the stranger's gaze, the pulling in of shaggy brows. "Inglesby? Blond-headed feller? The wife expecting soon-like? Pretty green eyes?"

Alphus, who'd started to nod, leveled a glare at the trader, who held up a palm. "A man can't help noticing a set of pretty eyes. Reckon they left these parts before word of Logan's raids reached us. And I mean *right* before. They'd come late and missed Harrod's party, and he was in a hurry to catch 'em up. Wouldn't wait for a boat to be built but traded his Conestoga for a smaller wagon to go over-mountain to Wheeling."

Alphus stared at the man. "He took a wagon over the Alleghenies?"

"Set out to anywise. Down the pack trail yonder." The trader lifted his shoulders but forbore showing any further sign of opinion on such doings.

Alphus was busy berating himself. *Lord, help.* He ought to have tried harder to persuade Philip of his folly in thinking he was in any way suited to the frontier. He'd told himself they'd be with James Harrod, who by all accounts was imminently suited. Had they ever found the man?

". . . then word of Logan's murdered folk come and that scout of McKee's decided to go after 'em, see could he find 'em on the trail, help 'em did they need it."

Alphus reined in his attention as a cart went rattling into the fort, near the busy gate of which the two stood talking. He waited for the conveyance to pass and stepped nearer the man. "A scout went after them, you say?"

"That's right. On his way to Cornstalk's Town with a message from McKee. He ain't come back neither, so either he found your kin and got 'em through to Wheeling or . . ." *Buried the remains and went on his way,* Alphus read in the man's eyes.

"This scout have a name?"

"Ring—Jeremiah Ring. Virginia-born, I think, but one of them adopted Shawnees. Don't know what he goes by with them, but he's back and forth through Redstone couple times a year, running messages to or from the Scioto towns. Speaks a fair number of the heathen tongues."

"Ring." Alphus frowned over the name, but in the seconds that passed before the trader snagged another man passing, he couldn't place where he'd heard it or why it struck a chord in his memory.

He waited while the two spoke in hushed tones, casting looks at Alphus the while. The second man's expression flattened, but he gave the trader a nod.

"This here's Isaac Pentland, come from Wheeling," the trader said of the man in a battered hat who looked to be in his thirties, though his face was haggard. "He and his family came over the trail your people took."

Pentland cleared his throat. "Ye say ye're looking for kin, gone west in a wagon not long since?"

"Inglesby, Clare and Philip. Have you seen them? Did they make it to Wheeling?"

Pentland shook his head. "That I don't know, but . . . reckon I seen the wagon, if not the kin."

The grim line of the man's mouth sent a spike of dread through Alphus's chest, but he was jiggered if he knew how to interpret that sidelong flick of eyes, or the look in them—guilt?

Alphus clenched his fists, one of which held his rifle. "Whatever you know, spill it."

Pentland took a step back. "Maybe better I show ye. Come over to our camp. Ye need to have a word with my wife."

The Pentlands' makeshift camp was tucked between pines a stone's throw from the fort gate, little more than a fire ring and a canvas shelter cluttered with packs and pans and red-headed children. The Pentlands had come in from a homestead twenty miles south of Wheeling with whatever they could carry on their backs and that of two horses, a mule, and a goat—plus a little something they'd picked up along the way.

Pentland's wife, the source of her brood's coloring—and well along with the next addition to the ginger-haired clan—wore the same guilty look as her husband, who stood by while she rooted among the family's scattered possessions, at last finding what she sought at the bottom of a meal sack: a china cup, blue-flowered and rimmed in gold, chipped and battered.

"They was more of'm, all busted up in a box. This'un was the onliest still whole and seeing as tweren't no one to say me *nay* and I always fancied me a purty cup . . ." The woman lifted rounded shoulders. "I took it."

"Wagon was busted," Pentland added, sounding a shade defensive. "Team and anything of use gone. Reckoned what was left was free for the picking."

Alphus heard the man's nervous prattle, his gaze on the blue-flowered cup. He lifted that gaze to the woman's, questioning. She handed him the cup. He turned it over, thumbing the chips in its rim. He'd never drank tea from one of these, or even handled them before. Clare had kept them safe atop a hutch in the farmhouse, out of Jacob's reach.

She'd loved those cups. All six of them.

"Listen," Pentland was saying. "They's likely holed up in Wheeling now even if we didn't cross paths with 'em, forting up safe. Or maybe they went upriver to Pittsburgh to wait a spell afore heading down to Harrod?"

Alphus looked at the man. "Tell me everything you recall—about the wagon, where you found it. What you found."

"About two days back along the trail, nigh a little crick and a clearing. Plain what the trouble was—broken wheels, busted axle. There was a fire ring and a shelter, but it was deserted. No sign of struggle. Just like they all up and walked away."

"Figured they put what could be toted on the horses and went on by foot," said his wife.

"Or maybe that scout found 'em and guided 'em over," Pentland added. "That has to be what happened."

But they all knew that didn't have to be what happened. Alphus handed the cup back to Pentland's wife.

"Keep it."

The woman's ruddy brows rose. "You sure 'bout that?"

"I'm sure." He thanked the couple, cast a glance over six . . . *seven* small freckled faces, then turned on a boot heel and headed back to the fort, where he'd left his horse watering.

He'd no need to see the broken wagon to know it was Clare's. That cup was proof enough. Likely too much time had passed to hope some clue survived to where his niece had gone when she and Philip and Jacob left the wagon behind, but he knew better than to presume so. And that scout—where *had* he heard that name, Ring?—if he had found and helped them along to Wheeling, would he have had the foresight to leave some sign for someone who might come looking?

Without seeing that wagon with his own eyes, he'd always wonder.

So focused was he on getting to it and what he'd find when he did, Alphus reached his horse and was about to loosen its hitch before the stir sweeping through the fort gained his attention.

Leaving the horse, he strode to a knot of men gathered round a speaker on the veranda of an officer's cabin, who turned out to be a messenger sent not from Pittsburgh with yet another rumor of an Indian raid but from the governor in Williamsburg with, finally, a concrete answer to those raids and the upheaval they'd occasioned.

"Governor Dunmore has written to the officers of the frontier counties," the man, still begrimed with the dust of travel, was saying between swallows from a flask someone thrust into his hands. "He's calling up the militia for a campaign against the Shawnees and the Mingos. The governor will lead an army westward to put down this uprising. There are to be two divisions of said army, a Southern and a Northern. Colonel Andrew Lewis is ordered to muster militia from the southern counties—Botetourt, Fincastle, and Augusta—to assemble on the Greenbrier River."

Alphus Litchfield, captain in the Augusta County militia, took a moment to absorb the news, reaching the conclusion that duty now compelled him to retrace his trail south—right after he found that wagon, abandoned down the trail, and had himself a good look round. Then he would return to Staunton, settle his affairs for a longer absence, recruit the requisite company of men, and lead them to the muster on the Greenbrier.

Not for Dunmore. Not primarily. First priority for Alphus Litchfield, however far west fate and Governor Dunmore's campaign might take him, was to find his niece and her family and return them to Virginia.

Else discover the means of their deaths and wreak his righteous vengeance.

17

Clare thought she'd grasped the extent of the cultivated fields surrounding Cornstalk's Town the day of her arrival but realized now she'd only seen a portion. The cornfields stretched what seemed for miles along the creek, their true extent revealed the morning she and Crosses-the-Path, her daughters, and Wildcat set off from Falling Hawk's lodge and walked . . . and walked . . . along a path populated with women and children making for the fields. The sun was barely risen, but on that muggy morning the exertion had sweat springing up on Clare's brow and down her back beneath Pippa's cradleboard.

Women were already in the fields, crouched and digging around the evenly spaced hillocks created by topsoil hoed into mounds. Out of each mound three or four cornstalks grew, most around knee-height that early in the season.

Though an acre accommodated dozens of hillocks, it didn't strike Clare as the best use of space, planting them thus. She'd have planted the corn in neat, tight rows—as she'd done on Uncle Alphus's farm.

They halted before a patch of the sprawling communal fields nestled between a threading stream and a row of massive tree stumps left to rot away.

"You make?" Looking earnestly at Clare, Crosses-the-Path gestured to the patch while her daughters waited, each clutching a leather pouch, the smallest dancing foot to foot in impatience. Clare was pondering what was meant by the words *"you make"* when Wildcat tugged on her wrist to draw her aside.

"Time plant beans and . . . squash? Pumpkin?" The boy waited until she nodded, though she'd no notion whether he'd found the words he sought. "This her field. She give you . . . patch. You make food for husband, baby."

Crosses-the-Path was giving her a portion of her field to tend, and its eventual yield. The woman was treating her like family—what she'd be had she truly married Jeremiah Ring—and not wholly out of duty. Crosses-the-Path looked genuinely hopeful her offer would be met with pleasure.

Clare flicked her gaze to the sacks the girls clutched. Seeds for the beans and squash? That was why so much space was left between the hillocks—they were planting all three crops together.

"She like you," Wildcat added with one of his infectious grins.

The boy had visited Clare several times for English lessons. When she learned about them, Crosses-the-Path had asked to be included. Wildcat pretended to be learning when all he really needed was the chance to practice. Though Crosses-the-Path was far behind the boy in her facility, she and Clare had developed a means of communication that included a few Shawnee words, a growing vocabulary of English, and much gesticulation.

Clare smiled at Crosses-the-Path and nodded, despite her unease at accepting the gift. Surely she wouldn't be living among the Shawnees when this corn was ripe for harvesting, but it would be good to have something to fill the time while she waited.

Waiting was what her life had come down to, and she chafed over it, certain she would go mad not knowing how Jacob was faring in Nonhelema's Town, however far beyond the creek it lay.

That was a question she hadn't dared ask, fearing if the distance was small she'd be overcome by the temptation to cross it, despite Mr. Ring's warning that doing so would alarm Rain Crow and make it harder for him to get Jacob back.

But how would the situation be resolved if she stayed on one side of the creek and Rain Crow stayed on the other? What, exactly, was Mr. Ring waiting for?

The man had other matters worrying him now; despite Cornstalk's disapproval, some forty young Shawnee warriors had crossed the Ohio to raid along the river, striking at isolated cabins raised in what they considered their hunting grounds.

As grave and immediate were such matters, not even that could preoccupy Clare enough to stem the grief of missing her son, the constant worry that he was well on his way to becoming another Wildcat, the spinning of plan after plan to get him back—plans that, if she voiced them, Mr. Ring found reason to dismiss as unsuitable.

Round face brightening at Clare's acceptance, Crosses-the-Path gestured to her daughters, who scampered into the field to begin the days' work. Wildcat and their mother followed. Clare came last, hearing a smacking of lips from Pippa and the small, urgent grunts that were precursory to a full-throated wail of hunger.

She settled near the hillock where Crosses-the-Path had begun digging, removed Pippa from the cradleboard, and put her to a breast.

She caught the other woman casting glances her way. Clare hadn't bothered to cover herself; many of the women in the fields wore nothing but a skirt, their brown backs already glistening in the morning sun. With some surprise Clare realized she'd grown used to the sight of so much bare skin, to the point she no longer felt awkward about nursing her baby openly. At least in front of the women.

Crosses-the-Path's covert gaze had nothing to do with such matters; the look of baby-hunger was the same anywhere—a Richmond parlor, a Shenandoah farm, or a Shawnee village. Unless they'd lost a baby since, it was four years since her last child was born. Perhaps she longed to give Falling Hawk a son, though Clare had the sense that daughters were valued as much as sons among these people.

Deeming it too intimate a subject to inquire about on their short acquaintance, Clare remarked, "I've never seen crops planted like this, together in one field."

Crosses-the-Path paused, dirt clinging to her hands and her small digging tool, then nodded. "*Wesah*. All together."

"Good for each type of plant?" When the woman nodded, Clare asked, "How is it good?"

This took longer to answer, but eventually Crosses-the-Path explained her people's planting method.

With the cornstalks grown sturdy enough, the beans, planted around their bases, would use the growing stalks as a climbing pole. Squash and pumpkins would be planted around the edges of the mound. When they matured, their broad leaves would shade the ground, inhibiting weed growth, thus reducing the work the fields would require in coming weeks.

"I do declare," Clare said, impressed by the wisdom behind the method. "I wonder why everyone doesn't plant that way."

Pippa was finished feeding. Clare returned her to the cradleboard in hopes she would sleep. "Would you mind keeping an eye on her while I work?" she asked Wildcat, who'd lingered nearby, listening to their conversation.

Crosses-the-Path's youngest daughter, paying attention to this exchange with an intensity that revealed her effort to comprehend it, looked instantly relieved when the boy went to sit in the shade of one of the big stumps, against which Pippa's cradleboard was propped. The little girl held her bag of seeds close, as if she feared its loss.

Thinking no more of it, Clare moved to the part of the field intended for her. She could hear Crosses-the-Path repeating a few new English words gleaned from their conversation.

The woman learned quickly. More quickly than Clare was managing to pick up her language. Or her ways.

She'd made a few inroads with the women of Cornstalk's village, beyond Crosses-the-Path. It could hardly be helped with a fortnight come and gone since she first saw the trader, Cheramy, at the creek. She'd returned each morning and evening since, hoping to encounter him again. When she hadn't, she'd allowed herself to be engaged by whichever Shawnee woman made an effort to speak to her. Talking with the women gave her cause to linger and wait for Cheramy. Thus far in vain.

The warm morning was turning into a hot day. Sweat coursed down Clare's temple. She swiped it away before it stung her eye, looking up to find Pippa wakeful, Wildcat tickling the baby's nose with a blue jay's feather, dutifully engaged in his task of minding the infant.

She returned her attention to the work at hand.

Before they'd washed up destitute at Uncle Alphus's door, Clare had had no experience in matters of the soil. Since her father was a physician as well as a businessman, they'd lived in the heart of Richmond; garden plots were the extent of the Litchfield family's planting, and they'd slaves to tend the work and its yield once it reached the kitchen-house. Yet Clare had taken to life and work on the farm with more readiness than Philip, who'd grown to manhood on a proper plantation. Philip had been at home with ledgers and figures, a proclivity Uncle Alphus had pointed out when her husband fixed on Kentucky as the answer to their financial difficulties.

Her thoughts drifted to Uncle Alphus as she moved around the hillocks, digging holes for seeds Crosses-the-Path's daughters planted and tamped down.

From her earliest memories, Alphus Litchfield had been besotted with her, his only niece. To her he'd seemed the epitome of the romantic adventurer. He'd settled in the Shenandoah when it was still the frontier, fought in the old French War, been a long-hunter, spending whole winters ranging the wilderness for furs, seeing and doing all manner of things a little girl accustomed to the parlors of Richmond society could hardly imagine—save during visits when he told her tales of his frontier life with a skill to keep her rapt with suspense.

Was he at work even now in his corn-dusted mill, with its grinding stones and splashing waterwheel, imagining her somewhere deep in Kentucky busy about the hard work of making a home? Or had he heard of the unrest on the frontier and worried for their very lives?

She was certain her reality was worse than anything he'd imagined.

Uncle Alphus couldn't help her now. She'd thought Jeremiah Ring would be the man to do so, but now there was Jean-Paul Cheramy. Or she hoped so. So much time had passed since that encounter at the creek that she'd begun to wonder if she'd conjured the man from thin air and desperation.

She looked up from her digging to spot Wildcat, only to find that Crosses-the-Path's youngest daughter had taken over minding Pippa after all. Wildcat stood at the field's edge with a band of boys stopped along the path. Each carried a bow and quiver of arrows.

Perhaps planting and minding babies wasn't a thing males typically did.

Clare blinked aside memory of Jeremiah Ring asleep with Pippa on his chest just as—sure enough—Wildcat cast a half-guilty look at her. She waved him away, and he hurried off with the boys, one of whom carried a small hoop fashioned of grapevines. Off to have some sort of competition, like as not.

Everything was a competition with males, it seemed. Philip had been of that mind-set, trying to regain what he'd lost, including his place in Richmond society, instead of settling for a simpler life on a farm in the Shenandoah.

At least they'd have both been alive to live it.

It struck her that of all the men she'd known, Jeremiah Ring seemed to have the least bent in him toward competition. He wasn't quite Shawnee in his ways. These people loved games, games of chance with bone dice, or games requiring what seemed half the village to play on a field set aside for the purpose, and would drop everything on the instant to play them, yet she'd never seen Mr. Ring take part. Nor was he like any white man she'd known. He'd no desire, seemingly, to own his own land, to farm, to learn a trade, even to marry and raise a family. His work for the Indian agents at Fort Pitt seemed a casual thing, done when he chose to do it.

He seemed adrift between those worlds, red and white, bearing his messages from one to the other, a threaded needle stitching them together. But what of dreams and desires? Had he none?

The sun had traveled up the sky and begun its descent before they left the fields, making for the creek to wash. Though covered in the dirt and sweat of labor, Clare felt a satisfaction in the work. Not as much had she believed she was providing for herself and her children.

Thought of Jacob, never more than barely held at bay, flooded back full force.

At the creek the women waded in to wash, most stripped naked, but Clare remained on the bank, half her attention on washing, half on the brush across the bank.

Once again she saw no sign of Mr. Cheramy.

Crosses-the-Path stayed with her while her daughters waded in, washing in the shallows by dipping water to sluice their arms and faces. No longer quiet or shy with Clare, the woman had kept up a chatter in Shawnee all the way back from the fields, with enough English sprinkled in that Clare now and then took her meaning. Now she seemed to be talking about her daughters.

"Children watch. Bean. Squash. Keep away bird. Deer."

"Yes . . . *wesah*," Clare murmured, nodding though she barely took in what the woman was saying, for just when she'd consigned another day's passing to hope deferred, she'd glimpsed the man watching from the brush across the creek.

He was looking directly, intensely, at her. With the barest tip of his head downstream, Jean-Paul Cheramy backed into shadow.

No one else seemed to have noticed him.

Clare waited until Crosses-the-Path became preoccupied with her daughters, splashing each other now rather than bathing, then took up Pippa's cradleboard and slipped away downstream, past the concealing clump of wild rose.

The creek's level had fallen over the past days, there having been little rain. Clare crossed to Cheramy, needing only to remove her moccasins. Now she stood before the man, who explained his long absence by saying he'd been across the Scioto River in Kispoko Town, trading there. "But now I am come back to look for you, Madame, to tell you I have seen your son. He is the one called Many Sparrows?"

"Yes," she said, a little breathless. Seen close up, Jean-Paul Cheramy reminded her more strikingly of Philip, only his eyes were a piercing blue instead of brown. "His name is *Jacob*. Jacob Inglesby."

"Not your own name—Ring? Ah, but he will have another father, not Jeremiah Ring, who I take it is the father of your new *bébé*?"

The trader went on before Clare could respond.

"But tell me, Madame, how come you to be in Cornstalk's Town and yet your son is in Nonhelema's Town, being called Many Sparrows, the son of Rain Crow?"

Hoping to form some sort of bond with this man, Clare spilled the story of her plight—Philip's death and Jacob's capture, Jeremiah Ring's arrival and Pippa's birth, their trek over the mountains to Wheeling, then following Jacob's trail at last to Cornstalk's Town to find him already adopted.

"Mr. Ring wishes me to give it time, even to *befriend* Rain Crow. But no amount of showing myself friendly is going to make her give up Jacob if she wants to keep him. And how am I to do any such thing when I'm on one side of this creek and she on the other?"

Mr. Cheramy, who had listened to her unfolding tale without interruption, wasted no time on exclamations or sympathy. "And yet, Madame, here you stand on *this* side of the creek."

Clare looked at her bare feet, wet in the pine needles. Feet at which the trader also looked.

"But what good will it do?" she asked, warmth blooming in her cheeks. "I cannot go marching into Nonhelema's Town uninvited. Rain Crow would drive me right back out."

"Even though your *husband* is her brother?"

She'd caught the emphasis he'd placed on the word, that subtle note of doubt. Ought she to trust him with the truth? Maybe it would help persuade him of her need.

Desperation and hope made her reckless. "Actually . . . he isn't my husband, Mr. Cheramy. We aren't married."

Silence wrapped around them, heavy and uncertain, as Clare searched the blue eyes regarding her.

"This I had already surmised. At least that he could not possibly be the father of this second child. Not if you met when you say. Yet you pretend to a marriage. Why?"

Because he didn't sound shocked, or condemning, merely curious, she said, "Mr. Ring says it's for my protection and my acceptance. And for all I know he's right, so I would ask you to keep the truth between us."

The admonition seemed to surprise—perhaps offend—the trader. "You will see, Madame. I am a very good keeper of secrets. Also I am a man who understands your lack of patience with Indians. As for this Mr. Ring, who has promised to help you, it is his own Shawnee family from which he must get your son away? That much you have said is true?"

"It is. He promised his help before he knew Falling Hawk, his brother, took Jacob to give him to their sister."

Mr. Cheramy shook his head, tailed blond hair sweeping his shoulders. "Then maybe this is not a thing within his power to do for you, however much he wished to." The trader held her gaze, eyes warming. "For I think, Madame, were I in his place with you, I would want to render you this service if I could."

Blushing again, Clare averted her gaze but couldn't deny the force of his words, the hope they kindled.

"And as it happens," he went on, "I know where your son may be found."

She looked up sharply. "In Nonhelema's Town."

"No, Madame. I know where he is *en ce moment* and will take you to him if you can come with me now. Shall the *bébé* keep quiet a while, do you think?"

Clare's heart was in her throat, robbing her of speech. Mr. Cheramy must have taken her silence for mistrust. "You needn't fear that I will harm your efforts to retrieve your son or do anything to make matters worse for you. For in this I and your Mr. Ring are in agreement—you would do well for the present to keep your distance from Rain Crow. That does not mean you cannot look upon your son, see that he is well. I will take you to a place where you may do so, though I caution you against approaching him or allowing yourself to be seen."

Clare saw the man through a shimmer of tears as he took her shoulder in a gentle grip.

"Can you do this, *ma chère*—for now only to look?"

Only to look. Hidden with Mr. Cheramy at the wood's edge while her son played with a band of Indian children on the fringes of another cornfield, Clare was doubting the wisdom of her choice. Seeing Jacob from afar like this, unable to touch him, speak to him, grab him and run with him and the baby on her back until they were far away, was agony, yet she couldn't tear her gaze from the small blond figure, shockingly sun-browned, wearing only a breech-clout and moccasins.

Now and then one of the children would dart into the field to chase away a bird or rabbit.

"The children guard the fields," she murmured, recalling Crosses-the-Path's words.

She heard laughter and knew it for Jacob's—sweet music to her soul in one breath; with the next a piercing of grief and frustration. He was happy, but he was happy playing with *those* children. Was he happy with Rain Crow as his mother?

Even as she thought of her, the woman came striding into view from what must be the direction of the town. She called out in Shawnee, words Clare recognized. *Many Sparrows.*

She clapped a hand over her mouth. *Don't go to her,* she willed her son. She'd only watched him for a moment. Not long enough. It could never be long enough. Not like this.

Jacob's back was to the woman, his face in Clare's view. She knew that stubborn look, that set of shoulders, stiff and slightly raised. Her son was ignoring Rain Crow.

Some of the children were pointing, speaking. Telling him his mother was calling?

Jacob's shoulders slumped.

Clare tensed, willing her son to outright defiance, but Jacob left the other children and crossed the cornfield to Rain Crow, who smiled and held out her hand. He took it. They walked away together through the corn.

Clare felt her knees threaten to buckle.

Mr. Cheramy gripped her arm. "Come. I will lead you back."

Pippa was making fretful whimpers as Clare stumbled after the trader, vision blurred, barely able to put one foot before the other. Mr. Cheramy took her by the hand and led her through the trees to the creek, where she found the will to speak.

"Is there anything you can do to help me leave this place with my children?" He'd all but offered it already. "Please, Mr. Cheramy."

The trader regarded her with consideration. "It is not right for a mother and child to be kept apart. Let me think on this situation."

Gratitude rushed in, but she needed more than his promise to think about helping her. "I am truly desperate. If there is *anything* you can do . . ."

Mr. Cheramy winced, as though pained by her unmasked need. "Here is how it is with me, *ma chère*. In three days' time I am leaving the Scioto. I meant to go westward, but . . . I could change those plans. This I am willing to do for you, if you wish it of me."

Taking her again by the arm, he ran his fingers down it until he'd clasped her hand in his. Gooseflesh rose where he'd touched her despite the sticky warmth of the day. She searched his eyes and read in them a look that both alarmed and heartened her. The man found her appealing.

"Wh-what are you saying?" Perhaps he wanted something from her she wasn't willing to give? But what wouldn't she give to have Jacob back, to be away from this place finally? To be safe.

Not that. *Please, don't want that.* Her heart slammed against her ribs.

Mr. Cheramy's gaze softened. "All I am saying is this, that in the time I remain in Nonhelema's Town I will befriend your son. I will speak to him as often as I can so that he is easy with me, so he knows me. Give me the three days for doing this and then, in the middle of the third night, I will bring him out of the town with me. I will meet you here on the bank of this creek—on this side. We shall leave all together, you, me, and your children. What say you to this, Madame?"

Once again the man had stolen her speech. *Three days.*

"I know we are not long acquainted, *ma chère*," he said. "But you may trust me. There will come no harm to you or your children. This I promise you."

She'd striven so long for this chance, the path blocked every way she'd attempted to pursue it. Suddenly, almost without trying, the way lay open before her. Surely she was meant to meet this man, the one who would get Jacob back for her.

"Yes! Oh, thank you. I . . . thank you so very much." Tears choked her, keeping her from saying more.

Mr. Cheramy gave her hand a pat and released her. "Go now. On the third night I will meet you in this spot. Your Jacob will be with me. You can slip away in the night, you and the *bébé,* and not be seen or followed?"

"I can. I will." Somehow she would manage it.

Pippa was starting to fuss in earnest. Clare turned toward the creek, thoughts spinning, but before she had a foot in the water, she looked back.

Mr. Cheramy was watching her go. She asked a question that had been nagging at her.

"Why will you not come into Cornstalk's Town?"

Mr. Cheramy smiled, giving a lift of his shoulders. "About that, Madame, this is how it is. When I come to the Scioto for trade it is in Nonhelema's Town I abide. I am, shall we say, *unwelcome* in Cornstalk's Town these days."

She dared not acknowledge the niggling of doubt that rose in the back of her mind.

"Unwelcome? Why?"

Mr. Cheramy brushed the matter aside. "A misunderstanding. It happened years ago when I was less skilled in the art of trading with Indians. With these people it is easy to offend, easy to misstep, no? Not so easy to regain their trust."

"Certainement," she said in heartfelt agreement and quickly removed her moccasins to wade the creek.

18

Logan had come to Cornstalk's Town, still wearing Inglesby's scalp on his belt. Jeremiah had spent much of that day in the *msi-kah-mi-qui* trying, along with Cornstalk and others, to persuade Logan to cease his raiding across the Ohio before more Shawnees followed his example and drove the nation nearer the precipice of war.

"It is too late to hold back what is coming; we are already over that precipice and falling," Logan told them, gazing around the smoky council house at their furrowed brows and questioning stares. "Is it I who bring you this news?"

"What news do you bring?" Cornstalk inquired, though Jeremiah doubted he was the only one making a reasonable guess.

"The Long Knife governor, Dunmore, has sent word to his captains in the west to gather their men." Logan's eyes shone in the firelight, glinting like glass. Seated around him, his warriors, most wearing their own scalping trophies, leaned forward as one, intent on his words. "He means to come into this land. Will the Shawnees sit and wait for him to come and burn their lodges down around their heads? Shall Puckeshinwah, your war chief, or you, Cornstalk, do this?"

Answers to these questions were evaded with more questions, but they gleaned no further details from Logan about the Virginians. Logan didn't know the intricacies of Dunmore's plans, or didn't care enough to recall them.

Could it be just rumor? Major Connolly at Fort Pitt had proven himself an embellisher and outright fabricator of tales of violence for the purpose of stirring up such a war.

Cornstalk sent runners eastward to find out.

Jeremiah left the council house knowing he would return to Pittsburgh to discover the truth for himself, if not for Clare. He doubted she could be persuaded to leave without Jacob. He still didn't know how he was going to get the boy back without doing irreparable damage to Rain Crow's soul and to his relations with the only family he had.

He'd been honest about that with Clare early that morning when she'd confronted him, impatient for him to do something, letting her know that while he hadn't given up, that he believed Jacob should be returned to her, he simply wasn't certain how to proceed. So he was waiting.

It hadn't gone over well.

"Waiting for what? For *whom*?"

"On the Almighty, Clare. He'll show us the way. The best way. In time."

She'd glared at him with the look of one betrayed, then left the lodge, and him, in a fuming temper.

Maybe it was time now. Time to cross the creek and have another hard conversation with Rain Crow. Or was he allowing himself to be pressured by these rumors brought by Logan?

He knew the voice screaming at him to *do* something, to set things to rights, clamoring for heedless obedience. He'd been in its grip before. He shut it out and listened for a quieter Voice.

And thine ears shall hear a word behind thee, saying, This is the way, walk ye in it, when ye turn to the right hand, and when ye turn to the left.

He didn't hear a command to go left, right, or forward. What he heard was, *Be still.*

Words Clare did not want to hear. He'd sent Wildcat off a while ago to find her. Not to disturb her if she was working with the women, untroubled. Just to be sure her path didn't cross that of the man who killed her husband and was still parading the evidence.

The boy had yet to find him again, but he assumed she was in no distress.

Though he'd encouraged her toward it, Clare's absence from the wegiwa had left him uneasy even before encountering Logan. He'd wondered at that until admitting he simply missed her and Pippa. Upon leaving the council house, he'd hoped to find Clare inside the lodge, perhaps with a kettle over the fire.

The lodge was empty, the fire cold.

He ducked outside and set off through the village in the general direction of Falling Hawk's lodge, searching for sign of her. Clare was free to come and go as she pleased, but he needed to be sure of her whereabouts. Seeing Logan would upset her—how could it not? He'd been relieved Clare chose today to go out into the fields with Crosses-the-Path. Falling Hawk told him his wife meant to give her a portion of the field to plant and work for him.

And for Wolf-Alone, he mentally added. But primarily a woman tended crops for her husband and children.

Despite the tension in the wegiwa and those times in the night when he heard Clare's muffled sobs, there were moments, going about the business of living, when it felt like they *were* married. He liked those moments. Maybe more than he should.

Clare wasn't his. He was a means to an end for her. Nothing more. Besides, he knew the dangers of letting down his guard. You opened your heart wide for life's arrows to pierce it, and there were always arrows coming. Yet the heart, willful thing, could still long to bare itself to such attack, to take that terrible risk for the chance of such exquisite reward.

He paused near a lodge where an ancient grandmother sat on a buffalo hide watching him, for he'd spotted Clare coming along the creek path in his direction.

She didn't appear troubled. In fact, her demeanor was a stark contrast to when she'd left the wegiwa that morning.

Radiant was the word that came to him. He caught his breath. Hearing a snort from the level of his knees, he glanced down. No mistaking the old woman's amusement. Her features were all but lost in a maze of laughing wrinkles, dark eyes peeking like puddles in the cracked mudflats of a drying river.

Face warming, Jeremiah strode off to intercept Clare.

She was smiling when he reached her, though behind her in the cradleboard Pippa was anything but happy. The baby was working herself into a full-throated wail Jeremiah recognized for her hungry cry.

Looking unfazed by the noise, Clare greeted him with shining eyes, their green intensified by the newly sun-burnished hue of her brow and cheeks. A breeze was springing up to cool the day. A strand of hair escaped its braid to blow across her face, pale against her skin. It snagged against lips so full Jeremiah had to resist the temptation to brush it back simply to touch them.

She pushed back the strand, tucking it behind an ear. "Mr. Ring, I suppose Pippa isn't the only one hungry by now?"

He was bereft of speech, until the baby's angry cries jarred him back to his senses. "I can get something started while you tend Pippa."

"Would you?" Clare started for the wegiwa, and Jeremiah followed, captivated by her change of mood, thoughts of guarding his heart spinning away into fragments.

Wolf-Alone came to the lodge long enough to eat with them, then went out again, giving Jeremiah a meaningful look, acknowledging their tacit agreement not to mention Logan by name. Clare was preoccupied, though whatever distracted her seemed a source of pleasure rather than concern. It couldn't be Logan, still troubling Jeremiah.

Logan had had on his person a letter to Michael Cresap, whom he still blamed for the murder of his family. It was written for him by a white man his warriors had taken prisoner. Logan had allowed Jeremiah to read it.

To Captain Cresap. What did you kill my people on Yellow Creek for. The white People killed my kin at Conestoga a great while ago, & I thought nothing of that. But you killed my kin again on Yellow Creek. Then I thought I must kill too; and I have been to war three times since but the Indians is not Angry only myself.

Jeremiah had offered to take the letter to Pittsburgh, where it might do some good toward convincing the Virginians that the majority of the Shawnees weren't in favor of war.

Logan refused. He would leave the letter where he chose—some future scene of slaughter—once his vengeance was sated.

"It is too late to hold back what is coming." Despite what Logan's letter proclaimed, Jeremiah had witnessed more than one Shawnee warrior's heart abandon hope for peace and harden toward war, hearing such words.

If war came and they were still on the Scioto, what was he to do? Let Clare and Pippa flee with the women and children should that become needful? He was willing to fight, but on which side? He'd be viewed a traitor no matter which he chose.

A gurgling squeal from Pippa banished such troubling thoughts. Seated cross-legged on his bed furs, Jeremiah looked to where Clare, pacing before the fire, was attempting to coax Pippa to sleep.

"Not having any of it, is she?"

"She's wide awake," Clare said around a yawn, patting Pippa's back as the baby rode her shoulder, little hands pressed against Clare's collarbone, head lifted. "And I need to mend a moccasin before I sleep."

She turned, bringing Pippa's gaze in line with Jeremiah. The baby gave him a gummy smile, a sight to which he unfailingly warmed. She had an expressive face for a baby, often playful, as if she knew more than she was letting on and it amused her.

"Want me to give it a try?"

"She still settles better for you, doesn't she?" With an oddly wistful look, Clare gave the baby into his keeping.

Pippa didn't protest the exchange. Full of milk, clean-clouted, she reflected her mother's seemingly contented mood, which Jeremiah was finding contagious. He put their troubles—Logan, war, even Jacob—from his mind, stood with the baby in his arms, and took up pacing. Clare settled by the fire to stitch a gap in the seam of her moccasin with an awl and sinew he'd supplied.

"Did Crosses-the-Path teach you how to do that?"

Clare glanced up. "With Wildcat's help. But I knew how to stitch a seam before today," she added with a hint of a smile, even teasing in her tone.

He felt a rush of pleasure, though mention of the boy returned Logan to mind. "See Wildcat today, did you?"

"Early on." Clare paused to cut the sinew with the knife she'd taken to wearing in a leather sheath around her neck, as Shawnee women wore— another item he'd supplied to her. "He went to the fields with us and watched Pippa for a while. Then he left to shoot arrows with some other boys."

It was shortly after that, Jeremiah guessed, that he'd left the council house to find Wildcat and instruct him to intercept Clare if she looked likely to cross paths with Logan. Wildcat hadn't let Clare know he had returned to watch her, else she probably would have mentioned it.

He'd make a good hunter, that one—already he showed promise of it, according to Wolf-Alone, who often took the boy with him when he hunted along the Scioto.

Pippa wasn't settling. She held her head erect as she'd done with Clare, though it had a tendency to pitch sideways, bumping his jaw. The baby turned her attention to that jaw, twisting to put a hand to it, seeming to like the scratchy feel. He let her pat him awhile before pretending to nibble her fingers. She was too young to understand the game, much less engage with him, but he provided the requisite snarls and lip-smacks until he caught Clare watching him.

"Do you know anything about him?" she asked.

"About who?"

He'd tensed, thinking she meant Logan, but relaxed when she said, "Wildcat. Where he came from. Who he was. He claims to have no memory of it."

Pippa took an interest in his ear, pressing her wet mouth to it. "I was here when he was brought in by the hunters who found him."

"Found him?" Clare paused her stitching, giving him her full attention.

"On a homestead in the mountains, near the Yadkin River, down in Carolina. The people there had died in a cabin fire—or something of the sort. He was hiding in a barn with some kittens, all of them half-wild. He was maybe three years old at the time. There was no one around to claim the boy, he was hungry, so the hunters fed him, then decided to keep him."

Firelight accentuated Clare's frown. "There must have been someone, somewhere, who would have wanted him."

Someone white, she meant.

"Just as likely the hunters who found him saved his life in taking him." Pippa was gnawing gummily at his ear now. Snorting with laughter, he shifted the baby away.

Clare smiled briefly at her daughter's antics. "What happened to his mother—Red-Quill-Woman, I mean?"

"She sickened and died last winter. She was elderly, like Split-Moon."

"Is that why you and Wolf-Alone take such interest in Wildcat? Because Split-Moon is so old?"

"Partly . . ."

It had caught him off guard, how sudden they'd come up against a part of his past he'd yet to share with her, that he'd thought of sharing a dozen times, but . . . how was he to explain that Split-Moon and Red-Quill-Woman had started out his enemies, much as Rain Crow was to her, but had become his friends despite his doing everything so wrong? She would ask why that should be and he would have to tell her everything. He would have to talk of Hannah and the part he'd played in her death.

"Wolf-Alone has a special liking for the boy. Teaches him as an uncle would."

He didn't wonder at her interest in Wildcat. Likely she saw in the boy what Jacob might become should she fail to get him back.

Then he wondered a thing that hadn't crossed his mind until that moment; if Rain Crow never relinquished Jacob, would Clare be willing to remain with the Shawnees to be near her son, even if she couldn't have the raising of him?

Remain with him, Jeremiah, as well?

The idea was a flame, drawing nearer the possibilities that had fluttered lately around the edges of his thoughts. He liked that she was trying to live among the People, to give herself the chance—as he'd once done—to see more in them than the savages his raising, and initial experiences, had led him to see. That had taken courage, a yielding of soul that hadn't come easy, a forgiveness only the Almighty had been able to work in him. And the grace to accept forgiveness in return.

Maybe he ought to tell her everything, what was done to him, the mistakes he'd made, who he'd been before he was Panther-Sees-Him, or even Jeremiah Ring. And what his willfulness had cost him in the end, why he was trying so hard to get it right this time.

Time. That was what had covered over those wounds, but what if he bared them to Clare only to discover they weren't truly healed? Even if they were, dared he take such a risk again? Let himself love again as he'd loved once before, this time with full knowledge of what he risked?

Love again. The thought drew him up short.

Did he love Clare Inglesby?

Holding her baby in his arms, looking at her in the firelight, blond head bent to her work, he felt the stirring of body and soul and thought if she chose to stay with the Shawnees, and would have him, he would marry her in truth.

And then he would give her his heart. Everything.

He lay Pippa on the sleeping platform and sat beside her, letting the knowledge settle in his soul, alternately warming him and shaking him to his marrow.

Clare stitched on, none the wiser to the workings of his mind—thankfully. The baby kicked her legs and cooed. He felt a stab of pity for Philip Inglesby as he bent and grasped a tiny flailing foot and rubbed the tender sole against his scratchy chin.

Pippa made a squeak of surprise. Grinning, he did it again.

The next sound that erupted from Pippa's mouth captured his heart and wrapped around it like a clinging vine.

"Clare," he said, turning to find her staring, face shining with firelight.

Thrusting aside the moccasin, she rose and came to bend over her daughter. "She laughed. That was a *laugh*."

"I believe it was," he agreed.

"Jacob didn't laugh until nearly twice her age."

For several moments they stared at Pippa, as if expecting her to do it again, until Jeremiah's focus shifted from the baby to her mother; Clare was bending close, their bodies brushing.

She seemed to grow aware of it and straightened. She looked down at him in the strangest way, as if with regret.

"You want her back?"

"No, Mr. Ring. You may continue to amuse her, if you wish. She doesn't seem tired, does she?"

It was safer looking at the baby. "She's bright-eyed and bushy-tailed, certain sure."

Clare laughed. "Bushy-tailed?"

Jeremiah felt absurdly pleased to have made both Inglesby women laugh in the space of minutes. "Never heard the expression?"

"Never."

"It's something my mother would say."

"Your mother?"

He looked up as her gaze sharpened. But if he'd stirred in her some curiosity, she seemed to brush it aside as she went back to the fire.

He wanted suddenly to tell her about himself, about the farm in the Shenandoah. His parents, both dead now. Even Hannah. But maybe she didn't care to know. He was trying hard to fathom her mind. It wasn't but two months since her husband's death, yet when she cried in the night he didn't think it was for Inglesby. But she must be mourning him in her way. At least mourning the life she'd had.

He gazed at her now, wondering again what it would be like if she was his wife. She wouldn't be calling him Mr. Ring, for one thing.

As if she knew what he was thinking, she raised her eyes to him, and he saw the color rise to her cheeks. He wasn't the only one sensing the growing intimacy between them, but it seemed to fluster her.

That wouldn't do.

"Clare, this arrangement we have going is in name only, for the purpose of—"

"Getting Jacob back," she said so promptly he knew he'd been right in surmising the reason for her discomfort.

"Aye. And I don't mistake it for anything else, but . . . I do consider myself your friend."

After a moment she nodded, accepting that. She seemed as distant as she had all evening, but guarded now. No longer serene. He wished he could read her mind, her very thoughts, and *where* had he been going with this?

"With that in mind, I was wondering . . . would you consider calling me Jeremiah?"

Her eyes flared in the firelight. She seemed to weigh the request, the silence stretching, making it seem more complicated than the simple thing it was. But who was he to judge what she found complicated? Her request to him must have seemed the simplest thing in the world when she'd made it. She'd lost her son. She wanted him back. He was able to help her, and he'd agreed to do it. Yet look how tangled it had become. For both of them.

"Not Panther-Sees-Him?" she asked, a slight teasing note in her voice, as if she was trying to lighten their mood again.

"I'd rather you called me Jeremiah."

When he said no more, she gave a hint of a shrug, as if it mattered little. Or she wanted him to think so. "I'll call you so if you wish . . . Jeremiah."

He let the sound of it wash over him, almost wishing he'd asked her to call him the name by which he'd been known in Virginia, a name he hadn't heard since . . .

A rustling at the door caught their attention.

Wildcat poked his head inside the lodge. He took in the sight of Jeremiah on the sleeping bench and started to speak, then noticed Clare by the fire and said, "I was looking for Wolf-Alone. He is not here?"

"No," Jeremiah replied, though he didn't think this was what the boy had begun to say.

Wildcat shot another look at Clare, who smiled in welcome. "Would you like to come inside? You could tell me how your bow-shooting went today."

"It well," the boy said in English. "Thank you."

He ducked back outside, leaving Jeremiah taken aback. Wildcat and Clare had been spending time together, along with Crosses-the-Path, practicing English. He thought the boy liked her, but his behavior just now had bordered on the rude. Unless . . . had he wanted to speak to Jeremiah alone?

Pippa's eyes had grown heavy-lidded at last.

"Mind if I go out for a bit?"

Clare stood, looking puzzled by the boy's behavior but not terribly troubled. As if that, too, didn't really touch her.

"I don't mind." She put the moccasin alongside its mate and came toward the sleeping platform.

Jeremiah headed for the door-hide.

Outside in the late summer dusk, the boy was walking away, though with dragging feet. Jeremiah called to him.

Wildcat turned quickly, as though he'd hoped to be followed.

Jeremiah closed the distance between them. "All right. What is it?"

He led Wildcat away until they were well out of earshot of anyone who might overhear. Then the boy answered his question.

19

It was the third night. The moon was high and bright, the sky a web of stars against the black. Though her path was well lit, it took longer than Clare planned to traverse the maze of lodges without arousing the alarm of man, woman, or dog. Wishing to kindle no suspicion by setting aside provisions, she'd brought little besides Pippa and her cradleboard, into which she now secured the sleeping baby, the noise of the procedure covered by the chatter of the creek at the wide bend where she intended to cross. She had clouts for the baby, a blanket from her bed, a wildly beating heart, and, contrarily, a weight of regret that had increased with each step taken from Jeremiah, asleep in Wolf-Alone's lodge.

She didn't like to dwell on what he would think when he found her gone. He'd proven himself a good man, despite his choice to live among heathens. She'd been fortunate he'd come along in her time of need. But things had taken an unexpected turn at Yellow Creek. She understood why he'd failed to keep his promise. So now that she'd taken matters in hand and would soon be reunited with her son, why did she feel as though *she* was failing in some way?

She would sort it out, but not tonight. Tonight only Jacob mattered. And escape for them all.

With Pippa secure in the cradleboard, she removed her moccasins and felt her way across the stones of the creek. She didn't slip. Pippa wasn't jarred awake. She reached the other side, donned her footwear, and made her way downstream to the spot where she was meant to meet Jacob. As she crept along the creek bank under the starry sky, stepping cautiously for fear of snakes and roots, it was all she could do not to call his name, aching to hear him call back from the riverine darkness ahead.

She would miss Jeremiah. She'd let down her guard with him these past days, much more than she'd intended to do. Without the constant strain of her need and his inaction souring the air between them, she'd felt free to simply *be* with him. She'd found a surprising pleasure in his tenderness with Pippa, how he'd been the one to illicit her first laugh. He could be gruff at times, aloof for no apparent reason, but he was also calm and patient and—

Ahead in the darkness a stick snapped.

A voice spoke. Another answered, sharp with surprise. Both were masculine, and they went on speaking, barreling over each other, rising with unmistakable anger and challenge until she could make out their disputing words.

"You won't do it again!"

It took an eternity to cover the last brushy yards and emerge into the clearing where Jean-Paul Cheramy was meant to be awaiting her. He was there, with a string of laden pack mules—Clare smelled them before her eyes picked out their bulky shapes. The trader's pale hair identified him, struggling on his knees in the grip of . . . was it Wolf-Alone?

A third figure stood over him, moonlight glinting off the knife blade held to the trader's throat.

"Clare—keep back!"

Jeremiah.

She advanced on the trio, looking wildly about at men and mules bathed in silvery light that obscured as much as it revealed.

"Jeremiah? What is going on? Why are you here?"

"Madame, he—" Mr. Cheramy's attempt to speak was cut off by a flurry of rough handling from his captors.

"Stop—what are you doing to him?" She halted a mere pace from the men, their faces now visible in the night. "Where is Jacob?"

Panic writhed up from her belly, wrapping around her brain and confounding her thoughts. She didn't see her son, didn't hear him.

Jeremiah passed the knife to Wolf-Alone and reached for her, fingers closing hard around her arm. "I said stay back. I don't want you hurt."

She yanked free. "Where is my son? And *what* are you doing to Mr. Cheramy?"

"Him?" Jeremiah's contempt was unmasked. "Keeping you from throwing your life away on him."

"My life? What are you saying? Mr. Cheramy agreed to help me! Why won't you release him?"

"No," Jeremiah said, a command to Wolf-Alone as much as in answer to her. "He never meant to help you—or Jacob, who is still asleep in Rain Crow's lodge."

"He's still with Rain Crow?"

Everything was shattering. Again.

"Yes. Now *listen*—"

"No. Jeremiah, no! I don't understand. Mr. Cheramy was to bring Jacob to me tonight and lead us out of this place, back to the Ohio. I've waited for you to do the same." Her plan spilled out as if speaking it would keep it all from flying to pieces. Keep her from coming apart. "I understand why you cannot help me now. They're your family. She's your sister. But I want my—"

He grasped her shoulders. "Clare, be silent!"

"I'll not be silent. I—"

"Perhaps if you will not be calm and listen to Panther-Sees-Him," a voice said from the darkness, "who is trying to tell you what is happening here, maybe you will listen to me?"

It was a woman's voice, rich and deep and Shawnee, though one who'd long since mastered English. Jeremiah released Clare as a tall, lithe figure stepped from the shadowy wood.

Even by moonlight Clare recognized Nonhelema.

Jeremiah seemed as startled by her appearance as was Clare. Wolf-Alone stood, dragging Mr. Cheramy up with him so they were all on their feet before Cornstalk's sister, whose teeth flashed white as she smiled at Jeremiah and his brother.

In the moonlight it seemed a feral expression, more warning than warmth.

"I am not surprised to find the two of you here, though I think you did not expect to see me this night. I will tell you how I come to be here. Then you will tell me the same." With a brief sweep of her hand in the semi-dark, Nonhelema indicated the trader. "Together we can decide what is to be done with that one."

"Je vous en prie," Mr. Cheramy began, an edge of desperation in his voice, but that same commanding hand raised against him, bidding him to silence and implying threat should he fail to heed.

Clare clamped a hand across her mouth, overcome by tears of disappointment and mounting remorse. Why had she thought this would ever work?

"This man," Nonhelema went on, to Clare's surprise and mortification addressing *her,* when all she wanted now was for the night to swallow her whole, "this one who I have much liked in the past—he is good to look at, is he not? And charming in his speech—him I have allowed to come into my town for trade even after my brother turned him away. This man, with whom you have allied yourself, went to the sister of these warriors and sought to purchase the boy who was born to you, who is now hers. She would accept no price for him. This she told me when she came to me as the sun was setting yesterday."

Clare gaped at the trader, standing rigid in Wolf-Alone's grip, head raised. Proud, it seemed.

She had surmised he'd meant to take Jacob without anyone knowing, that there would be subterfuge involved. He'd been so confident this could be done that she hadn't thought to question *how* exactly he meant to do it.

Mr. Cheramy had tried to *buy* Jacob?

"So," Nonhelema continued, "I set a watch on this man, and when it was told to me he was leaving in the night with all his mules and headed toward my brother's town, where he is forbidden to go, I rose from my bed and followed." Cornstalk's sister turned to address them all. "Now here I find you gathered, and I am ready to be told what this is about . . . though I have a good idea already."

Mr. Cheramy was shaking his head. "No, Madame. This is not what it appears. I had only the truest intentions of aiding this woman. I came here to tell her . . . of my failure."

The man now hung his head, though it seemed a calculated gesture. And his words, somehow they now rang false. Had anything he ever said to her been truly meant? Maybe none but this last. *Failure.*

"You are lying," Jeremiah said. "You came to entice her away regardless of this failure, with some flimsy promise of fetching her son away eventually if only she left the Scioto with you tonight."

"This is not true!"

Nonhelema gave the trader's protest no heed. "It is with regret that I tell you, Cheramy, that as it is in my brother's town so it is in mine: you are no longer welcome. You may do your trading across the river among Puckeshin-wah's people—if he still welcomes you. I did not want to believe it of you, but I see now that what the people of my brother's town have said of you is true. You are a man who lures women away to do them no good."

Clare remained as baffled by this turn of events as she'd been the moment she stepped into the clearing, ignorant of whatever the rest of them seemed to know full well. All she knew was that the trader didn't have Jacob, hadn't kept his promise.

And she had been a fool to trust him.

At Nonhelema's request, Wolf-Alone was preparing to escort Cheramy and his mules away. The ripe scent of fresh droppings filled the damp night air.

Pippa, long since awakened in the cradleboard, started to cry. Jeremiah took Clare's hand to lead her back toward the creek and Cornstalk's Town.

She halted, balking as any mule. "Is no one going to explain any of this to me? I at least have things to say to you!"

Jeremiah never slowed his step; she was forced to move again or be dragged off her feet.

"We'll talk," he told her. "Or rather I'm going to talk and you're going to listen. But not here."

Inside the lodge, Clare waited in seething silence while Jeremiah fed the fire—surely for light rather than warmth, for the night was muggy and close. Methodically he laid stick after stick over the embers, watching them catch flame, until she could take it no more.

"Jeremiah?" Speaking his given name still felt awkward, but it was satisfying to say it through gritted teeth.

He didn't rise from his crouch. "Give me a moment, Clare."

Her gaze dropped to his hand as he placed the last stick on the flames. It was shaking. She glanced up in alarm, but if he was angry enough to tremble, his face didn't show it. His features were expressionless.

Too expressionless.

She wanted to clench her fists and scream. To blame someone for this night's failure. Only she didn't understand what had gone wrong or who to blame. Mr. Cheramy? Rain Crow? Jeremiah? Nonhelema? Herself for daring to hope again? The Almighty—for letting any of this happen in the first place?

Taking a sleeping Pippa from the cradleboard, Clare settled her on the bed platform, putting her back and the tears she couldn't stem to Jeremiah Ring. Wishing him to berate her and get it over with, if that's what he meant to do.

When he spoke at last, his voice was strained. "I'm going to tell you something about Cheramy, something you should know."

She felt the burn of his gaze on the back of her head. No longer certain she wanted to know, she asked, "What of him?"

Jeremiah spoke readily now, apparently having found the words he'd sought, or the self-control to speak them. "Not long after I came here—about a year after—Cheramy came to Cornstalk's Town for the first time. He was a young man then, generous with his goods. Generous in many ways. He quickly became a favorite, especially of the women."

Clare wiped her tears and forced herself to face Jeremiah, though she would rather he couldn't see her now.

"As is the way of the French," he went on, seeming to find no difficulty holding her glare, "Cheramy found himself a willing Shawnee girl and married her. But he didn't go away and leave her to remain with her kin, as is their usual practice. He claimed their marriage was more than a formation of kinship ties to aid his trade. He loved her and wanted her by his side. So she left Cornstalk's Town when his trade here was done—and none who knew her ever set eyes on her again."

Clare couldn't see what this had to do with Jacob, but she wasn't liking it at all.

"His young wife had died in Montreal, so Cheramy told her family when he came again to the Scioto towns. I don't recall what sickness he claimed, but such is common enough. The tale was taken as truth, and before he left, weeks later, Cheramy found himself another woman willing to marry him and, like the first, persuaded her to leave her family and travel back to Montreal. Months later Cheramy returned alone with another tale of tragic death. Childbirth, this time."

Jeremiah's gaze bore into her. "The mothers and fathers of those women began to suspect the man of lying, but how could it be proved? Their daughters might as well have gone to the moon when they left for Montreal."

Kneeling by the fire, hands balled on his thighs, his voice had grown more ragged as he spoke, the edges fraying.

"The third woman, Tall Doe, he didn't even marry but enticed her away with . . . whatever women see in such a man. Charm, I suppose."

Charm is deceitful. Clare's face burned hot with humiliation. Though it had been their fathers who arranged their union, Philip's charm had swept her off her feet when they first met. And for many months after.

"Tall Doe was the only child of Split-Moon and Red-Quill-Woman," Jeremiah was saying, gazing now into the fire. "They begged her not to go with Cheramy, fearing never to see her again. Of course that's exactly what happened."

Split-Moon and Red-Quill-Woman. The old Shawnee couple who had adopted Wildcat. The sinking in Clare's middle seemed a harbinger of worse to come.

"When Cheramy dared show his face in Cornstalk's Town without Tall Doe, Cornstalk himself turned him away. Though Cheramy protested his innocence, he was no more welcome to ply his trade and entice away their young women to sell as slaves in Montreal."

Clare could keep silent no longer. "Slaves? How could Cornstalk know that?"

Jeremiah turned to her, his long face fire-shadowed and bleak. "As I said, it cannot be proven, but Cheramy wouldn't be the first to do such a thing."

His words chilled her, yet they kindled outrage. "Then how do the Shawnees justify what *they* do, stealing white children from their parents?"

Jeremiah stood, unruffled by her agitation. "Whether their ways are right or wrong, they're what we have to contend with. I just wanted you to know what sort of man you chose to put your trust in."

Clare stood too. "Whatever happened to those young women he led away, you don't think Mr. Cheramy meant *me* harm?"

"Clare . . . with or without Jacob, Cheramy would've taken you away this night and you'd have wound up in Montreal. Maybe he'd have kept you and rid himself of Pippa. At best—*best,* Clare—if Cheramy managed to procure Jacob through trade or purchase, he'd have held your son hostage until you repaid him many times what he paid to ransom him from the Shawnees. Had Wildcat not followed you at my request, seen you with that scoundrel, and told me of it . . ."

He stopped, the look of fear that crossed his eyes startling in its intensity. Then he looked away as if he couldn't bear the sight of her.

"Tell me this, then," she managed to force out on the wave of bitter regret this night had become. "Why didn't you let me go with him, even without Jacob? It would have relieved you of the trouble I've brought upon you. You could have been done with us. Free of it all."

His head jerked back as if she'd slapped him. His brows rose, then plunged over eyes that flashed as he faced her again.

"Clare. I— *You* . . ."

Now she'd done it. Angered him so thoroughly he couldn't even speak. Why had she even opened her mouth?

Pippa was stirring, not crying yet, but Clare seized the excuse and settled on the bed, turned her back and lay down with the baby to nurse. Behind her, Jeremiah was silent for so long she thought the conversation over, if not resolved. It wasn't quite.

"Had he taken you and Pippa, I'd have come after you with Falling Hawk and Wolf-Alone and any other warrior willing to follow me."

The hair on the back of her neck stood erect. "And if you'd found me?"

"Cheramy would have died. And I'd have brought you and Pippa home."

Home? She didn't know where *home* was anymore. It wasn't this place. This place was her prison.

Wildcat was outside the lodge the next morning. Ignoring him, Clare marched off toward the creek with empty waterskins, Pippa left in Jeremiah's care. The boy followed her on the path.

Dawn's light hadn't dispelled the night's crushing disappointment. She was appalled at the frightful risk she'd been willing to take for Jacob, shaken that what she'd thought a solid solution had turned out to be riddled as worm-eaten wood. Her feelings, especially toward Jeremiah, were a maelstrom. Humiliation, resentment, gratitude, frustration. What was she meant to do now, beyond kneeling on the stones of the creek filling the waterskins for another day?

And waiting.

She didn't believe in Purgatory, but if such a place existed, she suspected it felt like this. Trapped. Caged. Suffocating.

"Clare-wife?"

She dipped the skins without turning to look at Wildcat. Creek water rushed cool over her hands. "What?"

"I sorry you angry, but what Panther-Sees-Him say of that one, Cheramy, it true."

She rose and faced him, ignoring the curious stares of other women come to the creek to bathe or draw water.

"Does your spying extend to listening outside our lodge?"

The boy puzzled out her words, then vigorously shook his head. "He tell you? *I* know before of my sister I not know . . ."

He trailed off, brows puckered, at a loss to express himself.

Clare needed no explanation. Of course Wildcat knew the story of Tall Doe, his sister, though he'd never met her. He knew she'd been taken by Mr. Cheramy and in some manner mistreated. Did his sister live still, a slave, a wife by force? Or was she a prostitute long since dead of the profession?

The evil of it all.

She relented, having no strength left to be angry with anyone but herself, especially not this child. Who could say but that his part had been the saving of her and Pippa?

"I'm not angry with you," she said, fighting the sting of tears.

The boy looked at her, pained beyond his years, then nodded and went away, steps dragging.

The women glanced at her, then quickly away, as if they knew what she had tried to do. She hoped they didn't know. Surely there would be more than curious glances if they did.

She couldn't fathom these people. She didn't want to. Hateful, hateful people, to steal her son and keep him for their own, to rename him and remake him into their image. To drive her to such foolish desperation to undo it all.

Jacob would be waking up under Rain Crow's roof now. Had he already forgotten her? Was he calling Rain Crow *mother*?

Refusing to look at the women, she gazed hopelessly across the creek toward Nonhelema's town until her vision blurred. Then she dropped the waterskins and put her hands over her face, unable either to cross the creek or go back into the town among her enemies.

"Clare?"

Crosses-the-Path didn't stand back as Wildcat had done. She came and put her arms around Clare's waist and laid her head against Clare's back. Next Clare knew she was keening into the shoulder of one of the women she despised, weeping into long black hair that smelled of smoke and bear grease.

Crosses-the-Path, oblivious to the loathing rippling through the one she sought to comfort, crooned low in her throat and stroked the hair Clare hadn't bothered to braid.

Clare made no protest. She knew what she had to do. It would have to be Jeremiah's way or no way at all. From that moment she would be the most convincing Shawnee wife and sister and friend she could force herself to be.

She would die for Jacob. Lay down her life readily. She could die a little every hour, every day, could she not?

Mastering herself, she pulled back from the embrace, caught the searching gaze of Falling Hawk's wife, and forced herself to smile. Forced it all the way to her eyes.

20

Sometimes it seemed more livestock than men had assembled thus far at the spot christened Camp Union, where the Kanawha Trail met the Greenbrier River. Captain Alphus Litchfield and his company of thirty-seven able-bodied Augusta County men—ranging in age from a tenderfoot sixteen to a battle-hardened sixty—were among the first to arrive at the rendezvous for Governor Dunmore's Southern Army. Most of the company were familiar faces, neighbors or acquaintances from annual militia musters, with a handful gathered along the one hundred mile march they'd made from Staunton west into the mountains.

Other Augusta County captains had assembled with their men, but they still awaited most of them as well as their commanding officers.

Colonel Charles Lewis would command the Augusta County Regiment, and his brother, Colonel Andrew Lewis, the entire Southern Army. Dunmore himself planned to lead the northern division, assembling at Fort Pitt. The two divisions were to converge on the Ohio River at the mouth of the Kanawha, the Northern Army coming by water, the Southern along the Kanawha Trail, from thence to march as one into the Ohio country against the Shawnees.

Also assembled were a smattering of the Botetourt County Regiment companies, but of the Fincastle County companies Alphus could find no sign as he trudged through the hodgepodge of men sorting through supplies coming in by pack trains, chopping wood, raising tents, or tending the growing herds of cattle and horses.

He was keen to find a particular Fincastle company, the one James Harrod was purportedly raising; Daniel Boone had found Harrod at his settlement and given the warning to come in and fort up. That was all the news Alphus could unearth about the man.

The cattle filled the air with their bawling and Alphus's nose with their stink. They were intended to be driven down to the Ohio, feeding the army on the move. That wouldn't be a fast march, but Alphus was acquainted with the pace of armies, administratively and otherwise. Normally by now he'd have settled his soul in patience to endure the tedium of camp life, but he couldn't seem to quell his zeal to march.

He'd no eagerness to be killing Indians and no particular dislike of them, save when they brought harm to the innocent. But that sort of meanness came from individuals acting on their own baser impulses, not the designs of a whole race of people. No more than those who preyed indiscriminately on Indian lives represented every white man's notion of living peaceably on the frontier.

It was memory of that busted, abandoned wagon giving him no rest; he'd no better notion how to get word of Clare than finding James Harrod, who he prayed would bring his company in soon, eager to make safe the path to his chosen settlement.

Mayhaps Philip himself would be among their ranks and all this fret could be swept aside.

The sun was setting across the western ridges, bathing the clanging, thunking, cussing, bawling, whinnying, smoke-and-cow-scented camp in gold as Alphus left off watching the trail for late arrivals and made his way to his men. They were busy frying up their supper. It smelled of bacon.

His boots scattered grasshoppers through the weeds dotting the clearing where the army was convening as he came in sight of the oiled canvas shelters belonging to his men—and that solitary canvas strung off the ground between two trees. The sight still made him smile.

Geordie Reynolds, youngest of the company, had defended his hammock in the face of thirty-six incredulous stares and jibes about his thinking he'd joined His Majesty's Navy instead of Dunmore's Army.

The boy had claimed he couldn't catch a wink of sleep on the ground no matter what he did to pad his bedroll. "But I sleep like a tucked-up baby slung a few feet above it."

"Waking every hour bawling for hunger, ye mean?" Tom Woodbane had retorted, to the guffaws of the men and a blush from Geordie.

Eldest of the company and Alphus's lieutenant, Woodbane couldn't let a chance to rib the young'un pass, but everyone knew it for good-natured. Alphus had heard the promise Woodbane had made to Geordie's mother, a cousin of some degree, to bring the lad home alive, Geordie being his mother's youngest.

All in all, Alphus was pleased with the camaraderie grown among his men, the easy respect they afforded him as their captain. He was more than pleased by their marksmanship and—hammock aside—their fortitude on the march thus far.

He came unnoticed to the gathering, those doing the cooking and those waiting to eat it. Bacon it was, and proper biscuits to put with it, now they'd fresh stores of flour. He stood in the shadow of a nearby poplar, arms crossed. Woodbane, the watchful old scout, took note of him after a second or two but didn't call attention to his arrival as he listened to talk pertaining to news gleaned from camp.

"I'm telling you true," Ezra Baldwin was saying. Nigh thirty, white-blond as a young'un, the man nodded toward the encampment of a newly arrived company. "Heard it from one of the Botetourt fellas. There's more'n a few settlers stayed on their Kentucky claims despite the Indians raiding over the countryside."

"Better they come in," said another, watching the bacon sizzle in the pan. "Help put down the uprising, then go back to their cabins."

Baldwin bobbed his head. "What one man can't do, all us together can."

"And what would that be?" Woodbane inquired with the lift of a grizzled brow.

"Whoop every red scalawag from here to the Miami River, that's what. Send 'em west across the Mississippi."

"And if they whoop you back instead of turning tail and running west?"

Baldwin laughed at that. "When have they ever?"

Braddock's name came to mind, but Alphus's thoughts snagged on what began this line of talk. The stubbornness of certain settlers, refusing to budge off their land. Would Philip be of a mind to force Clare and the children to remain at Harrod's settlement, when Harrod himself had retreated east? Alphus feared he might be. Rarely could you tell Philip anything he didn't want to hear, no matter if you saw clear the cliff he was rushing toward and he didn't.

The conversation shifted; someone had heard from someone else that several companies of the Northern Army had already headed downriver to Wheeling Settlement.

"They planned a campaign up the Muskingum," the man—Baldwin again, in the know this evening and enjoying it—said with a barely contained grin. "Hear tell they've carried it out."

Alphus stepped forward into the brightening ring of firelight. "A campaign into Shawnee country already? Who's in command, Private?"

Baldwin straightened at the address. "Colonel by name of McDonald, sir.

Took four hundred up Captina Creek to the Muskingum, to some Shawnee towns up that way. They was some fighting, but the Indians fled, so they burned the towns and the cornfields and came on back down to the Ohio."

So it had begun.

Alphus didn't like to think on Clare and her family being taken from that wagon by Indian hands and carried off to some village across the Ohio—far better to imagine that scout leading them somewhere safe—but neither dared he dismiss it. Might she have been there on the Muskingum?

"You happen to know the names of those Indian towns?"

"Can't say I heard 'em all named," Baldwin replied, still basking in the company's attention. "Though I recall to mind Snaketown was one."

He paused, brightened, then added, "And another was called something like Wah-kah-toe-mee-kah."

21

The dancing to celebrate the summer's first corn harvest—the Green Corn Dance, Jeremiah called it—had begun at sundown the previous evening and had lasted deep into the night. Nearly everyone, including Clare, kept wakeful by the beating of drums, was red-eyed and wincing as they tended roasting pits and kettles the next morning.

Only Crosses-the-Path was bright-eyed as they gathered in her lodge to prepare more food to add to the mounds of corn, roasted or milky-fresh from the husk, the people would consume during the coming days. Confined to the lodge where Shawnee women spent their menstrual cycles, Crosses-the-Path had missed the first night's dancing.

Falling Hawk was sprawled asleep nearby, so they kept their voices low, his daughters muffling giggles as Clare made a show of being repulsed by what Crosses-the-Path was stirring into the kettle hung over the fire.

In truth her disgust wasn't merely to amuse the girls; she suspected their mother knew it though she didn't seem to mind. Crosses-the-Path enjoyed introducing Clare to her native foods and instructing her in their preparation, as well as the language barrier between them allowed. That barrier continued to shrink due to Crosses-the-Path's diligence in learning English, though Clare doubted words in any language could render appealing what was going into that kettle.

"Yellow jackets?" she'd said in disbelief upon identifying the little roasted brown things Crosses-the-Path's oldest daughter had prepared while her mother was sequestered in the women's lodge.

Her little sister snatched one from the heaping bowl before their mother could get them into the pot of seasoned broth, popping it into her mouth. Grinning while she chewed, the girl picked up another of the insects and held it out to Clare, who gazed with dismay at the repulsive offering nestled in the little palm.

Reminding herself she was making friendly with this family for Jacob's sake, Clare took the roasted yellow jacket, spoke the Shawnee word for thank you—*Niyaawe*—and put it in her mouth.

It crunched like a piece of chicken skin fried to a crisp. It had a little of that flavor too, with a slight nutty component. None of which overcame her repugnance, but she forced it down with a moue of distaste she tried to make look comical, as if she didn't really mean it.

The girls tittered. Crosses-the-Path hushed them, but it was too late. Across the lodge their father groaned and sat up on his sleeping bench.

Not only was Falling Hawk haggard from the night of dancing, he was still sporting the evidence of having been the one to procure the ground-dwelling yellow jackets. Yesterday morning he'd come home triumphant with the night-dormant hive, reeking of the smoke he'd used to procure it and spotted with welted stings. He'd put the hive on a heated stone at the fire's edge and parched it. The girls had removed the dead insects and fried them in grease.

Returned that morning from the women's lodge, Crosses-the-Path had dressed his welts with wet tobacco leaves, even though he'd danced half the night away with the stings untended. Now he sat blinking at them, face, neck, arms, and chest spotted brown as well as red. Seeing them staring, he grinned. Clumps of dried tobacco fell from his face.

Finding this sight hilarious, his daughters laughed loud enough to startle Pippa awake.

Clare welcomed the distraction; Falling Hawk's presence was a keen reminder of what happened the previous evening, the other reason she'd managed little sleep.

Wolf-Alone and Jeremiah had gone to the dance, the latter assuring her he wouldn't stay long. Having the lodge to herself, she'd decided to bathe, including her hair. Despite the drumming already begun, she'd gotten Pippa to sleep. Leaving the baby hedged with rolled furs and blankets, she'd hurried out to fetch water, taking the largest kettle she thought she could manage to haul back full from the creek. The sun had vanished over the horizon. Ribbons of orange fading to purple streaked the sky above the town. Shadows stretched among the lodges.

She knew this was a time of celebration for these people; still the deep rhythmic thrumming of the drums and the shaking of gourd rattles, the stomping of feet and the shrill voices of the singers, combined to unnerve her. She didn't linger at the creek. She'd reached the darkened edge of town with her heavy kettle when Falling Hawk stepped abruptly across her path.

"I hab here my sister wish talk wid oo," he said, face distorted by swelling, including his upper lip, which had impeded his speech.

She'd caught one word: *sister*.

Arms weak, Clare bent to set the kettle on the path outside the deserted lodge where Falling Hawk had stopped her. By the time she straightened, he'd stepped back. In his place stood Rain Crow.

Even in the twilight Clare could see the woman was as striking as she remembered, but there was too much bone in her face, too little flesh. Rain Crow was painfully thin, all but swallowed in a beribboned blouse belted over a deerskin skirt that looked as soft as butter. Twin spots of red, some sort of dye, colored her cheekbones. Clare didn't know what the spots signified but felt the heat in her own cheeks burning up to match them.

Rain Crow broke the drum-filled silence. "I must say to you a thing before the dancing."

Her voice was as supple as her flowing hair, her English as flawless as her skin. Clare at once feared this was going to be about Mr. Cheramy and her attempt to steal Jacob back from her.

"Say what to me?" she asked, every nerve taut.

"Say to you that I forgive."

Rain Crow hadn't stuttered or hesitated. Her words were clear. Still Clare could hardly take them in. "Forgive? Who?"

"You." Rain Crow gave a nod, sharp and quick. "For your bad behavior when you tried to take my son from me. Both times."

Clare felt the wind go out of her, as sickening as a punch in the gut. With effort she kept from bending double. No matter that it was clear Rain Crow knew about the trader. She had said *her* son.

How dare this woman say such a thing?

Rain Crow flashed her a searching look and, apparently having said all she meant to say, hurried into the shadows where Falling Hawk awaited her, before Clare could recover enough to say anything at all.

Falling Hawk gave her a long look before turning to follow his sister toward the beating of drums.

Jeremiah found her in the lodge soon after, unwashed and weeping beside the kettle, which she'd had the presence of mind to carry back. Without speaking he knelt and wrapped his arms around her, as Crosses-the-Path had done that day at the creek. She was too overcome with misery to care. It felt good to have a man's shoulder to cry against, to feel strong arms around her, never mind he wasn't truly her husband. Never mind there was nothing he could do to heal her heart.

"Rain Crow is here," she said against his shirt.

"Aye. I saw her dancing."

She pulled back to look at him. "And Jacob? Did you see him?"

"I didn't." He took her by the shoulders and gazed into her face—a face likely as swollen as Falling Hawk's. But Jeremiah's eyes in the firelight were tender, not appraising. "What did she say to you?"

"That she forgave me." Clare choked the words out. "For how I acted when I saw Jacob, the day we arrived—and what I tried to do with Mr. Cheramy. 'Bad behavior' she called it."

"Ah," Jeremiah said, as if this made all the sense in the world.

She pulled away, making him drop his hands, and wiped beneath her nose with the back of her own. "Why would she say such a thing? You seem to know."

He rose to sit on the edge of her sleeping bench, careful not to disturb Pippa in her nest of blankets. "It's the Green Corn Dance. For Shawnees to take part in it, they must come with a right heart. A clean heart free of resentment, of grudges. My sister was trying to make her heart right."

"Make *her* heart right?" Despair was a pit, and she teetered on its edge. She went to the water she'd left unheated, scooped a handful, and splashed her face. "Didn't you tell me Rain Crow lived with the Moravians? What is she doing taking part in a heathen celebration?"

For that matter, what was Jeremiah doing taking part?

He stood, reached for her hand, and guided her to the table to sit. He did likewise. "This is my sister's first Green Corn Dance since returning from the town Reverend Zeisberger started a couple years back, the first one west of the Ohio."

"A couple years? Didn't you tell me she lived half her life with them?"

"She did. Her mother chose to follow Christ when Rain Crow was a girl. They left the Scioto to live in Pennsylvania at another Moravian town until

Zeisberger went west to start the new ones. Rain Crow and her mother went with him to Gnadenhutten. By then Rain Crow—she was called Abigail then—had married a Delaware Christian, Josiah."

Jeremiah paused, glanced at Pippa, then said, "I visited them there once, just after their son was born. My sister was happy, fervent in her love for the Almighty. Then sickness came and she lost both son and husband and now is but a shell of the sister I first met. What Falling Hawk did, bringing her a son—"

"My son," Clare cut in.

"In bringing her Jacob," he went on relentlessly. "It wasn't done out of malice. He did it out of love for our sister. To see her healed."

Bitterness burned in Clare's throat. "And I suppose she was—until I arrived and spoiled it all?"

"No," Jeremiah said flatly. "Not in the way she needs to be." He didn't expound on that but studied her soberly. "I'm telling you these things to help you understand why we need to be patient, to allow the Almighty to work. My sister is His. He will speak to her, in His way and time."

"But she came to the dance," Clare persisted. "If He should speak, what's to say she will listen?"

"I know her faith has faltered," Jeremiah said, "though I did think she might have stayed back from the dance tonight, stayed across the creek with most of those who came from the Muskingum towns."

He paused again, as if to allow Clare to reach her own understanding of why those he mentioned would have chosen not to take part in a celebration that required clearing one's heart of bad feeling toward others. She didn't have to reach far.

It was but ten days since Wakatomica and other towns on the Muskingum River had been attacked by Virginia militia. The soldiers—the Shawnees called them Long Knives—had skirmished with the warriors while the women and children fled. Finding the towns deserted, the Virginians burned them and the surrounding cornfields, then hurried back south to the Ohio. The Indians hadn't returned to their ruined homes. Some had taken refuge in the Scioto towns until Wakatomica could be rebuilt, likely someplace farther west.

Soon after, a prominent chieftain of the Senecas, Guyasuta, and the Delaware chief, White Eyes, came to Cornstalk's Town to urge the people not to take up the war hatchet against the Virginians, despite this invasion and loss. Many gathered in the council house to hear their words, but all knew it was too late for speaking them. Cornstalk had his scouts out. The Shawnees knew Governor Dunmore was mustering a larger army than the few hundred that had come up the Muskingum. What exactly he meant to do with this army, and when, remained to be seen; though Cornstalk and Nonhelema hoped to avoid a full-scale war, the present peace felt as fragile as a flower tossed on the edge of a blaze.

Clare suspected Jeremiah wanted to make the long trek to Fort Pitt, to speak with the Indian agents. Since he hadn't mentioned leaving the Scioto, she hadn't brought it up, afraid of what his answer would be.

Across the table she met his gaze. "Did everyone from the Muskingum towns stay away from the dance?"

Jeremiah shook his head. "I saw a few there."

Did that mean those few had found a way to forgive the Virginians for destroying their homes, their food for the coming winter, everything but what they'd managed to carry away when they fled? Some had lost husbands, sons, or brothers, for there had been casualties in the skirmishing.

The sound of drumming had faded to the edges of Clare's awareness while Jeremiah spoke of his sister. It swelled again now, an incessant thudding that grated on her nerves. It commanded her heartbeat fall into rhythm, as though it were the collective will of these people who'd taken her son, her life. She couldn't tell herself the drums had nothing to do with her, for she was there, among them, held fast by her own heart's tether. How long before the beating of celebration turned into the beating of war? Would it sound any different to her ears when it did?

Exhausted, she'd risen from the table. "I'm going to sleep."

But she hadn't. She'd lain awake into the night listening to the drums, rehearsing that encounter with Rain Crow, until Pippa woke and cried to be fed.

Later, as she trailed Crosses-the-Path's family and their kettle of noxious soup onto the council house yard, Pippa riding in a sling across her front, Clare scanned the crowd gathering at the communal baskets of roasted corn for one small, fair-haired figure.

This time Jacob spotted her first.

"Mama . . . Mama!"

She heard his urgent cry a second before his little body slammed into her side. Only Pippa in her sling kept Clare from hoisting him into her arms.

"Jacob!" She put her hands to her son's head as he tilted his face up to her, sun-browned and smiling. His hair, longer than she'd ever let it grow, was a shock of white-blond in contrast.

She was aware of searing this moment into her memory, certain it would be fleeting. And it was. Rain Crow's voice called out the Shawnee words Clare recognized now as *Many Sparrows*. She pretended she couldn't hear, but Jacob's smile faltered.

"Mama, why I'm not with you? Why don't my other mama let me see you?"

Other mama. The words were a knife in her heart.

"Many Sparrows!"

Clare wrenched her head up and saw not only Rain Crow advancing on her but Jeremiah and Wolf-Alone. Crosses-the-Path looked apprehensively over her soup kettle. And there came Falling Hawk as well, hurrying toward them.

Before anyone could reach her, Clare removed her hands from Jacob and took a step back. Her mouth trembled as she fought for control.

"I hope to see more of you soon, Jacob."

Jacob's gaze dropped to Pippa in her sling. "Is that my brother?"

Her heart was breaking as she smiled. "This is your baby sister. Her name is Philippa Joan, but we're calling her Pippa."

Jeremiah's face had flashed through her mind when she spoke, but that wasn't right. That wasn't *we*. There was no *we*. A searing of grief for Philip caught her off guard.

"Pippa?" Jacob's face lit with interest. "Can I see her?"

It was all she could do not to kneel in the dirt and let him see his sister. But this wasn't the time or place. "She's sleeping now and—"

"Mama, let me ask you something," Jacob cut in. "Where's Papa?"

Her son gazed up at her, waiting for her answer. A stone lodged in her throat. She couldn't bring herself to tell him. Not now. "It's all right, Jacob. It's all right for you to be with Rain Crow for a while. I love you. I miss you."

Those last words nearly choked her.

"Many Sparrows, come to me!" Rain Crow had spoken the command in English this time; it couldn't be misunderstood.

"Love you, Mama," Jacob said and turned away.

Clare's heart swelled and soared and broke as her son scuffed across the trampled ground to Rain Crow, who waited for him. Though many voices hummed and laughter was going up, silence surrounded Jeremiah's troubled kin, tense and uncertain. Feeling their scrutiny, Clare stood straight under the weight, and when she was certain she would neither weep nor beg, turned to Jeremiah and smiled.

Her son knew who he was. He knew who she was to him. *"Love you, Mama."*

Of their little group, Falling Hawk moved first, striding after Rain Crow, calling to her. Rain Crow stopped to listen, clasping Jacob by the hand.

Clare shifted Pippa higher as the baby stirred awake. "What is he saying?"

Jeremiah was studying her. "He's asking our sister to sit with us at the feast."

While Falling Hawk spoke, Rain Crow looked at Clare, as if to discern whether this request had initiated with her, a ploy to be near Jacob.

Infused with a hope she tried not to show, Clare turned to Crosses-the-Path, offering to help carry the kettle, and from the corner of her eye caught Rain Crow's change of posture, her nod of acquiescence.

The feasting had abated. In the west, across the Scioto, thunderclouds piled, but thus far the sun still shown down on this first day of celebration.

Clare held Pippa as the day's sticky heat cooled and the first rumble of that distant storm trembled the air. They stood at the edge of a field where men and women were playing a rough-and-tumble game that centered around possession of a ball the size of a large melon, made of deerskin stuffed with grass, weighted with a stone at its center.

The players were divided into teams. At the moment, one team was attempting to put the ball through posts at the far end of the field—as best Clare could see craning around other watchers crowding the sidelines, chattering and shouting at the players—while the other team tried to prevent them. There was a great deal of shoving, jostling, and falling, so it was difficult to be sure, but she'd noted how the teams were set apart because members of one wore red cloth bands tied around their upper arms, while the other team wore none. Score was kept on the sidelines with small sticks driven into the ground; since Wildcat had assumed that job and was in too much earnest about it to be distracted, it was left to Crosses-the-Path to explain the game.

"Oh!" Clare said as a woman on the field made a spectacular leaping catch of the ball, which had been kicked high in the air by a man on the opposing team. "She caught the ball with her hands, but the men are only kicking it."

Crosses-the-Path raised her hands, palms out. "Woman hand touch ball—good. Man—bad." She shook her head for emphasis. "Only man foot touch. What word you say?" She made a motion with her foot, barely missing Wildcat hunkered on the grass before them, oblivious to everything but the game unfolding.

"Kick," Clare said, and missed whatever happened to cause a collective groan to rise from half the onlookers.

Jeremiah, on the field with both his brothers, was on the ground but laughing, being hauled to his feet by Wolf-Alone, who played for the opposing team since his muscular arm was tied with a red band. Jeremiah wore no band. He also wore no shirt, leggings, or moccasins. Nothing but a breechclout, just like the warriors and even the women taking part in the game. No one seemed the least concerned about that, so she was trying not to be either, but whenever a group of them went down in a tangle of limbs, she felt a searing heat in her cheeks. Especially when it was Jeremiah.

She had never seen him take part in a game like this before. It surprised her that he was often in the thick of things, his lean frame remarkably agile as he ran and dodged and kicked the ball to Falling Hawk or another member of his team.

Watching him, Clare thought back to something he'd said to her at the feast. At some point he'd noticed she'd barely touched the mounds of roasted corn before them.

"Clare," he'd said softly while those around them chattered and ate. "Are you all right?"

She had thought she'd been doing a passable imitation of it.

The Indians around her were consuming prodigious amounts of food.

These people knew times of hunger, she'd come to understand, though even when food was plentiful they tended to eat in moderation, each family sharing what they didn't need rather than hoarding it. But this excess . . . she could never hope to match it, having no appetite at all.

She hadn't lifted her head from Pippa. The baby wasn't fussing, but keeping her head down meant she wouldn't have to see Rain Crow and Jacob across from her. She'd thought she was ready to endure anything for another glimpse of Jacob—and she'd had so much more than a glimpse—but seeing him fed and mothered by another woman was agony.

"I'm fine," she'd said, not fooling him for an instant.

"Trust the Almighty, Clare. He'll work this out for good in the end."

She'd looked at him in time to see the expression in his eyes, seeming at odds with his words. A look of pain. Blinking back tears of despair, she'd murmured, "Was I deemed unfit to raise him?"

Jeremiah had reached for Pippa in order to lean in closer. "I didn't hear you."

She'd let him take the baby, watched him plant chubby feet on his lap, supporting Pippa between his strong hands. "Does God not want me to be his mother?"

She'd glanced up in time to see Rain Crow pop a bite of cooked squash into Jacob's mouth, see him make a face, then reluctantly chew and swallow. Jacob hated squash.

"Trust Him, Clare. A moment at a time."

"I cannot."

Jeremiah had leaned sideways until their shoulders touched. "Looks to me like you are."

There'd been a tug on her sleeve—Crosses-the-Path's youngest daughter, grinning shyly. With Clare's lap free of Pippa, the girl had claimed it for herself, climbing up to nestle against the empty sling. Clare's arms had come around the girl, who was nearly Jacob's size.

Separated from her by only a pile of corn ears and drifts of shed husks, Jacob had noticed. He'd glared at the girl. Rain Crow tried to distract him with more food, but Jacob was stuffed full and couldn't be enticed.

Clare hadn't known if she should put the child away from her. Crosses-the-Path had gone to talk with other women and wasn't there to intervene.

Rain Crow had decided the issue. She'd taken Jacob by the hand, rose, and led him to a group of boys his age playing a game with throwing sticks. The boys welcomed him, and he was soon engaged in their game.

He seemed so at ease among these Indians.

Clare had summoned the memory of their exchange before the feast. He'd wanted to see his sister. He'd asked after his father. *"Love you, Mama."* She'd clutched Jacob's words tight to her heart. He wasn't lost to her. Not in mind or in heart. Not yet.

The crowd at the edge of the playing field erupted in a roar, recalling her attention. Wildcat drove in a stick to mark a score, but Clare couldn't remember which group of pegs belonged to which team.

"Which side is winning?" she asked Crosses-the-Path, gesturing at the sticks. One side had three. The other two.

Crosses-the-Path frowned. "Side?"

Was there a Shawnee word for *team*? "With armbands or without?"

Falling Hawk's wife stared blankly, then looked beyond Clare, who turned, startled, to find none other than Rain Crow beside her.

"It is Panther-Sees-Him's team that made the score. They are winning. You were watching. You could not tell?"

Thunder rumbled, distant still, on the heels of Rain Crow's words. Clare was thunderstruck to find the woman standing there talking to her, as if she'd been any other woman asking the question. She forced herself not to look for Jacob.

"Is there a prize for the winning team?"

"The losing team gathers firewood for winners." Rain Crow's attention shifted back to the game. Without taking her gaze from the players on the field, she said, "My husband played this game when young, before he listened to the Moravians. Before he left his Delaware people."

Josiah, who had died among the Moravians and the Indians who lived with them. Along with their baby. Did Rain Crow know she knew this?

"It's hard," Clare said. "Hard to trust when a husband is taken. And a child. Even if . . ."

She didn't know what she was trying to say. This was the woman who had custody of the child in question. Her child.

She saw acknowledgment of this in Rain Crow's guarded eyes.

On the field another score was made, to judge by the cheers and groans of onlookers. Clare saw a tangle of men and women getting up off the ground, some being congratulated. Jeremiah was again in the midst of them. Falling Hawk slapped him on the back as he got to his feet.

"It is over." Rain Crow said. "Your man has won it for his team. Wolf-Alone will gather wood for you this night."

Wildcat sprang up and hurried onto the field to meet Wolf-Alone coming in. The boy seemed about to make a gesture of consolation, but the big warrior laughed and squeezed his shoulder, making light of his team's loss.

"Clare!" Jeremiah was still on the field, warriors around him, but he was looking at her, his smile a blaze of triumph, his usually sober face animated, gleaming in the light of a westering sun moments away from dipping behind the rising storm clouds.

The look of him captured her gaze, and she felt herself returning his smile, for a moment forgetting who stood beside her. Then she glanced sidelong.

In the seconds her attention had been caught by Jeremiah, Rain Crow had melted away into the crowd dispersing back into the town.

22

A drizzling rain settled in for the remaining days of the Green Corn Dance. On the final soggy day as the moisture at last drifted eastward, Rain Crow moved her lodge to Cornstalk's Town.

"She didn't tell me she meant to do so," Jeremiah said hoarsely from his pallet of furs. Suffering a summer ague since the previous day, he was resting at Clare's urging, though she suspected he'd be up and about as soon as she left the lodge.

She turned to Wolf-Alone, tending the fire, and asked in her halting Shawnee, "Sister tell you?"

Wolf-Alone shook his head, said something brief to Jeremiah in which Clare recognized the names of Wildcat and Falling Hawk.

"Apparently," Jeremiah said at her questioning look, "Wildcat's the one in the know this time."

Wildcat had come to them the previous evening babbling that Rain Crow and Jacob had left Nonhelema's Town, crossed the creek with all their things on the back of a borrowed horse, and were setting up a lodge near Falling Hawk's.

Clare hadn't rushed straight out to see for herself, having already made plans to visit Crosses-the-Path the following day; still she'd slept little for relief and eagerness. And curiosity. She and Rain Crow had barely spoken after their conversation on the sidelines of the game. The next day Rain Crow had gone back across Scippo Creek, taking Jacob with her.

"I've my suspicions as to why," Jeremiah said, the words followed by a coughing bout.

Clare frowned as she settled Pippa in her cradleboard and propped it against the lodge wall to lace it up, as Wolf-Alone rose from the fire and made ready to leave as well. He was going hunting with Wildcat, who was making sure Split-Moon had all he needed for the days the boy and Wolf-Alone would be away.

"It's to do with you," Jeremiah said once the coughing passed. "How you conducted yourself during the Green Corn Dance. You did well, Clare. You put everyone at ease."

Jeremiah didn't say "I told you so." He didn't look as though he was even thinking it. Clare appreciated that.

Finished with the cradleboard, she flashed a look of appeal at Wolf-Alone, who came and helped her don the contraption.

"Like you're doing today," Jeremiah added, nodding at the small, tightly woven basket she'd picked up. It held dried currants. "Being friendly with Crosses-the-Path. Falling Hawk says she enjoys your company."

Clare was surprised how much it pleased her to hear it. "I like spending time with her too. And her girls."

Though she'd eaten little during the feasting, she'd sampled something she'd liked, cornmeal cakes sweetened with dried fruit and maple sugar. They were the nearest thing to a proper tea cake she'd had in months. Crosses-the-Path had offered to show her how to make them, and she was looking forward to it . . . until she remembered. This friendship was a facade, with one end in mind—creating sympathy for herself and her desire to regain Jacob in the minds of the people holding him captive.

There was no more to it than that, she reminded herself.

At the door-hide she looked back at Jeremiah lying in his bed furs. She'd fixed him a bowl of broth and a tea of herbs Crosses-the-Path said would be good for his cough and slight fever. Both sat beside him on a rush mat, untouched.

"You'll be all right on your own?"

Catching a half-concealed grin from Wolf-Alone, Clare blushed. She'd sounded like a wife certain her husband hadn't the sense to take care of himself in her absence.

"I'll be fine," Jeremiah assured her with a grin. "Likely I'll sleep—once you both clear out and give me a little peace and quiet."

With his back to Jeremiah, Wolf-Alone rolled his eyes and went about his packing.

Marginally reassured, Clare went out into the town.

Split-Moon and Wildcat were coming along the path from the creek, each carrying armfuls of firewood. Split-Moon stumbled and dropped a portion of his burden. Clare, spotting them, hurried to their aid.

"Let me get those for you." She gathered the sticks, but didn't give them back to the old man. To Wildcat she said, "I'll carry these back to your lodge for you. I think Wolf-Alone is nearly ready to go."

The color in Wildcat's sun-browned face deepened as he responded—not with the fluency of which she knew him capable. "It good, Clare-wife. *Wesah*."

Returning Split-Moon's curious gaze—the man had little English, as far as she knew—she trailed them through the village to their lodge. Split-Moon set down his load outside the trade blanket that hung across the doorway and motioned her to give him what she'd carried.

She handed him the smaller bundle. He nodded his thanks.

She supposed she'd have left them then had not Wolf-Alone appeared from around a nearby lodge, stopped at sight of her, then raised a hand in greeting to Split-Moon and called to Wildcat.

Face lighting with eagerness, the boy darted into the lodge. He was back out seconds later with bow and quiver, a hide bag and rolled blanket slung across his chest. He spoke a farewell to his father and raced off to follow Wolf-Alone on their hunting foray.

Clare caught the old man's expression as he looked after his adopted son. Sadness curved the lines of his face. And loneliness? Wildcat was the only family he had since the loss of his daughter and the death of his wife.

Did the old man still think of Tall Doe? Still wonder at her fate?

Would *she* ever stop thinking of Jacob?

Sorrow for the man wrenched her heart. For the first time she was glad he had Wildcat to console him.

"I wish we could speak of these things, Grandfather," she said, using the term of respect Shawnees showed to older men. "I wish we had the words. Perhaps you would have some wisdom for me."

Split-Moon gazed at her, frowning, and Clare sighed at the language barrier. Then, brightening with a notion, she smiled at the old man staring at her with puzzled eyes.

"But I'm going to come back and see you later, and I'll have something for your supper, if all goes well."

It went very well. The cakes turned out so scrumptious that it wasn't easy to set a few aside, wrapped in cornhusks, to take to Split-Moon as she'd promised. Accompanied by a tea Crosses-the-Path steeped with her favorite herbs, mint foremost among them, the coos and gurgles and occasional laughs of a contentedly fed Pippa, and the giggles of two little girls vying to amuse the baby, it felt like a continuation of the Green Corn celebration.

Perhaps drawn by their laughter or the smell of baking, Rain Crow pushed aside the door-hide of her brother's lodge as they were diving into second helpings.

Crosses-the-Path waved her in with a glance at Clare, who looked immediately for Jacob. Her heart gave a leap when she saw him, but Rain Crow grasped his shoulder and spoke to him.

Clare didn't need to know the Shawnee words to recognize a mother telling her child to stay outside and play. With a look at Clare, in which she read confusion, then resignation, Jacob obeyed.

Disappointment. Envy. Rage. Clare's heart burned with such feelings and more, but she was smiling when Rain Crow let the hide fall shut behind her and sat with them by the dying fire to share in cakes and tea. At first she spoke little, but she seemed interested in Pippa, peering often at the baby nestled between the girls' knees, resting on her tummy but pushed up on her arms to look around. Biting back reluctance, Clare asked, "Would you like to hold her?"

Crosses-the-Path went still at her words. So did Rain Crow, who looked at her in open surprise.

"Yes," she said.

Crosses-the-Path's oldest daughter picked up the baby with practiced ease and brought her to Rain Crow, who held her against a shoulder until Pippa squirmed to see the rest of them. Rain Crow turned her and planted her little bottom on her lap.

It was all Clare could do not to snatch her baby from those hands that had pushed her son out the lodge door. She schooled her face as Rain Crow met her gaze.

"I saw you before, with Little-Cat-That-Scratches and his father, carrying the wood for them."

It took a moment for Clare to recall that other way of saying Wildcat's name.

There had been a question implicit in the words. Did Rain Crow think she was drawn to the boy because he was another adopted white? That was true enough. But today it had been Split-Moon's daughter on her mind. She hadn't been able to ask the old man about her, but she still had questions—some of them about Mr. Cheramy, questions she'd never brought up to Jeremiah again. Could Rain Crow know more about him, more than Jeremiah had shared?

"It's sad what happened to Split-Moon's daughter, Tall Doe, making it so he and his wife felt the need to . . . take another to be their child."

Crosses-the-Path hadn't grasped her words that time. Rain Crow noticed this and spoke to her in Shawnee. The women exchanged a look that left Clare puzzled.

"Is it really true, what they say Mr. Cheramy did to those young women he married? And to Tall Doe? Did he really sell them as slaves in Montreal?"

Again Rain Crow translated her words. The silence that followed grew ever more awkward, as if both women debated how to respond, or whether to respond at all.

Clare knew she'd taken a risk in mentioning the trader, but Rain Crow didn't appear angry or suspicious. Only cautious. Still she feared she had blundered, though in what way exactly she couldn't be certain.

What was wrong with her? Every time she gained a little ground with Rain Crow, earned a modicum of acceptance, she did or said something to lose it again.

"That much bad time," Crosses-the-Path said at last. "After other daughter die."

Though her tone had been polite, her expression had communicated censure, as though Clare had erred in mentioning not Mr. Cheramy but Tall Doe. But now her curiosity was too greatly aroused to keep silent.

"Other daughter? Split-Moon and his wife had two daughters? Jeremiah told me they had only the one; that's why they wanted Wildcat."

She'd spoken in English again, but Crosses-the-Path seemed to understand the gist of what she was asking. "Panther-Sees-Him not say you his woman?"

"I don't understand." Clare looked to Rain Crow, whose eyes flashed over Pippa's head at Crosses-the-Path with something close to reprimand, then with resignation she met Clare's questioning gaze.

"Of all these dead ones my people do not speak. But I will tell you some of it because you do not know our ways and maybe . . . maybe it is good you know of it.

"Before Little-Cat-That-Scratches came to be their son," she went on, "Split-Moon and Red-Quill-Woman adopted the one who was wife of Panther-Sees-Him. This was when Tall Doe was maybe nine summers, still a girl, and not a strong one. Little and slight like her mother, Red-Quill-Woman. They wanted an older girl, stronger, to help cook, help work. Hannah came with the promise of a baby to come. That was welcome too."

Clare gaped at the woman holding her daughter, trying to make sense of what she'd said.

"Jeremiah had a *wife*? A Shawnee wife? But no, you said . . ."

Hannah. Hannah . . . Ring?

Somewhere beneath the shock of it all, bells were ringing in her memory. And the half-forgotten name of *Bloom.*

Crosses-the-Path looked blankly at her, but Rain Crow was staring, understanding dawning on her face.

"He did not tell you about her? It is painful for him. And for Falling Hawk because Panther-Sees-Him betrayed him and his Shawnee people. For Hannah."

Rain Crow's words only added layers to Clare's confusion. "Jeremiah betrayed Falling Hawk?"

Rain Crow held Pippa out to her. Clare took her daughter but didn't take her eyes off the other woman, who stood and brushed down her skirt.

"Maybe you should know this. But it is not for us to tell you, that is what I think now. Ask Panther-Sees-Him to know. I am going."

She went, leaving Clare and Crosses-the-Path and three little girls sitting in silence.

Split-Moon wasn't at his lodge, so Clare left the cakes wrapped in cornhusks beside his hearth. When she reached Jeremiah's lodge, he was still lying where she'd last seen him, sound asleep. That surprised her. Was he feeling worse than he'd let on?

She'd been eager to get to him, to unleash the questions rising on her tongue like floodwaters. With equal parts frustration and concern, she realized she must hold that flood at bay, but as she stood over him with Pippa still in the cradleboard on her back, the memory she'd been trying to capture since hearing the name *Hannah* in connection with his burst into clarity.

She knew this man—or knew of him—had known of him long before their meeting by the wagon on a mountain trail in the midst of her labor with Pippa.

Why had he never told her?

The need to know vied with the impulse to let him sleep, but between getting Pippa out of the cradleboard and settling her to nurse, the baby erupted in howls of hunger.

Jeremiah woke. Looking decidedly unwell but no longer fevered, he propped himself on an elbow. Clare put her back to him while Pippa nursed but could feel his gaze.

"Have a nice visit with Crosses-the-Path?" he asked, voice raspy.

"Yes. Until Rain Crow joined us. She said . . ."

"Something about Jacob?" he prompted when she hesitated.

"No. About you. And your wife."

Silence followed her reply. She turned to face Jeremiah, dragging up a corner of a blanket to cover herself.

"I know who you are, Jem Ringbloom."

23

Jem Ringbloom. He could almost see the name hanging between them, shimmering like the ghost of the man it had belonged to. It swelled and filled the wegiwa until the air for breathing was squeezed right out. Who had told her? Rain Crow? But his sister didn't know that name.

Then he remembered where she'd said she lived the past few years. In the Shenandoah, near Staunton.

He swallowed over a throat still raw. It was long past time to tell Clare his story, the whole of it, but he'd been waiting for her to *want* to know. He'd hoped interest, even care, would be what prompted the resurrection of that name and the life that went with it, after letting it lie like river-bottom silt for nigh on a decade.

The silt was stirring now, muddying the waters above.

"I haven't been that man for a long time."

"But you *are* him—Jem Ringbloom," she insisted. "You lived not five miles from Uncle Alphus's mill on Lewis Creek. You and your wife. I remember now. She was taken by Indians when she was . . ."

"About six months along with our first child," he finished when she hesitated.

Jeremiah sat up, rubbing hands over bristled cheeks. Back in Wheeling she'd mentioned an uncle called Alphus. A miller on Lewis Creek? His mind produced an image—a man around forty years then, weathered, hair salted gray. Not tall but tough as seasoned hickory. A former militia captain who'd fought with Braddock and Washington. He'd heard the man tell his stories.

Memory tossed up a surname. "Alphus Litchfield, the miller, was your uncle?"

"He's my father's younger brother," Clare said. "But we aren't talking about me now. What wouldn't Rain Crow tell me?"

He'd stalled long enough. "I doubt my sister knows the whole story of how I came to be Shawnee. She'd gone to live with the Moravians by then."

Clare watched his face, more intensely focused on him than he'd ever known her to be. "Will you tell me?"

"I'd meant to." He lay his head back and closed his eyes, finding it easier that way to untangle the memories. So many layers. So much easier to tell it as if he spoke of someone else.

"Once upon a time a young farmer lived down the road a piece from a gristmill belonging to your uncle," he said, and wondered why he wasn't more amazed at this long-ago connection between them. "The farmer had a wife, a baby on the way. One day he traveled to that mill to have his corn ground, and when he got back home found his wife gone, his cabin wrecked, out in the yard . . . tracks of moccasins leading off. He grabbed rifle, horse, what food was to hand, and set out to follow, hearing along the way that a raiding party of Shawnees had been through. That daunted him, certain sure, but he learned all he could and pressed on westward, following the Indian paths toward the Ohio—"

He paused as a fit of coughing overtook him. His lungs had a rattle, not bad but annoying. His throat felt like he'd swallowed sand.

Clare was frowning. "Jeremiah, I know you aren't well. If you'd like, I could wait."

He could tell she didn't want to do that. Nor did he. He cleared his throat. "I'd as soon get this out."

"Once Pippa settles I'll make tea."

"For which I'd thank you kindly. I'll keep talking, all right? I just got to pace myself."

"Take your time," she said, clearly impatient to have the tale in full.

He smiled a little at that. "That young farmer made it across the Alleghenies and the Ohio River and all the way up the Scioto to this place. By then, of course, he'd been taken prisoner himself. He'd been caught the second day out by some of the warriors who'd taken his wife—a few had remained behind to watch their back trail for pursuit. They'd surrounded him and his horse, and he'd surrendered, hadn't fought them, for he'd come to realize it was the only way he was going to find his wife—or survive, if they showed him such mercy. Desperate as he was, he was no frontiersman. He could never make it so deep into Indian country, find his wife, rescue her, lead her back to safety, without coming to harm. He'd have to share in her captivity, pray they didn't kill him, and hope for the chance to get near her."

While he spoke, Clare rose and lay the baby down. Almost instantly Pippa was asleep. Clare shifted her focus to the fire.

Watching her, in the back of Jeremiah's mind a good feeling was welling up, a contentment that strengthened him to go on telling how that young farmer was taken to Cornstalk's Town, but not in company with his wife, who arrived some days ahead of him. How, once he'd glimpsed his wife there, he'd managed to communicate his desire to live among the Shawnees at Cornstalk's Town. How he was made to run the gauntlet and earned a modicum of respect for surviving it. How soon after, with his wounds still healing and his fate still undecided, a warrior called Falling Hawk took him along on a hunting foray.

Returning to camp one evening, Falling Hawk had caught a panther creeping up on the farmer, sitting by the fire and unaware of being stalked. Falling Hawk had scared the panther off and, being one who enjoyed a good joke, been highly amused by it all. That was how the farmer got his name, given a few days later when Falling Hawk adopted him as a brother—so he could go on laughing at him, apparently.

"During this time the farmer's heart was being wrenched in two; he'd been forced to stand by, helpless to stop it, when his pregnant wife was adopted by a Shawnee couple who wanted another daughter."

"Split-Moon and Red-Quill-Woman," Clare said, now tending a boiling kettle of corn soup over the flames. "That much I know. But I'd wondered how you got that name."

Jeremiah managed a half-smile. "Not for anything noteworthy save my inattention. I like to think that wouldn't happen now."

"Hmm," she murmured, leaving him wondering did she mean something by it. When he couldn't catch her eye he picked up his tale again.

"The farmer never let on that Hannah was his wife, her child his. They'd yet to speak to one another, though he knew she'd seen him there in the town. He was much talked of, the hapless white man who wanted to be Shawnee. He'd had no firm plan in mind, aside from watching for a chance to get near Hannah. Time wasn't on their side. The baby was but a month away from being born, and the longer he waited, the less likely Hannah would be able to travel. But as chance would have it, they were provided the opportunity of escape a week after his adoption."

"How?" Clare interjected.

"She was beginning to be trusted, allowed to do simple tasks alone, such as draw water at the creek. The farmer was trusted like a brother and could go where he wished by then. He took advantage of that, of the kindness and trust of his new brother, stashing a hatchet, a blanket, other items of use, in a hollow log a mile upstream along the creek. Of course when the moment came, one morning before dawn, they had to leave with next to nothing, save a desperation greater than their wisdom. Still they made it a fair ways before . . ."

Jeremiah paused, watching Clare move from the kettle to the cup of tea now steeping on a stone at the fire's edge. "Before?"

"The baby came two days out from Cornstalk's Town," he said. "Though the farmer did what he could, his wife and newborn son . . . they both died."

Clare had stilled, letting the soup bubble, the tea steam, the fire crackle on. She stared at him, absorbing the stark words.

"Jeremiah . . . I'm sorry." Comprehension filled her gaze. "That day at the wagon, when you found me . . . ?"

"I was plumb terrified. I knew the worst that could happen."

"But you faced it. One or both of us might well have died if you hadn't."

"There was no choice, Clare. I couldn't have left you. The Almighty lent me the courage I needed. And I'm thankful."

"You are?" she asked, as if he couldn't possibly mean it.

He held her gaze. "Of course I am."

She was the first to look away. "What happened then?"

"Falling Hawk and a few other warriors came after us. Found me sitting by the bodies, still stained with blood. He took us back, and I didn't resist. Hannah and the baby were buried in their custom."

He was no longer speaking as if of another, but Clare didn't seem to notice the change. She'd risen and brought him the tea, which he took, warm in his hands, and sipped.

It hurt going down, but the honey was sweet.

"I don't recall this next part well. I mind telling Falling Hawk the truth, that Hannah had been my wife, her child mine. I'd come among them to take her back. No other reason. He was furious, hurt, but he let Split-Moon decide my fate since Hannah was his daughter. I think they'd come to love her, those two, for the short time they had her."

He told this part as quickly as he could. How Split-Moon hadn't believed

Jeremiah's taking his daughter away was the cause of her death. It would have happened no matter where she was at the time. He told Falling Hawk what he wanted done with Jeremiah. *"Send him away. If he comes back, he is Panther-Sees-Him, a Shawnee, and a brother. If not, he is a Long Knife and an enemy of no matter and no name. Then if we see him again we will kill him."*

"They let me decide," Jeremiah said, still feeling an echo of the amazement he'd felt then, not quite dulled by shock and grief. "I left and wandered eastward, hardly caring where I aimed. I was ready to wander till death found me and I could go be with Hannah, our son. That might've been how the story of Jem Ringbloom ended had Logan not stumbled across me. Literally, I mean. But this part you maybe don't want to hear?"

Clare's gaze had sharpened at mention of her husband's murderer; a crease formed between her brows, but she said, "You once told me Logan was your friend. I want to know why."

So he told her.

Weakened from hunger, exposure—it was late November with winter closing in—he'd laid himself down on a thread of a path, somewhere east of the Muskingum River, deciding that was far enough. He was done. Buckskins covered in frost, he'd appeared to Logan and his hunters like a rock lying across the trail. Logan, in the van, stepped on him as one would a rock.

"He felt the give of flesh beneath his foot and went down in a tangle with the warrior coming behind him. Both fell atop me."

He smiled faintly, again not really remembering that part. Logan had told him of it later, once he had Jeremiah carried to his hunting camp, warmed and fed and forced to go on living.

Logan had saved his life, but more than that. He'd taken Jeremiah back to his lodge, given him a place to heal, a space of time to think, many nights of talking and listening and smoking around the fire, when certainly the man had more pressing matters to attend to with winter coming and kin to provide for.

But he'd never once made Jeremiah feel there was anything more important than listening to his rambling on about his losses, his pain, his path.

In the end Jeremiah had known he didn't want to go back to his old life in Virginia. Not without Hannah and their child.

"But I had another place, another people, if my heart was big enough to embrace them, accept them. Forgive them. Logan helped me see that; he'd already suffered losses at the hands of whites and yet he remained committed to friendship between our peoples."

Ironic, given the turn things had taken back in spring. And tragic. But back then Jeremiah had taken Logan's example to heart. He'd chosen forgiveness and, in returning, accepted it from Falling Hawk.

For a while, the first year especially, he'd made that choice to forgive many times. Eventually he'd learned to appreciate the Shawnees' way of life, to see their strengths as a people. Their devotion to family. Their generosity. Their fierce loyalty. Their ability to live off the land without overburdening it. Their love for and deep connection to that land.

Not long after, he began to meet the traders who crossed the frontier, from Pittsburgh and points east. They told him how he could be useful to the Indian agents at Fort Pitt. If he wanted to be.

He made the journey back east his second summer living as a Shawnee, told his story in brief, and before he left Pittsburgh had offered his services as an interpreter, guide, and message bearer when needed.

He'd given his name as Jeremiah Ring.

"And that's how our paths came to cross," he said, ending his story at last. "Yet I've never believed any of it was happenstance. I knew the Almighty was guiding things. It's just . . . we don't always see the path clear, much less any other path that crosses it or runs alongside it for a time. We don't get the eagle's view. Sometimes we look around and it's like being hemmed by a thicket of thorns. But it's there."

He longed to lay back and rest now but waited. Clare had set a bowl of corn soup down by him and taken her own to the low table, but hadn't touched it yet.

"What is there?" she asked.

"The way forward. It'll be shown us."

Talking had wearied him, but telling her of Hannah hadn't hurt as deeply as he'd expected it to. He felt ready to lay down the past, leave it there, and move on. If Clare and Pippa—Jacob too, God willing—would be there for him to carry instead.

Though he was long in coming to this place of healing, of looking ahead in the way of the heart, it would be foolish to expect Clare to have arrived with him. She was still in the midst of her turmoil as he'd been so long ago. Yet for the first time since Hannah's death, he yearned to be a covering for a woman. To protect her. Provide for her. Let her into his heart as far as she wanted to come.

Philip Inglesby had broken her trust. Circumstances had tested her faith nigh to its breaking point. Would she ever find it in her to trust a man again? Or for that matter, the Almighty?

24

Clare knew it was inevitable if she remained among the Shawnees long enough, but she hadn't expected it so soon; two days after sharing tea and cakes with Crosses-the-Path, it became necessary for her to spend time in the women's lodge, sequestered with those waiting out the days of their monthly courses. She'd no choice in the matter. No woman was allowed to be near men or come in contact with their possessions during this time. It didn't matter that she wasn't Shawnee. The women would force her to comply with their custom, Jeremiah had warned her, else the warriors would be incensed.

Though she didn't know any of the women present when she arrived, and none spoke English, having brought Pippa into the lodge with her seemed all the bridge needed to span the language chasm. From the youngest to the oldest, each wanted to coo over Pippa. Those few who had nursing babies found it amusing to place the naked little ones side by side to compare their looks.

Clare indulged their curiosity, until toward evening when Pippa became fretful.

Shifting the baby from shoulder to shoulder, Clare paced the crowded lodge, trying not to infringe upon another woman's space. Pippa's crying kept many wakeful, for which Clare apologized repeatedly, having learned those Shawnee words early on. The women lifted weary heads in the firelight or grumbled and turned over in their furs, no longer charmed by the fussy white infant.

Clare thought of Jacob through the wakeful hours, but now her mind was nearly as filled with thoughts of Jeremiah. Her heart was heavy for all he'd endured, the grief and guilt he'd lived with—though he hadn't expressed the latter, she sensed he carried that weight.

The night passed with little sleep for anyone. In the morning the door-hide was moved aside as several of the women left and a new one entered—Rain Crow.

By then Clare was fraught with exhaustion and rising apprehension, and Pippa was flushed with fever.

"She's got whatever Jeremiah had." Though still plagued by that rattling cough, Jeremiah had been up and about when Clare left for the women's lodge.

"Panther-Sees-Him is well," Rain Crow informed her, having spread her bedding on a nearby sleeping bench. "Your baby will come through too. She is white."

The words seemed unsympathetic, until Clare recalled having heard that Indians died more easily than whites of some sicknesses. Rain Crow likely meant it as a simple statement of fact. But Pippa was so tiny. As the day passed, Clare hovered over her baby, ignoring the women who chatted or sewed or tended the communal kettle of corn soup. Pippa wouldn't nurse for more than a moment before breaking off to cry pitiably. By the end of that second day, her fever hadn't broken and there was a rattle in her chest when she breathed.

"We must do something," Clare said to no one in particular. "I should leave."

"Do you bleed still?"

She looked up to find Rain Crow at her side. "Yes, but—"

"Then you must not leave." Rain Crow turned to talk with several women nearby.

"What are you saying?"

Rain Crow ignored her until the conversation concluded.

"We talk of what to do. That one," she said, nodding toward a young woman who, her time there ended, was gathering up her belongings. "She will bring what is needed."

"Medicine?"

"You will see."

Clare ground her teeth in frustration. Pippa awakened, and she picked her up, a hot, whimpering bundle. She knew she needed to pray but feared the Almighty wouldn't wish to hear from her after holding Him at arm's length for so long.

Desperation won out over shame. *If You really do care about sparrows, then surely my baby means something to You. Please make her well.* Clare shot glances at the women who watched her. *And keep these women from doing anything that's going to make Pippa worse.*

Feeling trapped and at their mercy, she trembled with fatigue and dread for whatever they had planned.

She hadn't long to wait.

Voices outside the door-hide heralded the arrival of several women, among them Crosses-the-Path, bearing a steaming tin cup.

"This fever tea." With Rain Crow's help, Crosses-the-Path communicated that Clare should get Pippa to swallow as much of the cup's contents as she could. Even a few mouthfuls would help.

"Willow bark," Rain Crow said, sniffing it. "With maple sugar, I think."

Clare nodded, her own pounding head in need of such a tea, as other women came in and out of the lodge, carrying smooth river stones. They took them to the fire and lay them in the embers. Others brought woven mats, which they unrolled and spread against the bark walls above the sleeping benches, sealing any cracks. Still others had water in skins.

Crosses-the-Path had carried in a tight-woven basket. It held water too, but she didn't put it near the fire as the rest of the women were doing. She poked a finger into the water and said, "Cold. You put on baby?"

She produced a wad of cloths and made motions of submerging them in the water.

Rain Crow joined them. "She fetched that from a spring. It will stay cold longer. Soak those pads and put them on your daughter to cool her fever. She will not like it, but do it. Then steam will help her here." Rain Crow put a hand to her chest.

"Steam?"

"We are making this a sweat lodge for your baby. Everyone agrees it is best for the breathing to clear."

Clare had heard of sweat lodges but had thought they were a thing men used—for ceremony. "Will that work?"

Rain Crow offered no reassurance. "We will see."

Clare had given up trying to stem the tide of sweat making runnels down her face and neck, soaking her shirt until it clung like a second skin. The warmth of the lodge was stupefying. So far it didn't seem to be helping Pippa; her fever had broken after applying the cooling compresses, but her little chest still rattled with labored breathing.

The women endured the discomfort with diplomatic fortitude. A few, stripped to their skirts, had stayed awake into the night to heat stones or pour water over them to create the steam. Once they'd gotten the steam going, Clare had slept from sheer exhaustion, while Rain Crow watched over Pippa, but between the heat and worry she'd soon awakened.

Two other women were awake, one still in her teens, the other older than Clare by a few years. That one was minding the steam but also rocking where she sat and murmuring to herself, a sound like the distant drone of bees.

"What is she saying?" A portion of the fire still burned for the heating of their food and the stones, but it had sunk to embers. The smoke-hole in the bark roof above was covered. Clare could just make out Rain Crow's features as the woman turned to her.

"She prays for your daughter's life."

Clare blinked, sweat stinging her eyes, making the dim figures around her swim. "Prays to whom?"

"The Great Spirit—Moneto." Rain Crow stared at her, eyes glinting with challenge, but just then it didn't matter that Clare believed the woman prayed to a being that didn't exist. She couldn't stop the tears that welled.

The praying woman glanced up, as if she knew they spoke of her. Clare reached for her, grasping her hand all slick with sweat, and gave it a squeeze. *"Niyaawe,"* she said, thanking her.

Rain Crow was staring at her hard when she pulled back, the taut skin of her face glistening with sweat. "You are not offended?"

"That she cares enough about Pippa to pray for her?"

Rain Crow cut the thick, humid air with a motion of her hand. "That is not what I mean. Do you not pray to Jesus and the Almighty, as Panther-Sees-Him still does?"

Jeremiah prayed. She knew that. Their lodge was small and it was impossible to hide such things. But her own faith, or lack thereof, wasn't a subject Clare wanted to discuss with this woman.

"I pray to the Almighty," she said, for it was strictly true even if her prayers for Jacob's return had gone unanswered, all her prayers for her life with Philip come to naught. "I prayed for my daughter."

Even she heard the doubt in her voice.

"You do not believe the Almighty will heal her?" Rain Crow asked.

"I hope so."

"Hope." The word sounded desolate on Rain Crow's lips. Her baby had died of sickness a little over a year ago, along with her husband. What sort of sickness had it been? Something like what Pippa had now?

"It was the spotting sickness," Rain Crow said, as though Clare had asked the question. "That is what killed my husband and son. It took away many, leaving those it did not kill covered in horrible scars."

But not Rain Crow. Her skin was smooth, unblemished by illness.

"I'm sorry," Clare said, knowing not what else to say.

Rain Crow's face hardened. "Why?"

"Because I know such pain. My husband was killed in the mountains before my son was taken. The Mingo, Logan, killed him."

"Whites killed *his* family. They killed mine."

Clare flinched at her vehemence. "Didn't you just say it was smallpox—spotting sickness?"

"White man's sickness. More deadly to my people than soldiers and guns. Why should I pray to a God who favors one people over another? Who makes one strong and another weak? He is the God of all peoples, the Moravians say. So my mother believes despite everything we have lost. A God of forgiveness and peace! Why then do His people not follow His ways? Why do my people melt like morning dew before such a bad-behaving people as yours?"

The woman who had gone back to her praying fell silent. She got up and went to her sleeping place, leaving them alone by the steaming stones with Pippa.

Clare's face heated, as if she'd been unfairly slapped. This woman who held her son captive was talking about the bad behavior of *her* people?

Yet it was true what she said. Indians hadn't fared well in the face of ever-encroaching settlement. They were pushed westward, or they tried to become like the whites, whether from sincere desire or out of desperation to survive. Had not she and Philip been on their way to claim a piece of what had been their hunting grounds south of the Ohio River? She opened her mouth but was at a loss to answer such piercing questions. Or the pain behind them. She lifted her hands in helplessness.

"I don't know why your people have lost so much. I don't know why *you* have lost so much. I don't know why Philip was killed and Jacob taken from me. I don't know why Jeremiah found me or why you of all people . . ." She shook her head. "I don't know why the Almighty let it happen. I don't know what He means by any of it."

She'd stood on this precipice of doubt before, staring down at the raw pit. But when had that pit so widened?

Maybe the better question was when had the first crack in her faith occurred? Surely long before Philip's final foolish notion of leaving Virginia for the wilds of Kentucky. She'd grown increasingly disillusioned over the course of her marriage—not just with Philip but with the Almighty and His care of them. She'd had a strong faith in God until she married Philip. Or so she'd thought. Had it only been untested?

"We don't always see the path clear," she blurted, and wondered where those words had sprung from, until she recalled Jeremiah speaking them as he lay sick. "Sometimes we get hemmed in by . . . by a thicket of thorns, and there's nowhere to go . . . but the way will be shown."

Rain Crow didn't scoff at the borrowed, comfortless words, as Clare had expected. She opened her mouth, then shut it and looked away.

Clare thought their conversation at an end, but after a moment Rain Crow said in a tone less hostile, "When my husband lay covered in sores, he said a thing to me this talk of paths makes me remember. He said it comes down to whether or not we believe God is what He says He is, a Father with a good path for His children to walk, no matter what that looks like to us on this side of death, whether it be a hard steep path full of stones or a long dry trudge or a gentle path through rich grasses by streams of water to drink. Or all of that at different times. There is nothing that can separate us from His love."

Clare clung to the words, those of a man who had known his path through this life was ending at a hard place, yet who obviously hadn't felt himself abandoned by the God he'd left his people to serve. The pain in her chest was raw.

Silence hung, broken only by the snores of women sleeping badly and the rattle of a sick baby's breathing.

"Do you believe that?" she finally asked.

Rain Crow looked at her, sweat running down her face like tears. "Do you?"

"I want to." Clare looked the other woman in the eyes and finished silently, *But you have my son.*

Gray edged the door-hide before Pippa's breath caught and she made a choking sound. Clare had dozed sitting up. Jarred awake, she reached for her daughter. Before she had Pippa to her shoulder the baby coughed. A wad of mucus shot from her mouth to land on the packed-earth floor. Pippa's wail was interrupted by a further string of coughing.

Rain Crow started awake, saw what was happening, and retrieved the pads they'd used to cool Pippa's fever and began wiping up the mess.

"Wesah," she said, even as she winced at the wracking cough that kept thwarting Pippa's cries.

Around the lodge other women stirred, murmuring to each other, blinking like sleepy owls at the baby propped on Clare's lap.

Clare patted the convulsing little back, soothing her, bracing her. Gradually the women began to set about making food or bathing. No one heated the stones again. Hopefully they wouldn't be needed.

Pippa settled down to nurse after a time, though she continued to cough, and finally fell into a more peaceful sleep, the rattle in her chest less pronounced.

Arms shaking, ears buzzing with fatigue, Clare lay the baby down.

"She will be well," Rain Crow said, coming to set a corn cake baked in ashes next to Clare. "Though if that rattle doesn't go away by tonight . . . more steam, I think."

Clare felt a hot, tight pain in her throat and knew it wasn't from sickness. "Thank you."

Rain Crow pretended she hadn't heard.

Another day passed. One of the women left the lodge. Three more arrived. Crosses-the-Path came to the door and was told of Pippa's improvement. She went to tell Jeremiah, who was, "Much worry you, baby."

Clare and Rain Crow sat near Pippa, talking little, listening to the chatter in the lodge.

Night fell. Pippa's chest sounded little better. They heated the stones and made more steam. The women around them resignedly stripped to their skin, most of them, and lay down to sleep as best they could.

Into the long silence Rain Crow asked, "The father of Many Sparrows who is dead. Will you tell me of him?"

Clare stared at the woman, debating asking why Rain Crow wanted to know—she having stated that talking of the dead was not a thing Shawnees habitually did—but swallowed back the question.

"His name was Philip Inglesby. We married when we were very young. I was nineteen." She fumbled her way through, not knowing what about Philip or the troubled patchwork of a life they'd stitched together would be of interest to a Shawnee woman who didn't know that world, whose only exposure to whites was the Moravian missionaries, traders, and men like Jeremiah.

Rain Crow listened in silence, taking Pippa on her lap at one point and patting her, wiping up after each coughing spell.

When Clare stopped, having come to the point where Philip refused to wait in Redstone for a boat to be built to take them down the Monongahela to

Pittsburgh, Rain Crow was silent so long Clare decided that was the end of the conversation.

"My husband was born Delaware," she said at last, "but the name he had among them I will not speak. He was known to the missionaries as Josiah."

Not letting on she knew this already, Clare watched Rain Crow as she spoke. The woman kept her gaze fixed on the top of Pippa's head, where blond hair lay plastered to her tender scalp. She bent her face as if to kiss Pippa's crown, then stiffened and drew her head erect, meeting Clare's gaze.

"We had a son born to us a year after we married. The day he was born I looked into his eyes and saw the man he would be. The good things he would do. Three moons later, when he was the age your daughter is now, all that was taken away."

Rain Crow pressed her chin to the top of Pippa's head, holding the baby in cradling arms. She didn't seem to want or need Clare to say anything. Especially not *I'm sorry*.

Clare wasn't sorry. Or if she was, it was drowned by her rage. She wanted to scream at the woman. *If you understand such pain, why are you trying to take all of that away from me?*

She knew she mustn't say such words. Must not—*must not*. But she had to say something or burst.

"Why do you call him Many Sparrows?"

Rain Crow's gaze sharpened as her head lifted. "That is his name."

"I mean why did you choose it? Do you know the verse in Scripture that speaks of sparrows falling?"

Rain Crow shook her head. "That is not the reason for the name."

"What then?"

"You must know," Rain Crow said impatiently, as if coming so near to acknowledging Clare's maternal connection to Jacob was a source of disquiet. "He chatters like many birds all together. Like a flock of sparrows in a field."

Clare put a hand to her mouth, but couldn't hold back the startled burst of laughter that escaped. In a voice pitched high to mimic Jacob's she exclaimed, "Mama—Mama, let me tell you something!"

Other women broke off conversations to look their way. Clare was only dimly aware of them. Her vision was full of Rain Crow, of the mirth filling her eyes and curving her mouth in a smile she tried hard to suppress, but couldn't.

"Yes," she said. "Like that."

And Rain Crow laughed with her.

Pippa was nearly over her cough and long over the fever the morning Clare left the women's lodge, abandoning Rain Crow to another day of confinement— two, if Clare was lucky. She went straight to the lodge of Crosses-the-Path, arriving as the woman was feeding her daughters and Jacob, who she was watching for Rain Crow. Seeing Clare at the doorway, he abandoned his food. She pressed him close, all sun-browned and sun-bleached. "Jacob."

"I'm called Many Sparrows now," he reminded her.

Clare's smile faltered. "You're still Jacob—to me and to your sister. Remember your sister?"

"Pippa!" He craned his neck to see the baby in the cradleboard.

Clare didn't bend down. Crosses-the-Path stood by the fire, watching them uneasily. Clare's heart thudded as she said, "I'll be taking Many Sparrows with me now. He'll stay with me and Panther-Sees-Him until Rain Crow . . . until she is able to care for him again."

She was both thrilled and angered to be saying the words. She hadn't dared to ask for such a thing, though the thought had crossed her mind and she'd been sorely tempted. Then, moments before she left the women's lodge, Rain Crow had stopped her and said, "Many Sparrows is staying in Falling Hawk's lodge, but you may take him to yours—until I am done here."

She'd added that last sharply, looking hard at Clare, who understood this was some sort of test. Could she be trusted to give this son of contention back when Rain Crow demanded it?

"Rain Crow not say me this—yes or no," Crosses-the-Path said with patent reluctance. "She say you yes?"

Clare kept her hand buried in Jacob's long curls, wanting with all her heart to scoop him into her arms and run like the dickens—far past Jeremiah's lodge.

"Moments ago. You can go to the lodge and ask her for yourself."

Crosses-the-Path spoke briefly to her eldest daughter, who rose from the fire and slipped out of the lodge. The girl was back in moments, nodding her head vigorously at her mother's question.

Crosses-the-Path shrugged and smiled, waving her off, and Clare headed to Jeremiah's lodge with both her children in her care for the first time since Pippa's birth.

If only for a day. Maybe two.

If she could have stopped time that day, she'd have done so. Jacob's incessant questions made her feel more like herself than she had since they'd left Uncle Alphus's farm. While she cooked or mended clothing, or Jacob played with his baby sister or explored the unfamiliar lodge, he talked and talked and Clare listened. So did Jeremiah who, reassured that Rain Crow had given her consent to the arrangement, entered into their conversations and their play, carrying on with Jacob when she needed to tend to Pippa—who's appetite had returned and then some—showing the boy his rifle and hunting pouch, Wolf-Alone's bow and arrows.

Where Wolf-Alone was Clare didn't know but hoped he would stay there. She liked it, the four of them together.

That night Clare didn't fall asleep as soon as Pippa was settled, as was her custom. Not even when she lay Jacob down, talked out and exhausted at last. She was afraid to close her eyes, afraid to miss a moment with her son. In the past few months he seemed to have grown inches in height. It filled her with pride even as it broke her heart.

As she watched him sleep, that familiar bone-deep longing nearly overwhelmed her—to take him up and start walking, through the bark lodges, out through the fields standing ripe with corn, with Pippa strapped to her back. And just keep going.

This could be her only chance.

Yet what chance was there really? It would take weeks to get back to the Ohio on foot, with two small children to keep alive, countless perils between, including an army of Virginians purportedly marching westward to do harm to these people, therefore more Shawnees than usual running about the countryside keeping an eye out for them. Not to mention wild animals, starvation, accident, and who knew what other perils?

Even in the face of all reason, the temptation was strong.

"Clare?" She looked across the lodge to where Jeremiah sat at the table. "I wish it could be so simple. I do."

Her every thought must be written on her face.

Sighing, she dropped her gaze to her son, having to content herself with the sight of his sprawled limbs, his sweat-dampened hair, his little mouth fallen slack in sleep. However fleetingly hers.

"I know," she said.

Rain Crow was at the door-hide the next morning, demanding her son's return. Clare gave him over with a smile that seemed to take Rain Crow, and everyone gathered to watch the exchange, visibly aback. Had they expected a battle? The only battle raging was the one inside her heart as she stood outside the lodge,

Pippa in her arms, and watched as Jacob looked back after Rain Crow summoned him to her side. Mildly confused, he raised a hand and waved to her. "'Bye, Mama. 'Bye, Mr. Ring. 'Bye, Pippa!"

Rain Crow's face stiffened, but she pretended not to have heard what Jacob called her.

Clare hadn't allowed herself to think that Rain Crow would let Jacob stay with her one moment longer than necessary. Yet the crush of disappointment felt unbearable.

"Clare? I'm so—"

The warmth of Jeremiah's hand on her arm made her yank free of him. "Don't tell me you're sorry. Not now."

She was fighting for control, fighting the doubt that seethed like waves against her heart. She was doing what Jeremiah said she must, but it seemed to be making no difference. This tiny taste of what she'd lost only broke her heart afresh. Was this the best it was ever going to get? Now and then a stolen moment, an hour, a day with her son, watching him grow up Shawnee, calling Rain Crow *mother*?

Provided that army of Virginians would leave them in peace. Or was that coming army the thing that would set them free?

"I wasn't going to say that," Jeremiah told her. "I was going to say how proud I am of you. That was a hard thing, but you did it with grace."

She opened her mouth, but no words came. Only tears, swelling in her nose, burning her eyes, blurring her vision. Still she saw the arms held out to her.

Moving purely on instinct, she walked into them, felt them come around her, warm and solid and strong.

She let Jeremiah Ring hold them both until the weeping passed.

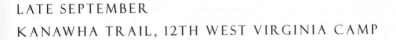

25

LATE SEPTEMBER
KANAWHA TRAIL, 12TH WEST VIRGINIA CAMP

Captain Alphus Litchfield left a meeting of the officers frustrated enough to curse. James Harrod's Kentucky Pioneer Company hadn't arrived at Camp Union before the Augusta County Regiment was ordered to begin their march westward—a methodical winding over terrain both mountainous and heavily wooded. Now, he'd just been informed, Harrod's company—having arrived at Camp Union the day *after* Alphus's departure—had remained behind when the Botetourt Regiment marched. Once again Alphus was prevented from speaking to the one man who might have some notion of what had befallen Clare and her family.

With every day's passing, his worry deepened, no matter how often he told himself Philip wasn't so great a fool as to leave his wife and children undefended against the depredations of raiding Indians.

Truth be told, he wasn't sure on that score.

Lord, help. Alphus lifted another prayer for Clare, as he did whenever she crossed his mind, morning, noon, and night, then shoved those anxieties to the side and set his thoughts to the business at hand, with which there was plenty to contend.

The regiments were encamped where the Elk River joined the Kanawha. While awaiting Colonel Lewis and the rest of the army, the Augusta Regiment had built a fortified supply camp. While the remaining cattle would come along the trail, from that point canoes were to carry the Southern Army's supplies more swiftly to the mouth of the Kanawha at the Ohio.

Twenty-seven large canoes, all of which must be built.

Following the rhythmic bite of axes, he found half his company grouped around the base of a broad cedar. Having over half the tree left to cut, they broke off to gather around their captain, eager for any news or orders he might impart.

Before Alphus could do either, young Geordie Reynolds piped up, "Mustn't be good news, Capt'n. You got your stormy face on," and blushed scarlet when Alphus leveled him a look and the rest hushed him.

Drawing a breath laden with fresh-cut cedar tang, Alphus gazed round at his men. "It's troubling news, right enough. You'll have noted the Botetourt companies come in to lend a hand with these canoes."

"Yes sir, we have," Ezra Baldwin cut in, ax in hand, pale hair darkened with the sweat of his labor. "About time, too."

Alphus forced a smile as the rest of his men grunted approval to the pronouncement, then proceeded to pass along what he'd learned at the meeting with the Colonels Lewis and the regimental officers thus far gathered. "There's been some changes to our orders."

This was met with the grumbling Alphus expected. He raised a hand to stem the questions he saw forming on the lips of Baldwin and others prone to talk before thinking. "Governor Dunmore reached Pittsburgh early in the month to lead the advance of the northern army, but he's changed his mind about the rendezvous at the mouth of the Kanawha."

That had been where the two wings of the army were meant to converge before crossing the Ohio and marching up the Scioto to attack the Shawnee towns on the Pickaway Plains.

"The governor has it in mind now to try talking with the Shawnees and Mingos one more time." More grumbling, but others did the shushing and

Alphus went on. "Seems some Delaware chiefs—ones that might hold sway over the Ohio Indians—aim to head straightaway to the Scioto towns, convince the Shawnees to meet at the mouth of the Hocking River for a council. That's to be in early October."

"Is that where Dunmore wants us to go?" Ezra asked.

"Where *is* the Hocking?" asked a young man, Judah Sawyer.

"Empties into the Ohio," Alphus said. "Above the Kanawha some seventy miles."

All the men stood staring, silenced by this, until Baldwin asked, "So what's it mean for us? Do we continue on to the mouth of the Kanawha?"

"Soon as we get these canoes built, that's exactly what we're meant to do." Alphus could see most of them had held hopes of leaving off the laborious job.

"And after we reach the Ohio?" Sawyer queried, but that was a question even Colonel Andrew Lewis hadn't been able to answer; the commander of the Southern Army had been none too pleased about the muddled change in orders and hesitant to commit to them.

"Runners are going between," Alphus said. "Like as not there'll be a message from Dunmore waiting for us when we arrive at the Ohio, if one doesn't find us sooner." But the question he couldn't put out of his mind was what Dunmore might have decided to do by then—send them all marching back to Virginia? It wasn't as unlikely as it might have seemed a few weeks ago. "One thing's certain: we and all our victuals have to reach the Ohio."

"What about Harrod, sir?" Baldwin asked. "You get to speak with him?"

Gazes shifted in the awkward silence that followed. In the distance the chopping of axes sounded loud as other companies worked at felling trees.

Alphus let his silence speak.

"Did the colonels have anything to say about the ruckus back east in Massachusetts?" someone behind Alphus asked, the voice he recognized as that of Jon Lawson, last to be recruited into the company. The others turned to look at him, some with blank gazes, some questioning, some dark with knowledge of said ruckus.

Alphus was of the latter group. "Where did you hear that?" he asked, turning to eye the man.

Lawson shrugged and wiped at the sweat on his neck, smearing it with the dirt and tree bark clinging to his hand. "A Botetourt man's spreading it about. Got the news afore they marched."

No point letting rumor spread.

"It's true, right enough. Round the first of the month a General called Gage sent soldiers to seize militia arsenals in Charlestown and Cambridge, Massachusetts."

Lawson asked, "Them Bostonians ain't going to sit back and let themselves be overrun by Crown troops, are they?"

"I cannot speak for the people of Boston," Alphus said. "What I know is that we now have us a Continental Congress, which has met in Philadelphia."

"A congress?" Geordie asked. "Of what?"

"Delegates from the colonies, including Massachusetts. I reckon there'll be answer to Gage, and a great many other grievances, directly. If there hasn't already been."

Again silence fell, in which Alphus could tell the attention of the men had suddenly divided. West toward the Indian problem. East toward the British problem.

"Sir?" Lawson ventured. "Any hope this council on the Hocking will end things here for us? Let us head back home and tend to matters there?"

"And them that wish it go about settling the Ohio," Baldwin added, being of the latter sort.

"Let's hope so," was the best Alphus could say to that. "For now, men . . . make those wood chips fly."

Alphus heard only one or two muffled groans at the order, though most of the men muttered to each other about all he'd conveyed—Dunmore's puzzling change of plans and the ruckus back east, as Lawson had phrased it.

The river wasn't running high now. Though its banks were still clothed in summer's tired green, here and there a tiny flame of the coming fires of autumn had kindled. The hills were steep, rising up from the banks in rounded crowns thick with tangled woodland. A peaceful setting, at first glance seemingly devoid of any life save that of bird and beast and biting bugs.

Alphus knew better. They were being watched—had been as far back as Camp Union on the Greenbrier. Whether it was Mingos, Shawnees, or both, Alphus didn't know, but there'd been some wounding of men who'd strayed too far from camp alone, and one night some horses had gone missing.

Behind him came a shout and the great, tearing crash of a falling giant. The earth shuddered beneath his boots, and the displaced air of the fallen cedar swept past. He was turning back toward his men, ready to pick up a blade to assist, when he sighted the figure on the river's far bank.

Drawn no doubt by the noise they were making, the tall Indian had brazenly shown himself, stepping out from tree cover to stand and stare, risking a rifle shot, for while the river was wide, it wasn't wide enough to guarantee a miss.

They know we're coming. And our numbers. Hang it all, they likely know our names and what we ate for breakfast.

Across the distance the Indian scout held Alphus's gaze with a force so strong the river between might have shrunk to a bitty creek. Then the Indian moved back into cover, gone so quick he almost seemed to vanish.

The hair on the back of Alphus's neck stood stiff.

Maybe it wasn't a bad thing Dunmore had changed his plans. Might make it harder for the Indians to anticipate their next move if half the army hadn't a clue what that next move might be. But a thousand men, their cattle and victuals couldn't be expected to dart about the wilderness like a flock of parakeets. They were a ponderous thing, easily overtaken.

It was all well and good for Dunmore, still safe up along the Ohio, to jump from plan to plan as the fancy took him. Alphus only hoped the Southern Army of Virginia wasn't moving straight into an ambush.

26

Wolf-Alone was away scouting, down along the Kanawha River where the southern division of Dunmore's army was making its slow progress toward the Ohio, but Jeremiah and Falling Hawk were present in the council house, where the chiefs of the Shawnee towns and their warriors had assembled. Each had had a chance to speak. Now all were listening to their principal chief, Cornstalk, address them on the issue of war with the Virginians.

Jeremiah sat to the side, on a raised platform. From there he could see through drifting pipe smoke the upturned faces of those men seated in the forefront of the gathering, arranged in a half circle around the open space where speakers stood. Among them was Puckeshinwah, war chief of the Shawnees, come from across the Scioto River. A thick-set man and muscular, his broad face was set, the mind behind it fixed, Jeremiah was certain.

There were Delawares present, among them the war chief Buckongahelas.

Though Logan wasn't present, there were Mingos.

Around the half-circle sat the Shawnee chiefs Black Hoof, Blue Jacket, Black Snake, and the brothers of Cornstalk—including Silverheels.

Directly across from Jeremiah on the far side of the half-circle sat Nonhelema, come to listen on behalf of the women, who had yet to declare whether they were in favor of their men going to fight the Virginians. She hadn't spoken, but nearly all who had addressed the assembly had done so in favor of meeting the approaching Long Knives head on.

Not Cornstalk, who was making a final plea for diplomacy and warning of the losses they would suffer if it came to battle.

Jeremiah couldn't be the only one wondering what losses such an attempt to placate the Virginians would bring. Dunmore was angry; Wakatomica's destruction was proof of that. And determined. Even if the governor could be made to agree to a peaceful solution, he would place grievous conditions upon such peace. No outcome now could guarantee the people would be left alone, their hunting lands unthreatened. Dunmore wanted land for Virginia.

"So why not meet them in battle and take from them the chance to take from us what is not theirs to take?" Puckeshinwah stood to demand the instant Cornstalk relinquished the place of speaker. "We are strong. Together with our Delaware and Mingo brothers we are stronger. The Long Knife army is divided. The half in the north have only begun to come down the Spaylay-witheepi, while those from the south come along the Kanawha as slow as children at play with all their cattle and supplies! Let us attack one or the other of them. If we defeat that half, then we can talk of peace and come to that talk with more to bargain with. Or we can go on to fight the other half of the army if that seems best."

Mutters of agreement arose, even a few enthusiastic yips from younger warriors tired of talking, ready to strike the war post outside, don their paint, and be about the business of slaughtering the coming Long Knives.

Puckeshinwah sat down amidst the approving clamor, letting it underscore his words.

When no other made to rise in the silence that fell, Cornstalk again stood to his feet.

"I have said all I have to say on the matter of the Virginians. You warriors know my heart is not for war, for many of our best men dying. I ask you, Puckeshinwah, and all you warriors, to go from this place and think on that, on what all that dying will mean to your women and children in the coming winter. In all the coming winters, until your sons are grown to replace you. But if your minds do not change, I will bow to the will of the people. That includes the will of our sisters."

Turning to the woman who had sat quiet while man after man had spoken, he said, "My sister, you have yet to speak on this matter of the Long Knives. We must stop them—this I do not argue against—but by what means would the council of women wish that to be done?"

Nonhelema rose to her impressive height. Her hair was loose about her face, which still held hints of its former beauty though she was nearing fifty now. The murmuring at Cornstalk's final words fell away as every man quieted himself to hear what she would say.

"In this matter my heart and my brother's are one." Nonhelema's voice rose clear and strong as a warrior's, carrying to all present. "I would try for peace before I consent to war, unless the hearts of my sisters are against mine. As my brother says, we will do the will of the people, even if it proves to be a bloody path the Shawnees wish to walk."

She paused to let those words sink in.

"Today I call my sisters to the high ground across the creek. Let the women of Cornstalk's Town gather in my town tomorrow and make their voices heard."

At the council's breaking, men drifted out into the sunlight of early autumn. Some warriors not from Cornstalk's Town had chosen to remain, ready to fight the Long Knife army, already presuming what the women would decide.

Jeremiah overheard them as he and Falling Hawk stood outside the council house speaking of Wolf-Alone. They hoped to see their brother back soon from his scouting across the Ohio. Jeremiah had wanted to go with Wolf-Alone, but in the end hadn't felt right about leaving Clare. Or Jacob. Not now he'd begun to develop a friendship with the boy.

Though their mutual adoption made them kin, Jeremiah had kept his distance from Jacob Inglesby, apart from the contact Clare was allowed—until Rain Crow asked him to act as uncle to the boy and teach him the things he needed to know to grow into a useful man. Of all her brothers, adopted or otherwise, she'd asked this of him, and Clare had been so encouraged when he'd sought her thoughts on the matter, so moved with hope that it meant Rain Crow's heart was softening toward her, he'd been unable to decline the offer.

Not that he'd wanted to decline it. He shared Clare's hope. But there was another reason he'd wanted to accept. Clare had told him what Rain Crow said about choosing the name, Many Sparrows, and he was coming to think it as fitting a name as he'd ever known a Shawnee child to be given. Jeremiah doubted he'd spoken so much in the past year as he'd done since he'd begun teaching the boy to use a bow, to read tracks in the forest, to learn the ways of the animals he would one day hunt—whether he remained Shawnee or not. Clare was eager to hear about their time together, and Jeremiah indulged her. He liked the way she hung on his every word of her son. He liked the intensity of her attention.

Liked it far too much.

Was that liking preventing her from releasing control of this tangled situation in her heart?

Things had been better this past moon, as the nights were growing cooler and the harvest coming in—better between his sister and Clare. The women were working together in the fields most days, and there had been no incidents of tension between them. Rain Crow was allowing Clare and Jacob to converse as they wished—under her watchful gaze.

After parting from Falling Hawk, Jeremiah found Clare in the lodge settling Pippa to sleep. He entered quietly, and she greeted him with a smile, looking past him for Jacob, who more and more could be found trailing in his
shadow, much as Wildcat did Wolf-Alone. But not today.

Her disappointment was visible as she stood from the sleeping bench and
crossed the lodge. "The council went long. What was decided?"

"The other chiefs will go against Cornstalk. It remains now for the women
to decide. They're the last chance for peace. They'll meet tomorrow morning
at Nonhelema's Town."

Clare raised her brows at that. "They could stop the men going to war?"

"They could."

"And if they do?"

"Cornstalk will send a message to Dunmore asking to meet in council."
Perhaps he'd be the one to take that message, let the white half of his world
know he hadn't fallen off a cliff or drowned in a river somewhere. Curious to
know her thoughts, he asked, "What do you think will happen?"

"I think there'll be fighting." When he looked at her sharply, questioning,
Clare added, "I hear the women talking. I understand more than they think I
do." She pulled her lower lip between her teeth, studying him. "What will you
do if the men go to fight?"

There was a tightness in his chest. "It might be different was I away running messages. I could maybe avoid having to choose. But I'm here and . . . I'm
Shawnee, Clare."

"But you're still a Virginian, too, in the employ of the Crown."

"I am. Though by now they must've written me off for dead."

Her face went white at that, and he wished he'd phrased the sentiment
otherwise. He hadn't meant to unnerve her or throw a shadow over her heart,
and yet . . . did that look of apprehension mean she cared whether he lived or
died? Or had he simply reminded her of Philip?

He'd managed thus far to avoid having this conversation, distracted as she'd been with Jacob. Truth to tell, he was as torn between his identity as a Shawnee and a Virginian as he'd been torn between Rain Crow's heart and Clare's.

"What will you do?" she asked again.

Jeremiah searched his heart, standing there before this woman he'd never expected to enter his life. He knew what he wanted to do. He wanted to stay with her. Protect her. And everyone she loved.

But what would he do?

The women were having their council at Nonhelema's Town, but neither Clare nor Crosses-the-Path had attended—Clare because she had no place there, and Crosses-the-Path because she was too unassuming to voice her opinion in such a setting, whatever that opinion might have been. She hadn't chosen to share it with Clare, other than to shrug and say in Shawnee, "The women will decide what they decide, with me there or not."

Whether or not she intended to have an active say in matters, Rain Crow had crossed the creek to attend the council, for when Clare arrived at Falling Hawk's door-hide, no smoke ascended from the roof-hole of the neighboring lodge.

"Did she take Many Sparrows with her?" Clare asked before she and Crosses-the-Path and her eldest daughter got down to the business of slicing the squash and pumpkins harvested the previous day and laying them out to dry in the sun. On a blanket nearby, Crosses-the-Path's youngest daughter sat with Pippa who, at nearly five months, wasn't yet crawling but needed to be watched.

"She no say me keep," Crosses-the-Path said in English. "So maybe."

Disappointment stabbed. If Shawnee women could talk at such a venue as long as could their men, did Rain Crow expect a boy his age to sit still so many hours?

His age. Four years old, but not for long. Clare wasn't certain of the date but thought it still September. Jacob's birthday was the twelfth of October.

She'd ask Jeremiah if he knew the date when next she saw him. Might he help her with a gift? Perhaps make Jacob a bow of his own? He'd been using one Wildcat had outgrown.

There was a prodigious amount of squash and pumpkins to cut and dry, including the seeds, removed with the pulpy innards. Their talk was sporadic as they worked, leaving Clare with space for thinking. Jeremiah hadn't given her an answer about what he meant to do if the rest of the Shawnee men left to fight. Including his brothers. What would happen to her and Pippa and Jacob if he did go off to fight?

She glanced aside at the young woman working diligently beside her, outwardly unruffled by what her Shawnee sisters across the creek were that moment discussing.

"Where would you go?" Clare asked, raising the back of a pulp-covered hand to brush away a tickling strand of hair come loose from her braid. "You and the children, if Dunmore's army comes here?"

Crosses-the-Path looked up from the pumpkin slices she'd been arranging on a rack of thin wood strips. "Come threaten this town?"

"What if they do here as they did at Wakatomica?" She looked round at the lodges nearby, quieter with many of the women and children gone to the council. She couldn't imagine it in ashes. Didn't want to imagine such a thing.

"Women, children hide—or go." Crosses-the-Path waved toward the creek and the lands to the west. "Maybe come back, build again. Maybe not."

Clare had deduced as much from observing the refugees from Wakatomica, most of whom had left their temporary lodging in the Scioto towns for a new site where Wakatomica had been rebuilt, somewhere to the west.

"But what about this?" Clare asked, spreading shiny hands over the vegetables before them. "And the corn we've harvested? You couldn't carry it all away even with the warning of a week."

The people had horses that could carry some in packs, but likely they would be used to carry people, the weak, old, and sick. Some, like Nonhelema and her brothers, had herds of cattle, cumbersome to drive away ahead of an attacking army. Then there were all these lodges and everything they contained.

Crosses-the-Path nodded. "Much lost when soldiers come. Hunger follow. But we run. We live."

Clare didn't voice her underlying fear that she would be pushed along with them if the people were forced to run, she and Pippa and Jacob borne like flotsam on a tide deeper into the wilderness. Unless Rain Crow finally gave Jacob back to her and Jeremiah led them away from such turmoil.

She was running out of time.

When she took up Pippa on her hip and left Falling Hawk's lodge for the day, she paused to stand gazing at Rain Crow's lodge. She detected no sign or sound of Jacob within.

The need to set eyes on him, to know he was well, turned her feet toward the creek instead of Jeremiah's lodge.

Though he'd left early to hunt with Falling Hawk and others eager to get meat for their families before the need to fight was upon them, Jeremiah had promised to return by nightfall. No doubt he would be hungry. Likely Rain Crow had taken Jacob with her and any searching for her son would be time wasted. Still she had a few moments to check the creek where the children liked to play. If Jacob wasn't there, she would return to the lodge.

But Jacob was at the creek, crouched on the ground with Wildcat and several other boys, poking at a pair of toads one of them had captured.

"Jacob!" she called, just as she caught sight of Wolf-Alone coming toward the boys from the opposite direction.

At her call the boys broke apart, one of them taking up the toads, as Wild-cat greeted Wolf-Alone and Jacob sprang up and ran to her.

She knelt with Pippa clasped to her side and gave her son a one-armed hug, reveling as always in the little boy smell of him, sweat and dirt and sun and grass, the feel of his small body alive with vigor.

"What have you been doing all day, and who have you been doing it with?"

"You smell like pumpkins." Jacob stepped back and looked her over. "I was with Split-Moon and Wildcat and those other boys. Listen, Mama—we found toads! Come see!"

He'd taken her by the hand to lead her back to the boys, then saw those with the toads had scampered off. Still he led her toward Wildcat and Wolf-Alone.

"Why were you with Split-Moon, not Crosses-the-Path?" she asked, feeling the deprivation, knowing she might have spent this day with Jacob had she but known where he was.

"I don't know," Jacob said.

Before she could inquire the same of Wildcat, Wolf-Alone addressed her in Shawnee. "Panther-Sees-Him wishes to speak with you."

She looked up at the tall Indian, struck as she sometimes was by his imposing face with those fiercely slanted brows that, in her opinion, kept him from being quite devastatingly handsome. Except on the rare occasions he smiled. "He does?"

"Yes. Now." To Clare's surprise Wolf-Alone took her by the arm and steered her away from the boys, speaking to Wildcat again in Shawnee, telling him to look after Jacob.

It seemed whatever Jeremiah wished to say to her was urgent.

"All right," she said, gripping Pippa to her side. "Jacob? I'll see you soon."

She looked back and caught a last sight of her son as he called, "'Bye, Mama!"

Pulling from Wolf-Alone's grasp, she hurried to match his pace back to the village.

"Your Shawnee is improving," he said as they walked, speaking low and in English so none but she would hear.

"Niyaawe," she said, surprised by the compliment. "You're just back from scouting?"

"I am. I haven't been to our lodge."

"Then how do . . . ?" She halted, shifting Pippa to her shoulder. Wolf-Alone halted as well. "Has Jeremiah returned from hunting?"

"Hunting?"

"He left this morning." She frowned, enlightened and annoyed. "Jeremiah doesn't wish to speak to me. *You* do."

Wolf-Alone nearly grinned. "My brother always wishes to speak to you. I think you know this."

To her mortification, Clare blushed. "What is it you wish to say?"

Wolf-Alone's face sobered. He glanced around, saw no one was near enough to overhear them, then leaned toward her slightly. "It's about Wildcat. If anything happens to me, if I don't return from the battle . . ."

Alarmed, Clare cut in, "Battle? The women haven't come from their council, have they?"

Wolf-Alone shook his head. "But that army's coming on, well supplied, many men. They don't come westward for a frolic in the wood."

Clare looked back toward the creek, but Wildcat and Jacob had gone off to play elsewhere. The need to find her son, to have him within reach, was nearly irresistible. "What were you going to ask about Wildcat?"

"I want you to look after him, take him as your own, if I don't survive."

She jerked her head around sharply, meeting his amber gaze. "What of Split-Moon? Surely he won't fight?"

"Whatever happens to Split-Moon, I want you and Panther-Sees-Him to take Wildcat with you when you leave the Shawnees."

The man was full of surprises today. "Why do you say we're leaving? Has Jeremiah said something to you?"

Wolf-Alone raised a hand. "He hasn't spoken of it to me. But you will leave. Both of you. This isn't the place for you, and I think . . . I think the place for *him* is wherever you are. And I don't want Wildcat to remain here without me."

Clare's thoughts were in a spin. Jeremiah's place was with her? And he didn't want Wildcat to live with the Shawnees?

What was it about that boy this warrior was holding so closely to his chest?

"Wildcat has no memory of any other life," she said, "and he has a father here. Why shouldn't he stay?"

"It will break that old man's heart, but . . ." Wolf-Alone again hesitated, looking on the verge of telling her something more. Then he grasped her hand and held it firm. "Clare, please. Promise me you'll take him with you, back to Virginia."

Whatever else he'd meant to do, Wolf-Alone had thoroughly rattled her. She'd never seen such emotion in the man before. Nor had she ever heard him sound less like an Indian. Even his cadence of speech had changed.

"I cannot take that boy from his father. I won't."

"Split-Moon isn't . . ."

"Isn't his father?" she prompted when he hesitated. "Is that what you were going to say?"

"No. Never mind it, Clare. Just, please, think about what I asked." Wolf-Alone gazed down at her, his scrutiny hard, then he nodded once, let go her hand, and strode away.

She could have made no other response to the astonishing request than she had, she thought. Right or wrong to begin with, Wildcat was Shawnee now. Taking him away from Split-Moon would be no better than kidnapping— unless she had some means to learn who his white parents were. If Wolf-Alone knew, he'd have said so, wouldn't he?

The warrior hadn't told her everything. She was certain of it. But she also knew that pressing him would serve no purpose. Either he would choose to tell her or he wouldn't.

What she ought to have asked about was what he'd seen down on the Kanawha, how near he'd come to the approaching army, whether he might even have glimpsed her uncle.

But no. That was just as pointless. Wolf-Alone wouldn't know Alphus Litchfield if her uncle stepped from the woods to hail him.

27

The day after the women's council ended with a declaration of battle, Clare went to the fields to harvest more pumpkins with Pippa in her cradle-board strapped to her back. Crosses-the-Path and her daughters went with her, as did Jacob. Suffering a headache that made the sunlight unbearable, Rain Crow had remained in her lodge to work on preserving produce already brought in from the fields.

The threat of coming violence sought to press upon Clare's spirit and fill her thoughts with anxiety, but just now—this blissful now with Jacob scouting the sprawling vines and hillocks for ripe pumpkins—she could almost believe he was hers again, that at day's end he would return with her to Jeremiah's lodge, eat food she prepared, then sleep under her watchful eye.

Crouched in the morning chill with a buckhorn knife in one hand, a pumpkin's spiraling stem in the other, she raised her face to the autumn sun, bright through closed lids, and was rocked by a contentment so deep she thought maybe she could live this life—be Shawnee—if that was what it took to have both her children near like this. Had the Almighty not answered her pleas for Jacob's return because, for whatever unimaginable reason, He wanted *her* to be Shawnee?

Wolf-Alone didn't think so. *"This isn't the place for you."*

Jacob's voice broke into her thoughts.

"Found one, Mama! *Wesah.* Come see!" he came running, hair shining like flax, chattering in a hodgepodge of English and Shawnee.

"Did you, clever boy? Let me cut this one first. But no, first I'm going to *hug* you!"

She dropped the knife and scooped her son into her arms. With Pippa squealing in her cradleboard at the sudden movement, she stood and swooped him high into the autumn sky, the both of them laughing.

But her boy wasn't tiny anymore. He was sturdy and solid. She couldn't hold him aloft as once she'd done on a farm far to the east.

Back on his feet, he raced off to stand guard over the pumpkin he'd found lest Crosses-the-Path's daughters claim it.

Clare knelt to sever the one at her feet, thinking more soberly now but as intensely: could she truly be content thus? Raising Pippa among the Shawnees, living with them? With Jeremiah . . .

Married to Jeremiah? She wasn't blind to his feelings for her, though she could tell he tried to hide them.

It was a question she set aside for the present, afraid to delve into her heart and discover there some unexpected desire. It would only cloud her thinking. She must do what was best for her children first and keep her own needs, her wants, out of it.

Jeremiah might try to hide his feelings for her, however deep they went, but to his feelings for Pippa he'd given free rein. The man was besotted with her daughter. That time she'd come upon him holding her, the two of them asleep, hadn't been the last such moment she'd witnessed. Now that he'd been allowed to see Jacob, to act toward him as an uncle in the Shawnee way of reckoning, it was clear he was fond of her son as well. He'd good things to say of Jacob, and it warmed her heart to hear them, yet it pained her to see her son adapting to Shawnee life.

This wasn't the life she'd choose given the freedom—and possession of her children—to do so. But if Jeremiah could be a part of Jacob's life, and through Jeremiah she to some degree, then her son would never forget entirely who he was, who *she* was. He would never forget who Jacob Inglesby had been.

Could she somehow live with that?

Clare carried the severed pumpkin to the others they'd collected at the field's edge, then turned back toward her son. Glancing beyond him, to parts of the field where other women worked and little ones ran among the harvested cornstalks, she was stabbed with longing for homes built of timber and stone, for mills and churches and shops and carriages. For the sound of English spoken in the streets. For her parents. Her uncle. The society and the family she'd left behind. A world her children might never know.

Contentment evaporated. Anxiety filled her heart, even as she smiled at her son and bent to cut the pumpkin at his feet, sending him off to look for the next.

Lord, how long?

When nothing but silence greeted the prayer, her mind sought refuge in that abyss of desperation, churning with schemes and plans. Was there something she'd yet to think of, something to do or say that would turn Rain Crow's stubborn heart?

Things between herself and Jacob's adopted mother had been better of late. She'd never call what was between them friendship, but there was forbearance. Rain Crow had allowed Clare to take custody of Jacob today, not Crosses-the-Path.

Dared she do it? Come straight out and again ask the woman to give back her son? The temptation was consuming.

Wait a little longer. A few more days. Possess your soul in patience . . .

But war was looming. Crosses-the-Path had told her what would happen if they were attacked, but she hadn't said what such moments were like. Did a mother ever lose track of her child during such a hasty exodus?

Whatever came, she would have to stay near Rain Crow, wherever she went, subject to her every whim, as long as she held Jacob.

Such helplessness was not to be borne. After they came in from the fields that day, she would ask Rain Crow to give back her son before the warriors left to fight. She would get down on her knees and beg the woman if she must. Find the words to make Rain Crow see it was for the best. For them all. Then Jeremiah could lead them away, back across the Ohio, avoiding all those soldiers.

Or lead her *to* them? Maybe that's where she'd be safest. Especially if her uncle was among them and she could find him. Alphus Litchfield would know what to do to see them safely back to Virginia. Then Jeremiah could go on his way, do whatever he felt he needed to do for his Shawnee family, without the complication of her and her children in his life.

Would she never see him again?

She tried to ignore the ache that tightened her chest at that thought. She couldn't think of what she might want if only things could be different. She couldn't let her heart open in that way. Not now. Now she had to get her son free, and that was what she would do. Today.

The determination rooted itself in her mind seconds before the scream ripped through the bright air.

She bolted to her feet to look for Jacob, who'd gone off to find another pumpkin. She didn't see him. Nor who had screamed.

Scrambling up the nearest hillock, she clung to the cornstalks at its crown and looked in the direction she thought the scream had arisen, off near a line of forest to the east, blazing with autumn color still shy of its peak—yellows, oranges, ambers, reds.

Other women had found higher perches for a view. One of them was Crosses-the-Path.

"What is it?" Clare called to her. "What's happening?"

Crosses-the-Path lifted a hand but kept her gaze trained on the tree line. Another scream arose, followed by shouts.

"Soldiers come!" Crosses-the-Path exclaimed, then disappeared from sight.

Clare remained frozen on her perch, heart thudding, looking frantically for militia emerging from the wood, for their hunting shirts, their cornered hats, their long rifles.

Nothing but a breeze stirred the trees.

How could Dunmore's army have surprised them so? These people had scouts out watching the progress of the Virginians, who were meant to be far down the Kanawha River, many days' march away. Why no warning?

Panic swept over the fields like a line of oncoming rain. There were more screams, the calls of mothers looking for children, the crying of children looking for mothers. On her back Pippa began to wail.

Jacob.

As she slid down the hillock, Crosses-the-Path came running through the ground vines, dragging her youngest daughter by the hand, her eldest coming behind. The older girl caught a foot in the vines and fell, crying out to her mother, who turned back to yank her to her feet.

More than anything, Crosses-the-Path's patent fear made Clare believe in what was happening. "Where is Jac—Many Sparrows?"

Crosses-the-Path halted, gaze darting about. "No see . . . not . . . him!" English failing her, she grasped Clare's arm and spoke in Shawnee too rapid to translate. Finally, tugging hard, she said, "You come. Town."

"Not without Jacob!" Clare tore free to dodge through the hillocks, calling Jacob's name. The rustling, thudding passage of women and children swept past her, all seeking shelter in the town among the warriors. She ignored them.

"Jacob! Where are you? Answer me!"

Her son didn't answer.

Beneath her breastbone, panic bloomed, hot and commanding. Pippa screamed in her cradleboard. Sweat sprang up on Clare's face, beneath her arms, down her back. "Jacob!"

"Mama!"

"Jacob?" She barreled through the hillocks to find him standing in a declivity that hadn't been planted. He was clutching a lizard in his hand. She swept him off his feet and, carrying him like a sack against her side, followed the last of the women darting like frightened deer back to the town.

How many soldiers? Where was Jeremiah? Jacob was growing too heavy to carry. She set him on his feet.

"Take my hand!"

Alerted by the women, warriors sprinted toward the field and the wood beyond to engage their enemy.

There was no shooting. No sound of an army marching behind her. Were the Virginians advancing? She didn't look back to see; she'd spotted Jeremiah coming toward her, seeking her among the women and children running his way.

"We're here!" she called.

He saw her. "Clare! It's all right."

She reached him, panting, not yet registering his words for the panic buzzing in her ears. "Where do we go? What do we do?"

He grasped her shoulders. "There's no army. A woman thought she saw a man in a hunting shirt in the forest and gave the alarm, but it wasn't a soldier. Just a deer."

"What? A deer? You're sure?"

He was still holding her, his grip firm. "I'm sure, Clare. Just a deer."

Jacob was crying. Clare pulled from Jeremiah's grasp to kneel.

"Jacob, it's all right. No army, Jeremiah says. Just a deer!"

She was shaking now, so badly she feared she'd never get back to her feet. She wrapped her arms around Jacob and held him, trying to catch her breath.

"Many Sparrows, come to me!"

Rain Crow's voice cut through Clare's relief. She looked up into Jeremiah's hovering face. He helped her to her feet as Jacob stood, looking first at her, then Rain Crow, who came marching to them, raised a hand, and for the second time in their acquaintance, struck Clare across the face.

"You will never keep him so from me. Do you understand? Never!"

Humiliated, bewildered, Clare sputtered, "I—I didn't keep him from you. I couldn't find him. I had to search the field. We came back as soon as—"

"You did not know where he was?" Rain Crow narrowed her eyes in rage and disbelief.

"For a moment only."

Rain Crow made a sound in her throat like a growl, took hold of Jacob's hand, and led him away without another word.

Too stunned to call after her, Clare looked mutely at Jeremiah. She could see he, too, was rattled. "My sister was afraid you'd been captured, or that you'd taken Many—Jacob and run with him to the army they thought was coming. Try to be—"

"Be what? Patient? Understanding? I don't know why I should be such things!" Before Rain Crow disappeared into the town, she started after the woman.

Jeremiah moved to block her path. "I'll speak with her. You'd best let her go for now."

Pippa was still wailing. Clare wanted to wail more loudly still. She turned her back to Jeremiah. "Take her out for me, please."

She felt the tug and pull of the cradleboard's unlacing, then Jeremiah was placing Pippa into her shaking arms. She didn't look at him again. She took her crying baby and headed for the lodge.

28

Two Delaware chiefs had journeyed west from Governor Dunmore to the Shawnees at Cornstalk's Town. They bore an unexpected invitation: come to the mouth of the Hocking River and talk peace.

The Delawares, the well-respected White Eyes and another called Captain Pipe, had spoken in the council house nearly bursting with warriors and Shawnee chiefs. Few of those were of a mind even to hear such an invitation, much less accept it, but all listened in cold politeness.

When the two finished speaking and sat down amidst silence, war chiefs like Blue Jacket, Puckeshinwah, and Black Snake looked to Cornstalk, seated beside Nonhelema near the front of the gathering. The principal Shawnee chief rose to his feet and faced the gathered Indians.

Like all present, except perhaps White Eyes and Captain Pipe, Jeremiah knew what Cornstalk would say. He watched the older man closely, but Cornstalk gave no hint by word or expression that, had he been able to choose for himself alone, he'd have accepted this invitation to talk with the governor now leading armies into Shawnee lands.

"I am sorry to disappoint you, brothers," Cornstalk told the Delawares. "But these are the words you must take back to Governor Dunmore. We will not come and sit with him to talk of peace." Pausing, he looked hard at the warriors looking back at him, satisfied that he wasn't standing in opposition to their will, then he added, "Maybe after we have put many of his soldiers on the ground in their blood, and many of our warriors lie in theirs, maybe then we will do this thing you ask. But not before."

Cornstalk waited until White Eyes and Captain Pipe departed with his grim message to Dunmore before talking of battle strategy with Puckeshinwah and the other war chiefs.

He began by saying, "We will hear the scouts who have lately come in say what they have seen, where each of these armies camp at present, how swiftly they move. Based on what they have to say, we will march to the Spaylay-witheepi and meet one or the other of them before the halves can join, for our numbers are less than half theirs. Whichever army you chiefs think it best to meet first, my sister and I will lead you into battle against them."

When some reacted in surprise to these words, knowing well Cornstalk and Nonhelema opposed war, Cornstalk came as near to losing his self-possession as Jeremiah had ever seen.

"Did you think I and my sister do not wish war because we fear battle or have no heart to lead you as we have done in times past? If you did not hear our true hearts the many times we spoke to you before this day, you have no ears to hear now. I have just sent away those two who came with a last offer of peace. You will have no more chance to choose that path until much blood is spilled, and maybe most of it will be yours!"

Seeing the man's mouth tremble with the passion of his words, a chill raced down Jeremiah's limbs, and a foreboding he couldn't conceal.

Falling Hawk and Wolf-Alone waited for Jeremiah outside the council house. They had heard the words of Cornstalk and others as, weighing in one by one with their thoughts, a plan of battle had been agreed upon. Wolf-Alone had spoken for the scouts who spied on the Southern Army along the Kanawha River, the half led by Colonel Andrew Lewis. Those soldiers had reached the mouth of the Kanawha at the Ohio and were camped on a point of land there between the rivers, building a supply fort and sending messengers back and forth to Dunmore, still up north many miles distant getting his troops and supplies across the Ohio.

It would be the Southern Army they attacked—over a thousand men, while the Shawnees and their allies had barely eight hundred—an army of men from the Shenandoah Valley and the frontier beyond. Men Jeremiah once called neighbors.

"We did not speak to you of this until we were certain it would happen," Falling Hawk said. "Now we go to fight the Long Knives and the governor whom you still serve. Will you fight beside us or choose to stand to the side?"

"We know you will not fight against us," Wolf-Alone said. "But we have wondered about that woman in my lodge, whether you would stay behind with her. If you felt your heart drawn to her now more than to us."

Jeremiah let out the breath he'd been holding. He'd put this off as long as he could. It was no less difficult for the waiting.

"I know what I am going to do about this coming battle, brothers," he said, a heaviness in his chest. "But I ask you to let me tell it to her first."

Falling Hawk and Wolf-Alone exchanged a look.

"Find us, brother," Falling Hawk said, "after you have spoken to your woman. You must know what is in our hearts. We cross the river to fight. We know that for you to do so and be captured would be a bad thing. Worse than for us. Still we hope to have you beside us. Together we are stronger."

Falling Hawk spoke a grim truth. Were he captured fighting among Cornstalk's warriors, he would be identified as Jem Ringbloom, a Virginian, or as Jeremiah Ring, in the employ of the Indian agents at Fort Pitt.

By either name a traitor.

Desire to take Clare and Pippa—Rain Crow and Jacob too if he could persuade her—and flee the coming conflict, guide them to some safe place, beat drum-urgent under all his thoughts.

In the lodge he found Clare, if not the words to tell her what was going to happen in the coming days and what his part in it must be.

He didn't have to. She straightened from the fire, glanced at Pippa asleep on the bed platform, and asked, "When do you leave?"

The words trembled on the wegiwa's warm air.

"Tomorrow. We'll cross the Ohio to where the Southern Army camps, attack them before they can join with Dunmore's troops and come against us here in a force too great to face."

She came to him, features riddled with fear. "Have you considered my uncle is likely part of that army? If I know Alphus Litchfield, he's raised a company for Dunmore."

He'd thought of it and said so.

Green eyes flashed frustration. "But you're going into battle anyway. With your brothers."

"It's not what I want, Clare." What he wanted was never to be parted from her. What he wanted was to make the charade they'd lived a charade no more. But her heart was focused on Jacob; since the scare in the cornfield, she hadn't been allowed near her son. Rain Crow was threatening to take Jacob back across the creek to Nonhelema's Town. Perhaps across the Scioto to the town of Puckeshinwah.

He searched her gaze, aching to see something more than her fears for Jacob, her impatience and need. Something for him.

"I won't abandon them to fight without me. I'd rather see the Shawnees preserve their land by peaceful means, but when has that ever lasted? Has any treaty been honored for long?"

Pleading entered her gaze. "Jeremiah, these aren't your only people."

"I know," he said, voice husky with the pain of it. "But they need me more than the Virginians do."

"And what about—" Something flashed in her eyes; for a giddy second he thought it might be longing.

She was breathing hard, as though they'd been wrestling, but though they stood less than a pace apart, he hadn't touched her.

"Say it, Clare." *Please, say it.*

"I cannot," she whispered. "Not now. First I . . . Jacob . . ." She shook her head, then looked at him, imploring. "It would do no good to argue with you, would it?"

"No. I'm sorry." For so many things. Most of all for having to leave her now.

Her voice hardened. "Never mind then. Do what you must do. I'll manage alone. But have you any opinion about what we should do, Pippa and I, should you fail and the army reach us here?"

He felt things vital inside him breaking at her choice of words. *Alone. Fail.*

"You won't be alone, Clare. Stay with Crosses-the-Path. Go where she goes."

She didn't like that answer. "And Jacob? I cannot control what happens to him, where *he* goes."

"You've never been in control of this situation. Nor have I," he added, seeing accusation fill her gaze. "The Almighty is in control."

"And a fine job He's done of things thus far!"

"Clare." He wanted to shake her in her stubbornness. He wanted to hold her in her distress. He wanted to kiss her until they forgot everything else. Discover if that hint of longing he'd seen was only the tip of things. Instead he said, "Don't go judging the Almighty by your own understanding. We're rarely given eyes to see the whole of what He's doing in our lives or through us. That's why we're called to walk by faith, not by sight."

"Jeremiah, I've tried," she protested. "All I do is stumble about, making everything worse. I see no way through this—"

He held up a hand, stopping her. "I've been where you are. I've felt what you're feeling. But you must surrender your will and your wisdom to the Almighty, give it over to Him once and for all and stop blindly groping about for what to do next. Why not try doing *nothing*?"

She looked at him uncomprehendingly.

"I don't think you grasp what it means to wait on the Lord," he said. "To let Him come to your rescue. To completely, utterly trust."

"And you do?"

It felt as though she'd struck him. Whether or not she'd lost faith in God, she'd clearly lost whatever faith she'd had in him. Maybe that was how it had to be. "Clare, please. I don't want to leave you like this. I don't want to leave you at all."

They gazed at each other, and gradually the hard, hunted look of her softened. "I don't want you to go," she said, but when he tried to close the small space still between them, she stepped back.

She wasn't the only one struggling to wait on the Almighty's timing. He ached to take her in his arms. If he did, could he ever do what he had to do in the next few days, the next few seconds?

"I'll say one more thing about Jacob; then I need to go find Falling Hawk and Wolf-Alone. Please hear this, Clare." *And hear my heart,* he added silently. "The Almighty is good, and He's working all things together for your good. And Jacob's. Either you believe that or you don't."

Tears welled and coursed down her cheeks. "Haven't I been waiting for Him to *do* something good for me all this time?"

Do again. If only she could simply *be* and let whatever the Lord granted be enough. Let God Himself be enough.

Be enough for me now, Lord.

"You're saying the right words," he said, "but only you can know whether you truly trust Him."

Pippa, disturbed by their voices, whimpered and came awake. Clare turned from him and picked up the baby, put her to a shoulder, and patted her. She wiped at her tears and looked at him again, eyes unguarded, and he was almost certain he saw in them what he longed to see.

A need that had nothing to do with Jacob.

He didn't want to leave her with so much between them frayed, but he meant to spend the night preparing for battle with his brothers, set apart from their families, each seeking strength and guidance in his own way.

"I'm going to fight to my last drop of blood to keep harm from you, from this place," he told her. "Dunmore's soldiers will have to get through me—and eight hundred other warriors—to reach you."

His words seemed to bring her no comfort. There was so much more he wanted to say that he feared she wasn't ready to hear. But what if he never had another chance to say it?

"Clare, never think I regret a moment of what's passed since I came upon you at that wagon, about to birth that sweet baby girl you're holding. I'd lay down more than a few months of my life for you. I'd lay it all down. All my years. This body too, if you need it."

He raised his hand to Pippa's head, not daring to touch her mother as he longed to do. She caught his gaze, a stirring in her eyes, then she stepped back from him.

"Jeremiah," she said, her voice a bare thread. "Please come back."

"You know I cannot promise it."

"I know." Gratitude flashed across her eyes, though for what he didn't know.

He went to pack the things he'd need for the coming campaign. They were few and gathered quickly, but in the process his hand encountered something in his knapsack he'd all but forgotten he placed there. He withdrew it, stood, and held it out to Clare.

She stared at the object in his hand, the timepiece that had been Philip Inglesby's, handed down from his grandfather. Still crushed. Still unopened.

She took it. "Didn't I throw this away, back in the clearing where Pippa was born?"

"I fetched it out of the weeds while you slept. Thought you might change your mind and want it back."

He watched her face as she looked from him to the timepiece, all that was left to her of her former life, save her children. Pain and sorrow sharpened her gaze, but there was more there. Acceptance, resignation, maybe even peace.

"Thank you. Maybe one day it can be Jacob's, if ever I have the chance to see it mended."

He stood at the door-hide a moment, setting the sight of her and Pippa to memory. She watched him back with equal intensity.

"God keep you, Clare," he said at last and went out to find his brothers.

"And you," she'd forced through a throat too tight for speech, though she didn't think he'd heard her. The air of the lodge seemed to buzz with his passionate words. So did her head. And heart. Why hadn't he touched her? He'd plainly wanted to. She wished he had, even if it wouldn't have changed a thing.

Would she ever see him again? He hadn't promised, and for his honesty she was thankful, and yet . . . for the first time in her life she wished a man had lied to her, had told her what she wanted to hear, had promised her a future, a hope, all the things he'd just said he wanted. With her.

All my years . . .

Instead he'd handed her Philip's timepiece and walked out of the lodge to go fight a battle that stood between them and all their years.

Almost she went running to the door-hide. Almost she gave in to the need to call him back. But where would it lead? What would a few more moments solve? He had to go, though she knew he would never willingly abandon her. Her only regret was that he'd likely left thinking she believed that's what he was doing.

She looked at the timepiece, thought of the man who had cherished it, and realized she no longer mourned him or the life they'd had. There was sorrow for its tragic ending, for all the failures that had led to that ending—hers as well as Philip's—but the grief didn't pierce as it had. Nor did the regret. And she knew why.

Jeremiah.

But she couldn't open her heart to him yet, couldn't let such passions distract her when she needed to be as single-minded as he.

It was going to take all she had, mind and heart, not to let Jacob slip through her grasp again as her world turned upside down.

29

OCTOBER 9, 1774
POINT PLEASANT, VIRGINIA COLONY

At noon on the first Sunday spent at the encampment at the mouth of the Kanawha River, the men of Colonel Andrew Lewis's command gathered for their customary religious service, led by the Southern Army's chaplain.

Looking around at the faces of the men assembled to hear the exhortation, Alphus Litchfield detected little pleasure in their expressions, though it hadn't to do with anything the man behind the makeshift log pulpit was saying.

Alphus reckoned it a good thing they'd dubbed their camp Point Pleasant before they'd found the message from Governor Dunmore.

Not that the place wasn't deserving of the name, situated on a triangle of land on the north bank of the Kanawha where it flowed into the Ohio. The rivers formed two sides of the triangle, while a high ridge, at the base of which flowed a creek aptly named Crooked, created the third and longest side. The densely forested hills were ablaze in autumn tints, the ground beneath a carpet of leaves so thick that to walk those wooded aisles made a man feel encased in a tunnel of gold.

The rivers were low, the Ohio at that point nigh as calm as a lake, reflecting the sky and the fiery ridgeline opposite clear as a looking glass. Across this scene, flurries of wind-driven leaves whirled like amber sparks.

Upon arrival, many of the men briefly forgot the purpose of their being there, transported by the enchantment of the place—a spell broken when a scout discovered the letter from Dunmore concealed in a hollow tree. Assembled in his marquee, Colonel Lewis informed his officers of the letter's content; orders to move the Southern Army upriver to the Hocking still stood, to everyone's dismay.

A messenger was sent with a letter entreating Dunmore once again to adhere to the original plan and come downriver to Point Pleasant.

Meanwhile the army went about the business of mending clothes and equipment, fortifying the encampment, securing supplies, caring for livestock.

Days passed, thinning the patience of officers and men alike. Finally that morning more messengers sent from Dunmore arrived—with yet another change in orders.

The Shawnees had rejected the governor's invitation to a peace council on the Hocking. Dunmore now purposed to take his troops directly across the Ohio and begin the march toward the Scioto towns. Lewis's army was to meet the governor at a ridge somewhere southeast of the Pickaway Plains.

Reactions among the officers to this vague rendezvous in the middle of hostile Indian territory had ranged from consternation to blazing outrage. They couldn't abandon their present encampment before the Fincastle Regiment and the rest of the army arrived from Camp Union. Leaving Point Pleasant and pushing deep into Shawnee lands with their smaller numbers would be inviting attack, with their enemy having the advantage of knowing the terrain. Did Dunmore mean to sacrifice his Southern Army, deliberately leaving them open to attack?

And what were they to make of these continued rumors, also brought by Dunmore's messengers, of militiamen in Massachusetts battling British soldiers?

Alphus Litchfield wasn't the only one frustrated at not knowing who or what to believe, cut off from the colony and about to face a fierce and implacable enemy.

At least that latter concern didn't seem to overly distress the men, Alphus thought as he looked around the little clearing where the meeting was taking place. They felt themselves in good position, there in the forks of the river. As long as they could remain on the Virginia side until Dunmore saw fit to join them, they didn't fear attack.

"Let 'em cross the river and try us," he'd overheard Ezra Baldwin boasting around the fire. "We'll send 'em back with their tails tucked."

Sitting on a log as the preacher preached, with the murmur of the rivers in his ears, dazzled by the leaves burning like flames along the ridgeline, Alphus tried to clear his mind of everything but this place, this campaign. Perhaps after this assemblage broke up he'd take Lieutenant Woodbane and a few others and scout that twisty little creek and the high ridge beyond it. He wanted to know the lay of this land. Felt the need in his bones to learn it intimately.

He'd a sense that men were coming, but not necessarily Dunmore's.

CORNSTALK'S TOWN, OCTOBER 9, EVENING

Cornstalk and Nonhelema, along with their brothers and the war chiefs, had led the warriors east toward the Ohio, with Jeremiah, Falling Hawk, and Wolf-Alone in their ranks. Unable to bear the solitude, Clare had gone to Rain Crow's lodge, hoping to see Jacob, but once again Rain Crow refused to let her in—or Jacob out.

"She fear," Crosses-the-Path explained when Clare found admittance into her lodge. "She fear soldiers come, you take Many Sparrows, run to army."

With shaking hands Clare set Pippa on a buffalo hide for Crosses-the-Path's girls to entertain, then knelt by the fire and looked imploringly at their mother.

"I'm not going to do that." Even as the words left her lips, Clare knew their dishonesty. If the opportunity presented itself to do exactly that, she might take it. But the chances of that happening seemed almost nonexistent.

Crosses-the-Path looked miserable and torn. Clare was sick to her soul of her plight doing that to everyone who held any sympathy for her.

Jeremiah. There was so much she should have said to him, this man who'd put his life on hold for her, borne himself with dignity through an impossible situation. Why had she let him go into battle without telling him what that meant to her, what *he* meant to her?

"You're saying the right words, but only you can know whether you truly trust Him." Those words had plowed deep, turning up the soil of her heart, unearthing doubts and fears.

How could she lay down the need to regain her son? Her *son*. How did a mother do such a thing? The very notion filled her with a panic so visceral she could barely breathe.

There was but one directive of Jeremiah's she could obey.

"Stay with Crosses-the-Path."

She saw Crosses-the-Path chewing at her lip, anxiety mirrored in her round face. She was worried for Falling Hawk, for all the warriors gone to face the Virginians. Clare felt a kinship with her as never before.

"May Pippa and I stay with you?" she asked. "Until the men are back? I don't want to be alone in that lodge."

Of course they were welcomed. Crosses-the-Path rarely said no to anything Clare asked of her. But Clare caught the glint of question in her gaze. Was she really asking to stay so she might have a better chance at seeing Jacob? Of *taking* Jacob?

Questions that thankfully went unasked.

ALONG THE OHIO RIVER,
OCTOBER 9, NIGHTFALL

The warriors had come down to the trail that ran along the Ohio, but Jeremiah knew they wouldn't cross opposite the point where the Kanawha joined its waters to its flow. Concealed by the wooded ridgeline, they followed that trail three miles upriver, where a few of the warriors and youths who had accompanied them would remain with the horses and excess belongings the warriors left behind; they would take nothing but weapons and waterskins with them over to the other side.

They crossed the river by raft, under cover of darkness, coming ashore in small groups at the mouth of a creek where once a Shawnee town had stood, long ago abandoned.

They knew from their scouts that the Virginians couldn't be surrounded, but they could be trapped, there on that point of land between rivers, if the Shawnees could make themselves a long advancing line, come upon them in the twilight before dawn to attack the camp and block escape to the east.

Many, they hoped, would have no time to raise a weapon or even emerge from their tents.

Once across the river, they camped at the old town creek. Dressed for war, stripped to breechclout and moccasins, they'd been divided into units of sixty warriors. Jeremiah, Falling Hawk, and Wolf-Alone would fight under Cornstalk's leadership. Others would fight with Nonhelema, Blue Jacket, Puckeshinwah, Black Snake, and the rest of the war chiefs.

Wolf-Alone approved his chief's strategy. "He is thinking like a white general thinks."

"Do you know how white generals think, brother?" Falling Hawk asked. Clouds had covered stars and moon so that his face was unreadable, but there was teasing in his voice.

"It may be I know something of it," Wolf-Alone said.

Jeremiah felt more than saw Falling Hawk turn to look at him, seated on the ground in a bed of leaves. They were well used to their brother and his mysteries, but tonight Jeremiah wanted to push beyond that wall Wolf-Alone kept raised.

"So here we are, and tomorrow maybe one of us, or all, will stand before Creator," he said. "Do you not think it time to tell us who you were before you rose out of that creek like a fish sprouting legs?"

"You did not come into being that day," Falling Hawk said, perhaps catching what stirred in Jeremiah's heart, that sense that this could be their last chance to speak of such things.

Wolf-Alone was silent for a while. They waited.

"Brothers," he said at last. "It is not that I do not wish you to know who I was before. But truly that man is no more. It would be like speaking of the dead to mention his name. Will you be content that you have a brother, Wolf-Alone, who will fight beside you as the sun is rising, who will do all he can to keep you whole and bring you back to your women and children?"

Jeremiah swallowed, finding a lump had formed at the base of his throat. Falling Hawk too might have found such an obstruction, for he didn't speak at once. Jeremiah saw his hand lift, catching the glimmer of moonlight through the clouds. It came to rest on their brother's broad shoulder.

"It is more than enough. Let us sleep now."

Around them others were lying down in the leaves and grasses of that place Shawnees once lived. Were any of them thinking of those lives lived there? Were they thinking of the towns back along the Scioto and how easily they could be swept away, leaving no more than a memory on the land?

What were the Virginians thinking as they took to their bedrolls just a few miles to the south? Jeremiah was sick at thought of killing them—and trying not to think of Clare's uncle among them—but just as Cornstalk was doing what he must, because it was the will of the people, he too would do what he must to keep safe those who held his heart in their hands—his brothers, his sister, Crosses-the-Path and her children, Wildcat, Pippa and Jacob. *Clare.*

Just don't let me come face to face with Alphus Litchfield. Any man but that one.

Sometime before dawn tinged the sky above the ridges and mountains to the east, Wolf-Alone shook him awake as others around them were stirring.

One by one, eight hundred warriors fell into file and began their advance to the place where they would spread their line between the rivers. Heading down one of the low ridges that ran along the Ohio, which flowed now on their right, they crept through the predawn wood toward the base of a much higher ridge, where a mist was rising, spreading from the twisted creek bottom.

30

Alphus Litchfield came awake in his bedroll and stifled a groan as old aches gave themselves new voice. Hips, back, knees, and more protested, having marched a hundred and forty miles over rugged terrain. It was yet an hour, best he could tell, before he needed to be sitting up, so he lay still, eyes shut, inviting sleep's return, but he couldn't shut his ears to the call of a pre-dawn bird or the snores of his men.

Another company would be rising now, heading to relieve those on sentry during the night past, doubtless by now staring into the murky dark of the wood, bleary-eyed, fighting to stay wakeful.

Was it Captain Russell's Fincastle men on sentry duty this morning? *No, ought to be McClanahan's.* Tonight it would fall to Alphus's company again, if they were still encamped there.

No help for it. His mind was up and running, busy with the doings of the day about to break. Would they spend it waiting for Dunmore to change his mind again or cross the Ohio and make for his vague wilderness rendezvous?

Last he'd heard, Colonel Lewis hadn't decided.

Instead of speculating, he traced in memory the two short sides of the triangle that was their camp, where tents stretched along the rivers, including his own company's on the Kanawha side, along with the rest of Augusta County Regiment, some of the Botetort companies and others—among them William

Russell's company of men who'd come up from the Overmountain country near the Tennessee River.

Alphus had heard those men talking the evening before as they sat around the fires, about how they'd formed themselves an independent colony, though they were careful not to name it so. The Watauga Association, they called it. It was needful, they said, with the North Carolina seat of government so far off to the east, no decent roads to connect them to the rest of the colony, cut off for weeks at a time when snow fell with no one but themselves to depend on for aid in the face of Indian threat. Why not govern themselves while they were at it?

He'd listened and wondered whether it was Crown approved or something of a little rebellion going on across those high Carolina mountains. Those men—Russell, Shelby, Sevier, and others—had had a lot to say about what was purported to be happening back east, particularly in Massachusetts.

"Might be independence is coming for the rest of the colonies," Isaac Shelby had remarked.

"Especially with Crown-appointed governors who cannot even settle on a rendezvous," one called Valentine Sevier quipped, to the wry chuckles and dark assenting looks of his listeners, none of whom were pleased in the slightest with the turn Governor Dunmore's campaign had taken.

Alphus didn't express his agreement openly, but listening to the Over-mountain men, he had, for the first time in years, felt the old wanderlust stirring—that urge to turn his back on the settled east, climb a ridge, and look away westward. To sell what he could, load up a horse with goods enough to get by on, and just set out.

The report of gunfire, distant but sharp, dispelled his drifting thoughts like mist before a gale wind. He strained his ears as its echo died away. North-eastward, he made it, upriver along the Ohio-facing ridges.

He was out of his tent and running, rifle in hand, struggling to sling

cartridge box and powder horn across his chest, even before the solitary soldier
came stumbling into camp, his progress just perceptible in the graying dawn,
frantic in his shouting.

"Then the fog parted, and right afore us was a whole line of 'em, Colonel—
Indians stretching far as I could see, coming on toward the camp." The young
private, Mooney, who'd been out hunting turkeys in the dark, gasped in air
between the words. "One of 'em shot Hughey! Shot him dead, I think."

Colonel Andrew Lewis's set expression didn't alter at this news, the truth
of which every officer who'd managed to assemble outside his tent had already
surmised.

"How close?" he demanded.

"Still out past that big ridge, sir. Mile and half off but likely coming on fast
behind."

Alphus, who'd scouted that land yesterday, had its lay still sharp in his
mind. The high ridge to the east rose about a half mile from where they now
stood, thickly wooded save where boney knuckles of stone protruded. It rose
over two hundred feet, in some places its slopes almost vertical. At its foot,
Crooked Creek made its meandering way to the Kanawha, coming down the
low ground between the high ridge and two lower ridges to the west. Those
ridges ran parallel to the Ohio. It would be along those the Shawnees were
coming.

Alphus said so but added, "Not fast. They'll come on cautious now they've
been seen."

"They mean to pin us in," Colonel Lewis's brother, Charles, in command
of the Augusta County Regiment, said. "Here in the river fork. We cannot let
them."

"We don't know that for certain, sir," said a voice behind Alphus. "Private Mooney couldn't see the entire line. Could be just a skirmishing party."

Andrew Lewis raised a hand to halt the debate. "How many *did* you see, Private?"

"Acres of 'em, sir. Thick as ticks on a dog."

Every man present drilled Private Mooney with a stare, likely thinking the same thing. Had it only *looked* to Mooney—shocked, affrighted, half-blind in the misted dark—like a full army of Indians?

Andrew Lewis hadn't the luxury of dismissing the prospect. He pulled a pipe from his coat and put it to his lips unlit. After a pause that seemed eternal, he ordered his drummers to beat "To Arms," signaling the army to assemble. Then he gave his orders.

Two columns would advance up the Ohio, a hundred men in each. His brother, Charles, would lead one, made up primarily of the Augusta County companies. Colonel William Fleming, commanding the Botetourt County Regiment, would lead the other.

Charles Lewis turned to find his captains, those who'd made it out of their tents—Dickinson, Harrison, Wilson, Skidmore, and Alphus Litchfield. "Choose you twelve, thirteen men each, whomever is awake and ready. We advance on Fleming's right, a parallel course along those low ridges, aiming for the spot Mooney saw the Indians. Fast as you can muster!"

Cornstalk's plan had been to reach the low-lying land along the creek at the base of the high cliff, then spread out in a line between the rivers, cutting off escape for the Virginians. Scouts had returned to the chiefs in the night to inform them of where sentries were posted. Not a one had been detected. But no one had anticipated soldiers venturing out past the sentries before dawn.

"Looking for something to eat besides beef and biscuits," Jeremiah had murmured as, the element of surprise obliterated by a warrior's shooting one of the soldiers, they'd listened to the panicked shouts of the other soldier and the crackle of his scrambling down the wooded ridge in the dark, diminishing into distance.

There'd come a moment's hesitation, a sense of the warriors around him hovering on the verge of turning heel and abandoning the attack before it had begun. At the crucial second, Cornstalk had spoken, and the word passed quickly along their ranks; they would meet the militia in battle even without surprise. Most of these warriors, save the very youngest, had hunted over this land countless times in their younger years, before the whites had pressed so far west. They still had the dark and the terrain on their side. And, with a little luck, they could re-create that surprise.

Cornstalk had led them forward, along with Nonhelema and his captains, Puckeshinwah, Blue Jacket, and the rest, each commanding a unit of warriors, leaving some in the rear as reserves. Some units took position on the low ridges, burying themselves in leaves or finding concealment in logs or behind trees. Others sought the low ground where the creek flowed, at the base of the steep-faced ridge, in an attempt to get round the soldiers if possible and block their retreat up the Kanawha Trail.

Jeremiah and his brothers had started out on the easternmost of the low ridges, crouched in hiding as darkness began to lift, listening long after the cries of the man they'd surprised fell silent.

Then had come the beating of drums and, with the dawning of the day, a column of soldiers creeping up the wooded ridge through the mist as the sun crested that highland to the east.

At first their ambush seemed to work with surprising effect, as if these Virginians had forgotten the manner of Indian warfare and expected to meet an orderly line of warriors waiting in the open to be shot at. The Shawnees' first volley, fired after springing out of cover, had so stunned the Virginians that the Indians had time to reload for a second firing before the militiamen scattered for cover.

More gunfire, attended by the tremolo screams of warriors, erupted to Jeremiah's right, over a hundred yards away; there'd been a second column of Virginians creeping along that ridge nearest the river.

Now powder smoke drifted with the rising mist. The yellow-leafed earth was spattered red with gore. The Virginians were firing back, though not all together, not by command. Man by man, each side sought for targets among the shadowy wood, beginning to blaze with morning's advance. Soldiers and warriors sprang out of hiding to take a shot, then dove back to reload before an enemy could overrun his position. As was their way, the Shawnees targeted first the commanding officers whenever powder smoke cleared enough to see. They were not hard to pick out. They were the ones standing up and shouting.

One or two voices doing most of the shouting made it clear whomever was still alive among their officers was trying to form a battle line. If there was a line at present, it was like a snake in its death throes, writhing across the broken landscape, pushed ahead by the Virginians or pushed back by the Shawnees.

The din of gunfire and screams rang in Jeremiah's ears as he discharged his rifle, then ducked back beside Wolf-Alone to reload.

Wolf-Alone fired, then he and Jeremiah switched places.

"See the log with the moss thick on top, red leaves piled below?" Wolf-Alone asked as he ran the ramrod down the length of his rifle barrel and yanked it free. "Down the slope ahead of us. Long Knives lie behind it. Three, I think. One is wounded. I do not think I killed him. They have seen where we hide."

"I see it." Powder smoke had drifted between the log and their position higher up on the ridge, acrid in Jeremiah's nose, stinging his eyes, thin enough to make out the log but barely. He waited, darting looks from behind the tree, making sure no soldier was rushing their position or creeping in for a closer kill.

In the near distance, lost from view in the fiery foliage, he could hear the high, strong scream of Nonhelema fighting, nearer still the commanding voice of Cornstalk exhorting the warriors to be strong, to press their advantage. That voice had seemed to be everywhere as the morning and the battle advanced, moving from ridge to ridge, always exhorting, lending courage, giving direction.

Indeed it seemed the Virginians were being pushed back toward their camp. The Shawnees had gained the ground where the first of them had fallen, and more ground besides.

Just as Jeremiah dared hope it would be a swift victory for the Shawnees, the Virginians were no longer falling back but holding strong. Even when they were shot and killed, their numbers seemed to increase.

"They've sent reinforcements," Jeremiah shouted to Wolf-Alone beside him and to Falling Hawk crouched behind a stump off to their right.

Falling Hawk didn't hear what he'd said but, apparently thinking it something important he should hear, broke from cover and sprinted across an open space between them.

He almost made it before a musket ball took him in the shoulder, spun him hard, and knocked him to the churned leaf mold, sprawled across the body of a Virginian killed in the first volley and scalped.

He didn't get up.

"Shoot at them, brother!" Wolf-Alone shouted.

Assured Jeremiah would do so, he lunged from cover to grasp Falling Hawk by the ankles and dragged him behind their tree, while Jeremiah aimed at the crown of a hat poking above the log down the ridge and fired. He'd his tomahawk in hand, gaze darting about in case other soldiers had them in their sights. Then Wolf-Alone was back behind their tree, laying Falling Hawk down, crouching to reload; Jeremiah did likewise before he looked to see if Falling Hawk lived.

31

Of the Augusta County officers who had advanced in the first column, few were still able to command. Colonel Charles Lewis, shot early on, had retreated back to camp with help. Dead or living now, Alphus didn't know. Of the captains accompanying the column, Wilson was dead, Dickinson and Skidmore wounded. Harrison was alive somewhere off to his right along the ridge, from whence his bellowing could now and then be heard.

Alphus had struggled to wrangle the men around him, most belonging to other companies, and direct them in the fight. When attacked from the front, they were meant to wheel forward, each file away from the other, to form a line at the fore of the column—an impossible maneuver once every man dove for cover under the Indians' fire. Many thereafter refused to obey his command, either to advance or form any semblance of a battle line—either from stubbornness or loyalty to their captains lost in the confusion, wounded or dead. Some out of abject terror had refused to fight at all, crouched in cover like frightened rabbits. Others had turned tail and fled back to camp at the first volley.

Along with Harrison, Alphus had cursed, exhorted, threatened, and somehow managed to stay alive and unscathed through the initial clash and beyond, when most of the men recovered from shock and began fighting like frontier Virginians, picking their Indian targets from behind trees and logs and making their shots count, giving ground only when too hard pressed, taking it back where they could.

Thin face streaked by powder smoke, young Geordie Reynolds had stuck to Alphus's side since Lieutenant Tom Woodbane fell. True to the promise he'd made the boy's mother, Woodbane had shoved Geordie from the path of two musket barrels aimed at the lad. The first ball clipped the boy's shoulder and embedded itself in a stump. The second had taken Woodbane through the neck.

The graze hadn't slowed the lad. Nor had the shock of Woodbane's death. He'd hardened that stark, dirty face and was reloading and firing his rifle with cold accuracy, teeth bared in a rictus of rage and grief.

Alphus thrust his own grief aside, having no thought to spare beyond the crises of the second. This was no skirmishing party but a full-on army of Shawnees, and they weren't fighting in their usual manner—a hard strike and a hasty retreat. They were dug in along the ridges, down in the bottomland too, not just holding their ground but pressing their assault.

Leaving their dead behind to be scalped, the Virginians had given ground. Some four hundred yards of it by Alphus's estimation.

More of the screaming devils kept coming, yet even the shouts and yips and ululations one would expect from such a force seemed subdued. Alphus sensed their intent not simply to harass and intimidate but utterly annihilate the whole of the Southern Army, to break through their line and overrun the camp and slaughter them to a man.

But thanks be to the Almighty and Colonel Lewis, reinforcements were streaming in and they were able finally to push back, at least here on the ridge where Alphus commanded.

To his relief, some of the reinforcements were of his company, ready to obey. He ordered them to fill any spots where men had fallen, then caught sight of another encouragement—over to their left the Botetort men had regained better order, creating a rough but discernable line, the near end of which Alphus glimpsed through the trees.

"We got help now!" he shouted to any near enough to hear, wishing he could project his voice like the Indian he'd been hearing all morning from across the battle line, higher up on the ridge, moving from place to place. Always shouting the same words. He wondered what they meant when he'd time to think of such things and who it was shouting them. Then a painted face would show itself, aiming a rifle his way, and he'd have no time for idle speculation.

"I see 'em, sir!" Geordie exclaimed at his side, craning his neck along the ridgeline. "Botetort men?"

"Right. Others coming up behind from camp. Make your way back out of this now, if you want."

Through its mask of grime and blood, the boy's expression darkened. "No sir! I'm gonna fight long as there's redskins to kill. Woodbane . . ."

He choked on the name and said no more.

The kid had hunted squirrels since he was big enough to tote a rifle. Though he'd wordlessly taken over Woodbane's guardianship of the boy, at times it felt to Alphus as if Geordie Reynolds was guarding *him*.

"All right." He'd no idea how much time had passed since Private Mooney came rushing into camp. Felt like hours, though he thought it still morning.

Something was changing now. Indians to their left were falling back before the press of reinforcements sent up to the Botetort column. Virginians rushed the incline, up into a newly vacated hollow choked with wounded.

Fire, reload, move from tree to tree. A slow but dogged pursuit.

Soon the Indians in front of Alphus seemed likewise to be giving way. But he was cautious. He'd known Indians to feign retreat to lure unwary soldiers too far, then surround and slaughter them.

Alphus took a chance and advanced several yards up a leafy slope, Geordie on his heels. They reached a moss-covered log high enough to hunker behind once a couple of dead soldiers were pushed out of the way.

One of Skidmore's company joined them. Between them Geordie settled in, panting for breath.

"What's happening now, Capt'n?"

"Lord only knows, but Colonel Lewis is doing something right."

The firing directly before them had tapered off, but he could still hear fighting ongoing to left and right. It was only a momentary lull, however, before a rush of warriors had them firing fast and ducking to reload.

He'd never known Indians to press an assault with such tenacity. For hours it went on, the sun climbing high, making streaks through the fiery woods that half-blinded men trying to spot their enemy darting through the trees, using the light to their advantage.

No matter how quick or clever, the Indians revealed themselves each time they fired by a spurt of flame and smoke. Then a dozen Virginia marksmen took aim, needing but a hand or foot to make a target. Protected by the covering fire, a few braver souls darted or crawled forward to where the musket had flashed and finished off whomever they found lurking behind tree or log.

The battle line in its coiling throes had gradually pushed back northward after that initial loss of ground; the Indians were falling back, but every yard of ground they gave came at a cost in Virginian blood.

Shouts came along the ridge to Alphus's left. Captain Evan Shelby, commanding the Overmountain Wataugans, had come up with more men and was taking command of the field, bringing the Augusta County men into his line.

Hailing him, Alphus rallied those men still following him, Geordie at his side, as Shelby himself came darting through the wood to hunker behind their log.

They were, Shelby informed him, fighting from the Ohio River eastward all the way to the flanks of the high ridge. They'd enough men in the field to hold the line, but while the Botetort companies were pushing the Indians farther along the western ridge, there on the next ridge over the Indians had again become entrenched; the opposing lines had drawn near each other, near enough to hear individual voices.

And there was that clarion call Alphus had heard intermittently throughout the battle, still shouting strong. A yard to his right, crouched behind a thicketed stump, a Wataugan private inquired of that voice and what it was saying.

"Be strong," another said. "*Be strong.* That's what."

Another Indian voice rose, nearer, taunting. This one spoke in English, epithets his only vocabulary in that tongue apparently.

Others in the enemy ranks took up the same taunts, here and there a warrior brazenly showing himself to the Virginians less than twenty yards away.

Off to Alphus's right a warrior came screaming straight at the gun barrel of a militiaman who couldn't load in time. He whipped out his belt ax and met the warrior's attack. Alphus caught but a glimpse before another warrior rushed him in like manner.

For some time after, it was a jumble of ducking and scrambling and hacking, the smell of blood and leaves and earth, of flesh and sweat and gunpowder. The screams of dying men and those doing the killing. The fierce features of savages and the blades of their tomahawks and the spiked ends of their clubs.

From the corner of his eye he was keeping track of Geordie, but the lad was holding his own, fighting viciously.

Woodbane would've been proud.

Alphus emerged bruised, bleeding, and half-dazed to find Geordie alive still, having killed three more Indians to Alphus's two. The battle at that point had become a scattering of individual combatants, as Indians and Virginians raced each other to reload or prevailed over each other by strength, speed, or plain ferocity.

Then once again the line of battle thinned and receded northward as the Indians fell back farther.

Alphus found a breath of space to take stock of the immediate situation. More Virginians had fallen, a few dead, more wounded. Some thirty yards ahead on the ridge, figures were moving, Indians dragging their wounded and dead back with them as they retreated, not quite concealed in the sun-dazzled woods, hazed with drifting smoke.

Geordie saw them too, and something Alphus had missed.

"Sir! Is that—it's a white man with 'em. Fighting with 'em. Look!"

Alphus looked, even as he was thinking he'd fought as long as a body his age could be expected to fight and then some. Lord, but it felt like suppertime, though it couldn't be that late in the day. Whatever the time, he didn't know if he had it in him to make one more rush after their enemies.

But the boy was young and grieving and freshly riled. He'd his rifle loaded and was already swinging it toward the trio of warriors, two of which were supporting the third who sagged between them, clutching their long firearms in their free hands.

Along the crest of the ridge, other Indians were doing the same, bringing off dead and wounded comrades as they withdrew, but only among these, dressed like them in breechclout and war paint and little else, was the unmistakable pale skin of a white man. He was one of the two supporting the wounded warrior. The other was an Indian, tall and well-muscled, his hair unshaven. The three were about to pass between two towering yellow-leafed oaks and disappear over the crest, down the other side.

Alphus felt a seething at sight of that long white back.

"Take him down, Geordie," he said, voice rasped with shouting, throat gritted with smoke.

"Gladly, sir." The boy leveled his rifle and fired.

Falling Hawk lived, though his wound was deep and bleeding heavily. For a while he'd sat upright behind the tree while Jeremiah and Wolf-Alone continued to fire. Jeremiah had seen too many acts of bravery and fortitude to count on the part of the Shawnees and Mingos, far beyond what these warriors were accustomed to committing to in a battle. They'd lost valued men in the doing of those deeds, some of them chiefs. Puckeshinwah, the war chief, and Silverheels, Cornstalk's brother, were counted among the dead. Many besides Falling Hawk were wounded.

At some point in the afternoon, word had come that more Virginians were on the Kanawha Trail; runners had been sent up to alert them of the battle and hurry them along. Even if the Shawnees defeated these soldiers, more were coming. And there was still Dunmore's Northern Army to reckon with. If they didn't triumph here, that army would likely sweep them west beyond the Scioto, if they weren't all killed first and ceased to be a people.

So they'd fought longer and harder and taken more risks, all these brave warriors, than they would have if the consequences of failing weren't so high, but the afternoon was passing and hope for victory with it. The pushes forward had become less frequent, the fallings back deeper. The Shawnees couldn't break the Virginians' line, and they were running out of powder and ball.

Falling Hawk, though conscious, was slumped against the broad oak behind which Jeremiah and Wolf-Alone still took aim. They had wounded more Virginians from that spot, but Falling Hawk needed to be taken off the field.

When there was a lull, Wolf-Alone and Jeremiah got their brother up and, supporting him between them, made as hurried a dash as they could to reach a point of better cover. Jeremiah recalled a hollow beyond the crest behind them, just a few yards distant, that would lend cover. They'd get Falling Hawk well back, then return to help hold off the Virginians while the wounded retreated to the river and the rafts that would carry them across.

The three reached the lip of the hollow amidst the leaf-ripping of musket balls, the shouts of soldiers and warriors, the screams of dying men. Wolf-Alone descended a short way first, reaching back to take Falling Hawk's weight as Jeremiah steadied him from above.

He never heard the shot—his ears were in a state of constant ringing—but a fiery pain seared the flesh above his right hip, and he stumbled under the impact, lost his grip on Falling Hawk, and tumbled down the leaf-strewn forest slope into the hollow below.

He fetched up hard against a stony outcrop. Wolf-Alone lost his grasp on their brother, who likewise fell, landing atop Jeremiah, who had to roll him aside in order to get to his knees.

"You are hit?" Wolf-Alone had leapt down into the hollow to crouch beside them, desperation marking that face so habitually composed.

"I am." Jeremiah's voice issued breathless as he tried to cover the blaze of agony arching through his side, above the cord of his breechclout. He reached his hand down and found leaves plastered to the wound, held there by his blood. "Just a graze."

He barely looked at the wound, so he didn't know whether he spoke the truth, but fear nipped at his mind as he got to his feet. He dropped a glance to his side. Blood was spilling down his leg.

Wolf-Alone hadn't noticed, busy getting Falling Hawk back on his feet while Jeremiah reached to brace their brother beneath a shoulder. He made it a few yards beyond the hollow, following the low ridge back the way they'd come in the predawn, before he staggered, his right leg giving under him.

"You are bad hit?" Wolf-Alone asked, taking Falling Hawk's weight.

Jeremiah went down to one knee. "Get our brother to safety. I can walk but cannot carry anyone else."

Again somehow he was on his feet, but Wolf-Alone protested, "I will not take him and leave you!"

"I will be coming." When Wolf-Alone still hesitated, Jeremiah found the strength to give his arm a push. It nearly sent him reeling off his feet. "Go!"

He could see the reluctant decision made in his brother's face, while Falling Hawk raised dark eyes to him in a dazed, wordless look of . . . not farewell but something near to it.

"I will return for you," Wolf-Alone said, and the two started away.

Jeremiah made it to a tree and looked back but saw no sign of militia following them over the lip of the hollow. Not yet. They would come, but cautiously.

He made it three steps alone, four . . .

The earth hit hard as he fell. Almost at once he roused, fear coursing through him. He would be overrun by Virginians if he didn't draw off farther or . . . could he hide himself?

On his knees he looked about. No hollow logs or stumps met his gaze but there . . . a drift of leaves at the base of a tree. He crawled toward it but didn't reach the leaves before his arms buckled.

A musket ball whizzed past his ear as he fell facedown again. He was in someone's sights. He rolled onto his back, nearly screaming with the pain.

Briefly he thought he heard Cornstalk's mighty voice shouting to his warriors to be strong and to fight. Some would be holding the line to let the wounded and those who helped them retreat.

Cornstalk's voice—if it had been his—faded.

Others replaced it, shouting in English. The Virginians were about to overrun him.

Wolf-Alone would not be back. Not in time.

He felt his blood flowing out onto the ground and tried to gaze along his ribs but couldn't raise his head to see far down his body. Blood spattered the fallen leaves near his face. Small blotches and pools of it, red on gold. Or were those red leaves among the yellow?

Beyond them warriors lay, three in a tangle of limbs. He hadn't noticed them before. He knew their faces. He'd be among their number soon. He was dying, leaving something undone. Some important thing he'd been meant to do.

Many Sparrows. No, Jacob Inglesby. Clare. *Father in heaven, help her . . . Clare.*

Still lying on his back, no longer hearing shouts or gunfire or even the crackle of leaves as booted feet approached him, he turned his face to the boughs above, eyes struck by the light of a westering sun. It slanted in beams through a canopy speckled every shade of gold imaginable. If he couldn't see Clare again before he died, those green eyes, her smile, then this was a good sight to end it with.

Until it was blotted out by a shadow coming between, indistinct in form with the blaze of sunlight behind it.

He blinked. The shadow resolved into the faces of two men looking down at him. Both were white, one more boy than man, though he'd a man's hardness about the eyes. The other was older than Jeremiah. Begrimed with soot and streaked with sweat, both wore the same twisted look of disgust, as if he were an insect one of them had stepped upon.

The older one was speaking. Leastwise his mouth was moving. Jeremiah couldn't make out the words. There was something about that face, those eyes, something he maybe ought to know. Or remember.

Something chill and wet struck his brow. At first he thought the men were crying over him, ludicrous as that seemed, but the wetness pelted him again and he knew it for rainfall. It was the last he knew before darkness rolled over him.

32

With the rain's onset, the Indians had fallen back a final time, with enough skirmishing to convince Colonel Lewis to send three companies scrambling up the high ridge to the east to fire down on the retreating Shawnees, encouraging them to keep going—all the way across the Ohio. The rest of the army, ordered back to camp, brought with them the battle's casualties.

All told they'd lost upwards of eighty men, nearly twice that wounded. Alphus had been appalled at the lack of tending the latter were receiving as darkness fell. Overwhelmed by sheer numbers, their sole army surgeon had conscripted anyone willing to help, no matter how unskilled, but some of the wounded had expired for neglect.

Bone-weary after nearly twelve hours of battle, after carrying in the white man found fighting with the Indians and leaving him bleeding outside the hospital tent, after helping bring in the dead—including Woodbane—after sitting with Geordie Reynolds while the lad bawled his eyes out for that old soldier . . . after all that, Captain Alphus Litchfield slept like one dead himself, straight through the midnight arrival of reinforcements into camp.

In the predawn gray next morning, he joined his men at the fire. Most had risen early despite fatigue, half-expecting the Indians to attack again. Thus far stillness had prevailed in the mist-shrouded wood and along the foggy rivers.

The only sounds were the clanking, hawking, cow-bawling, fire-crackling, and steam-hissing of an army encampment coming awake.

They were a subdued lot, his company. Besides Woodbane they'd lost two others, Jon Lawson among them. Most of the rest bore some manner of wounding. One or two moved with evident pain.

Ezra Baldwin laid a seared slab beef on a tin plate, handed it to his captain, and as Alphus took it said, "Don't know if'n you heard, Capt'n, but that fellow you been keen to find? He come in late last night with the Fincastle companies fetched in by Colonel Lewis's runner."

Judah Sawyer, next in line for a steak, muttered, "Too late to be of help."

"Better late than never," Baldwin countered. "Who's to say we won't need 'em in the next half hour?"

It had taken a moment for Alphus's tired brain to spark to life and grasp what Baldwin was saying. "Are you speaking of James Harrod? He's here in camp?"

Baldwin stabbed at a steak over the fire, ready to serve it up. "That's the one, sir. Here with his Kentucky men. They pitched over on the Ohio."

Alphus thrust his plate at Sawyer and took off at a trot for the Ohio side of camp. He found the newly pitched tents deserted, the fires in their stone rings dying. All but one. Outside the last tent, he found a private no older than Geordie sitting on a log, clutching his belly, his color ashen-green.

He stopped before the lad, who blinked up at him. "Private, what's your company?"

Through gritted teeth the lad replied, "Capt'n Floyd's . . . sir." He started to stand, or try to.

Alphus motioned him to sit. "Where's your company, son? And the rest come in last night?"

The boy licked his lips. "Colonel Lewis sent 'em up the Ohio . . . not ten minutes past . . . to see where the Indians've got to. I was too sick."

Alphus waited, pitying but impatient, while the boy vomited on the other side of the log. "Might want to get yourself over to the hospital tent," he said, pity winning out.

The boy straightened, wiping his mouth. "No sir. I know what ails me. Et some berries on the trail I knew better'n to. It'll . . . pass."

Alphus gave the boy a wry smile. "Don't envy you meantime. But tell me one thing, is James Harrod's company gone with the rest upriver?"

"Cap'n Harrod? Yes sir. I seen 'em go."

"All right then, son. Take care of yourself. Drink some water."

Alphus took off at a lope, headed out of camp. His better sense told him to wait, that Harrod's company would return in a few hours, either with word that the Shawnees were gone or else they weren't and there'd be more fighting directly. A few hours more wouldn't change whatever had become of Clare and Philip.

But if there was to be fighting, he had to find Harrod before some Indian's arrow took him out. Maybe Philip himself was among the company ahead. He ought to have asked the boy that.

Along the easternmost low ridge he ran, nearest the river, ground he hadn't covered in the battle. Much sooner than expected, he spotted the tail of the Fincastle companies ahead through the trees and hailed them. Two men bringing up the rear turned, halting as he reached them, others ahead on the trail pausing to look back.

"What's afoot back in camp?" asked one. "We been recalled?"

Alphus sucked in air, attempting to steady his voice. "No. Just me looking for James Harrod."

The man who'd spoken raised his brows. "Capt'n Harrod? What's he wanted for?"

Alphus didn't bother replying but stepped aside and looked down the line of men, most still trudging off toward the river and called, "Captain James Harrod!"

More men looked back at his shout, but only one peeled away from the file and doubled back. He was tall and young, dark-haired, strong-jawed, and bright-eyed beneath his hat brim.

"I'm James Harrod," he said upon reaching them. "Who's asking?"

"Captain Alphus Litchfield, Augusta County Regiment." Alphus saw the name meant nothing to Harrod, save it gained him a nod for his rank. No reason it should. Clare might never have mentioned him. "I'm looking for a man, I hope of your company. My niece's husband. They were aiming to catch you up at Wheeling Settlement, back in April, meaning to claim Kentucky land."

Harrod's brows tightened. "His name?"

Alphus felt a fool for not having said at once. "Philip Inglesby. Married to Clare. They'd a boy, Jacob. She was expecting another babe. It'd be some months old by now."

Harrod's blank expression hadn't cleared. "Ingles, you say? Some kin to them at Ingles' Ferry?"

"Inglesby. Clare and Philip . . ." But Alphus saw his answer in Harrod's gaze before the man's head began to wag. He'd never heard of Philip Inglesby. Or Clare.

It left him feeling poleaxed, how quick and utter that flame of hope long-nourished had been quenched. *Lord Almighty, I got no more trails to follow. Give me something. Some sign. I need a trail.*

Alphus didn't hasten back to camp but picked his way through the battle-churned wood, gaze falling only half-seeing over the castoff bits left behind—a broken powder horn, a severed leather strap, a bloodied moccasin, a feathered arrow sunk in a tree. His stomach growled with hunger.

His need to know was a sharper pang. Dead or living, what had become of Clare and her family? And the question nearly as haunting: why had he ever let her go into the west with a man who'd no idea what he was getting himself into?

Some of the company were still at breakfast when he reached the fire, but Alphus's dazed attention sharpened at sight of Geordie standing apart, nearly hopping foot to foot.

"Capt'n!" The boy rushed to intercept him out of hearing of the others. "I been over to the field hospital. Went to see if'n the prisoner we brought in died in the night." Color crept into the lad's cheeks as he rushed on, "On account I got to thinking maybe he weren't a traitor exactly. Maybe he were one of them taken a young'un and made to grow up Indian. Maybe he ain't ever known no other way. I got to feeling bad for how we left him lying and thought I'd see did he speak any English, if he was alive."

Alphus, having waited out this explanation, asked, "And is he? Does he?"

Geordie nodded vigorously. "Is and does, sir, but he's done lain out all night more or less untended."

Alphus wondered at the concern in the boy's voice. "You saw how overrun the surgeon is. Our men came first, no doubt."

"I know, sir. But you ain't seen him. Took me a while to find him 'cause he's been moved over by the . . ." Geordie hesitated, swallowing. "By the dead ones. I think someone drug him there hoping he'd die, maybe used their fists to help it along. He's roughed up a sight more'n when we left him. I tried asking his name, but he only moaned and said . . ."

The boy hesitated again but seemed finally to be getting to the point.

"It sounded like he said the name of that niece you been looking for. If'n I remember right and her name's Clare."

Alphus stared at the lad, trying to wrap his mind around those last words. "You heard him speak of Clare?"

"That's her name?"

"It is." Forgetting his empty stomach, he took the lad by the shoulder and steered him away from the fire. "Show me to him. Right now."

Traitor or not, it was disconcerting to find his erstwhile prisoner lying among the dead, still clad in nothing but breechclout and moccasins, still caked in his blood. While a binding had been placed around his torso, makeshift at best, it was soaked through and likely dried to the wound, which apparently had been neither cleaned or closely examined, only the bleeding slowed. Contrary to even such slapdash tending, fresh bruising covered the man's torso and face. One eye was swollen shut. Also swollen, his nose had bled down over his mouth and the blood had dried in dark rivulets, mixing with smeared war paint.

"I see."

The man was conscious; when Alphus spoke, he opened his one good eye and fixed on him a look of such beseeching need that Alphus knew why Geordie had been stirred to pity. Holding such feeling at bay, Alphus knelt beside the man, who spoke a word too softly rasped to hear.

"Say again?"

"He's asking for water, sir," Geordie said. "Asked me earlier."

The man held Alphus's gaze, fear and need in that dark eye.

"Geordie, fill a canteen and bring it here."

"Yes sir," the boy said, though reluctantly, and left them alone with the dead waiting to go in the ground.

"Thank you."

Though the man's voice was a thread, Alphus didn't detect the accent of a native Shawnee. He didn't think this man had lived his whole life among them. "Who are you?"

"I . . ." The man's voice caught. He closed his eye.

Alphus felt the beginnings of alarm. If this man knew of Clare—a wild unlikely *if*—he didn't want him dying before he spilled whatever he knew. Why hadn't he brought his own canteen?

"While we wait for that water, I'm going to have a look at your battle wound."

The man didn't flinch or protest when Alphus began cutting away the binding around his lean torso. He'd guessed right, the linen stuck. He'd have to soak it off else risk reopening the wound to fresh bleeding.

Geordie came running up, clutching a dripping canteen. "Got it, sir. And I saw the surgeon. He's been working all night and still at it, with more of our men yet to tend. He ain't gonna get to this one."

Alphus got the man's head raised, and he swallowed down enough water to satisfy what must have been a raging thirst.

"All right now. I expect you can talk, and that's what I want from you. Geordie here says you got a woman on your mind. A woman with an English name. Just you tell me that name now."

The white Indian opened his eye and gazed at him, and there was to Alphus's surprise something like recognition in the gaze.

"You know Clare?" he said, voice slightly less of a rasp. "Clare . . . Inglesby?"

Geordie's eyes were wide. "How does he know your niece?"

"I do not know." Though he was beginning to have an idea.

Alphus reached for the canteen the boy held and, holding it aloft, addressed the prisoner, whose gaze fastened with longing on the source of water. "Listen. I'll give you this and even tend your wound, see if we can keep you alive—"

"So the army . . . can shoot me?" the man interjected, wryness in his tone.

So he was a traitor, or thought they'd view him as such.

Alphus considered the man lying before them, in no wise warming to him but needing him to live.

"That remains to be seen. Just you give answer to that boy's question, then we'll see what happens next. How is it you are acquainted with the name of my niece, Clare Inglesby? And—" Despite his resolve to reveal nothing of his desperation to this man until he got from him what he needed, he hadn't kept the catch from his voice. "Does she still live?"

33

News of the battle reached them two days before the warriors did, coming up the river trail with their wounded and their dead. Runners came ahead to spread the word and prepare the people of the Scioto towns. Few learned anything certain about the husband, son, or brother they'd sent off to fight, only that some weren't coming back and more were coming back wounded. One of those dead was Cornstalk's brother, Silverheels. Another was their war chief, Puckeshinwah.

As for the battle itself, as Clare understood it from Crosses-the-Path, the Shawnees had inflicted more casualties on the Virginians than they'd suffered, but it hadn't been enough. More Virginians had come down the Kanawha to join the survivors of the battle while Dunmore's Northern Army, still at full strength, had crossed the Ohio and was headed their way.

Many talked of leaving the Pickaway Plains, of finding a new place to live beyond the reach of grasping Long Knives. Here and there Clare noticed a lodge standing empty where some elder and his wife, maybe a grown daughter or two, had made it home. She wondered where they'd gone, who else might follow, what she and Pippa were to do if Jeremiah didn't . . .

He would come back. *He had to.*

She stood outside Crosses-the-Path's lodge, staring at Rain Crow's, hoping she would emerge. The day was chilly. She'd left Pippa inside, watched by the girls, but she didn't want to go back in. The lodge had begun to feel too small, the air thick with worry. Crosses-the-Path and her daughters were as anxious for Falling Hawk's safe return as she was for Jeremiah's.

She thought about seeking out Wildcat, knowing the boy awaited Wolf-Alone with equal concern. It would be something to do to pass the time crawling by so agonizingly slow.

She'd made up her mind to go to Split-Moon's lodge and look for the boy when the hide flap over Rain Crow's lodge shifted and the woman looked out. She saw Clare and for a moment merely stared, as though making up *her* mind about something.

Jacob's voice rose inside the lodge, asking something in Shawnee. Rain Crow said something sharp in the same tongue over her shoulder.

He didn't speak again.

Clare felt a burst of anger that the woman should speak to Jacob so, but when Rain Crow let the door-hide fall and came striding toward Clare, alarm replaced indignation.

Rain Crow halted in front of her, face set, dark eyes smoldering with feeling.

"I would know a thing from you," she said in English. "Before my brothers return."

Clare's heart was already racing. "What?"

"If the Almighty is a good God, as the Moravians say—as my mother and Panther-Sees-Him believe—why does He let happen all the bad things? Why so much sickness? So much death? Why do warriors spill their blood in battle and still that army comes? You tell me this."

Clare realized her mouth was hanging open, no doubt making her look as dumbstruck as this woman had rendered her. What could she say to such things? She had no words. None with any conviction behind them.

Someone else had, however.

"The Almighty is good, and He's working all things together for your good. Either you believe that or you don't."

She opened her mouth to parrot Jeremiah's last words to her, but they formed like soap bubbles on her tongue, bitter and empty. What spilled out instead was, "I don't know! Is that what you want to hear from me? Fine then, I admit it. I still don't know why my son was taken, or yours died, or both our husbands are gone. Is any of it fair? None of it *feels* fair."

Unmoved by her honesty, Rain Crow raised her chin, defiant.

"Why then follow such a God?" she demanded but didn't wait for an answer this time. Turning on her moccasined heel, she strode back toward her lodge.

Clare knew she'd again fallen short, again failed. Said the wrong thing. Done the wrong thing. Did it really matter now what she said?

Rain Crow had nearly reached her lodge when Clare knew she must say something more. The compulsion to do so was like a hand prying open her jaw, loosening her tongue.

"Why? Because He knows how we feel." The words tore out of her like bits of her own flesh ripped away, trailing blood. "Abigail—He knows!"

Speaking her Christian name had the effect she'd hoped it might. Rain Crow whirled to face Clare.

"What do you mean? *Who* knows *what*?"

"The Almighty. He knows how it feels to lose a son. Don't you remember? His own Son was lost to Him, hanging on that cross. Don't you remember when the sun went dark? Don't you remember what that meant? He took the punishment for it, all of it, all the evil that men do, all the pain of this fallen world. He was broken so that we can be whole. He held nothing back."

Rain Crow's face was for once completely unguarded. The defiant mask had fallen to reveal a look of pain and need and fear so raw that Clare was stunned.

It was her own heart staring back at her.

But something else was happening now, something in Clare's soul was shifting, opening, filling. And it hadn't to do with Rain Crow. Not directly. Her voice when she'd started to speak of the Almighty had been weak, pleading. By the time she'd finished, something had rushed in to fill the emptiness carved out in her heart, carved again and again during the years of her failing marriage to Philip and in the months since his death.

Where there had been emptiness, now there was hope. Not the thin, desperate thing she'd called hope these months past, not the fretful worrying wishes and wants that had dominated her every thought and deed. An absolute certainty. A knowing. As solid as the earth beneath her feet.

It was all going to be right in the end. She did not know how. She did not need to know how. She only needed to know who was going to make it so.

Like a flood, assurance swelled and the fullness of it empowered her so that the last words out of her mouth had been spoken with a conviction she'd thought she would never again feel.

He held nothing back.

But she had. She'd withheld her trust. She'd withheld her heart. For so many years now she had curled up her soul in fear. But that wasn't how she wanted to live. How she wanted to be. She did believe God was good. That He cared about the sparrows. Each one. That He saw her and Jacob and Pippa. And Jeremiah. And Wolf-Alone and Falling Hawk. And Crosses-the-Path and her daughters and Wildcat and Rain Crow, whose heart was broken by grief. He'd proven it, and she believed it. And yet . . . *Lord, help my unbelief!*

Rain Crow continued to stare, though something in the woman's resistant posture seemed to soften; she took a step toward Clare and started to speak but got out only two words before a cry went up from the direction of the creek that flowed between Cornstalk's and Nonhelema's towns.

Other women emerged from lodges, looking in that direction. Crosses-the-Path came out of her lodge and asked something urgently in Shawnee, to which Rain Crow replied.

"What is it?" Clare asked, though she'd already guessed.

"Warriors come from south." Crosses-the-Path took her by the arm. "We go over creek."

Clare didn't resist as Crosses-the-Path pulled her inside the lodge, where Pippa would need to be strapped into her cradleboard for the journey. She glanced back to see that Rain Crow had vanished inside her lodge.

Clare's heart lurched, but she settled it with a deep breath, quieting her racing mind. She'd heard those two words Rain Crow spoke before the cry from the creek arose.

"I remember," she'd said.

34

The first of the warriors, the chiefs and those on horses, had reached the council house at Nonhelema's Town when Clare and Crosses-the-Path arrived. Clare doubted she would ever forget the sight of Cornstalk's face or that of his sister, so grim and set with bitter grief. She didn't look to see where they went or try to understand anything they said to the distraught crowd gathering around them. Like most of the Shawnee women, she was watching the warriors still coming in, those on their feet and those helping them, then the litters and the travois and . . . There was Wolf-Alone, supporting Falling Hawk who was on his feet but sagging, one shoulder stained with blood.

Crosses-the-Path cried out in dismay. The women ran to meet them, Clare searching but not seeing Jeremiah. When she finally captured Wolf-Alone's attention, the look he gave her answered her question before she could ask it.

"Where is he?" He made no reply, for she'd spoken in English. Near to screaming with anxiety, she repeated the question in fumbling Shawnee.

Wolf-Alone replied, something about Jeremiah not making it back across the river. Something about his being shot. She must have looked as she felt, near to swooning, for the warrior reached out to grip her arm.

She managed to find the one Shawnee word she needed. "Dead?"

"I do not know."

"What do you mean?" Again she'd spoken in English.

Wolf-Alone gave his brother over to the care of his wife, who couldn't support his weight for long alone, then hastily bent near her ear and in hurried English said, "We're going to listen to Cornstalk speak. Go to my lodge. Wait for me there. I will tell you all when I come."

Then he was striding away toward Nonhelema's council house, and she couldn't follow because Crosses-the-Path was calling for her help. Clare got a shoulder under Falling Hawk's arm, and together they began the slow, painful process of getting the wounded warrior home. She didn't think he was mortally wounded, but he was nearly unconscious by the time they reached the creek.

When Falling Hawk was safely on his sleeping bench in his lodge, Crosses-the-Path's daughters came rushing in to see their father and help their mother tend him. Still Clare lingered, though her worry for Jeremiah was nearly driving her to distraction.

And where was Rain Crow? Where was Jacob?

"You go," Crosses-the-Path told her, breaking off from tending Falling Hawk's shoulder wound. "He not too much hurt."

"Thank you," Clare said, hardly knowing why she was thanking the woman, and slipped out to find Rain Crow and Jacob, needing to be near her son, needing to see him if not Jeremiah.

Jeremiah shot. And captured? Wolf-Alone hadn't said he was dead. *Please not dead.*

She called at Rain Crow's lodge but got no answer.

Clare grasped the door-hide. She was prepared to be shouted at, ordered out, verbally abused, physically assaulted, anything but what she found when she moved aside the hide.

The lodge was empty.

She'd never been inside Rain Crow's lodge, never seen her possessions or Jacob's, the places where they ate and slept, but to her eyes it looked stripped. Hastily so, as if a woman and boy had taken only what they could gather quickly, what they could carry away on their backs.

Not wanting to believe what her eyes were telling her, she moved to the fire ring in the center of the lodge. Though the flames had died, it radiated shimmering warmth.

She turned in a circle, searching shadows, then hurried out to find Crosses-the-Path at her fire, Falling Hawk tended and resting on his sleeping bench.

By force of will she kept from blurting out her news and asked, "Will he be all right?"

She kept her voice low, though it shook. Crosses-the-Path heard her distress and frowned as she said, "In time. But what wrong? You hear of Panther-Sees-Him?"

She looked braced for the worst of news, but Clare shook her head.

"No. I'm still waiting for Wolf-Alone to come from the council house, but . . . Rain Crow is gone. So is Jacob. I went inside. Her things are gone. Did she go back to Nonhelema's Town?"

"And we not see?" Crosses-the-Path asked.

She waved her oldest daughter over and asked her a question in Shawnee, in which Clare caught Nonhelema's name.

The girl, who had stayed behind in Cornstalk's Town when Clare and her mother crossed the creek, now shook her head as she replied. When Crosses-the-Path looked at Clare, it was like that meeting of eyes she'd had with Wolf-Alone before he told her of Jeremiah.

"Rain Crow hear of battle. She say if Long Knives attack, it bad for her. If Shawnees talk peace, it bad for her. They take from her Many Sparrows." She heaved a sigh, deep and troubled. "She go with others, far from here."

The last of Clare's denial shredded. "She took Jacob away?"

Crosses-the-Path lifted her hands in helplessness. "She not want him go with you or army."

Clare stood with all of them watching her. Her breath came short. Her heart felt crushed, beating like a thing long trapped having worn itself out.

"You said far from here. Where have they gone?"

Crosses-the-Path shook her head. "She not say."

Who would know where she'd gone? Who could she ask? Wolf-Alone? But he wouldn't know. He was just returned from the battle.

The weight of Pippa on her back was like a stone. Even if she found someone who could tell her where Rain Crow and Jacob had gone, she couldn't go after them. Not without Jeremiah.

Turning from the staring eyes of his brother's family, she went out to wait for Wolf-Alone.

He wasn't long in coming to the lodge.

She'd laid Pippa on the sleeping bench, kindled the fire, and started a kettle of corn soup heating, when the door-hide pushed inward and Wolf-Alone entered.

All the things she needed to ask, to tell, crowded hard and fast on her tongue, but in the end she said none of them, for he crossed the lodge and stopped before her and took her shoulders between his hands.

"Clare, forgive me. I promised I'd go back for him, and I didn't. I'm sorry."

The big warrior dropped his head, anguish on his face. She reached up and touched that face, seeing that it bore bruises and a cut across the brow. She looked him over, but he seemed to have come through the battle unscathed save for these minor wounds. No easy feat from what she'd seen of the survivors in Nonhelema's Town.

"Wolf-Alone, I know you would have gone back for him if that's what you promised to do—you would have done it if you could. I'd believe nothing less of you. Look at me."

The man raised amber eyes to hers. "Clare," he began, then swallowed, hesitating.

"Sit down," she told him. "Soup is heating. Tell me what happened. Tell me—" She tried to say Jeremiah's name but couldn't. "Is he alive?"

"He was when I left him." Clearly exhausted, Wolf-Alone lowered himself heavily onto a block chair at the low table. He glanced aside at Pippa, waving tiny arms and making gurgling noises. "I washed on my way across the creek. May I hold her?"

To Clare's knowledge, Wolf-Alone hadn't held her daughter since the day they met, outside the council house in Wakatomica—unless one counted his lifting the baby and cradleboard off her back the day they arrived in Corn-stalk's Town.

"All right." She gave Pippa into his keeping before she went to tend the soup.

Pippa seemed fascinated by the man's eyebrows, her little fingers tracing those twin bold sweeps from her perch in his arms.

Clare smiled briefly at the incongruous picture they made, the big Indian and her little girl. Then he looked at her with grief and weariness etched into his face and started to speak.

As the soup in the kettle began to steam, he told her of the battle. He talked of its lasting for hours, of the long, terrible back and forth of it, with the fiery woods above and below and on all sides.

"Like being engulfed in flames," he told her. "Or a dream. That's what it seemed like, the things we were doing to each other in the midst of such beauty. A terrible, beautiful dream."

They'd made it through nearly to the end, he and his brothers, before Falling Hawk was wounded.

"We knew it was time for us to retreat and get our brother back to the river. That's what we were doing when Panther-Sees-Him took a ball here." Wolf-Alone touched his fingers briefly to his side. "I think it passed through, but I don't know. He fell down into a hollow, but he got back on his feet. He couldn't help support Falling Hawk, so he told me to get our brother back across the river and he would follow."

Clare had the soup warm enough. She brought him a gourd bowl full and took Pippa from him so he could eat it. But he only stared at the food as if it didn't register.

"Guess he thought he'd make it, or maybe he wanted me to think he would so I would go. I tried to go back, but by then nearly everyone was over the river and Cornstalk said all who could help the wounded were needed to get them back to the Scioto."

"Could he still be alive?" she asked, pacing now with Pippa because she couldn't stay still. "A prisoner?"

"Likely, if he lives. But there's maybe a chance he got away."

He didn't sound very hopeful of it. Clare paused her pacing with her back to the table, eyes closed, and drew a steadying breath. If Jeremiah was alive, there was hope, even if he was a prisoner. What should she do? Wait here? Try to find him? Or Jacob first?

Wolf-Alone would help her find Jeremiah, she was certain, but would he help her find her son? Whichever one she went after, would she be abandoning the other forever?

How was she to choose?

"Clare," Wolf-Alone said behind her. "What else is wrong?"

Pippa's head was resting sleepily against her shoulder now, but Clare didn't want to put her down yet. "Rain Crow has taken Jacob—she's gone and no one I've spoken to knows where. Do you?"

"If I knew where she'd gone," he said and held her gaze as he spoke, "I would tell you. Better, I would go and bring her back."

She put Pippa down, settled her, and straightened, gazing into the fire. Thinking too many thoughts at once. When the silence in the lodge registered, she looked at Wolf-Alone. He was looking at her, clearly puzzled.

"What is it?"

"I am . . . surprised," he said, a little warily. "You aren't anxious about this?"

Anxious?

"Oh yes," she said. "It's only that I don't know what to do. I don't know how to find Jacob. I don't know how to find Jeremiah. I don't even know which of those I should try first and . . . I suppose I'm taking a leaf out of Jeremiah's book," she said with no little surprise of her own. "I'm waiting for some guidance."

She was as astonished at herself as Wolf-Alone appeared to be.

"Do you love him?" he asked her.

"What?" She blinked, taken aback by the question. "Of course I love him. He's my son."

Wolf-Alone's expression didn't alter. "That wasn't who I meant."

Of course it wasn't. But she didn't give him an answer. How could she? She longed for Jeremiah. She wanted him there with her. But was it only for need of him because of Jacob? That need had been her guiding force for as long as she'd known Jeremiah Ring. If it were gone, would she feel this longing? If she had her son, would she choose the man?

So much had happened in so short a time that her feelings were an impossible tangle. So many longings. For home. For peace. For some semblance of the life she'd had. But could a life like that include a man like Jeremiah Ring? She was almost certain he wanted a life with her. But what sort of life? He'd been Jem Ringbloom. Would he ever want to be again?

He was also Panther-Sees-Him.

What life would he choose after this? If there would be life for any of them *after this*.

"What is going to happen now? What will Cornstalk do?"

Wolf-Alone studied her for a moment, as if her face might give answer to the question he had asked and she had not truthfully answered, then he relented and told her what Cornstalk had said to them in the council house at Nonhelema's Town.

"He stood there before his chiefs and warriors, some of them still with the blood on their flesh unwashed, and he said we'd failed to defeat one half of Dunmore's army and did we now wish him to lead an attack on the other half and see if maybe we could defeat it—those of us with strength and heart left for fighting." Wolf-Alone's amber gaze didn't fix on Clare as he spoke. He was seeing again that scene he'd come from witnessing in the council house. "I was near enough to see the shaking of Cornstalk's hands as he spoke. When no one answered him, he proposed that if they still chose war, we should first kill all our women and children, then go and fight until we'd all died. That would be the kindest thing."

Clare searched his face in alarm. "Surely not."

"No," Wolf-Alone was quick to agree. "He spoke in his grief, in his anger—anger with the warriors who are now showing themselves ready to seek peace from the Long Knives, but peace at such a cost! If you could have seen . . ."

Clare sucked in a breath, her thoughts of Jeremiah, what he might have seen, what might have been done to him. What he might even now be enduring.

"Still no one dared answer Cornstalk," Wolf-Alone went on. "Or even meet his gaze. So he spoke of how he'd done what they wished, instead of seeking peace with the Virginia governor. 'Now,' he said, 'I suppose you wish me to go and do that seeking, only we will come as beggars instead of the men we were before the battle.'"

That was, Wolf-Alone told her, exactly what the warriors now wished. Messengers had been sent to Governor Dunmore, who was coming their way with his half of the army along the Hocking River. They could only hope this entreaty would stop him coming to battle and cause him to want to talk instead. Come to terms of peace.

But so many lives lost. So many bodies maimed, and not just on the

Shawnees' side. How many from Augusta County had gone to fight, Clare wondered. Those who had been her neighbors. And family? Had Alphus Litchfield raised a company or joined one?

"Does this mean Jacob will be freed?"

Wolf-Alone nodded. "I'm sure that's why my sister ran. She saw this coming. Maybe someone in the army can help you if . . ." Pain lanced across his eyes, where Clare read the rest of the words he wouldn't say.

If Jeremiah is dead.

It was more than grief and weariness in the face of Jeremiah's adopted brother; it was devastation.

"He might be captured. You said that."

"I'll go with the chiefs to Dunmore," Wolf-Alone said. "I'm going to learn if my brother was taken prisoner, though what I'm going to do about it if he has been . . ."

His gaze held Clare's, anguished. "I'll check first with the militia, wherever I find them camped. If he isn't there, I'm going back to that battlefield. I'll change my dress, my speech, whatever I need to do. I can still pass for . . ."

He broke off, as if grown aware of what he was saying aloud. He could pass? For what?

Wolf-Alone's next words jarred such questions out of Clare's mind. "I'll take you with me, Clare. You and the baby. You need to leave this place, and maybe together we'll find my brother yet living. Help him, if he's a prisoner. They'll count him a traitor."

Which meant that even if Jeremiah had survived the battle, the Virginians would probably kill him for having fought with the Shawnees.

Knowing now what Wolf-Alone meant to do, she knew she had to decide—between two equally impossible paths. Run blindly into the wilderness after a son she'd scant hope of finding, or march with this Indian into a camp full of his enemies on the equally scant hope Jeremiah yet lived, could be found, could be saved.

Maybe she could tell them—the army, the officers, Governor Dunmore himself if need be—that his involvement was all down to her. It was her fault Jeremiah had been in this town these many months instead of back at Fort Pitt or someplace else where he could have avoided the fighting. He'd done it for her. Given it all. Maybe even his life.

Jacob, at least, wasn't in any immediate peril. Rain Crow cherished him. She would die before she let harm befall him.

"I'll go with you." The words were a wrenching to her soul. "Get me to the army. My uncle may be among them. If he is, he'll help us." Dazedly she began to move, gathering up her things and Pippa's, starting to think about food for the journey, wondering why Wolf-Alone still sat at the table staring at her.

"We're not leaving yet. We have to wait for word from Dunmore, whether he accepts Cornstalk's offer to meet and talk." He paused, looking into her face. "But you say you've an uncle in that army?"

"Most likely. Alphus Litchfield. He holds the rank of captain. Do you know what that means, captain?"

"I know," he said. "Maybe you and I don't need to wait then. I can take you to him and—"

There came a scuff of moccasins in the dirt beyond the door-hide, a boy's voice calling Wolf-Alone's name. Before the warrior could respond, Wildcat ducked into the lodge.

"Listening, were you?" Wolf-Alone asked, still speaking English.

"Yes!" the boy replied, arms crossed over his narrow chest. "I go with you, see army?"

"No," Wolf-Alone said. "You won't."

The boy's gaze narrowed. "You say no, I follow."

Wolf-Alone stood and crossed to the boy, who stared up with defiant eyes. "You mustn't follow. Stay back here at the town."

"I not fear Long Knives!"

"You should fear."

Hurt twisted the boy's features. "You take Clare-wife. Why not me?"

Wolf-Alone's fierce brows soared. "Do you know what those Long Knives would do if they set eyes on you?"

The boy thrust out his chest, one hand falling to the small tomahawk at his waist. "Run and hide for fear!"

For all the anxiety of the past days, Clare felt the urge to laugh.

Wolf-Alone didn't. "Don't be foolish. They'll take you away from me. From the People. They'll think I'm bringing you, a captive, back to them."

"I'm no captive. No one is taking me!"

"The soldiers won't believe that. So you must stay." The boy held his stance but with pleading eyes. Wolf-Alone placed his big hand on Wildcat's shoulder. "Listen. I won't be gone long, but I must see if my brother lives. And I must take *her* to him, to help him, if he does."

"Panther-Sees-Him," the boy said, turning at last to address Clare, regret in his gaze. "I am sorry Clare-wife."

She crossed to the boy and wrapped him in a hug. Far from spurning the motherly gesture, Wildcat clung to her, but when he backed away, Wolf-Alone put his hand on the boy's head. There was something changed in his expression, in the set of those fierce brows. His gaze still held grief, but something in it had lifted, some weight gone off him.

"When I come back," he said, "when there is peace and all is settled, we'll go hunting, you and me and your father. Falling Hawk too, if he is well. We will make it a long hunt, many days. But only if you stay now."

Clare watched the boy wrestle with this offering, weighing it, finally deciding it was a compromise he could accept.

"All right," Wildcat said. He turned to Clare and grinned. "Good-bye, Clare-wife. I hope for you to find your husband still living."

She'd bid Wildcat good-bye and he'd gone out of the lodge before she remembered Jeremiah wasn't her husband. How used to the idea of it she'd grown. She turned to look at Wolf-Alone, watching the swaying hide across the doorway.

"Hunting?"

Wolf-Alone shifted his gaze to her. "It is likely Dunmore will demand *all* our white children back if a peace treaty is signed—not just your Jacob—even those who have lived all their lives with us. I'll need to get him away for a while."

"You mean to hide him," Clare said. "Yet you were willing Jeremiah and I take him, even knowing we'd have left the Shawnees."

"Only if I fell in battle," Wolf-Alone reminded her. "I didn't fall."

She stared at the man, attempting to fathom the workings of his mind. He wasn't like other Indians in his thinking, yet he wasn't like a white man either. He was a man apart, as his name suggested. Even more so than Jeremiah, it seemed. "Will you ever tell me what it is that ties you to that boy?"

Wolf-Alone held her gaze. "He's mine."

Clare needed a second to absorb that. "Yours? What do you mean? Not . . . *your* son?"

"He is not my son," Wolf-Alone said and almost smiled at her. "But still he is mine. And that is all I'm going to say about it, Clare-wife," he added, using Wildcat's name for her. "It's more than I've ever told anyone. Be content with it."

35

OCTOBER 24
SCIOTO TRAIL

The prisoner was struggling to maintain the pace Colonel Andrew Lewis had set. He'd struggled since they'd left that flaming, bloody point of land between the rivers and crossed the Ohio days ago, heading north into Indian territory. Alphus Litchfield had all the while kept the man in his sights, a pace or two ahead, bearing witness to every stumble and wince, and while his rifle wasn't exactly trained on Ring's back, he'd held it ready in case the man made a break for the entangling wood that edged the trail—however unlikely. Ring was exhausted, his wound healing badly for all the marching. In truth Alphus hadn't expected him to make it as far as he had.

Dressed in breeches and a shirt scrounged from among the company, the man looked a deal more like the Virginian he claimed still to be and less like the Shawnee Alphus was inclined to believe he'd become. That he'd been a Virginian, once upon a time, was true enough, though he'd gone by the name Jem Ringbloom then.

Not that the man admitted to it. Not while Alphus tended his wound. Not while he'd been interrogated by Colonel Lewis. Not in the days since, in camp or on the march.

But as the swelling in his face had subsided, his features jarred Alphus's memory clear; he'd known the man years back, had wondered along with everyone within fifty miles of Staunton what happened to him and his young wife after Indians carried her off and he went after to get her back.

Was it ten years ago? Longer?

He'd found the Indians, clear enough—and become one. With one foot still in the white world. One of the messengers running between Colonel Lewis and Governor Dunmore, a fellow called Simon Girty, had confirmed the man was known to the Indian agents at Fort Pitt as Jeremiah Ring. Known, respected, and valued for what he was.

What the Shawnees called him Alphus hadn't asked. He didn't need the man's story. He needed one thing from him—the safe return of his niece and her children. Preferably before the army Colonel Lewis was leading fast toward the Scioto, where Ring claimed to have left Clare, reached those towns and she was placed in mortal danger.

It had taken surprisingly little effort to convince Colonel Lewis to let Ring accompany the army north, while the rest of the wounded remained behind at Point Pleasant with a garrison building a stockade. The colonel's brother, Charles, had died of his battle wounds. The grief-stricken Colonel Lewis was distracted by his desire to strike at the Shawnees in retaliation; as long as Alphus took responsibility for the prisoner, the pair could come along and find his missing niece and her children.

There would be no finding Philip, months in his grave on a mountainside between Redstone and Wheeling. Ring had told Alphus how he'd found the man's mutilated body—one of Logan's casualties—then Clare in her desperate need, one child abducted, another making its advent.

"Merciful Lord," Alphus had uttered, pausing in wrapping a linen bandage low around his prisoner's torso.

He'd sent Geordie away, not wanting the lad to hear what passed between himself and Ring concerning Clare. For a flicker of an instant he'd felt gratitude for the traitor whose blood stained his hands.

He'd squelched that feeling smart-like. Whatever else the man had done, he'd fought against his own, no easy mountain of guilt to get around.

While he worked on Ring, the man had surfaced in and out of consciousness. Each time those dark eyes fluttered open, Alphus had been ready with questions.

"Why'd you think it was that Mingo, Logan, who killed Philip?"

"Did Clare press you to take her across the Ohio after Jacob, or was that your notion?"

"Why didn't you take the boy back from whomever adopted him and give him to his mother and be done with it?"

Ring refused to answer until he'd first bargained those answers, his knowledge of Clare's whereabouts, and his ability to bring her away from the Shawnees, in exchange for his life.

"Let me get her safe to you. Let me live that long. Then do with me as you will."

In no wise sure the man was in earnest about his disregard for life—or the devotion to Clare his words implied—but needing to know what he knew, Alphus had struck that deal.

Give him his due, Ring had answered every question about Clare put to him and seemed to have done so forthrightly, but Alphus couldn't be sure. Ring might be a skillful liar, able to read men and give them what they wanted—or feign to—having straddled two worlds for so many years.

Of course he'd have suspected as much no matter what the man said, but he sensed Ring was holding something back concerning Clare. It seemed he'd done a great service for his niece, but that just might be the shine he was putting on things. Clare might have another tale to tell. Surely Ring hadn't done it all out of the kindness of his heart. What had been in it for him?

"Who's given my niece shelter all this while?"

"I have," Ring told him. "In my brother's lodge."

"A Shawnee brother?"

"Born Delaware. Adopted, like me."

"All right. Just so I understand—Clare and her baby girl lived with you these past months, under the same roof?"

A guarded look had sharpened in Ring's eyes. He knew what Alphus was getting at. "And with my brother, as I said. Once I knew it wouldn't be an easy thing getting Jacob back, I thought it safer if my kin, all the Shawnees, thought of her as my wife."

Alphus wasn't liking this. At all. "She make objection to that?"

The man didn't look away. "Was she best pleased? No. But she saw the wisdom in it."

"It was more to you, though, wasn't it? More than a sham for her safety."

"Clare . . ." Whether from thirst, exhaustion, or emotion, the man's voice caught on the name. "For Jacob she was willing to do whatever she must, more than I'd have asked of her."

That didn't answer the question and raised a heap more in Alphus's mind, but he decided to let that subject lie until he could speak to Clare about it, get her side.

Having received permission to accompany the army across the Ohio when they marched, Alphus wasn't presently in command of anyone, save Ring. His men were part of the garrison left raising the fort at Point Pleasant. Geordie and the rest would be folded into another Augusta County company formed as the wounded recovered.

Alphus was now as single-minded as Andrew Lewis, though not to wreak vengeance on the Shawnees—unless Clare had come to harm in Ring's absence, at their hands.

That was another rankling, making him pin the back of Ring's head with his glare as they trudged along the Scioto Trail. He'd led Clare to the savages, then left her to go and fight against his own?

If he hadn't needed Ring so badly, Alphus likely would have shot the traitor himself.

Colonel Lewis was determined to attack the Scioto towns, and not even a direct order from Governor Dunmore, received on the march, had served to alter his course. The fighting was over. Peace negotiations, Lewis had learned to his dismay, had been underway for days. The Shawnees had already agreed to the governor's terms—to return all white prisoners and any African slaves they may have carried off; to cease hunting south of the Ohio; to no longer molest settlers traveling via that river; to give up their hunting grounds in Kentucky.

To return all white prisoners . . .

Jeremiah had felt a heaviness in his chest for Rain Crow as cheers and shouts went up from men around him, hearing of the capitulation, even as relief had swelled for Clare.

"What does this mean for her?" Alphus Litchfield had asked him, those steely eyes—green like Clare's—drilling into him.

"Jacob will be given back. She'll have what she wants."

Was this the answer to their prayers? Or was this merely one small good thing the Almighty was working out of the tragedy of war and death?

Good for whom? For Clare, certainly. But what about his sister, what about her good?

Jeremiah closed his eyes, seeking the truth of that, seeking it in his past, in what he knew, by hard paths, of the Almighty and His ways. And he realized it was best for Rain Crow as well, no matter how much pain it brought. She would never find the wholeness she longed for in a child, just as he could never have found it in his wife and son had they lived. His sister must find wholeness where any man or woman found it at last. Where Clare would find it. Where he was working at finding it now. Not in another person, frail and failing as all were, but at the foot of the cross, in a love that had no bounds. A love that bled and died to clear the path to that deepest of relationships severed long ago in a garden somewhere far away. Man and his Maker. Or woman and hers.

Exactly when those prisoners, and some who weren't prisoners but adopted sons and daughters, married wives and husbands, would be returned wasn't clear. There was to be a grand council in Pittsburgh in the spring to confirm the peace agreement. Perhaps it would happen then. Perhaps in mere days.

And what of Falling Hawk? Wolf-Alone? Did they live? Was Clare with them, under their protection?

Loving and not knowing was never going to be an easy burden to bear, no matter how many times he bore it. He'd thought he'd learned how, years ago, thought he'd had some wisdom to impart to Clare about it. But it came down to this: crying out to the Lord and clinging to His promise that He was vigilant enough, present enough, loving enough, and good enough to deal with it all.

Still his flesh was urging him to *do* something. To escape, get out ahead of that army of Virginians and find Clare, Pippa, Jacob, and Rain Crow, before they were swept along in the flood of refugees that would already be headed northward, for surely by now Nonhelema's Town, first in the army's path, had been evacuated, perhaps burned before its occupants fled.

Cornstalk's Town across Scippo Creek would be next.

Even if he wouldn't have been shot for trying to run, his strength was failing, his wound wasn't healing, and he couldn't figure Colonel Andrew Lewis's thinking.

The man had sent a message of defiance back to Dunmore via the scout, Girty. He wouldn't halt his advance.

Jeremiah judged they were several miles south of Nonhelema's Town when the first shot was fired. He felt a hand clamp his shoulder, then he was on the ground, face in the leaves, while Litchfield and the surrounding militia took cover and fired back.

Currently weaponless, he kept his head down.

It was a quick skirmish. The warriors—scouts he was sure, not a war party—had fired in warning, not to kill. The Virginians lost a bit of time but resumed their march when no attack materialized.

A mile or so on, another messenger from Dunmore found them, pausing the march again.

Thankful for the respite, though made as uneasy as the men around him by the obvious cross purposes of those meant to be leading this army, Jeremiah leaned against a nearby tree, trying to stay on his feet.

He must have dozed standing up; the suddenness of men stirring around him, cursing Indians, governors, and the very land beneath their feet, then the bark of orders getting them back in formation, brought him around bleary-eyed, dizzy, muzzy-headed. His fever was up.

"What's the stir now?" he asked Litchfield, who grasped him by the arm and yanked him back onto the trail.

"Dunmore's still ordering us to halt." Face grim, the older man nudged Jeremiah forward with the barrel of his rifle.

It was another half-mile of staggering before Jeremiah realized the army was still moving toward the Scioto towns, not altering its course as twice—was it thrice?—ordered.

He risked a look back at Litchfield. "Colonel Lewis still not complying?"

Litchfield's face was stony, those green eyes no little troubled. "It does not appear so."

Jeremiah tripped over a root in the trail, pitched forward into the man in front of him, who turned and shoved him back into Litchfield. Clare's uncle grasped him, kept him upright and moving, and by main effort Jeremiah focused on the bobbing ranks of militia moving ahead down the trail toward . . .

"Clare."

He realized he'd said her name aloud only when her uncle spoke behind him. "We will find her."

There was as much threat as promise in the words.

Just let me get her safe into his keeping, Jeremiah thought or maybe prayed—hard to know with his head swimming.

He wasn't certain how he was going to do anything for Clare, not now. Did she think he had abandoned her? Had Wolf-Alone or Falling Hawk survived to let her know he'd been wounded?

Maybe it didn't matter. *I'm not the one she needs to trust. God in heaven, help her. Let her know You haven't abandoned her or her children, no matter what she thinks of me.*

He was stopped on his feet again and swaying before he realized the army had come to yet another ponderous halt. He felt it around him like a collective groan. These men weren't easy about Colonel Lewis disobeying orders, though most seemed in favor of inflicting as much harm upon Cornstalk's people as could be managed.

Someone up ahead called back to those behind. "It's him!"

"Him who?" Alphus Litchfield hollered back.

"The gov'nor hisself, ridden in with a body of guards."

"Going to stop us?" someone asked.

"Let him try!"

"It's orders. Lewis has to stop. This war's over, such as it was."

"They're starting another up the trail—sounds like a proper row!"

In Jeremiah's ears the voices swirled and blended, clashed and broke apart. Much closer to hand that gruff voice he'd come to know said, "I'm going to sit you down before you fall down, Ring. No knowing how long this'll take, and I don't aim to hold you up indefinitely."

Litchfield got him to the ground, which was damp from a morning rain shower, then left to join the officers ahead on the trail to get what news he could.

Jeremiah drew his knees up and put his head down and didn't raise it until he heard that voice again—a moment or an hour later he never knew.

"It's the governor, come with a guard," Litchfield was saying to all within hearing, "and it was a row right enough he and Colonel Lewis had, but the colonel is finally turning back. Lord Dunmore thanks us for our service, and we are ordered back to Camp Union on the Greenbrier. War's over for us, though I reckon whatever's getting started back east will keep us all busy for a spell."

Jeremiah sensed movement around him. Men too stunned to speak, picking up their gear. Waiting to be told when to start retracing their steps.

He couldn't retrace his.

"No," he said when he felt that grip on his arm, urging him to his feet. "Clare."

"I said we'd find her, and we will," Litchfield said, as Jeremiah brought the man's face into focus. "Most of this lot is headed back south, but not you and me. We're going on with Dunmore and some of the officers to Camp Charlotte, on Scippo Creek. Lewis gave his permission, though Dunmore didn't like it."

Alphus Litchfield's mouth quirked in something near a smile.

"Between you and me, Ring, and the shining sun, I don't think Lewis is much bothered over what Dunmore likes or doesn't."

36

The Northern Army's camp on Scippo Creek was pitched six miles from Cornstalk's Town. The Virginia governor's troops had built council houses for the talks with the Shawnees; though many of the chiefs and warriors who took part in the talks lingered in the vicinity, including Cornstalk and Nonhelema, formal negotiations had ended.

With Wolf-Alone, Clare had attended those talks, on pins and needles until learning that as part of the terms of peace with the Virginians, the Shawnees were being forced to return their white captives. She would have Jacob back. If Rain Crow could be found. If someone would help her. If . . .

Clare forced her mind back from that twisted, fretful trail. How strange that without Jeremiah there to continually cast her care upon—her worry, her questions, her impatience, anger, fears—she was finding it easier, a very little easier, to cast that care first upon the Almighty. The One who asked for it. Who promised to carry it. Who called Himself good and claimed to have good plans for her.

Still her faith was a faltering thing. *Lord, do You truly see us? Are You watching? I have the will of the governor of Virginia on my side. But that is nothing without You. Where is my son? Who will find him for me?*

And where is Jeremiah?

There'd been no word of him, though Falling Hawk, recovered from his wound, had made his way to Camp Charlotte in hope, like Wolf-Alone and Clare, of somehow discovering Jeremiah's fate.

Where? was the cry of Clare's heart that wouldn't be silenced, even as she and Wolf-Alone debated whether they should remain at Camp Charlotte or journey south to the Kanawha and see if they could get word of him there, once the talks had ended.

Then, still in the midst of the talks, had come news that Colonel Lewis was bringing the Southern Army up to them.

They'd thought at first Colonel Lewis meant to join his commanding officer at Camp Charlotte, until panicked reports of Shawnee scouts claimed Lewis was bent on retaliation for the attack upon their Ohio River camp. Messages from Dunmore to halt his advance had been ignored. It had taken the governor himself riding out to head off Colonel Lewis to stop him, and now, at last, Dunmore was returning with his body of mounted guards.

And a few more besides.

"I know it's unlikely, but perhaps there's news of Jeremiah?" Clare couldn't help voicing the query as she and Wolf-Alone came up from their creek-side camp upon hearing of Dunmore's return. She was thinking of another as well; maybe somewhere among that Southern Army, Alphus Litchfield was numbered. The Augusta County companies had taken part in the battle at the place they were calling Point Pleasant. Had her uncle raised a company? Had he survived the battle?

Jacob, Jeremiah, Uncle Alphus. All these male creatures of hers gone astray. The comparison to corralling cats might have afforded her amusement had the need to find them and see them safe not been so wrenching.

"You're right," Wolf-Alone said, walking a half-pace ahead of her. "It's unlikely. But let's see who comes now."

As always when she showed herself, Clare caused a stir among Dunmore's companies—a white woman in Indian dress, a baby in a cradleboard on her back, escorted by a singularly tall and fearsome warrior everywhere she went. No one knew what to make of her, but she waded in among those gathering near the governor's marquee as he rode in on his trail-spattered mount along with his guard, some of whom carried extra riders.

"Do you see him?" she asked, knowing Wolf-Alone had the better vantage. Her heart banged hard with hope. "Jeremiah?"

"Of those I can see, none look like a prisoner."

Clare pushed past a knot of militiamen in hunting shirts to get a better view of the new faces, but horses and men milled too thickly.

She would have to wait, perhaps approach the governor again. She'd spoken to him briefly of her plight the previous day; Dunmore had expressed appropriate levels of concern, though of course he couldn't commit his troops to a wilderness expedition in pursuit of one Shawnee woman and a captured child. Nor had he any notion who had been taken prisoner by his Southern Army.

"Clare," Wolf-Alone said, catching up to her and taking her by the arm. "Come away for now. You'll have to—"

"Clare? Clare Inglesby!"

She'd turned to let Wolf-Alone lead her back to their camp when she heard her name shouted above the rumble of male voices.

"Clare!" Alphus Litchfield, trail-grimed and badly in need of a razor's attention, thrust aside the same knot of militiamen she'd just waded through and before she could believe what her eyes and ears were telling her had engulfed her in a pungent, bear-hugging embrace.

"My girl! Here you are. He said you'd be, if you could convince his brothers to bring you here and if not maybe you'd have come alone. I didn't half-believe him!"

The smell of unwashed male, the scratch of those lengthening whiskers. The solid embrace. The comfort and familiarity of that gruff voice. Clare's heart nearly burst with joy.

"Uncle Alphus! I'm so relieved to see you. *Who* said I would be here? Jeremiah?"

She looked past her uncle's shoulder, which stood not much taller than her own, to see him standing there watching their reunion—not looking well, but alive and on his feet.

Jeremiah Ring.

Not dead. Not dead. Not dead. The words resounded in her soul like a joyful bell as she pulled away from her uncle and, without a word, moved toward the man who had been her companion since he found her by the broken wagon and brought her daughter into the world.

Having no idea whether that daughter was asleep or awake in the cradleboard on her back, she walked straight into Jeremiah's arms and held him with a thankfulness, a tenderness, she might spend the rest of her life attempting to express and never manage to her satisfaction.

"Clare." He trembled as he said her name, then took her face between his hands and looked at her.

She looked back at him, at the bruising faded around one eye, the healing of a cut across his mouth. She looked at that long face—gaunt now but bearded like she first remembered it—at the astonishing sweetness and longing bright in his eyes, and in that moment knew beyond all scrap of doubt that the Almighty had been with her every step of this journey into the unknown, providing for all her needs, small and great, there to comfort her in those times when she despaired, if only she'd stilled her soul enough to believe it, embrace it, drink Him in like water to her soul.

And not just with her. With Jacob. Jeremiah. Rain Crow. Even—she knew this though it went against all reason—Philip. The Almighty had been with him in his final moments, whatever he had seen, whatever he had endured. Just as He would always be with her, working for the good of her eternal soul, no matter how events unfolded from that moment.

As if she'd been viewing it all through someone else's spectacles, ones not meant for her eyes, and had finally changed them for the proper pair, she could see it now. God's hand in all these paths that had come together and split apart, only to converge again in this place. And he'd used this man to do so much for her. This strong, tested, faithful, treasure of a man.

"Jeremiah." She touched his face, stroking her fingers down his beard. He was startlingly warm. His eyes, a little too bright, softened at whatever he was seeing in her face.

A throat's clearing behind her made her aware of the scene they were creating. She turned to find her uncle gazing at them, a mixture of surprise and disapproval on that face she knew well.

"Is he your prisoner, Uncle?"

"He is."

"Then I must insist upon taking custody, for I have need of him."

She glanced at Jeremiah to find him gazing down at her with amusement, and hope, and in full sight of her uncle and anyone else caring to observe, she took his hand in hers. Claiming him just in case there was any doubt left in anyone's mind.

Jeremiah Ring swayed toward her as though he might do more than merely clasp her hand. She squeezed his fingers, hoping to relay that such would be just a little *too* much for now.

"I see we've some catching up to do, Niece," said her uncle, "but first we best get this man a bed to fall into before he does so at our feet."

The words might have made little sense save that while Uncle Alphus was still speaking them Jeremiah had done more than sway toward her again. He was fairly slumping on her shoulder.

She'd thought him warm, but was he fevered? Injured?

"Wolf-Alone!" she called to the Indian who until now had stood back from them, just beyond Alphus Litchfield's notice.

He was at her side in a few swift strides, catching his brother in strong arms before he swooned.

37

The Mingo, Logan, had refused the invitation to attend the peace talks with Governor Dunmore, but he was camped nearby. The trader, John Gibson—whose wife, Koonay, and unborn child had died at Baker's Post—had gone to speak with Logan beneath a lone elm tree. Jeremiah, Wolf-Alone, and Falling Hawk went with him.

Unable to bring herself to approach Philip's murderer, Clare waited at a distance. With Pippa dozing in a shoulder sling, she stood with Uncle Alphus, who had no stomach for facing the Mingo chief either. Together they watched the scene, and she thought about Gibson, whom she'd met just that morning.

The man's little daughter, never found at the scene of her mother's murder, had survived in a strange twist of fate; those who killed her kin had for some reason balked at taking her life. The tiny girl had been carried off and eventually given over to Major William Crawford, with whom Gibson had finally found her. He'd settled the child at his trading post, where he intended to raise her.

Clare guessed he'd given Logan this news, for the two had embraced beneath the elm tree, and it looked as though Logan had wept.

Then came a time of smoking pipes and talking, after which Gibson took what appeared to be writing materials from a knapsack, knelt on the ground, and began putting them to use. Logan was speaking. He went on speaking for a time while the others listened and Gibson wrote.

Even from a distance Clare sensed the weight and solemnity of the moment. Her gaze went to Jeremiah, as it often did now when he was near. A day and a night's rest seemed to have helped him toward the healing the long march with the army had delayed. His color was better today, but she didn't like to see him on his feet so long, yet on his feet was where she longed for him to be.

No one yet knew where Jacob and Rain Crow had gone; it was a thing Jeremiah meant to discuss with Logan. It seemed unlikely the Mingo would know, but they were leaving no stone unturned.

Steadfast and true, Jeremiah was still bent on helping her find Jacob. He also greatly desired to find his sister.

Knowing his heart was heavy for the woman who held Jacob prisoner created in Clare a roil of conflicted feeling. Always uppermost was the longing to have her son back. That couldn't change. It simply couldn't. But in that moment of understanding, of finally believing God was in control—that He had been all the while—she'd begun to glimpse a larger canvas upon which He'd been at work over the past months, since that terrible April day Philip rode out of their lives. That canvas included Rain Crow. She was the Almighty's, one of His sparrows, of which there were many.

How, Lord? How will this work good for all of us?

"I do believe they're winding it up," Uncle Alphus said, recalling her attention to the gathering beneath the elm.

Gibson had put away his writing implements and risen. Logan gripped his arm, then Jeremiah's. The Mingo looked her way briefly, then put away his pipe and strode back toward his camp.

Falling Hawk and Wolf-Alone followed.

Jeremiah and Gibson made their way across the clearing to Clare and her uncle. She kept her gaze on Jeremiah's face as they neared, searching it for sign of well-being, distress, news good or bad.

The meeting of their eyes left her breathless at the sparks of warmth it kindled all through her, so that what she'd meant to ask fled her mind when he stood before her. Awareness of him left her feeling shy with this man whose roof she'd shared, this man she'd vexed, defied, thwarted, and to whom she'd showed the worst of herself. This man who, barely on his feet, was doing all he could for her and Jacob. And she couldn't even hold his gaze.

As she looked down at Pippa, the crown of her blond-capped head nestled warm against her breastbone, Uncle Alphus spoke for her.

"That Mingo have anything of import to say?"

He hadn't said *murdering* Mingo, but Clare heard it in his tone. She glanced up in time to see the look that passed between Gibson and Jeremiah.

"A good deal of import," Gibson said and swallowed over some deep emotion. He opened his mouth but seemed now lost for words.

"He'd a message for Dunmore," Jeremiah said. "And for you, Clare. We spoke of Jacob and my sister. Logan might know where she's taken him."

Hope seized her heart, that familiar, painful squeeze of dread and joy. She didn't know who reached for who first, but next she knew she was clasping Jeremiah's hand. "Where?"

"On the Scioto, north some thirty miles of Cornstalk's Town. Place called Seekunk. Some of Logan's people retreated there with captives and goods from their raids, so as not to have to give them back. We suspect that's where Rain Crow has gone."

She couldn't speak. Her whole being was a cry to the Almighty. *Please. Oh, please.*

"Is that what you were writing down?" Uncle Alphus asked Gibson. "Something about the Mingos running off with their prisoners?"

Gibson at last found his voice. "Logan meant to tell Dunmore of it, yes, but that's not what I wrote. He . . . has a message for the governor, but I think it's for anyone with ears to hear it, to hear the lament of a broken man's heart."

Uncle Alphus didn't alter his grim aspect. "That varmint begging forgiveness for his sins?"

Another look passed between Jeremiah and Gibson, who withdrew from his coat what must be the paper he'd written upon.

"I do not excuse what the man has done, especially to you, ma'am," John Gibson said to Clare as he unfolded the paper. "Understand that, please, before you hear what Logan had to say."

"All right," she said in a voice measured, braced. "I understand."

Gibson cleared his throat, stared mutely at the page, and finally thrust it at Jeremiah who, with no more than a brief pause, said, "These are Logan's words, as best as John could get them down.

"'I appeal to any white man to say, if ever he entered Logan's cabin hungry, and he gave him not meat; if ever he came cold and naked, and he clothed him not. During the course of the last long and bloody war, Logan remained idle in his cabin, an advocate for peace. Such was my love for the whites, that my countrymen pointed as they passed, and said, *Logan is the friend of white men.* I had even thought to have lived with you, but for the injuries of one man. Col. Cresap, the last spring, in cold blood, and unprovoked, murdered all the relations of Logan, not sparing even my women and children. There runs not a drop of my blood in the veins of any living creature. This called on me for revenge. I have sought it: I have killed many: I have fully glutted my vengeance. For my country, I rejoice at the beams of peace. But do not harbour a thought that mine is the joy of fear. Logan never felt fear. He will not turn on his heel to save his life. Who is there to mourn for Logan? Not one.'"

No one spoke when Jeremiah finished reading. They all felt the power of the words, even Uncle Alphus.

Clare was left stunned by their anguish, their defiance, the broken spirit behind them. She remembered the friendship the Mingo had offered Jeremiah long ago, how Logan had saved his life, and his soul, in his darkest hour. He truly had been a friend to white men, but white men had abused and betrayed that friendship one too many times, and friend had become enemy, murderer.

Logan had made her a widow.

Still, indirectly she owed as much gratitude as blame to that Indian. If his had been the hand to cause her loss, his had also been the hand to provide the means of aid in her darkest hour. He'd saved Jeremiah, helped make of him the man he had become, the man who had saved her, helped make of her what she was becoming.

For she was becoming, being remade—as they all were, by their choices—and though it remained to be seen all that that woman would be, she knew she would be stronger, and yet at the same time more aware of her weakness and the strength of her God, for having walked this difficult path.

Yet a part of her wanted to refute the words. Or some of them. Logan's blood wasn't utterly cut off from the earth, and yet maybe in a sense even those words were true. Logan still had blood kin. There was his niece, Gibson's daughter, but she would never remember her mother or anyone else who died at Baker's. She would never mourn as Logan mourned. Perhaps she would never even know her uncle. But she lived.

Jeremiah raised his gaze to Clare's, full of pain for this man once a friend. "Logan had something more to tell you, Clare. He said . . . well, his exact words were, 'Tell the mother I am sorry for taking the boy.'"

Uncle Alphus put his arm around her shoulders; she could feel his anger and indignation through the embrace, but something different was happening inside of her. Something hard and jagged was breaking open and melting, as it had been doing now for days. Since she uttered those words to Rain Crow?

"Don't you remember?"

She'd been remembering—that the Almighty didn't place the same degrees upon wrongdoing as men did. That she had murdered in her heart.

She knew what she had to do.

"I don't wish ever to see Logan again, Jeremiah, much less speak to him, but if ever you do—or you, Mr. Gibson." She looked to the trader, who had tears running down his face. "Would you give him these words from me? Tell him that I forgive him for taking Jacob. And tell him, though he isn't sorry for killing Philip, I forgive him for that as well. Would you do that?"

38

John Gibson had had more to relate to Governor Dunmore about the Mingos who'd rejected his terms of peace and fled to Seekunk. They planned to journey farther north with their captives in two days' time, to a new village near Lake Erie. Dunmore ordered Major William Crawford to take several companies of militia to stop them and liberate the captives. They would leave on the morrow.

Alphus Litchfield, present when these plans were made, came to Clare at the camp on Scippo Creek where she was staying with Wolf-Alone and Jeremiah, an arrangement that felt right and familiar—to her uncle's consternation.

"I've spoken to Dunmore," he told them after relating the particulars of the campaign, fixing Jeremiah with a drilling gaze. "While the governor hasn't expressly given you pardon, or permission, he's willing to turn a blind eye should you slip your guard—namely *me*—and be found no longer in camp come morn."

Relief and dread seized Clare simultaneously. Jeremiah was being given his freedom, but he would have to take it that very night.

Already the sun was setting, the short October day grown chill. Clare had a shawl wrapped warm around her and Pippa. She held her daughter close, looking from Jeremiah to Wolf-Alone.

"Can you?" she asked, for he wasn't yet recovered from his wound. "Will you?" She half-hoped he'd say no, was desperate for him to say yes, tried not to pin hope or expectation on either outcome.

Beneath the trees along the creek bank, Jeremiah stood straight, his gaze on her level and certain. "Of course I'm going after them, Clare. I'll get out ahead of Crawford's army if I can."

"How? You're not yet recovered."

"I will go with him," Wolf-Alone said when she turned to him in mute appeal. She felt a rush of gratitude and held his gaze in thanks.

"And then?" she asked, the question directed at Jeremiah.

"I'll do as God leads. Pray He enables me to bring Jacob back to you." Jeremiah gazed at her, calm and steady. She knew he was expecting her to demand to accompany him and Wolf-Alone, to help fix what was broken, as she'd demanded and insisted from the start beside that shattered wagon.

But she said nothing at all.

Clare left Pippa in Jeremiah's care and went down to the creek to walk along the bank as night fell, wrapped in the warmer folds of a blanket now. She paced and she wrestled—with her heart, with her God, with things said to her moments ago.

"There's no more you can do for Jacob," Uncle Alphus had said. "You have Pippa to consider, and winter's coming on. You'll only be a hindrance to the search if you insist on going."

Though he didn't say it, Clare knew Jeremiah was of like mind. She also knew she was well able to fight both his and her uncle's will and prevail. She'd learned much about the limits of her determination, and stubbornness, when it came to achieving her heart's desires, to seeing her will be done. Both were terrifyingly boundless.

She also knew she'd far more reason than those her uncle had cited to hesitate following the demands of her heart, which yearned after her firstborn as desperately as on that morning she found the wagon empty, her arms emptier. Since that moment she'd grasped and clutched and striven to fill them again by any and every means possible, to no avail.

She was done grasping.

Which meant that for Clare Margaret Inglesby, widowed at twenty-six years of age and aching for the return of her child, there was but one other course of action to take. With every breath she must deny the desire that screamed within her to fix what was shattered, demand justice, make it right. Instead she would stand still and be silent and open her hands, holding her heart's desire there, unprotected and submitted. And she would wait.

Not my will be done, but Yours . . .

The choice of surrender was a tearing in her soul. Bent with it, she hunkered on the creek bank, the blanket around her, and rocked and wept and released her little boy to the Almighty and to His chosen vessel, Jeremiah Ring.

"I will trust, I will pray, and no more," she whispered into the blanket's muffling folds. "Even if it means I must grieve Jacob and pass through life and death to see him again. I believe You have him, have us all, in Your hands. You're doing what You will, and it will be for the best."

But help my poor battered heart. Give me strength to do this.

She remained so for a time, listening to crickets in the brush, the murmur of water flowing by, the wind in fading, papery leaves clinging to the branches above. When she was ready, she stood and went back along the creek and up the bank and found Jeremiah standing alone by the fire.

She didn't ask where Wolf-Alone or her uncle had gone. She saw Pippa asleep inside the tent but didn't go to her. She walked into the circle of Jeremiah's arms, weeping spent, and laid her head against his chest.

"Clare."

She loved how he simply said her name, for there was so much in it, layer after layer of feeling, of history, of hope. She felt his hand splayed warm on the back of her head, his breath against her hair, his heart beating beneath her cheek where it was pressed.

"I'll stay with Uncle Alphus while you and Wolf-Alone go, but I will pray for you and for Jacob—and your sister—until I see you both."

She felt him draw a breath, deep and clean. "When I come to you again, it will be with your son or I won't come at all."

She hadn't expected that. Stepping back from the embrace, she searched his face by firelight, thinking of never seeing him again. Something wrenched beneath her ribs, as if one had sprung out of alignment.

It didn't go back.

She put her fingers over his lips. "I want you to come back to me. Even if you cannot find Jacob."

He seemed to know how hard that was to say. She hoped he believed her.

"I want to," he said, but whether he meant he wanted to find Jacob or come back to her, she didn't ask. It was enough. For of one thing she was convinced: Jeremiah would do God's will, even where it conflicted with his own. And if God willed for them to be together as she now wished, what could stop it?

She looked long into Jeremiah's eyes and knew a power of feeling unlike anything she'd ever experienced, even with her children. It was a bud unfurled as yet, as it should be, for winter was coming.

But spring always followed winter, did it not?

Voices were approaching, Uncle Alphus and Wolf-Alone returning from wherever they had gone—to gather supplies for the journey north, a glance at their laden arms revealed.

Jeremiah would be leaving in a matter of hours. That out-of-joint rib gave another wrench.

Maybe his had too, for he touched her face and said with plain regret, "It has to be tonight."

"I know." Then she said the thing that was most important. "Thank you. I can never say it enough. Thank you for all of it."

"I'd do it over again. A thousand times."

"If we had even once to do it again, I'd do it better . . . now." She'd carried one thing down to the creek with her, held it while she paced and prayed. Now she opened her hand so he could see it.

"Philip's timepiece?" he said, raising dark eyes to hers in question.

"I need to say this, need to tell you that Philip is the past. All those regrets, they are the past. I'm ready to move on with living . . . in that way," she added, holding his gaze with an intensity that made her tremble. "Do you understand what I'm saying?"

The longing in his gaze wrapped around her, made her barely aware of the two men who had joined them in camp. "After you have Jacob back? Is that what you mean?"

"No. Yes." She shook her head and smiled, self-conscious now but aching to make him understand, so there would be no question in his mind when he left her this night. "I want him back, of course. I'll always want that. But there are other things I want."

The light in his eyes let her know he understood. "Then I'll find you waiting for me?"

"You will," she said. "No matter what."

They were no longer alone, and the business of preparing for another journey must needs begin. With every breath, Clare clung to her hard-won resolve. *Not my will . . .*

There was one more farewell to make after getting her and Pippa's belongings together—she couldn't stay alone on the creek bank after Jeremiah and his brother left—and there came a moment when she and Wolf-Alone were together by the dying fire, she with Pippa in her arms asleep, and to her deep surprise the tall Indian touched her face and told her he would take care of Jeremiah.

"I know." His devotion to his adopted brothers was a thing she'd never questioned, though so much about the man begged for answers.

"Better still," he said. "God will help."

He hadn't said *your* God. "You're a Christian, aren't you—whatever else you are?"

"I am," Wolf-Alone said and smiled faintly at her unveiled surprise.

She gazed at the warrior, so strikingly handsome—except for those terrifying eyebrows—and she wondered again where he came from, why he'd chosen to live as Shawnee.

"Who *are* you?" she asked, thinking it possibly her last chance ever to do so. "What was your name . . . before?"

But Wolf-Alone shook his head. "I left that name behind long ago, and I won't speak it again now," he said and raised his head with a look in his eyes as if he could see past their dismantled camp on Scippo Creek, past the army's larger camp nearby, straight through the darkness to something in the distance.

He was staring in the direction of Cornstalk's Town, and it brought the boy, Wildcat, to mind.

"But I think," he added, half to himself, "maybe soon I'll have another name."

39

OCTOBER 28
CAMP CHARLOTTE, SCIPPO CREEK

Beneath her uncle's canvas shelter, Clare woke to a dawn cold and misted, the gray of it glimpsed through a slender gap in the tent's canvas opening. Pippa slept, warm in the blankets beside her, but even before Clare felt the bite of seeping air, her first coherent thought was of Jacob. Was he warm? Was he safe?

Her second thought was of the man gone to find him. She closed her eyes, calling up her last moments with Jeremiah.

When all was ready for their departure, Wolf-Alone and her uncle had drawn away, giving them a space of solitude, and she'd told Jeremiah something she'd been wanting to say.

"The day the warriors returned to Cornstalk's Town, after the battle, was the last time I spoke to Rain Crow, but I haven't been able to put it from my mind."

"What did you say to my sister?"

They'd stood close; the fire had died, the night was dark. The pack he would bear waited at the edge of camp. She'd wanted to touch him, hold him again, but Pippa filled her arms.

"I told her God knows how we feel, she and I, about our sons. About losing them. Because He lost His Son. I asked her if she remembered that. It was right then the warriors returned but . . . I'm certain I heard her say that she remembered too."

He put his hands to her shoulders and drew her and Pippa to his chest. His lips were warm as they touched her brow.

"Thank you," he said, the warmth in his voice greater still. "I have prayed long for her to remember."

"I know." She nestled her head against his chest. "But there's something more I wanted to say. It wasn't until I saw you again, here, that I really understood what that meant myself."

Not until she'd seen Jeremiah again, there in Camp Charlotte with Uncle Alphus, had she understood how deep her own mistrust of the Almighty went.

"What I wanted to say to Rain Crow, but didn't have the chance, is that there's a verse in the Bible—I cannot tell you where to find it exactly. It says, If 'he that spared not his own Son, but delivered him up for us all, how shall he not with him also freely give us all things?' It came back to me in that moment."

Jeremiah stepped back, though he didn't take his hands from her.

"You'd find it in Romans, the eighth chapter," he told her, a smile in his voice though it was too dark to see it. "And yes. *Yes,* Clare. He will give us all the good things, and all that He does give is good. If it doesn't seem so in this life, yet it will prove to be in heaven, where neither you nor I—or my sister—will turn to the Almighty in accusation and say, 'I wish You'd given me whatever it was I begged You for, or didn't give me that hard thing I didn't want. I wish You'd ordered my life otherwise.'"

She was beyond speech, in her throat a burn of longing and hope as she raised her face to his.

"The only promise I can leave you with," he said, his voice gone husky with the pain and the glory of such words, "is that we will never say such things to the Almighty. Instead we'll call His judgments right and true. Every single one."

"Jeremiah." She wanted to tell him to be careful, to be mindful of his safety as he went into the unknown for her, for Jacob, for his sister.

"I will," he said, answering her unspoken plea. Then he leaned down and kissed her mouth for the first time, and before he'd finished she was breathless and tingling down to her toes, longing for it not to be the last kiss but the first of many.

Then he bent lower and kissed the top of Pippa's head. "Take care of my girl."

His girl. She didn't refute the claim. She had joy in it.

"When you find Rain Crow, will you tell her what you just told me, about God's judgments?"

"I'll tell her," he said. "And more besides."

And then she'd let him go, to stand with her uncle and watch the two warriors vanish into the night, Wolf-Alone carrying the lion's share of their belongings until Jeremiah regained his strength.

And the stillness, the trusting, finally and truly began.

It wasn't late into the morning before a messenger arrived, sent from Major Crawford, who'd led his men north after the Mingos at Seekunk the morning after Jeremiah's departure. The news wasn't what Governor Dunmore—or Clare—had hoped for. While Crawford had attempted to surround the village in the night, in preparation for a dawn attack, one of his men was prematurely discovered by the Indians and many managed to escape.

"We killed us a few, took some prisoners, rescued a couple Virginians they was holding," the messenger related in Alphus Litchfield's hearing, which he'd related to Clare. But her uncle was quick to say neither of those captives had been a child. No word was to be had of Jacob or of Jeremiah, but with the raid on Seekunk, Lord Dunmore's war against the Ohio Indians had come to an end.

That day the governor began preparations for the return to Virginia.

Though Clare had hoped to wait at Camp Charlotte for Jeremiah and Jacob to return, that choice was taken from her as well.

"We have to go with them," Uncle Alphus told her. "We cannot stay here on our own, and as for you returning to the Shawnees, I'm sorry, Clare, but I simply cannot let you and Pippa do that. Your father would scalp *me,* and he'd have every cause to do so."

"I'm not asking for either," she said, holding Pippa wrapped in her shawl and gazing north, as if Jeremiah might come striding out of the trees, Jacob in his arms, if she but kept a vigil.

She started when a deer stepped into view, blood surging in eagerness even as her brain told her there was no cause. Then she turned away and let her uncle lead her back to the army's camp, where they began their preparations for leaving.

Not my will, Lord. Yours be done.

She heard the following morning that the Shawnees who remained at Camp Charlotte intended to ride with the governor on his return journey as far as Fort Gower, erected at the mouth of the Hocking. On the last day of October, mounted on a borrowed horse, Clare rode with the militia and that Shawnee delegation, which included Cornstalk and Nonhelema, along forest paths decked in fading gold, down the Hocking River until they reached the Ohio and the new fort Dunmore had left in his wake.

The air smelled of the river, the coming cold, the tang of fresh-cut timber. All around her—at least among the men of Dunmore's army—the talk was not of the west or Indians but of what was happening in the east, in Boston and Philadelphia. Even she with her great distraction of mind and heart could discern the discontent among men like James Harrod, John Sevier, and others over the issue of British authority and its bounds, and the Crown-appointed men like Lord Dunmore who had led the campaign.

Unlike the men around her, eager to return to their homes and take up their rifles, or their pens, in yet another brewing conflict, Clare Inglesby was leaving her heart behind in the wilderness, with her son.

And with Jeremiah Ring.

The day in early November the Shawnees departed Fort Gower, Clare stood in the sting of a chilling breeze and watched them go. Cornstalk, Nonhelema, the chiefs Blue Jacket and Black Hoof, many others, all with feathers twirling in the wind, black hair lifting, astride horses painted and bedecked for parade, to all outward appearances without grief or regret. But Clare knew the heartache, even despair, those regally composed faces concealed. They had lost sons and brothers and husbands. They had lost their lands south of the Ohio River. They would lose all those captives, many now family, that they would be forced to give back to the whites. With one exception, perhaps, and she wondered again what Wolf-Alone would do about the boy, Wildcat.

It was nearly as hard for her to stand and let the Shawnees ride away, out of her life, as it had been to watch Jeremiah vanish into the darkness without her, days ago. Beyond all expectation, she felt her heart break at the sight.

Perhaps Governor Dunmore was envisioning his newly inked peace leading to rich settlements for Virginia extending down the Ohio and branching south along Kentucky's many rivers. But how long until even Kentucky wasn't enough? Until restless, hungry eyes looked northward?

This will never end. Always men want more.

Before the last of the Shawnees' horses vanished around the bend in the wooded path, the warrior astride it looked back briefly. Around him all was burnished brown and drifting mist, the flames of autumn sunk to embers.

He wasn't a warrior Clare knew by name, but his face was familiar and it remained emblazoned upon her memory for many days after, along with that of Falling Hawk, Crosses-the-Path and her daughters, Split-Moon and Wild-cat, others she'd come to know. She wondered if she would ever see them again, all those fallen sparrows the Almighty was watching.

She hoped so. Until then she would wish them peace in which to heal their wings, that they might take flight again.

40

Snow fell in the night, blanketing the valley and the ridges rising to west and east, making their slopes seem higher and more remote, each wooded fold cast in sharp relief beneath a leaden sky promising more snow before day's end.

In late March such heavy snowfall was less welcome than it had been in late November when Clare and Pippa Inglesby and Alphus Litchfield returned to the mill on Lewis Creek, having made the journey from Fort Pitt down the Monongahela, then by horseback south along the wagon road Clare, Philip, and Jacob had traveled in spring. But to Clare, who lifted her face to the sullen heavens from the warmth of her uncle's horse-drawn sled, the breeze of their passing cold against her cheeks, it seemed fitting winter should linger, the earth continue sleeping, spring be deferred.

She'd spent the winter tending her uncle's house and hearth, lavishing upon the man the domestic attention he'd rarely known in his life of bachelorhood. It made her happy to see him dandle Pippa on his knee like a grandfather—though like a grandfather he was swift to hand the baby back if she cried or needed tending.

So she'd lived, worked, slept, and each morning awoke thinking: *Should evening come and they have not, Thy will be done.* Then she would arise and pray for her boy, for the man who sought him, for the woman who clung to what wasn't hers to claim.

Didn't she herself know the terrible wrench of releasing?

Afterward she went about the doings of the day, and it seemed to her the life going on around her—in her uncle's home, at his mill, in Staunton, in the colony beyond where revolutionary-minded men such as Patrick Henry spoke of liberty or death—was like the rim of a wagon wheel turning, its many spokes running inward to where she stood, the axis of the wheel that spun, alone with the Almighty in a stillness both temporal and eternal.

At Christmastide her parents had come from Richmond to entreat her to return east. She'd known it wasn't time to choose a path. She was at a cross-roads, listening for direction. Until she had it, she wouldn't take a step. She'd remained in the place where Jeremiah Ring had been the young farmer, Jem Ringbloom, with a wife called Hannah, and had known happiness; where once she had been content, none of them knowing how fragile was such happiness, yet to learn there was a joy deeper than circumstance, a joy that sprang from the seeds of trust, believing God was who and what He said He was. *Good. Sovereign. Father.*

Through it all she'd watched her baby girl grow. At nearly ten months, Pippa was as tow-headed and brown-eyed as her brother, grown chunky on the verge of taking her first unaided steps.

For Pippa, the sight—and feel and taste—of snow was as enthralling as it had been the first time she took note of it, though just now she was well-covered by the blankets in the sled, pressed close to Clare's side, sheltered from the cold. Nestled in an old buffalo lap robe from Uncle Alphus's adventurous long-hunter days, Clare watched the mountains and woods slip past, felt her daughter's small head butt against her side, and tried to recall exactly when her uncle began talking of hitching his team to the wagon and driving out to the farm, their present destination.

Had it been yesterday? Or the evening before?

That was it. He'd broached the subject over dinner of roasted chicken and dried apple pie. She'd fed Pippa small bites of the food, half-listening to him talk of riding out to check on things as he did periodically, seeing as the farm stood vacant. It had only been a week since he'd last done so; she'd been surprised he would again. More surprised still that he'd insisted she and Pippa accompany him.

There'd been something about the way he looked at her when he said it. Something in his gaze. Expectancy?

Whatever it was, he'd suppressed it too quickly for her to be certain. She suspected he'd some surprise for her there—perhaps he'd made something for Pippa. She decided to play along.

"All right, Uncle. We'll go with you." And in saying those words, she'd wondered, was she ready to take up residence there, alone with Pippa? Was that what the Lord had next for her?

She didn't know, but she would go with the idea in mind and see if He might tell her so when she stood again on that ground.

In the end it was the sled they hitched, not the wagon, and over the miles Clare had grown lulled by the hiss of runners, the muffled fall of the teams' hooves, the occasional *thump* of snow sliding from a tree bough, the passing of the last wooded mile before the farm came into view.

It had always struck her as abrupt, that falling away of trees as the track emerged from the wood—even in winter for the pines were densely spaced. The farmhouse would appear ahead, two-storied and whitewashed, the barn and outbuildings set amidst rolling pasture and fallow field.

Before the wood opened, she glanced at her uncle. He'd fallen silent over the last stretch.

"It's only been a week since you've been out here," she said, breath clouding briefly before vanishing in the wind of their passage. "Planning to give up your mill and turn farmer again?"

Uncle Alphus seemed to be trying to hide a smile. "Never crossed my mind, my girl. I've wondered whether you might."

She wasn't ready to admit her mind was circling the notion.

"Are you eager to have me and Pippa out from underfoot? Perhaps coming down with a case of the wanderlust after all these years?" When Uncle Alphus looked at her half-guiltily, half-startled, she laughed. "You've mentioned that Watauga Association at least a dozen times since Christmas, Uncle. I've expected you to come home from the mill one of these days to say you've sold it and the farm and are heading west again."

He'd told her in some detail about the settlements beyond the mountains to the south. Apparently he'd met men from that region during Lord Dunmore's campaign. It sounded as though another colony was going to be formed, or had been.

It wasn't likely to be a British colony, the way things were going. Spanish, perhaps. Or maybe American?

"I reckon old age isn't a cure for itching feet, after all," Uncle Alphus said as he guided the horses around a fallen limb.

"You aren't old!" Clare protested. "But I did wonder if perhaps you wanted me and Pippa to come along with you."

"That would be for you to decide, Clare, if the time should come. But I don't want you following after me out of some sort of duty or obligation. You're young and need to live your life, not mine."

Clare gazed ahead down the snowy track bending away through the pine-wood, blinking away tears the cold air stung from her eyes. They'd lingered at Fort Gower until the fifth of November, the officers who'd served under Lord Dunmore discussing the conflict with the Crown and, agreeing upon their sentiments, writing up a statement that was published in the *Virginia Gazette,* to the effect that if there was war with Great Britain, then the Americans would have an army. Having fought together as colonial militia on the frontier, they'd learned they needn't go in awe of men in red coats.

Live your life.

Where would that life be lived? What would be the shape of it?

Exceeding, abundantly, above all that she could ask or imagine.

The fragment of promise from the Scripture slid through her mind as the sled emerged from the wood, the view of the farmstead opening up in that sudden way it had. She knew at once that something about the scene was wrong.

Smoke ascended from the farmhouse chimney.

A child played in the yard, near a snowy woodpile.

A man was chopping the wood. Clare heard the *chunk* of the ax as he brought it down, the *crack* of the wood's splitting.

"Uncle? What . . . ?"

The man had his back to the coming sled; they were yet too far away for him to hear the hiss of its runners over the noise he was making. He hadn't turned to show her his face. But she knew him by his long, lean lines and by the way he moved, though like the child he was dressed warmly for the weather in clothing she'd never seen—a heavy buckskin coat, a furred hat, gloves, and thick winter moccasins.

Her mouth hung open as her body absorbed the shock, limbs and gaze and heart frozen, fixed on the man. Then in a heated thawing she looked again at the child.

"Uncle, stop the sled!" She couldn't get there any faster than the sled would bring her but she couldn't sit still another second. "Please!"

Alphus Litchfield pulled back on the lines; the horses slowed. Before they'd quite stopped, she'd bolted from the buffalo robe and hit the ground, managing to stay on her feet.

"Watch Pippa," she called and then was running down the untrodden lane through the fresh snow. "Jacob!"

The man thrust the ax into the cutting block and turned, and she laughed aloud with the joy of seeing Jeremiah's face. Though he was already striding toward her, the child bolted past him, running pell-mell to meet her at the edge of the yard.

"Mama!"

No sweeter sound ever graced her ears.

No sweeter pain ever squeezed her heart than when Jacob barreled into her and they fell with her skirts awry and snow in places it had never touched, the both of them laughing.

"Mama, we're back. We're home."

"I see you are! Oh, Jacob. My sweet boy." She was laughing still but crying too, when a shadow fell across them and she looked up, arms and lap full of her squirming son.

Jeremiah Ring's face was shining down at her, his beard dark, his teeth white, the tip of his nose red with the cold.

"Jeremiah, when? Where? How long?" She couldn't get a coherent question past her lips, but she didn't need to.

Jeremiah laughed. "I'll tell you everything, Clare. For now, it's so good to see you again."

His eyes were saying it was much more than *good*. He reached down and took her mittened hand in his gloved one and pulled her to her feet, all crusted with snow. He didn't let her go, but drew her in close and held her, and she melted into the warmth of his solid, sure embrace.

Home, she thought. *At last I am home.* Not the farm. Not even Virginia. It didn't matter how they lived or where. She could live anywhere with this man, anywhere he wished. In her world, or his, or somewhere altogether new.

Perhaps the Watauga would do for them all. There was time to decide.

Jacob bounced up as if he'd springs for knees. "Mama, he said you would come. Are you going to live here with us?"

"Live here?" she echoed, blinking first at him, then at Jeremiah. Was that what Jeremiah had in mind, to live there on that farm? What of his Shawnee kin? "Of course I'm going to live with *you,* silly boy. You're my son, aren't you?"

She'd been teasing but found she needed to hear him to say it.

"I am. Don't you remember?"

"I do remember. But look at you, Jacob. You're such a big boy now, I mightn't have recognized you."

Her son had grown since she'd last seen him, his features a little more the boy he was becoming, less the babe he'd been. She glimpsed how much he would resemble Philip in a few more years—years in which she would watch that change happen, day by precious day. God willing.

"They don't call me Many Sparrows anymore," he told her.

"They?" she asked, but just then Uncle Alphus arrived in the sled—he must have walked the horses, giving them time to reunite—with Pippa sitting beside him peeking out of a blanket.

Jeremiah's gaze fixed on the sled. "Speaking of getting big . . . Clare, *look* at her."

At the sound of his voice, Pippa uttered a squeal.

"She remembers you," Clare said, as something caught deep at her heart, something sweet and tender, made of memories in a clearing, along forest trails, in a canoe on a river, and in a bark lodge far away. Their history.

"I want to see Pippa!" Jacob dashed for the sled and clambered up to sit beside his sister, while Uncle Alphus held the horses still and gazed at them all, looking as near to tears as Clare had ever seen the man. She caught her uncle's gaze while her children became reacquainted.

It struck her that he wasn't the least surprised to find Jeremiah and Jacob at the farm.

"How long have you known?"

"Little over a day."

"Uncle," she said, thinking she should be aggrieved but unable to be for the joy overwhelming her and yet . . . "How could you not tell me?"

Her uncle looked a bit shamefaced. "I . . . well . . ."

"That was my doing." Jeremiah's dark eyes searched her face. "I came to him at the mill, day before yesterday, toward evening. I'd left Jacob at the farm but needed to let your uncle know we were here. I'd a question to put to him before I put it to you, Clare, because I knew I couldn't bear to see you without asking it straightaway. Forgive me for making you wait even one day more, but this question is of utmost importance. So is your uncle's blessing." He looked to Alphus Litchfield, still in the sled with the children. "You've had time to think on it?"

"I've brought her here to you," said her uncle.

Clare was trying to make sense of this. "Why did you come alone to the mill? Did you leave Jacob here at the farm on his own?"

That didn't seem a thing Jeremiah would do, not after he'd somehow— she intended to hear every detail of *how*—gotten Jacob away from Rain Crow and brought him home to her at last.

"Not on his own," Jeremiah said, and would have said more, Clare was certain, had not the door of the farmhouse opened and a young woman in homespun, wrapped in a woolen shawl, stepped out. A woman with black hair coiled on her head above a face like smoothly beaten copper. A face strong-boned and elegant, one that would have drawn every gaze even had her presence alone not been so compelling.

Rain Crow came to them across the snowy yard, looking almost other-worldly in the way she was laced and gowned, moving as if she floated across the snow, feet hidden beneath a full petticoat.

"Alphus Litchfield," Jeremiah said when Rain Crow reached his side. "Allow me to introduce my sister, Abigail Ringbloom. She looked after Jacob," he added, turning to Clare. "I'd never have left him alone, not even here."

Clare's mouth hung open again as she watched Rain Crow's slim brown hand lift to Jeremiah's arm, as if seeking comfort.

"Jeremiah, what is this? Why . . . ?" There was a tug at her shawl and she looked down into Jacob's upturned face.

"Mama," he said, as if she was unaccountably slow. "He wants to marry you."

"Exactly," Jeremiah said, with a laugh uncharacteristically nervous. "I went to your uncle's mill to ask his permission, Clare. And his blessing. I came away with the impression that he wasn't wholly against the idea."

He looked toward her uncle as he said this last. Clare didn't follow his gaze, but he must have seen something in the man's face to give him leave to press on with the matter. He still held her hand in his. He drew it close to his heart.

"Clare, you are a woman of amazing strength and courage, and I want you by my side. I want to make what we pretended to in Cornstalk's Town our truth. I love you. I want you for my wife."

She was vaguely aware that Rain Crow had stepped away from them, but she didn't take her gaze from the man before her.

"Jeremiah, I . . . You . . ." She shook her head, overcome. Her heart beat wild with the joy of it. But there were things she needed to understand before she could answer him truthfully. "Why have you brought your sister here? Why is she calling herself by your name? Can she not bear to be parted from Jacob—still?"

"No, Clare. That's not why. Not exactly. When I found her on Lake Erie with the Mingos that fled Seekunk, she was already repenting having left Cornstalk's Town and taken Jacob away from you. From us all. I told her what I told you—"

"About God's judgments being righteous and true?"

"That and more. She wept over it. She knew she couldn't keep Jacob, that he belongs with you. Yet she despaired, not knowing any longer where she was meant to be—with our brother or with her mother. So I told her . . ." Jeremiah paused, clearly uncertain how she would receive his words. "I invited her to come with us to Virginia, to come away from both those lives, take some time and see what the Almighty might have for her. By then winter had closed in, and I didn't want to risk travel. I knew you were waiting, and again I ask your forgiveness, but there was another reason I didn't want to leave Cornstalk's Town right away."

Clare searched his face, seeing in it now the marks of grief. A fresh grief. Dread tightened her belly as her mind flitted over the faces of those she'd come to know in that town far away on Scippo Creek. "What has happened?"

"We've lost Split-Moon and Wildcat. And . . . Wolf-Alone."

Their names landed like blows.

"Lost? You don't mean . . . ?"

"I do," he said, and squeezed her hand.

"How?"

He swallowed and told the tale. "After we returned from Lake Erie, Wolf-Alone and Falling Hawk took Split-Moon and Wildcat hunting. They didn't cross the Ohio, as per the treaty with Dunmore, but they were near it. In camp one evening they were set upon by whites, already trespassing across the river meant to hold them back."

They were fired upon, he told her, relating it as Falling Hawk had told the story to him. Old Split-Moon was shot and killed immediately. Falling Hawk, so soon recovered from his battle wound, had fallen as he tried to escape and took a musket ball in the leg.

"He managed to crawl off into a rhody thicket to hide but saw Wolf-Alone grab Wildcat, throw him over his shoulder, and go dodging into the darkening woods like a deer. They were pursued. Shots were fired."

Falling Hawk was left for dead. It took him days, but he made it nearly back to Scippo Creek when he was found by other Shawnee hunters and brought home to tell the tale. They retrieved Split-Moon's body and buried him, but Wolf-Alone and Wildcat were never found. Either they'd been captured or were killed.

"I cannot imagine any other reason they wouldn't have returned," Jeremiah said. "My family has been much grieved. I didn't want to leave them, Clare."

"Oh, Jeremiah. I understand." Clare felt the weight of grief herself, thinking of that old man, of the boy and Wolf-Alone, that enigmatic warrior, now not only was his past a mystery, but his passing.

Or might by some miracle he and the boy be alive somewhere? Unlike Jeremiah, she sensed that could be possible. She recalled her last exchange with Wolf-Alone, his talk of having a new name. Had he'd a presentiment of some wrenching change coming?

One thing she knew: Wolf-Alone would give his life to save Wildcat, in more ways than one.

"When I finally made ready to leave, me and Jacob," Jeremiah was saying, "Abigail announced she would go with me as I'd asked. She wishes to take my name for now and stay with us for a while. Until she knows her own mind, if you'll allow it."

Apparently the woman hadn't gone quite out of hearing during Jeremiah's recounting, for she was at Clare's side of a sudden, a graceful hand raised now to her arm, beseeching.

"Sister," she said. "I am sorry for the pain I've caused you, in keeping your son from you after I learned he had a mother. I was wrong to do it, but I did not want to see that for a long time. Now I am the one seeking mercy, for I do not know where I belong. Will you let me stay with you and my brother until my eyes are clear and I can see the path ahead of me again?"

Sister. Clare looked into the eyes of the woman who had tried to claim her son but didn't see the defiance, the pride, the anger she had come to expect. She saw grief. She saw confusion. And hope. She saw the woman she'd glimpsed that moment in Cornstalk's Town uttering those words, *"I remember."*

But it was the words she'd just spoken that echoed Clare's heart. *"I do not know where I belong."* Or her heart until a few moments ago.

She belonged at Jeremiah's side.

Yet deeper in her soul a sense of unbelonging remained. Where did any of them truly belong? Was it a question all humanity asked, to be answered only by eternity and in time they would reach it—those who came by the narrow way?

They were only pilgrims here, walking that narrow path. Should they walk it together, she and this woman? Even for a little while? Would she be safe in allowing it? Would her children be safe?

Rain Crow seemed to understand what was going through her mind. "I make no claim on your son. We have brought Jacob back to you. He is yours. I understand now why I wanted him. I . . ."

"I know," Clare said, when the other woman faltered, tears welling. Rain Crow had been using Jacob to fill the void of her grief. A void only the Almighty could fill. In her own way, so had Clare.

"You wish to be called Abigail now?"

The woman lowered her eyes, then raised them again, looking at Clare straight on. "I once told you never to call me that name, but I will be called so now. Names have power. Maybe I will become who that woman is, and maybe I will do that becoming here with you."

Jeremiah's sister dropped her hand from Clare's arm. "I will let you and my brother speak of these things. I will do as you decide."

She stepped away, turning to go back into the house.

When she was halfway across the yard, Clare called to her. "Abigail? Would you please take the children in out of the cold?"

The woman turned, face shining with a startled relief.

"I will," she said and went to the sled and took Pippa in her arms and, Jacob following, headed for the house.

Jacob chattered happily as they went, and while it was a wrench to let him out of her sight, Clare reminded herself he was back now. He was hers. Then she flung herself into Jeremiah's arms again and wept, and thanked him. Again and again. And he held her.

"Did I say you were a woman of strength and courage? Add heart to that, and grace."

Clare didn't hear her uncle start the horses toward the barn, but after a while she realized she and Jeremiah were alone. She pulled back, still in his embrace, and took his face between mittened hands. His beard had grown on the journey to her, though it was still short, hugging his lean jaw. She hoped he would keep it.

"She needs a refuge—how well I understand that, for you were that to me all those months and I didn't even realize it at the time. She may seek her refuge with us."

Between her hands Jeremiah's lips parted in a smile. He reached up and wiped away the residue of her tears with the tip of a gloved finger.

"That's one question answered."

"Did you ask another?" Clare replied, holding back a grin. "I seem to recall you stating an intention . . ."

His smile turned playful, but the look in his eyes was earnest, full of hope. "Clare Inglesby, *will* you marry me?"

"I will," she said. "And I love you, too, in case I haven't said it—but I think you know it."

They were already embracing. Such an easy, natural thing, the meeting of their lips. Jeremiah kissed her thoroughly, their breath mingling in the cold, until she heard the crunch of her uncle's footsteps coming up from the barn through the snow.

They broke their embrace. Uncle Alphus halted, studied them, then nodded, apparently accepting what he saw. He came nearer and, in his blunt way, addressed the practicality of the situation.

"What will you do, the two of you? Can you remain in Virginia safely?"

Clare felt a clutch in her middle as she stepped back from Jeremiah to gauge his reaction. She'd not thought of the battle between the rivers at Point Pleasant for weeks, but her uncle's implication was clear. Jeremiah had fought against the governor's troops and not been officially pardoned. He'd been taken prisoner. By either of his names he was known—as a traitor.

"I don't know," he said.

"I don't want you risking your freedom," Clare said. "We can go anywhere. Even back to the Shawnees if we must."

"Do you mean that?" Jeremiah asked.

"If that's where you need to be, I'll go there with you."

Alphus Litchfield looked alarmed at that. "Hold on now. Things being as they are—likely war coming, maybe even a break with the Crown—there may be no one left calling you a traitor. You could stay in Virginia. Or," he added, "there's always the Watauga."

"The what?" Jeremiah asked, then his face cleared. "You mean that independent colony, west of the Yadkin?"

"It's not exactly a colony," Uncle Alphus replied, "but they've drafted a plan to govern themselves, and it might be a good opportunity for a man—and his kin—looking to start afresh."

"I think Uncle Alphus has already made up his mind to sell the mill and this farm and head west again," Clare said, wondering if this was the path opening up for them all, at last.

"I've been waiting to see you settled first," Uncle Alphus said, "before I decided how to dispose of my doings here."

"You really are serious then? You'll go?"

"I suspect I've one last adventure in me. However, I don't necessarily fancy going alone." He caught Jeremiah's gaze. "Not if I had strong young kin willing to venture with me."

Clare looked at the two men, young and not-quite-old, both eminently capable, and felt that in their company she wouldn't be afraid to venture into the unknown. For Jeremiah it wouldn't even be the unknown. The frontier was home to him, its people his.

"The Watauga," she said, liking the feel of the name on her lips.

"I'd be glad to have you by my side in any case," Jeremiah said, nodding respectfully to her uncle. "Wherever we decide to settle. But no sense in rushing into anything," he added, his arm coming around Clare's shoulders. "We've a roof and a fire, so we'll seek the Lord on the matter, see how He leads."

"Besides which, we've a wedding to arrange," Clare reminded them. "First things first."

"Sounds like a fine plan," Alphus Litchfield said, nodding his approval.

Clare knew a peace in that moment, a contentment laced with the excitement of knowing life as Clare Ring—or Clare Ringbloom, whatever they ended up calling themselves—was going to be an adventure. Not an unguided one. Jeremiah would lead her with wisdom to match any danger life threw their way, would keep his word to her because he would never give it unless he was sure of it, and wouldn't drag her heedlessly down a path of reckless dreams.

From the shelter of his encircling arm, Clare gazed over the farm, thinking that while she'd known a fleeting happiness there, she liked the idea of someplace new to them both.

The idea of the Watauga was growing on her.

"And to think, Uncle," she said, "had you not chanced upon that conversation with Sevier and the others in camp that evening, we likely wouldn't be standing here contemplating heading overmountain into Carolina."

"Oh, I doubt very much it was chance," Alphus Litchfield said, gazing at the two of them. "Just the Almighty working things out, step by step."

The farmhouse door opened, and Jacob bolted outside, raced across the yard, and threw himself into the snow, where he proceeded to thrash about, making a snow angel. Abigail came to the threshold, Pippa on her hip, started to call him back, then shook her head and looked toward Clare, as if to judge whether she was displeased.

Clare couldn't stop smiling.

"We don't always get to glimpse His plan," Jeremiah said. "How He's working all the while, before and behind and beside us. Not in this life anyway."

"True." Clare watched her little boy playing in the snow, his laughter music on the cold air, while in the doorway Abigail, holding Pippa, returned her smile. "And yet sometimes we do."

READERS GUIDE

1. Clare Inglesby struggles with trust. Her disappointing marriage, Philip's death, Jacob's abduction, and the subsequent culture shock she experiences among the Shawnees create many layers of distrust around her heart. The peeling away of those layers is a process that spans this story. What are some of the key turning points on this journey for Clare?

2. Jeremiah Ring still finds it difficult to wait on God's timing when outside pressures tempt him to make hasty decisions. Why do you think this is? Is there something fundamentally impatient in human nature? Is there an area in your life where you experience this temptation?

3. The struggle over land between settlers and natives is a long one. Before you read this story, did you know about Dunmore's War and the struggle of the Shawnees to preserve their land? Did anything surprise you? What was the most interesting thing you learned about this pre–Revolutionary War period?

4. Two sides of a frontier collide in the pages of *Many Sparrows*. While the history of Dunmore's War, the Yellow Creek Massacre, and the violence that happened along the Ohio River during this era cannot be rewritten, as a writer I'm drawn to pen stories of men and women who face the perils of that cultural collision and overcome evil with good. Cite some examples of characters who do that in this story. Are there examples of characters who repay evil for evil instead?

5. There are two tragic figures in this story, one real (Logan) and one fictional (Philip Inglesby). Each man's fateful decisions set the story in motion. Could you understand the choices of either of these characters?

Could you sympathize with them? If not, what was your reaction to the life-altering consequences of their actions?

6. Indian captives on the eighteenth-century frontier met different fates depending on a wide set of factors. Some, like Jeremiah, chose to be adopted. What about those who didn't choose that life? Should they have been returned to their birth families, as the Shawnees were forced to do at the treaty signing with Lord Dunmore? What sort of challenges do you imagine such a person would face, readapting to white culture? Do you agree with Clare that Wildcat, with neither family to return to nor memory of another life, would be best left with his Shawnee father?

7. A little more seasoned in life than Clare, Jeremiah Ring has suffered his own painful past, which has left its scars. Did you understand his decision to remain with the Shawnees? What did he need to overcome in order to open his heart to loving a woman again?

8. When her every effort to reclaim Jacob fails, Clare is forced to remove her hands from the situation and allow God to fix it for her, and to accept it if He never does. How might this story have played out if she had reached that place of surrender sooner?

9. Rain Crow tries to fix what is broken in her life by her own wisdom and the traditions of her Shawnee people. Did you have sympathy for Rain Crow in her desire to keep Many Sparrows for herself? Did your feelings about her change over the course of the story? If you were Clare, would you have allowed Rain Crow to stay at the farm? Why or why not?

AUTHOR'S NOTES AND ACKNOWLEDGMENTS

World-building is a term used mostly by those writing in the fantasy genre, but world-building is essentially what I'm doing with my historical novels. Book by book, I'm weaving a broad eighteenth-century world in which a character from one story could (and probably will) wander into another. *Many Sparrows* is no exception.

Readers of my earlier novels may have recognized two of the characters living in Cornstalk's Town. I've introduced readers to Wolf-Alone and Wildcat before, under different names—Cade and Jesse Bird. For readers new to my books with *Many Sparrows,* if you're curious about these two characters and their mysterious past before they each became Shawnee, as well as what happens next in their story (which is far from over in these pages), you'll want to read *The Pursuit of Tamsen Littlejohn* next.

Clare Inglesby and Jeremiah Ring's story is woven around the events that took place along the Ohio River in that pre-Revolutionary War year of 1774. The massacre of Logan's family at Baker's trading post, near the mouth of Yellow Creek, really happened. In autumn of 2016 I spent a night in the hotel that now occupies the land where Baker's cabin and trading post once stood. I lay awake that night thinking about the massacre that happened there—the inciting incident from which the events of this story flow—before exploring next morning up the banks of Yellow Creek, and knew there was one question my story wouldn't answer: who actually killed Logan's family and the warriors who crossed the river to Baker's that fateful morning of April 30, 1774? Frontiersman Michael Cresap was initially blamed due to his reputation and previous threats of violence against the Mingos, but Cresap was innocent of these murders, as later came to light. The true culprit, leader of a gang of Long Knives who lured in and murdered these men and women—including Logan's sister and her unborn child—was a man named Daniel Greathouse.

After the letter of lament Logan writes at the end of this story (historians debate whether it is his own words, but I chose to let him speak them), little more is known about his life. He went on to fight with the British against the Americans during the Revolutionary War, hoping to drive the latter from his people's lands, and died before the war's ending.

Dunmore's War, culminating in the Battle of Point Pleasant between the Ohio and Kanawha Rivers, is also drawn from the pages of history. My go-to resource for this campaign, the battle, and the situation along the Ohio River that led to it, was the Osprey book by John F. Winkler, *Point Pleasant 1774, Prelude to the American Revolution*. Another good resource was *Dunmore's New World, The Extraordinary Life of a Royal Governor in Revolutionary America* by James Corbett David.

This book turned out to have a lot to do with babies and young children, with which I have little firsthand experience. So I asked questions. Thank you for answering them, Dr. Amarilis Iscold and Jennifer Major, both early readers of the manuscript with an eye toward childbirth, postpartum, and infant care details. You both added much to those scenes. Thanks also to new mommas Brittany Etheridge (for answering questions) and Jamie Boothby (for providing the real-life model for Pippa). Much of Jacob Inglesby's dialogue came straight from the mouth of my husband's namesake, Benaiah Brian Lucero, during a memorable hour in the car. Let me tell *you* something, buddy. God's got good plans for you.

My thanks to Joan Shoup (author J. M. Hochstetler, *The American Patriot* series) for her hospitality and being a most excellent companion for our mutual research trip across four states—Indiana, Ohio, West Virginia, and Pennsylvania. We took back roads whenever possible and saw the shape of the land. We met some interesting folk (from a cider-brewing Amish woman and a couple of small-town Ohio historians—all fans of historical fiction—to a descendant of the Shawnee Chief Cornstalk, who took time to tell us about him, her people, and their history). Along the way we talked story and characters like crazy. Let's do it again sometime, my friend!

As always, so much appreciation goes to the team at WaterBrook for your hard work and the clarity and depth you each add to my stories. For that and much more, thank you!

Wendy Lawton, I wouldn't want to do this without you. I'm thankful you looked past an overblown word count years ago and saw potential there. And for everything you've done since, most especially your encouragement and prayers . . . mwah!

ABOUT THE AUTHOR

LORI BENTON was raised east of the Appalachian Mountains, surrounded by early American history going back three hundred years. Her novels transport readers to the eighteenth century, where she brings to life the colonial and early federal periods of American history. These include *Burning Sky*, recipient of three Christy Awards, and *The Pursuit of Tamsen Littlejohn*. When Lori isn't writing, reading, or researching, she enjoys exploring the Oregon wilderness with her husband.